I0819980

BREAK THE STONE

CASSIE SWINDON

ISBN for paperback: 9798555967817
ISBN for hardcover: 978-0-578-84263-9

Cover Design by The Book Outfitter
Interior Formatting by DoElle Designs

Dedicated to:

Matt, because 80% love + 20% hate
Kyella, because of all your notes on my pillow
Bryson, because "Once Upon a Time..."

Trigger Warnings

Recommended for age 17+ due to mild profanity, mild violence, moderate sexual content, mention of sensitive topics such as PTSD that could potentially trigger the reader.

Read at your own discretion.

Playlist Inspiration

If you want to jump into Cassie Swindon's mood for a few different scenes, try playing these songs (without video)
There is also a Spotify playlist called "Break the Stone"

Chapter 1- Raelyn
"Burning House" - Cam

Chapter 2- Kody
"Jump"- Lupe Fiasco
"Persona 5 Soundtrack" - Shoji Meguro

Chapter 3- Raelyn
"Sweet Caroline"- Neil Diamond
"Traveler"- Chris Stapleton

Chapter 4- Kody
"Work"- Rihanna ft. Drake
"Call Of Duty Black Ops: Interrogation Room Theme"

Chapter 5- Raelyn
"Love the Way You Lie"—Eminem featuring Rihanna
"Say Less" - Dillon Francis featuring G-Eazy

Chapter 6- Kody
"Bojangles"- Pitbull ft. Lil Jon
"Enter the Maze"- Kevin McLeod

Chapter 7- Raelyn
"Unstoppable"- Sia

Chapter 8- Kody
Into You- Ariana Grande

Chapter 9- Raelyn

"I Will Wait for You"- Mumford & Sons

Chapter 10- Kody

Youtube- Action Movie Music - Epic Suspenseful Fight Scene
- FesliyanStudios

Chapter 11- Raelyn

"Dies Mercurii" – Martius- Hans Zimmer
"Dark Dramatic & Suspenseful Film Score Instrumental Music" - Vyapada

Chapter 12- Kody

"Three Days Grace" - Riot

Chapter 13- Raelyn

"Drowning Shadows"- Sam Smith

Chapter 14- Kody

Youtube- "Epic Dark Battle Music"- Rok Nardin

Chapter 15- Raelyn

"Shut up and Dance with Me"- Walk the Moon
"Evermore"- Dan Stevens

Chapter 16- Kody

"Love me Now"- John Legend
"David Garrett" - Dangerous

Chapter 17- Raelyn

"Stay with Me"- Sam Smith

Chapter 18- Kody

"Under Surveillance"- Steven Price

Chapter 19- Raelyn
"You Needed Me"- Rihanna
"Say Something" – A Great Big World and Christina Aguilera.

Chapter 20- Kody
"Beyond"- Leon Bridges
"Stairs and Rooftops"- Lorne Balfe

Chapter 21- Raelyn
"Gun In My Hand"- Dorothy
"Company"- Justin Bieber
"Perfect Illusion"- Lady Gaga

Chapter 22- Kody
"Close"- Nick Jonas
"Static Motion"- Kevin MacLeod

Chapter 23- Raelyn
"Wide Awake"- Katy Perry
"Heartbeat"- Carrie Underwood.

Chapter 24- Kody
"One Call Away"- Charlie Puth

Chapter 25- Raelyn
"You Have Been Loved"- Sia
"The House That Built Me"- Miranda Lambert

Chapter 26- Kody
"Extraction"- Alex Belcher

Chapter 27- Raelyn
"Industrial Cinematic"- Kevin McLeod

"Halo" - Beyonce

Chapter 28- Kody
"Stealing Cinderella"- Chuck Wicks

Chapter 29- Raelyn
"Stay"- Rihanna
"Converging in Athens" – John Powell
"Night Break"- Kevin MacLeod

Chapter 30- Kody
"Concept2"- 2CELLOS

Chapter 31- Raelyn
"Clash Defiant"- Kevin MacLeod

Chapter 32- Kody
"Day of Chaos"- Kevin MacLeod

Chapter 33- Raelyn
"The House of Leaves" – Kevin MacLeod

Chapter 34- Kody
"So Will I"- Ben Platt

Chapter 35- Raelyn
"Rise Up" - Andra Day

1

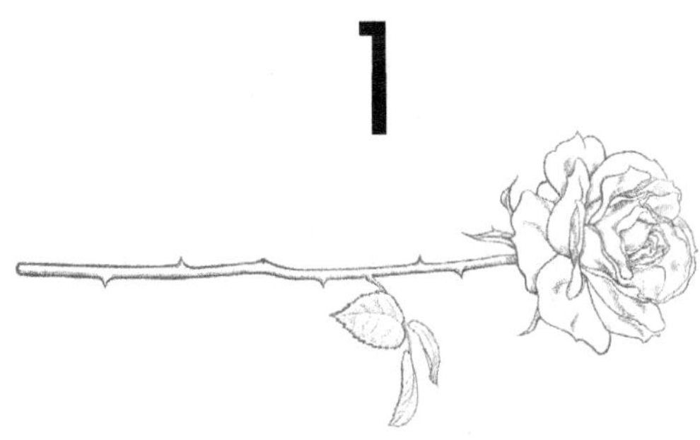

RAELYN BELL

Should I search up there or not?

Raelyn Bell stared up at the forbidden barn loft. Her truck's keys clanked against the ladder as she hovered one hand over the rung. The sweet scent of straw wafted through the autumn air.

I have to look. Maybe there'll be something of Ma's up there.

Bear placed his fluffy golden paws on the ladder, his sharp barks echoing throughout the barn.

"Okay, Bear, I'll go. But if Pa catches us, I'm blaming you." She pointed a finger right at his big brown eyes.

Raelyn's cowboy boots scuffed against the ladder. The higher she climbed, the whiter her knuckles turned from clenching the rungs so tightly. Once at the top, she stood alone in the abandoned loft. The emptiness around her felt familiar, paralleling all her current relationships.

While she looked around at the deserted space, Raelyn lost any hope of finding anything of Ma's. She sighed and poked her head over the side of the platform. Bear's rear wiggled back and forth on the ground, his whining bringing a faint grin to Raelyn's face.

"Don't worry, boy. You're not missing anything. There's only dust up here."

He barked and danced in a circle below.

As she turned, the toe of her boot caught on one of the slats of the floor, and she fell straight to her knees. The strap of her satchel rolled off her shoulder, spilling her journal onto the cracked beams. Mid-groan, she glimpsed the sunlight shimmering through the rafters, reflecting off something metal in the back corner. Raelyn crawled closer. A latch protruded from a warped, wooden door. The door whispered her name, its secrets creeping over her like a cold chill. Her pulse quickened. She jiggled the rusty handle.

Stuck.

Raelyn gripped it harder and yanked.

"Hun?" Pa hollered from below.

Raelyn jumped at the sound of his deep voice. After stumbling she started to hurry down to see what her father needed.

Wait! What about what I want?

Raelyn chose to ignore him for the first time since … ever … and moved back to the door. She accidentally kicked her journal. It soared over the side and landed on the barn floor with a splat.

Crap!

Raelyn held her breath for a beat, praying Pa hadn't heard it, and peeked between the wooden slats of the wall.

Thud. Thud. Thud.

Under the oak tree, Pa swung an axe down hard, splitting each log with one swift blow. Heart pounding at the thought of getting caught, Raelyn turned and pulled on the latch again.

Nothing.

She gritted her teeth and rammed into the door hard with her shoulder but fell back onto her side. Glancing around, Raelyn spotted her canoe paddle hanging on the wall. A soft grunt escaped her lips as she leaned off the side of the loft and pulled up the paddle.

Wedging the tip between the door and frame, she tightened her fists and pushed with all of her 110 pounds.

The door jerked open, sending her flying through the opening and tearing through a spider's silky web and into a tiny room beyond. The chopping sound of the axe stopped.

"Raelyn?" Pa's boots stomped and cast a bear sized shadow on the floor. The man others called William Bell, stood below with his broad stature filling the barn.

Raelyn hunkered down in the back corner of the secret space, struggling to quiet her panting.

Please don't look up.

Pa ran his hand through his thick, wavy hair. Bear sat right next to her journal, tongue hanging from his mouth. Raelyn silently dropped her forehead into her palm.

Pa squatted, picking up her journal. His strong hands made her journal look so small as he laid it on a barrel. "Where'd she go, boy?"

Why does Pa suddenly care?

Pa turned quickly and jogged back to the farmhouse, dialing his phone on the way.

See. He gives up easily and forgets about me.

Once his footsteps faded, Raelyn looked around. Behind a pile of dusty crates was a large trunk.

In her way rested a canvas picture of Ma standing among a line of a dozen young women who were all covered from head to toe in hijabs. Ma wore her typical journalist attire, her work ID badge reflecting the desert sun, showing her name Joanna Bell. The other women looked defeated and exhausted, but Ma's sapphire eyes hinted of hope—like she possessed a secret. Raelyn flipped it over, revealing the year 2004. Twelve years ago. She moved the canvas and walked over to the large chest. Scratches and dents marred every corner of the worn, wooden trunk. It was sealed with a rusty lock.

What's inside? Something of Ma's? Treasure? A skeleton?

When she kneeled in front of the chest, her jeans brushed dust away from a small metal oval. She bent down and rubbed harder, revealing a name:

Joanna Rae Bell

Raelyn froze.

Finally! I knew I'd find something!

She placed both hands on the top and blew out a big breath. Dust flooded the air like the faded memories swirling in her mind. Picnics by the lake, baking cupcakes, and planting strawberry seeds—all with the mother she had lost years ago.

Raelyn pulled on the lock, but it didn't budge.

Pa's axe!

She descended fast, staying out of view of the farmhouse windows and snuck around the side of the barn. The heaviness of the axe felt familiar from all the times she helped Pa around the yard. She lugged it back up the ladder as Bear watched the spectacle unfold. Raelyn raised it high above her head. Before swinging down, she peeked through the wooden slats again to check for Pa. She crashed the axe hard onto the lock, making her bounce back a bit. It didn't even make a dent. Bear barked.

Raelyn whispered, "You're right, Bear. The wood." She slammed the axe into the side of the trunk, creating a quick crack at the bottom. A hard grunt escaped her lips as she pounded the axe one more time, turning the split into a hole just big enough to fit her thin wrist through. Kneeling, she reached in and felt blindly.

There are way too many papers in here.

Raelyn tugged on a stack and pulled out a bundle of her parents' wedding pictures was wrapped with a rubber band. At the bottom of the pile, a thicker parchment stuck out. Raelyn cocked her head to the side, turning it over.

What is this a map of?

There were a bunch of handwritten symbols.

At the bottom, written in cursive, was one word: Zohaib.

Squinting, she read small numbers, potentially a serial number or USB code: 35.1415N and 79.0080W.

Raelyn snapped a picture of it with her phone.

"Raelyn!"

She shoved the map into her pocket and hurried down the ladder. A sharp piece of wood sliced into her fingertip, making her gasp, but she held in any signs of discomfort—as usual.

When she landed with a soft thump, Bear circled her heels. She crouched and kissed his forehead. "Don't you tell a soul."

His adorable growl brought a smile to her lips.

Pa strode around the corner of the barn. "There you are. I was worried."

Worried? No, Pa's never worried.

His scent radiated fresh wood. Pa always smelled of the forest. If someone ever mentioned the word hunting, the comfortable memory of his scent whirled through her mind. Raelyn looked up to him, her neck uncomfortably angled to meet his gaze.

"Don't disappear on me like that," he said softly.

Raelyn turned toward the log pile so he wouldn't see her eye roll.

Like he cares …

By her boot, a dandelion sprouted up from the hard-packed clay, tough despite all the odds stacked against it.

Raelyn scrunched her nose. "So, did you catch any fish earlier?"

"Trout. It's in the fridge. You're still making dinner?"

"As always."

After an awkward silence, Pa rubbed his back and stretched. "I feel old."

"Guess you're falling apart before you even turn forty."

Their conversation was longer than any of their interactions over the last week. She smiled and playfully pushed his sturdy shoulders. "Come on, Pa. You used to chop wood for hours."

"I'll just fix myself with some duct tape." Pa grunted. "Remind me what it feels like to be seventeen?"

His green eyes went vacant, like he had gone back in time. What was he thinking about? Probably Ma. She used to bring him lemonade whenever he worked outside for too long and then sit on top of the pile of wood, flirting in that gross way parents should never do.

He scratched his chestnut beard, which was peppered with hints of gray. Raelyn looked nothing like Pa, with her thin frame and high cheekbones. His emerald eyes didn't match her amber ones, either.

She twisted the heel of her boot and dropped her gaze to the ground. "Uh, so do you need anything?"

"Well, during my fishing trip, only one paddle was in the boat. Have you seen the other one?"

She wiped sweat off her brow and forced herself not to look to the loft. "Um. I'll look for it."

"Thanks." His callused hand pulled out a rolled-up newspaper from his back pocket. A page flipped from the warm breeze. The date in bold on top read,

September 23

The anniversary of the last time I saw Ma … so long ago.

Pa handed it over. "Can you check for any listings looking for handyman work? I could pick up some extra cash on the weekends."

He began chopping again, slamming the axe down strong. Raelyn's fingers grazed the nearby tire swing that her parents used to push her on—a reminder of a different time, when family laughter rang like a constant melody. Neglected for years, its only remaining purpose was to tether them to the past.

Some days, her memories with Ma felt like wounds from a dagger—not a thin slice that barely grazed the surface, but a deep cut that could pierce her entire soul.

Raelyn leaned against the barrel and skimmed through her journal, landing on her book wish list, full of stories about desert worlds and handsome heroes. She plucked a pen from her messy bun and placed it on a fresh page until gold ink bled.

My soul split between the options ahead
Searching
For a clue of what beliefs to shed

"Hey, Bear. What rhymes with 'shed'?" She tapped the pen to her round chin. "I wish Ma wasn't dead."

Bear nudged her leg softly, always knowing what she needed. Raelyn tightened the plaid shirt snug around her waist. She drew in a deep breath before she could lose the nerve, and fabricated a lie. "Pa, I have a project for class. I need to bring in a family heirloom."

"Use your grandma's little mirror."

Does he know about the trunk or not?

"Actually, I was hoping I could bring in something of Ma's. The project is about connecting with our ancestors, and I thought you might have something you could lend me."

His eyes hardened and flickered to the loft for a moment. "Got rid of all your ma's stuff years ago. Plus, you don't need Ma. You have me."

No. I don't have either of you.

Raelyn identified with the red leaf falling down from their oak tree, completely at the mercy of the wind—and alone.

As Pa turned, each stride he stepped away, he grew more distant from her heart.

She swallowed her nerves and raised her voice as she followed him across the yard. "You gave away everything?"

He marched into the house.

The scent of burning wood from the fireplace filled the air.

She stared at the compass hanging from his belt loop. "You still have the compass Ma gave you."

He squared his jaw. "That's different."

Raelyn pulled the crinkled map from her pocket. "What about this map? Was it Ma's?"

Pa hustled forward and tried to swipe it from her grip.

"What is it a map of?"

"Nothing. Just a souvenir."

"Can I keep it?" She pressed the map to her chest.

"No."

Raelyn raised her voice. "Why?"

"Give it here."

She reluctantly laid it in his hand. "Are you lying about–?"

Before she could finish, Pa ripped the map into pieces, marched to the brick fireplace, and chucked them inside. The paper turned brown, curling under the fierce heat.

Her heart pounded. "Why did you do that?"

Pa didn't look at her. "I love you. That's all you need to know."

No, he doesn't.

Raelyn looked out the window at the barn.

I need to see what else is in Ma's trunk.

2

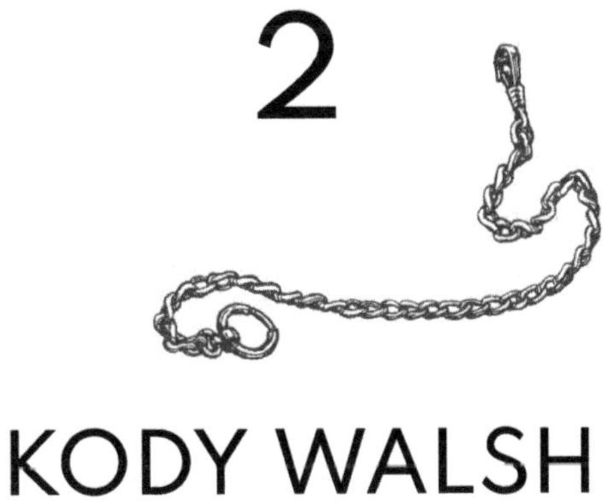

KODY WALSH

Specialist Walsh prepared for a practice jump with his airborne infantry unit. Kody grabbed his T-11 and MC6 parachutes from the Fort's equipment room while fellow soldiers bustled about. Kody checked his knife in its sheath, swung his gun in place, then picked up his oxygen tank. A new recruit fumbled with his equipment, dropping a metal piece that clattered against the floor.

Kody shook his head and frowned.

This kid's gonna die up there.

"Fix your harness. It's crooked." Kody bent over and double-knotted the laces on his combat boots, then followed seven fellow soldiers onto the C-130 plane.

The pilot radioed in, and the plane took off smoothly. Nothing else compared to the exhilaration of the next few minutes. He inhaled deeply, wishing they could reach the altitude faster.

Over the roar of the engines, the Lieutenant commanded the soldiers. "As you should know, you'll fall for about a minute, reaching 150 miles per hour, before activating your chute."

Kody leaned in, trying to hear over the engine's clamor but after limited success, resorted to reading lips.

"Check … altimeter!"

Once they reached twenty-thousand feet, the Lieutenant raised his fingers. "Jump two at a time. Five seconds apart."

Kody's muscles relaxed further the higher they flew. The rear door unbolted, unleashing the powerful wind, which ruffled his uniform. Kody couldn't help but grin.

It's go time!

The soldiers shuffled forward and hurtled out of the plane. His focused mind turned off momentarily, allowing the moment to take over.

Five.

Four.

Three.

Two.

One.

He leaped out. The air was sucked out of his lungs, stolen by the azure sky. His body shot headfirst toward the earth. Wind stung his cheeks. Faster. Faster, until a floating sensation settled over him like a blanket. All he could hear was his heavy breathing, full of life, full of power. Shades of blues above and greens below captivated his sights like whirling abstract art. He'd jump every day if he could.

The wind's force threw him a few degrees off course, separating him from the group. Kody focused on the drop zone, but his goggles fogged up, blocking his view. He whirled in circles, his pulse quickening. Chutes activated and bloomed below him.

The wind whipped his face. Kody tugged his ripcord. Nothing.

Shit!

Adrenaline spiked. He pulled again. Nothing.

Fuck!

Kody hurtled toward the ground. Buildings in the distance grew as he sped toward the terrain.

Eight seconds until impact.

His altimeter showed 1,500 feet. He reached for the reserve chute but fumbled his grip. He approached 1,000 feet.

Five seconds until impact.

Four seconds.

He found the lever and pulled the reserve again.

Whoosh.

The harness jerked him upward, pushing into his hips. His body flailed about, but he gripped the handle and steadied the canopy. Kody slowed on his way toward the ground but was still descending fast.

Too fast.

His feet slammed on the landing. Sprinting, he lost his balance and rammed into the dirt as his body rolled and thudded to a stop. He lay flat, covered in his chute's strings, panting. The floating chutes of his buddies above speckled the blue sky. The earthy scent of mud snapped him back into focus.

I'm okay.

After a moment, he put pressure on his palm to stand up, but needles of fire prickled through his shoulder.

Lieutenant Meadows ran toward him from the landing team. "Walsh? You okay?"

Not really.

"Yes, sir. My shoulder is just dislocated. Can you pop it back in?" Kody groaned, blinking his eyes.

Lieutenant Meadows pulled and rotated Kody's arm with a rough jerk.

Sharp pain.

Kody's bone grinded against cartilage when Meadows tried to reset it, but it didn't take.

"Sorry. One more time."

Kody grunted when Meadows finally popped it back into place. He released a big breath and slouched forward.

"Last one out of the plane and first to touch down." He patted Kody on the back. "You okay?"

"Yes, sir."

"Here comes the rest of your chalk." Lieutenant Meadows pointed to the other seven soldiers gliding down, each landing with a gentle jog. "Was that your first HALO jump?"

"No."

Great. I look incompetent.

Kody leaned forward to rise, but Meadows gently pushed him back down. "Sit for a minute, son. Need a medic?"

Kody pushed his chest out. "No, I'm fine."

"Tough guy. You're gonna do just fine overseas." Meadows grinned. "I may be on your flight to Iraq. How many days left until you leave?"

"Ten, sir." Kody took a deep breath and rolled his shoulder. "So, what's the sandbox like, sir?"

Meadows paused a beat. "It's intense when there's action. Otherwise, I bet it's something like being in prison … where you're both the guard and inmate at the same time." Meadows slapped Kody's back cheerfully. "Who's on your team?"

"Privates Dabbott, Huffman, and Daniels, sir."

"Wow. It's rare to have three Black soldiers on one team."

Kody read Meadows's face. "I don't think Daniels will care about us, sir."

"Good, good. Things were harder back in my day." Meadows lowered his chin. "Walsh, on another note, take some free advice. Don't stick your nose into dangerous business. Some soldiers got in trouble for snooping around the local village, but they didn't get as much of a consequence as *you* would."

"Yes, sir." Kody rubbed his shoulder. Talking wasn't his forte, but he was eager to have one on one time with his role model. "Have you been enjoying time with your family, sir?"

Meadows nodded. "Yeah, that's my daughter, Xeera, over there." He pointed to a brown-skinned woman with pouty lips and braids that were twisted tight in a bun. "She's pre-med in the National Guard, probably your age. How old are you?"

"Nineteen."

"She's twenty." Meadows patted Kody's back again., in a way his own father never would. "Actually, you and Xeera could hit it off. I'll introduce you when she visits overseas. The army only lasts for so long. You'll need something more sturdy than your team to keep you together."

"Yes, sir."

No way. Relationships are distractions. No commitments, no risk.

Kody glanced at his watch as he relaxed on the ground a bit longer. The crisp smell of grass brought back memories of when he and his little sister, Cali, played outside for hours as children. She'd catch snakes while he sat on a log, reading. Cali would dare him to jump off high branches or over rushing streams that were too wide for her. All their life, Kody's job was to coax her down from roofs or off the neighbor's motorcycle. The big brother's obligation was to keep her safe—no matter the cost. That motivation of keeping Cali safe led him to join the army in the first place. It didn't matter that colleges had offered him both academic and athletic scholarships. Kody owed it to his sister and every woman by becoming a reliable man—someone opposite of Walter. He'd make up for his father's mistakes in the only way he knew how, through strength, rules, and honor.

"Good recovery today, Walsh." Meadows helped him up. "You'll make your NCO proud."

"Yes, sir. I've only heard good things about Sergeant Snyder."

"You'll get to the top in no time with him."

Meadows handed him a letter and a sealed red envelope. "Actually, Sergeant Snyder sent this for you."

Kody knew it was against protocol, but a soldier's job didn't include asking questions, only to follow orders.

Gripping the sealed red envelope in his hand, Kody drove for hours from his Fort in North Carolina to a country town in the mountains. Kody pulled up to an old farmhouse where lace curtains blew out from an open window. He kept his Jeep at a distance and parked behind a set of oak trees, leaving his vehicle running–just in case.

Hopefully no one's home. I'll be quick.

Kody patted his Glock and swiftly moved past a blue Chevy with a dented-in door. It looked so run down that it probably couldn't even start.

Good. No one can chase me when I leave.

A tall, broad, lumberjack-looking man with a trimmed beard marched out the side door, out to a barn.

Shit!

Kody plastered himself against the side of the house, then snuck inside the open window. He scanned the study, taking inventory of the exit options: one closed door leading to the rest of the house, the window he just came through, and a chimney. He instinctively listed all the items that he could use as weapons.

Desk chair—blunt force trauma, non-lethal. Award hung on the wall—one quick slice from a shard of broken glass to the neck could do the trick if needed. Darts in the corner could poke out someone's eye.

An antique desk stood against a wall in the small room. Kody dropped the red envelope on top of the desk as instructed. Then, he started searching for the item Sergeant Snyder requested he find. His hands were jittery, but he kept repeating the same phrase in his head.

A soldier does anything for the team. Anything.

He sprang across the study and looked in boxes, under books, on top of the shelf, in the cabinets, and rummaged through the drawers. As he slid the bottom drawer out, the rollers got stuck and fell off the track, sending it down at an angle. A girl's voice started singing from the other side of the door. Kody's heart raced as he ducked below the desk.

Wait! There it is!

A white marble box was taped underneath. It had a gold compass shape engraved on the front with tiny red specs sparkling like jewels. Kody ripped it off and jammed it in his pocket.

Just follow orders. There's no other option.

3

RAELYN

RAELYN STOOD IN THEIR farmhouse kitchen, singing along to "Sweet Caroline" by Neil Diamond as it blasted from her phone.

The sunset's beams streamed through the lacy curtains of the windows, bouncing off the old picnic table outside where Ma used to drape her checkered blanket over the top. Spurts of a memory flashed by—stacks of peanut butter sandwiches and the three of them on a plaid blanket.

I can buy this house from Pa one day and raise my kids here—that way Ma will always be around.

The smell of fresh fish drifted through the house. Raelyn taught herself how to cook when she was in third grade, ever since she was tall enough to reach the stove with the assistance of a crate as a footstool. She tried to recall Ma's movements, from the way she held a spatula to which spices she used.

Most household responsibilities landed on her ever since Pa picked up extra shifts at the hardware store to save for her college tuition.

A splatter of hot oil flew over the side of the pan and dripped down the wall, streaking over the pencil markings that tracked her growth over the years. The most recent line stopped at five foot two inches and never went higher.

A clattering sound came from the study, behind closed doors. Raelyn froze in her tracks.

Isn't Pa outside?

"Bear?" Raelyn swiveled on her heels until she spotted her pup lying by his water bowl. She walked toward the study and held her hand over the door knob, twisting it slowly. Pa lumbered in the back door. She jumped and turned.

He scratched his beard. "Well, wanna play Yahtzee tonight?"

Her eyes widened. She hadn't expected him to ask that. "Of course!" It had taken him years to finally wake up and transition from zombie back to human.

"Great." He sat and started reading the newspaper.

Inspired by Pa's proposition to finally spend time with her again, rhymes soared through her mind. Her fingers hovered over dozens of pens crammed inside a mug on the counter; colors ranging from navy to crimson. Her fingers plucked a seaweed shade and wrote a poem in her journal.

Provide me faith to lower my guard.
It's not an easy task. This will be tough;
To show my true self will be really hard.
If I open up, will I be viewed as enough?

Raelyn tapped her pen to her chin.

Pa's cell rang, and he put it on speaker. "Hello?"

A crackled, old woman's voice started speaking. "Son, you need to help me convince your father to get his eyes checked. He can't find the remote," Grandma Viola screeched from the phone.

Pa winced and pushed the phone away a few inches.

"So … have you told my granddaughter yet?" Grandma asked.

Raelyn's heart raced. She tried to make eye contact with Pa, but he hurried away, cradling the phone between his ear and shoulder. Whispering, Pa grabbed the mail by the front door and enclosed himself into the study.

Raelyn whizzed across the room and pressed her ear to the study door, but only his muffled voice and the opening and closing of Pa's desk drawers could be heard. She raced out the back door and ran around the side of the house to listen through the open window. But Pa had closed it.

What does Grandma know that I don't?

The rose bush under the window was smushed down flat. Raelyn tilted her head, wondering how she hadn't seen that earlier when gardening. She gave up eavesdropping and went back to the kitchen.

Right as she was ready to serve the fish Pa stormed out of the study doors. "Let's go!"

Raelyn hopped when Pa's voice boomed off the kitchen walls. She lost control of the spatula, and it clanged to the floor. "Jeez! You scared me," she said. "What about our fish?"

"We're leaving!" Pa said with terror in his eyes.

She cocked her head. "Okay. Okay. I can wrap it up. A hike? I'll get Bear's leash."

Pa's towering frame powered toward her, emerald eyes darting around frantically. He rushed to his gun cabinet and grabbed his hunting rifle. "We're moving."

She laughed and scrunched up her nose. "What?"

"Go pack!" Pa waved chaotically.

Raelyn smiled. "Did Amy convince you to play some joke on me?"

"Who's that? No one's ever over here." His tone grew sharper, and his Southern accent grew more pronounced.

"Pa, I've known Amy since third grade."

"Get your backpack. Throw in food, water, and a change of clothes."

A lump lodged in her throat.

He's stressed about something. I'll fix it.

"I'll make a picnic. Picture the trees swaying." Raelyn imitated branches with her arms.

He turned and mumbled, "Never mind food. We can get it on the road."

She inhaled like someone was about to lock her in a coffin. "Pa, slow down."

He darted across the room, then disappeared around the corner. Raelyn scrambled after him through the halls, tripping on a chair leg and landed with a *thunk.* "We can't go."

Pa lifted her from the floor without missing a beat. "I got fired," he said in a strained voice.

Raelyn rolled her eyes. "Is that all? I can help you find another job. It's fine."

He threw his hands in the air. "No! We're leaving!"

She took a deep breath.

What's going on?

Raelyn's voice cracked. "We can figure this out." Invisible needles jabbed into her heart from all sides. "This is our home. We can't leave."

In a measured, serious tone, he said, "You've never been one to talk back to me. Don't start." A large vein started throbbing in his neck.

Her breathing quickened.

Mid-life crisis?

He picked up his pace, making the floorboards creak. "There'll be more opportunities for a college scholarship with the extracurriculars in a city school."

"You're not making sense. Are we moving because you got fired or for extracurriculars?" She crossed her arms. "I'm not going anywhere. Let me call Grandma." Raelyn pulled out her phone, snagging a hole wider in her jean pocket.

"I'm your father!" he yelled wildly and grabbed the phone from her hand. "This is my final decision."

The doorbell rang. Out their window, their trusty delivery man set a package down at the doorstep.

"Didn't the mail already come?" she asked.

Pa's face paled. He pulled her into the back corner of the room, putting one finger to his lips. Raelyn stared at Pa and opened her mouth to talk, but he shook his head and placed his hand softly over her mouth.

Her heart pounded. The scent of oil on his rough skin almost made her gag.

What is he doing?

"Stay here." He tiptoed around the corner and locked the front door, then closed the window, which cut off a cardinal's song.

"You're scaring me." Raelyn's chest tightened, and she struggled to draw a full breath.

Panic clamped down on her hollow gut. Outside, the mailman drove toward the field in the distance. Pa pulled her into the kitchen and yanked items off shelves. He bent over, thrusting open cabinet doors, grasping at the appliances and utensils. Bear's brow twitched, and he raised his fuzzy ears while watching Pa's odd behavior. Each item he tossed onto the counter, Raelyn eased back into a different cupboard.

He muttered, "One pot is enough, two cups, two forks, two glasses—wait, toothbrushes!"

I have to stop him!

"Pa? Let's sit and eat our fish. We can talk about this."

"No time," Pa murmured, looking around questioningly.

"Of course we have time."

"Where did those forks go? I put them right here." He ran a nervous hand through his chestnut hair.

"Let me find those for you. Why don't you go rest."

"No!"

"Then how about I ask some neighbors to come over? A poker game could help."

Pa ignored her and flung open the pantry door, then dug among the canned jars at the bottom. "No! This is important. We're leaving."

He's serious.

She could hear the desperation in her voice. "This is crazy! No one leaves their home after one bad day. Senior year already started!"

"There are thousands of schools in North Carolina."

"Where would we go?"

"Anywhere but here."

"If we're leaving stuff here, is there anything of Ma's that I can keep for myself?" She dug her fingertips into her palms. "I want one thing to feel connected with her."

He waved dismissively. "You can have her journaling award."

She rushed away to the study and breathed in the strong leather scent. Her fingers brushed away the scattered papers over the floor and desk.

What the hell happened in here?

Her fingertips grazed Ma's award on the wall, the one for her journalistic accomplishments. Pa had removed most pictures of her years ago, unable to bear the reminders of what they used to have. But the award, he kept. Apparently, Ma had worked tirelessly polishing one specific article night after night. The title read:

Sand Tunnels Disguise Secrets

The last piece Ma ever wrote. At least I have something.

Her attention diverted to the antique desk. All the drawers were open, and papers were spread across the floor. Pa wasn't a lazy guy. Why would he leave such a disaster? She crouched. One small, ripped piece of paper rested over a red envelope on the floor. Scribbled across the middle of the page read:

Give me J's

The rest was torn off.

Raelyn took the award off the wall and burst back toward Pa.

"Get in my truck." He raised two boxes onto his shoulders, one with each hand, then opened the squeaky screen door with his back. The same door he had installed years ago.

A list of all her upcoming plans whizzed in her mind. Amy expected her to watch the cheerleader tryouts tomorrow. The English teacher had a meeting scheduled to help her write a great college essay. Blue paint she had planned to redecorate her bedroom walls with still sat unopened on the counter.

Everything is taken away from me … again.

"Let's go! Now!" he snapped, jerking Raelyn from her thoughts.

While passing their tire swing, Pa stopped, put one box down, and tugged on his wedding ring. It didn't budge. He twisted it, wrinkling his skin, before pushing the band over the stubborn mound of his knuckle. Raelyn stared at the white circle around the base of his finger. He paused and pushed the ring back on. Shaking his head, Pa pulled it back off and chucked it far into the field.

"What are you doing?" Raelyn ran toward the area it may have landed and dropped to her knees. The long grass itched along her skin. Her fingertips turned brown while frantically skimming the top layer of soil. "Where is it?"

Another image flashed in her mind of Pa dressed up in his best plaid shirt for a date with Ma. She had twirled in their front hallway. The light from the lamp had reflected off Pa's wedding ring when he came up behind his wife and dipped her low to their hardwood floor. When Pa lifted Ma back up, she had kissed Pa's wedding ring and given him a look that made Raelyn's head tilt.

But Pa had just thrown all that away. He whistled for Bear to get in the truck. The dog bounded toward him obediently. "Raelyn! Come on!"

Raelyn's heart thudded wildly as she crawled around, groping for the ring. "No!"

His heavy footsteps approached behind, then Pa's rough hand rested on top of hers. "We need to let Ma go."

"How could you say that?" Her voice was barely a whisper.

Pa sighed. "There's no point in thinking about the past anymore."

Raelyn squeezed the strap of her satchel tight and stood. "Pa, please! What's going on?"

"Listen, hun." Pa's gaze darted to the road. "Before your Ma died … she left us. Uh … yes, that's it. I don't want you connecting with someone who abandoned us."

Raelyn's heart pushed hard against her chest. "That's not true. She wouldn't leave us."

His voice grew more certain. "Your ma was bored. She hated life at the farmhouse. She always wanted to change the world and make a difference. I held her back, and she moved on. That's what Grandma wanted me to tell you. When your Ma went on that work assignment to Tahil, she hadn't planned on coming back home."

Something was off in Pa's eyes.

"No. I don't believe it. You have no proof that Ma would leave. It's something else." Although tears welled in her eyes, Raelyn refused to cry.

Pa's gaze focused on the mountains. He sighed, and his voice softened. "I know what's best for you." He gently guided her to the truck and moved his hunting rifles to the back.

She slid into the passenger seat with her journal in hand. The unfortunate smell of grease overwhelmed her senses. "What did Grandma *actually* say to you in the study? Why was the desk such a mess?"

"Raelyn! Enough!"

Her leg jittered in the car. "Where are we going?"

"I have coordinates."

Coordinates? Is that what the numbers on that map were?

From habit, Pa swung his compass up from his belt loop. "Two hours east from here, in Oak City. I can get a job at another hardware store, and you can apply for a position at a different library. There are good high schools. We will be fine."

Raelyn swallowed hard.

Pa cleared his throat. "You know I love you no matter what, right?"

Sure. He proves that by taking away everything I love.

Raelyn turned away from him.

His truck sputtered a death rattle when he turned on the ignition. "Damn it! Drive your truck behind me. We'll take two cars just in case."

She huffed and reluctantly did as he said, each movement full of hesitation and increased concern. As she drove away, a cloud of dust rose. If the earth had a pulse, it'd start at the base of the mountains, but her precious slopes shrank into small hills in the side mirror as they sped further away. In the side mirror, Raelyn watched with tears prickling behind her eyelids as her house faded into the distance.

I have to convince Pa to come back.

4

KODY

DURING TRAINING AT THE Oak City Fort, Kody pulsed back and forth on the padded wrestling mat.

Kody's best friend, Private Huffman lunged forward and rocketed a punch. Kody arched back, spinning out of range.

Sweat dripped through Kody's shirt as air whooshed passed his cheek. Huffman swept a straight leg behind Kody's knees, knocking him down, but Kody rolled out of the way. His bicep pulsated under the tension of pushing off the ground. Huffman jumped on his back from behind. Kody flipped him and wrapped his arm around Huffman's throat in a chokehold. His friend grunted, tapping Kody's shoulder twice.

Lieutenant Meadows passed by. "Good PT today, soldiers. Hit the showers."

Good. He saw! Still undefeated.

Kody bent and kneaded his burning quadriceps with his thumb, digging in deep. Grunts and smacks echoed around the large gym as another platoon walked through the door.

"I'll get you next time, once we're in Tahil," Huffman smiled as they headed into the locker room.

After showering, Kody's phone vibrated inside the pocket of his folded fatigues. He read a text from his little sister, Cali:

If you say the word gullible slowly, it sounds like lemons.

The corners of Kody's lip curved up.

The date on his phone reminded him of his parents' twenty-fourth anniversary. Not that it mattered anymore.

I'll tell Mom about Walter—soon.

Thoughts of his father wiped the smile away.

Huffman's deep voice came from within the shower's steam. "I can see your frown from here, Walsh. Did someone die?"

Kody buried his phone back into his pocket and closed his locker. "Everything's good."

"Whatever. You'd say that if you were on fire." Huffman's silhouette emerged from the steam. "Anyway, did you see the news and that jackass's comment this time?"

Kody took a deep breath. "I'm glad we're flying to Tahil soon so we don't have to deal with the election here. If he wins the presidency, let's hope it's four years, not eight." He threw on his old Cubs shirt—always had to root for the underdog.

Huffman tossed his gym bag on a bench. "So, are you gonna have my back when Sergeant Snyder questions me later?" He threw a sock at Kody, who caught it in midair.

Kody paused, feeling the significance of the marble box in his possession. "What would Sergeant Snyder have to question you about?"

"I dunno, man. I probably didn't tie my shoe or something." Huffman slapped his back. "Dude, loosen up."

Huffman smiled. "Come on, hurry up. There's a hot girl by the conference room. And before you say it, no, I'm not talking about Dabbott."

"Aren't you engaged?" Kody spat out a bit too harshly, thinking of his father.

"I'm just looking. When's the last time you got laid?"

Kody mumbled, then strapped his M4 on the three-point sling. He hadn't been with a woman since his ex, Ivy, who broke off their relationship months ago. All her argument points had been valid—work was his priority. If she didn't understand that, it was her own fault. She probably did him a favor by ending things. A full year of his life had been wasted when he could've been spending that time gathering resources on how to better excel in the army. Failure wasn't an option.

Kody pulled an apple from his pack and crunched into it, spraying juice through the air. He and Huffman walked out together with their bags hung over their shoulders. Ever since his shoulder was dislocated from the jump, Kody hadn't been able to move as gracefully. While Huffman went to flirt, Kody looked out the window at the large oak trees, wondering how the dry, cracked desert would feel in comparison next week.

Huffman jogged back over. "Damn, Walsh. You don't have to try at anything, do you?"

Kody's lips twitched. "What makes you say that?"

"She's Lieutenant Meadows's daughter. Her name's Xeera. She's here for a week from the National Guard. I asked to borrow a pen, and you know what she said?" Huffman slapped Kody's back. "She said, 'Introduce me to that tall guy over there.'"

"No time for distractions." Kody shot the apple's core into the trash like a basketball.

Huffman playfully shoved him. "You could teach her how to handle a—"

Kody silenced his best friend with a sharp glare.

If anyone ever said that about Cali . . .

Sergeant Snyder's deep voice echoed from down the hall, booming like a bear's roar. "Walsh! A word."

The man reminded Kody of a hockey player whose face was plastered on a magazine for Hottest Athlete of 2016. He had a youthful face for a forty-three year-old, not one wrinkle. Snyder's slightly crooked grin charmed everyone on base and Kody was glad to be on his team.

Entering the office, Kody stood at attention. The aroma of coffee wafted through the small, cave-like den. Dead plants wilted away along the room's windowsills. Plaques of Snyder's two doctorates hung on the wall next to a magazine cover from years ago where he shook the hands of various leaders. One of the leaders caught Kody's attention, a short man with thick eyebrows and raven black hair that was slicked into a tight bun at the top of his head.

Snyder followed his gaze and rubbed a scar on his chin. "It's crazy to think I was born 'n raised in the mountains hauling hay bales. I worked damn hard to get out of such a small country town."

A dozen pictures of a young boy at tee-ball practice covered Snyder's desk. Without a window, the office gave off a vibe of an interrogation room despite the ecstatic little kid smiling at him through each picture.

"At ease. We're friends." Snyder nodded for him to sit, tapping his bony fingers on a folder. His long nails scratched the paper.

Kody waited.

"You were given a special ops assignment." Snyder studied him. "Did you succeed?"

His hand hesitantly brushed over his pocket. Whatever was inside the box must be important. But why didn't Snyder steal it himself? Who lived in that farmhouse? What was Snyder planning to do with the box?

From his pocket, Kody pulled out the white marble box. "Yes, sir."

Snyder's eyes widened as he took it. "Great job, soldier. You're just like me."

"What's in the box, sir? I wasn't informed—"

Snyder pocketed the box. "Don't worry about it. We're similar, my boy. You thrive under pressure."

"Thank you." Kody bowed his head.

"What are your career goals?"

Kody straightened. "Sergeant First Class."

"Ambitious. And what are your personal goals?"

Kody glanced at the family pictures on Snyder's desk, then shrugged. "Just focusing on work."

"You don't want a family?" Snyder smiled his twisted grin. "Fatherhood has its moments, let me tell you."

"I'm not sure I'm cut out to raise a son, not like you." He nodded at the tee-ball pictures on the desk.

Snyder's smug face went on overdrive with pride. "Two. I have *two* sons."

In each picture, there was only the one boy, who was probably seven years old.

"My boys are a lot of work. They scare me to death sometimes. This little guy almost fell into a ravine. His superhero mother caught him."

Kody fidgeted with his fatigues.

Snyder paused, studying him. "You should see my *other* wife in Tahil, though. I'm not letting *her* get away."

Kody curled his fingers around the seat of the wooden chair and stared at the wall.

Why does everyone think this guy's so great? He's just like Walter.

"Do you need anything else from me?" Kody asked.

Snyder rose and paced. "Yes. I need you to make sacrifices, Walsh. We all want power. So, sacrifices must be made."

Kody remained stiff in the chair.

"Any woman would be impressed and stay with the man who commands the world, am I right?"

What's he getting at?

Snyder's voice sounded like a snake's hiss echoing in a tunnel. "Once we're overseas, I need to make sure you're willing to make sacrifices to help me out. Can I count on you?"

"Affirmative." Kody moved to the edge of his chair. "Anything for honor and the team."

"Good." Snyder rubbed his scarred chin. "If you really want to get places, Walsh, I have a way. I was given a similar opportunity at your age, twenty years ago. It led me on the path to success." Snyder stared at the picture of his family. "I can promise you advancement and awards sooner than your peers if you help me at the first meeting with the Tahil locals. I want you to *NOT* follow my orders."

Kody cocked his head to one side. "*Don't* follow orders?"

The coldness of Snyder's voice sent chills down his spine, as he said, "Don't follow orders that day. And Walsh, if you pass up this opportunity, any promotions may be … delayed." He circled behind Kody's chair and pressed down on his shoulders.

This isn't an opportunity. It's a threat.

5

RAELYN

After Grandpa dropped off boxes of their clothes, Raelyn stood in her new closet, halfway unpacked. The range of colors paralleled the limitations of the experience her life had given so far. Shades of apricot, peach, wheat, straw, amber, tan, rice, seashell, and the wildest of them all, oat, matched her sandy walls. Yet her heart still belonged to the green mountains a hundred miles west.

"It's a big day, Bear. Brand new school."

She scribbled scarlet in her journal with broad strokes.

Heavy colors gloom in the clouds out west
Dragged to a new life that I'm forced under
Bursting with resentment, not at my best
Lightning in my veins, followed by thunder

After tucking her journal in her satchel, she joined Pa in the bare kitchen, where he paced around aimlessly. Raelyn knew she could convince Pa to go back home. She just had to get him in a good mood first.

Her gaze followed Pa's footprints tracking dirt over the old floors. "So, Yohaan's nice."

His eyes snapped to meet hers, and his lips twisted into a frown. "Who's Yohaan?"

"Our new neighbor. He brought over some cookies." Raelyn walked to the chipped counter, opened the container, and caught a waft of chocolate chips. She chomped a cookie in half and let the gooey chocolate melt over her tongue.

"You let a stranger in?!" Pa roared, bolting to the window. He tried to yank the broken shades closed, the dusty ones that came with the house, but the whole thing came clattering to the hardwood floor.

Raelyn picked it up. "He's just a nice cop."

"Don't answer the door. For anyone!"

Raelyn jingled her truck's keys. "I want to go back to my old school. Senior year started a month ago."

"Don't start again. We have a new home now."

She fidgeted with her hair that hung down to her waist and chewed the inside of her lip. "We're going back, though, right?"

"No."

The heaviness pushed down on her heart.

How is this real?

Pa glanced her way and took a big sigh. "Hold on one sec. This may cheer you up." He walked off into his empty room and came out with a box. "I got you a present for your birthday. You can have it early."

Her jaw dropped. "Really?"

He held it behind his back. "*If* you stop asking why we left."

Raelyn sliced open the tape sealing it shut with a short nail. Inside was a Canon camera. She had broken her last one junior year while trying to enter into a contest.

She smiled hesitantly. "Thank you! But we need mattresses and more food before something like this."

Pa looked out the window. "I've got money to take care of that stuff."

Raelyn laughed in disbelief while rummaging through her satchel. "Um, here. I'll give you something too. You can have one of my journals." She opened a page in her journal where a generic class list had been transferred into a whimsical scrapbooked page. She ripped out the few full pages that held her new poems and handed the rest over.

Pa held it like a bag of fleas. "Oh, uh. Yup. Thank you."

Bear stared at them both with sweet, milky eyes.

Raelyn idly stroked Bear's nose. "You wanna go outside before school, boy?"

"I'll come too." Pa grabbed his hunting rifle and stalked out in front of her.

She eyed him. "Uh, okay."

Outside their new rental, the acrid stench of spoiled meat wafted to her nose as Raelyn jabbed at litter with a stick, tossing it in a trash bin. After walking around the poison ivy, she slouched on the stoop next to Bear, staring at the surrounding porch pillars as if she were a caged animal. She nuzzled her face into Bear's forehead. The neglected piles of rotten leaves, overgrown weeds and the crooked mailbox were all in stark contrast to the pristine houses on either side.

Pa sat next to her in silence as Bear roamed the yard. He poked a baby rose with buds bursting into bloom, one of the few pieces of beauty in her current life. He almost plucked the flower off the stem, but she stopped his hand. In the center, new leaves huddled together, reaching for the chance of a new life. He left the flower alone as Bear lay by her feet, his slurping tongue licked his paws.

"While we finish unpacking, can you tell me if you find anything else of Ma's. The journalism article you gave me is great. But do you have anything personal of hers to pass down?"

Pa sighed deeply. "You're really not going to let this go, are you?" His eyes had dark circles underneath, probably from their night of sleeping on the floor. But there was also a dark shadow that seemed to lurk in his expression when he started to speak. "A long time ago, I wanted to give you her gold necklace, the one I gave Joanna as a wedding present with the big red jewel."

Raelyn jumped up. "That's perfect!"

"But I don't have it."

"Why?"

Pa slouched. "I should've told you this years ago." He palmed the compass hanging from his beltloop and stood.

He's finally going to tell me about that trunk!

Raelyn swallowed. "Told me what?"

Pa paced the yard, his boots crunching leaves. "You know I love you no matter what, right?"

Raelyn's eyes narrowed. "Told me what? If you are just planning on saying that Ma left us for work again, I don't believe it. Tell me the truth." She crossed her arms.

Seven cars drove by before he finally spoke. "I've been keeping something from you for a long time." Pa's eyes glazed over to that zombie-look she'd grown accustomed to. "You were so little. I couldn't tell you."

Bear nudged her with his nose, his breath hot on her knee.

Dread covered his face. "If I tell you, it won't change anything." His voice quivered slightly.

"Just tell me."

"I lied to you, about how Ma died." He winced.

Goosebumps prickled down her neck, and her heart quivered. "What do you mean? Ma didn't have an allergic reaction?"

Pa exhaled and squatted in front of her. She stared into his green eyes that started to glisten. "This isn't the best idea."

"Tell me! You don't share her with me. You expect me to forget about her, but Ma is a part of me. You can't keep her all to yourself anymore! I'll find out about her some other way." She grabbed her phone. "I'll call Aunt Aubree."

He reached forward quickly. "No, no, no. Don't do that. I'll tell you." Pa sighed. "The night I found out about your Ma, I had read you several books and tucked you under your unicorn blankets."

The night I lost everything.

Pa shook his head. "The phone rang, and some guy from the Department of State was on the other line. After confirming that I was Joanna's emergency contact, he said a car bomb struck at the local market and that Joanna was at the scene. The guy had to repeat himself four times before I understood what he meant."

Raelyn's jaw dropped. "A car bomb?"

Pa rubbed his beard. "She died from a terrorist attack."

The walls around her shattered as if a tidal wave were crashing through the yard. Wrapping her arms around herself, Raelyn squeezed her eyes shut.

"The guy said they'd send her personal items by mail, but the necklace never came. And there wasn't a body to return."

A buzz in her ear almost drowned out his words. "Who did we bury?"

"Just an empty coffin." Pa paused.

Raelyn's heart plummeted to the ground. "Why did you lie to me?"

"To protect you." Pa rubbed a hand over his forehead. His eyes were desperate. "I'm sorry."

Her insides felt like they were ripping apart. Raelyn sprung up and sprinted to her Chevy, snapping for Bear to follow. "I'm going to school."

"Raelyn!"

"Leave me alone."

"You can't bring Bear to Slate High."

"Watch me."

While peeling out of the driveway, her phone in hand, she scrolled through dozens of news articles about terrorist attacks near her worksite in Tahil, but none had been reported on the day of Joanna Bell's death. She tried to block out her feelings about how Ma died. She couldn't think of it yet.

Raelyn barely watched the road. Her thumb swiped open the picture she took of the map from the barn loft. She inserted the numbers to see if they were coordinates. The online search showed an old building only twenty minutes away. Two sides of her mind ping-ponged like a debate of whether she should check out the site or go straight to school. The first option lead down a new path, and the second confirmed Raelyn's personality for the last seventeen years—a good girl who followed the rules. After a moment of hesitation, she nodded at her loyal pup.

"We're ditching school, Bear."

He lifted one eyebrow at the sound of his name, then stuck his head back out the window. His golden ears flapped in the morning breeze.

Excitement whirled in her veins, but she shook her head from the realization that Pa had lied for so long. "What else is he hiding?"

Soon, they arrived at the coordinates on the map. Raelyn squinted into the sun as the truck rolled toward a line of trees.

"There's nothing here." She glanced down the deserted road; not one car had passed for a few minutes.

Bear wagged his tail.

"Okay, we can look around for a minute." She jumped out of the truck and let Bear sniff. He ran off behind the trees, and Raelyn chased after.

On the other side of the line of trees was a big hill. A boxy warehouse loomed against the bright sky. The building was at least four stories tall. At the base, a tall gate looped around. Raelyn moved closer and pushed the gate open. The rusty metal creaked at her touch. The wind whipped her long hair as they sloshed through the swampy puddles. She noticed a small graveyard behind a row of oaks, reminding her of Pa's story.

Ma's coffin was empty.

Raelyn shivered while following Bear up the steep hill. She scanned the large, steel doors that dotted the side. The furthest corner was crumbled into rubble from obvious fire damage. Bars lay across the windows.

She creeped closer to one of the doors. It was already wide open. Bear sniffed around the exterior, investigating the overgrown weeds.

Why would Ma's map lead here?

Raelyn slipped through the door. The glint of light on broken glass reflected into the dim room that was scattered with treadmills, weights, mats, and boxing bags. Elaborate graffiti designs decorated the walls with images over two stories tall.

A loud, metallic clank made Raelyn jump. She spun around on the balls of her feet. Across the room, a tall man in camouflage dropped from a pullup bar.

"Hello?" she squeaked out.

He didn't turn. Raelyn noticed the earbuds sticking out of his ears. He wouldn't be able to hear her.

At that moment, Bear rushed inside and raced across the gym and barked.

Raelyn raced after him, whispering, "Shh! Bear!"

The man turned. Immediately, he pinned Raelyn with his stern gaze, sucking all the air out of her lungs with those deep brown eyes. She absorbed the intricacies of his mahogany features, broad shoulders, full lips, and shaved hair. Raelyn's heart pirouetted, and the hairs on her arm stood on end. She immediately wanted to tear the camo t-shirt from his curved arms or run her fingers along his square jawline—either would be perfectly fine.

If desire was a fire, then Raelyn's escalated from a flicker to a wildfire in mere seconds. Rhymes and poems about soulful eyes swirling with intensity whirled in her mind.

The man snapped to Bear and pointed down, causing her pup to lie still at his feet.

Raelyn couldn't take her eyes off Mr. Rugged-Guy when she asked, "How'd you do that?"

No response. He just stared at her and pulled out his ear buds.

"This is Bear. I'm Raelyn." The goofy dog had laid straight on the man's combat boot and looked up at him with his tongue hanging out.

The man's deep voice wove through the air like silk. "What are you doing here?" He looked deadly, like Michael B. Jordan playing a James Bond character.

The distracting thoughts about gliding her lips over his shoulders were rudely interrupted by his question—the reality of Ma's true cause of death. The terrorists must have attacked her because of something in this building. They definitely wanted her map.

Why else would Ma have these coordinates saved? It must be important.

Raelyn frowned. "Uh. I'm looking for something."

Mr. Rugged-Guy said, "It's oh-nine-hundred hours. You should be in school."

Raelyn put her hands on her hips, a lie already felt like poison on her tongue. "I only have afternoon classes."

"You don't look old enough for college."

"That's for me to know and you to never find out."

Mr. Rugged-Guy's hard features were glued to his face, as if he were incapable of a smile. He had to be five years older than her with that muscle mass—probably twice her weight.

He nodded. "You're a senior, aren't you? I went to Slate High. Graduated in May last year."

"You look older than that. Do you go to State?"

His expression stayed cold. "No. I'm a Specialist."

Raelyn tilted her head, doing her best not to scan his sculpted chest. When the breeze blew in from the open door, she caught a whiff of his sweaty scent, which was somehow still obscenely sexy.

"Specialist of what?"

His face didn't change. "Army."

Raelyn gestured to his outfit and felt her face flush. "Right, yes. I see. Right."

A soldier in the army will know about terrorist attacks.

He started wrapping boxing tape around his wrists and forearms. "You're not afraid of me?"

She couldn't help but notice how his biceps bulged each time he moved his arm. "No. Should I be?"

Is he hiding a smirk?

"I'm not afraid. But, while I'm here, can you lock your gun away somewhere?"

"Sure." He walked over to one of the doors leading to an empty conference room and left his gun inside.

Raelyn scanned his broad back and shoulders that almost busted out of the tight t-shirt. She swallowed hard. Did he know what his voice did to her? Or his eyes, those lips? He riled her without even trying. Raelyn chewed the inside of her lip, trying to focus on what she came there to discover. Raelyn moved toward a brick wall and traced her fingers along the graffiti. "Enjoy your workout. I'm just gonna take a look around."

He followed. "This is private property."

"Do you always play by the rules?"

"Yes." His rich eyes fixated on hers.

Bear's nails screeched and scratched against the floor with every desperate attempt to get to Mr. Rugged-Man again, then the pup shoved his nose into the guy's crotch.

Raelyn felt her face warm. "Bear! Come here." She hurried over and tripped on a weight, landing on her knees and palms. A dagger symbol was engraved in the floor, slightly raised, like it was a button or lever. She wiped it with her fingertips, pulled, prodded, pushed, twisted. Nothing happened.

"Hey, soldier. Do you know what this is?"

He stooped next to her and brushed his hand over the dagger symbol. Their skin met briefly, sending a tingling jolt over her entire body. Their faces only inches apart, she held her breath. For a moment, nothing else mattered.

I need to kiss him. Now.

6

KODY

KODY HELD BACK A grin at the sight of this girl investigating the dusty warehouse floor on all fours, her head low and her butt sticking straight into the air. Her jean shorts and white t-shirt hugged her curves perfectly.

Why is she here? What is she looking for?

When her sharp, amber eyes locked onto his, all his questions faded away. It felt like his brain had been turned to mush, and nothing made sense anymore. Kody swallowed and glanced at the boxing bag. Her eyes lingered on his upper arms a second longer than they should have. Kody ignored her intoxicating coconut scent and moved away—fast. He grabbed two weights, crunching them up and down.

She tilted her head and arched her thick eyebrows. "You're a soldier."

"I am."

"Do you know how to read maps?"

"I do."

"A man of little words."

"The tiniest." He hunched down to see her adorable face more clearly just as she laughed. Raelyn's smile, button nose and her piercing amber eyes rattled his core.

Focus. Priorities.

Kody shook his head and started to turn away, gripping the weight harder as if he could willingly smash his attraction and smother it between his palms. "You should probably go, though. Your teachers will get upset."

"Not yet." Her angelic voice was almost a whisper. "Can you help me?" She pulled out her phone from her pocket. When the screen turned on, the light illuminated her golden skin.

No—average skin. Nothing golden.

To show a picture on her phone, Raelyn moved in so close that their hips connected, radiating an intense energy between them. He needed to put distance between them but couldn't—unable to fight the magnetic force drawing him closer. She showed him a map, and their forearms brushed against each other. He had to remind himself to breathe.

What's happening to me?

"Do you know what these rose symbols mean?" she asked.

"No, but this part here looks like an underground facility." He drew his finger in an arc that led around the drawing from the north to the west. "This one means there's a door to the surface." The excitement on her face was like how his sister looked at an amusement park.

He tapped his smart watch. "My team may be here soon. You should head out."

Raelyn wrinkled her nose. "Where did you park? I didn't see any cars."

"I ran here." Kody backed away.

His muscles burned from curling the weights so many times, but he had to keep his body's attention on anything but Raelyn. Sweat dripped from his temples. "My officers might discipline me if there's a civilian on army property."

Raelyn looked at the ceiling and toward the ends of the room. "So, this is a military place?"

Kody grunted as he lifted the weights over his head over and over. In between breaths he explained, "The guys call it 'The Castle' because of the pointy tower. It *used* to be an army facility for classes and training until the back area burned down twelve years ago."

"Do you know what Zohaib means? It's a word on this map."

"No. Time to leave, though. I'll walk you out."

Raelyn looked up at him from under her long, sweeping lashes. "You can't control me." She opened her perfect mouth as if to say more.

No, she's not perfect—snap out of it.

When he turned back around to set down the weights, she was already wandering and inspecting the room again. Kody smiled.

A curious one.

She petted the top of the dog's head as it followed her around the perimeter. Kody put his boxing gloves on and punched the two-hundred-pound bag with rapid jabs, pummeling it each time he pivoted. Shoving the bag with all his strength, he felt an inner rage rise whenever he thought about his father. Between jagged breaths, his fists thrashed until he gripped the bag and shook it fiercely.

Damn Walter.

When he turned for a backhanded hit, the sight of Raelyn balancing on a bench quelled his rage. She held a camera to her eye, the lens pointed directly at him. She lowered it quickly, revealing her gorgeous smile, then jumped down.

Something about the way this girl tilted her head completely unraveled him. His brain flashed warning signals, while his heart pushed him toward her. Meanwhile, his body sent all kinds of mixed messages, one specifically that he needed to cover up and fast.

Kody smirked. "Did you just take a picture of me?"

Her amber eyes widened in fake innocence. "Yes."

"Then you owe me."

If she's gonna stay, I may as well enjoy myself.

Kody raised his chin. "Can I teach you to box?"

Raelyn fidgeted with the strap of her camera. "I don't work out much. I mean, not like you, but it's always before sunrise if I do. And I usually hurt myself or—ya know what, I'm gonna stop talking."

He spotted an old pair of boxing gloves. "Put your camera down and grab those."

When Raelyn turned to follow his directions, her jean shorts snagged on the corner of the workout bench when she pivoted, showing the full length of her defined legs. Taking her small hand in his, he took his time sliding each into the gloves. Her invigorating energy sent his pulse racing.

She rotated her wrist as he slid on the gloves. "It's a little tight."

"Supposed to be." Kody stood behind her and held his hands an inch from her hips. "May I?"

"Okay," she whispered. A nervous dare radiated from her eyes, as if she wasn't even sure what she was saying. "Come on, show me."

At the sight of her biting her bottom lip, he became as stiff as morning wood.

There are so many things I wanna show her.

He shook his head. "After this, you need to leave. Deal?"

Raelyn raised her clenched fists to her round chin. "You'll have to make me." A strand of her chocolate-brown hair came undone, flapping into her vision. She tried to move it but couldn't grasp anything with the giant gloves. Puffing out her lips, she blew the loose strand, but it landed straight on her nose.

"Okay, rotate your hips." He moved her body. "This punch is a hook. Watch my elbows. This is an uppercut. Punch like you're hitting from down low."

She swung and made contact with the bag.

"Again!"

Raelyn leaned in with more force, making the bag sway.

"Again—harder!"

She caught on, falling over twice and swinging at the air a few times.

"I can't." She leaned over, panting. Raelyn's chest gently heaved. Smiling, she said, "Can you get these off of me?"

"You'll get the hang of it if you practice."

After he helped, she gave her hair a quick tug, letting her silky locks fall from the thick bun, cascading down her back like a wave. The top of her head didn't even meet his chin, and the scent of her shampoo filled his senses.

Coconut.

He let out a huge sigh when she moved away to wander around the room again.

Raelyn cracked her knuckles. "I'll stay longer just to train you. You need some practice."

"No, we made a deal. Time to go."

If this girl stayed any longer, he'd have a serious problem on his hands. All 110 or so pounds of her was controlling his every thought and movement without even knowing it. He needed an exit strategy, any option to get her as far away as possible. It was a good thing he'd never provided his name and that he didn't wear his whole army outfit that showed his tags. Raelyn needed to disappear from his life; she'd only serve as a distraction from what mattered.

"Woah! Check this out." She pulled the chord of an old pull-down chart in the corner, causing dust to fly.

He walked over fast but tried to calm his excitement to be near her again. When he could feel her body heat, the thought of touching her skin again sent a shiver up his spine.

"It's a chart. Are those names?" she whispered. "Wait, I don't even know your name."

He skimmed down the list. A familiar name on the list caught his eye. Kody's jaw tightened as a sudden realization struck him. "You need to leave."

"Why?"

"Just keep this place our little secret, okay?" His heart rate quickened as he took a picture of the chart with his phone quickly. "Don't tell anyone about this."

"What?" Her eyes grew wide.

The sounds of a car rumbling to a stop at the bottom of the hill and a door slam made Kody's head whip around. He reached for his gun but only felt his fatigues.

"Damn it." He gripped Raelyn's wrist hard, lowering her under a workout bench.

"Ouch! What are you doing?" Panic rose in her voice.

"You're in danger."

"What?"

"Shh!"

Rapid, heavy footsteps crunched on the gravel outside. Only one set of footsteps, quickening. Kody lifted a forty-pound weight and stood behind the door with it raised above his head. Loud panting came from outside the door.

The guy's out of shape. I can take him.

Kody loosened his grip on the weight, lowering it gently. Through the side window, a silhouetted figure stood, the sun reflecting off something, making it hard to see him clearly. The door creaked open an inch. A sliver of sunlight slanted on the floor, approaching the bench Raelyn hid under. The light almost hit her hand. A bolt of a gun slid forward, pushing a round into the chamber.

Kody wouldn't risk her safety. He raised the weight again, tightly gripping the cold metal in his grasp. The tip of the barrel protruded through the crack, pushing open the door further followed by the wielder's hands. With a grunt, Kody shoved the door shut on the man's arm, resulting in a loud groan from outside.

"Raelyn!" A large lumberjack looking man pushed the door open.

She gasped. "Pa?"

Shit!

Kody stumbled back. His muscles tensed.

"What are you doing here, hun?" The burly man dropped the rifle to the floor and sped over, kneeling in front of her. "Are you okay?"

"Yeah. How did you know I was here?" Her hands shook, and she glanced in Kody's direction.

Her father's ripped muscles flexed through his plaid shirt as he whirled around, reaching for his rifle, but Kody already had it in his grasp.

"Here you go, sir." He handed it back over, careful of where he pointed it.

Her father stood and met Kody's eye. "What did you do to her? Who are you?

Raelyn stood, moving away from her father. "Pa? How did you find me?"

"None of that matters." Her father's green eyes narrowed, and the lines of his face sharpened as he stared at Kody. "How old are you?"

"Nineteen."

"Why are you here with my underage daughter?"

Kody backed up.

Shit! Fuck! Shit!

Raelyn jumped between them. "I want to know more about Ma! You won't tell me what the map meant. The coordinates led to here."

Her father gently pushed her behind him. "I know that."

The strong woman Kody had witnessed earlier had disintegrated into a frail lamb in her father's shadow when she asked, "You know? What do you mean?"

"Never mind." A vein in his temple pulsed, and his eyes moved like a fierce hawk hunting its prey, taking account of every inch of his surroundings. "Boy! Explain why you're with my daughter. Now!"

Kody couldn't help but notice how the image of Raelyn's sweet, innocent face resembled delicate lace in his mind, a stark contrast to her father's hard features. "Sir, your daughter is a smart woman—"

He flinched. "Woman? She won't be eighteen for a few more months." William crossed his arms. "You don't know anything about us. I know what she can and can't do."

Overprotective. Got it.

Kody straightened his shoulder. "In the army—"

"What's your name?"

"Specialist Walsh."

Her father stepped forward with more authority than even Lieutenant Meadows. "Do you talk to commanding officers in this way?"

Kody paused. "No, but–"

"But you put a young girl in danger?"

"Pa! Stop." Raelyn stepped forward, rubbing her wrist, where a bruise was already forming.

Fuck! Did I do that?

Her father glanced at the bruise and pointed in Kody's face. "What did you do to her?"

Kody stood like a statue. "Sir, there's been a misunderstanding."

He stormed forward, his lips pulled into a tight line. "I don't want you near her again."

Kody glanced at Raelyn. "Yes, sir."

Raelyn's jaw dropped slightly.

Her father's hollow eyes held pain when he commanded, "Let's go." He ushered Raelyn outside and into his truck. Bear chased after.

Gravel rumbled under the pickup's tires. She was gone. Kody groaned and slid both of his hands over his head. He kicked a small table, sending it screeching across the stone floor.

If Mr. Bell made *any* complaint to a cop about him, like hinting at sexual harassment, most cops would believe him. Kody's mom had seen it before as a lawyer. Guys had been given years to serve without much evidence against them.

He could destroy my whole life.

Trying not to get sidetracked, Kody returned to the chart. His fingers brushed the bottom name, his Sergeant:

Sergeant Snyder — Zohaib.

I need to figure out what Zohaib means.

7

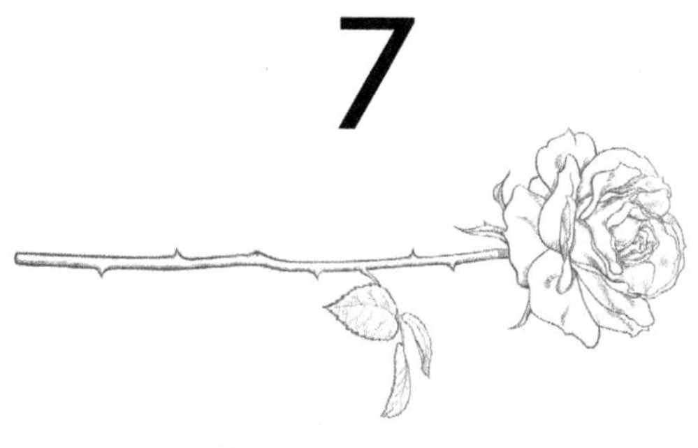

RAELYN

The last thing Raelyn wanted was to leave that soldier—a Specialist. Even his title sounded scrumptious. But she parked her Chevy in Slate High's enormous lot and hopped out, hesitantly stepping forward to a strange type of prison. Her foot slipped, sending her flat on the concrete. It was already the second time she had fallen before noon. At least this time, there was no giant soldier there to witness the atrocity.

"Ouch," she groaned and pushed away a skateboard, a wheeled culprit sent from hell to ruin her first day. "Why me?"

"Effin gumballs! Are you okay?" A bubbly, high-pitched voice came from above.

Raelyn met the spirited eyes of a smiling girl with skin almost as dark as a midnight sky.

The girl twirled her long, ebony braids between two fingers. "Are you alive?" A refreshing lemon scent wafted over from the girl's direction.

Raelyn stood, brushing off her shorts. "Yeah, I'm okay."

"Wouldn't want you breaking your tailbone. You're yummier than frickin' fried Oreos!"

Raelyn couldn't help but smile at her dramatic flair. "I'm Raelyn."

"I'm Cali Walsh." Playfulness bubbled in the girl's eyes.

"Aren't y'all supposed to be in class?" Raelyn asked.

"Y'all? Oh, I'm gonna like you." Cali grinned. "We're allowed to eat lunch outside. Come sit with us. I was putting on a performance on my grand ol' stage!" Cali guided Raelyn over the sidewalk that was dotted with old chewing gum.

A blond-haired boy wearing sunglasses tapped the end of his cane along the blacktop. "Cali, did you catch a newbie?" A slow grin formed when he held out his hand at a slightly off angle from where Raelyn stood. "Hi. I'm Mason."

Before she could shake Mason's hand, a girl pushed her way between them, the cigarette between her fingers almost lighting her red ringlets. "And I'm Natalie."

Raelyn clutched her books tight to her chest in silence and noticed the braille on the front of the one Mason carried.

"Are you in the photography club?" Cali asked, pointing to the camera poking out of Raelyn's satchel.

Mason's smile grew wide. "Oh, I'll join too. I'd freak everyone out. The blind boy who takes amazing pictures."

Natalie stepped between Raelyn and Mason, then held the cigarette between her lips. "New girl, you have a boyfriend, right?"

"Oh, no, I don't have anyone …" Raelyn shoved one hand in her pockets; lint rolled at her fingertips.

Cali's voice piped up behind them. "No way! A hot babe like you?"

"Uh, nice to meet y'all, but I need to figure out where the library is." Raelyn backed away, needing to research terrorists in Tahil.

Cali giggled. "What do you need at the library? Isn't it your first day?"

I can't tell her about Ma.

Natalie flickered her cigarette on the ground. "You got snatched by the infamous Calipescia."

Cali rolled her eyes. "I won't need to introduce you to more friends, Rae. Mason's all hot and bothered already."

Mason cleared his throat as Natalie's eyes widened as she pulled out her lighter, clicking it repetitively.

"Well, ladies, on *that* note ..." Mason cracked his knuckles and turned toward the brick school, tapping his cane along the way.

Silently, Natalie pulled lipstick from her pocket while narrowing her eyes at Raelyn. She popped her lips.

Cali rolled her eyes. "Natalie, you know Mason can't *see* your lipstick, right?"

"Whatever." Natalie trailed after him.

Raelyn's shoulders softened as the group around her diminished to only Cali. Amy was her only real friend in Ash Mountain, and Raelyn had never gotten used to crowded malls or busy parties or congested schools—like the one she was about to walk into.

"Um, sorry to ask, but do you know how to turn off trackers?" Raelyn held out her phone. My Pa—"

Cali swiped it from her grip. "Girl, don't ever apologize for shenanigans." She handed it back. "Done."

Raelyn giggled. "Thank you."

Cali stepped off the curb, then linked her elbow with Raelyn's. "Truth or Dare?"

Raelyn couldn't hold back a laugh. "We just met."

Cali faked an Irish accent. "Stick with me, and you'll never get bored again!" She waved her arms dramatically, and her black braids whipped through the air.

"Okay, fine. Truth," said Raelyn.

"How far have you gone with a guy? Or a girl?" Cali winked.

Raelyn's first thought rushed to the soldier's thick lips. They looked buttery soft and full; a little nibble tomorrow would be perfect. She gasped at her own idea and banged the base of her hand on her forehead. "Well, I almost kissed this guy named Matt one time at my old school. The football team had won a big game, and everyone carried him off the field on their shoulders. Afterwards he brought me to this beautiful view of the valley with all these flowers."

Cali leaned closer, her eyebrows raised to her hairline.

Raelyn continued, "He was cute. But he was dating my best friend Amy and shouldn't have flirted with me. Awkward, right?" Raelyn lowered her eyes and focused on her shoes. "I want to date, but I wouldn't know how to kiss."

"Time to practice! I can teach you to kiss. Come here." Cali puckered up.

Raelyn stammered, "Oh, it's okay …"

"I was just joking. I have my eyes on Breanna. You'll meet her soon. Let's go." She pulled Raelyn through the double door entrance, belting out lyrics from "Unstoppable" by Sia.

Inside, streaks from countless sneakers etched memories onto the floors, a record of the wars the halls and the students had battled over the years. Raelyn nervously scanned other students' outfits. Hers miraculously mirrored everyone else's despite having been found at a consignment shop. She breathed a sigh of relief. Her plain white shirt was tucked into her tight jean shorts, and the outfit was finished off with cheap sneakers. Her trademark blue plaid shirt wrapped around her waist was the only thing that didn't fit in. Raelyn tore it off and threw it in her backpack.

"It looks like Cali captured another one," a girl said jokingly in a knot of students by the lockers.

"Rae, this is Breanna." Cali leaned in to hug Breanna, holding her a moment too long after noting a boy with a football jersey had his arm wrapped around Breanna's waist. Breanna had Bantu knots, plump lips, and green eyes.

Cali chewed on the tip of a pencil. "Don't worry. You can forget everyone's names. Except Mason. He seems to like you. Remember that one. Mason, Mason, Mason."

Raelyn giggled quietly.

"I'll tell you everything you need to know about this school. What classes are you in?"

"AP English, AP Calculus, AP Physics—"

"Good golly molly." Cali whistled low. "How smart *are* you?" She pranced around, her charm bracelet jingling when she pointed to the picture collage on the front of Raelyn's binder. It showed close-ups of sunflowers and the view from atop Ash Mountain. "That's more fabulous than a squirrel's nest on Neptune! Can you make one of those for me?"

Raelyn lowered her imaginary shield and armor to open up. "Sure. I have a new camera now. Yours will look way better than this one."

Cali leaned in. "Amazeballs. Join the photography club. Plus, then you can go to Italy with me. All the seniors in art clubs like theater, pottery, photography … We all go to Tuzlicci for a trip at New Years. They do it every year."

Raelyn smiled. "That sounds—"

Cali tipped her imaginary hat. "Amazeballs?"

Raelyn smiled bigger. "Yes. Amazeballs."

Why is this going so well?

Cali batted her lashes at Breanna across the way. "Yo, sugar doodle, everyone's coming over to my place tonight. You coming?"

Natalie appeared, ramming into Raelyn's shoulder. "Don't invite the new girl. She's got a weird southern accent." Her breath smelled foul of cigarettes.

The bell rang, and the group dispersed, leaving her behind. Cali turned and tossed a paper airplane to her, doodled with her address and phone number.

Pa will never let me go. I guess everyone sneaks away. It can't be too hard.

After a boring day at school, Raelyn drove above the speed limit to Cali's house—another first in the rule breaking repertoire. She kept glancing at the clock on the dashboard.

Pa will be at his new job for a few more hours. He won't notice I'm here.

Each time she made a turn, a cop's car trailed after her. Raelyn continually glanced at her odometer and checked the rearview mirror but was unable to see the officer's face. When she chugged into the suburban neighborhood full of three-story houses with their brick mailboxes and perfectly trimmed grass, the squad car disappeared. Raelyn parked in between Cali's white convertible and a green Jeep, both collecting golden leaves on their hoods. She sighed and stared up at what seemed like a castle compared to her house. A shiny basketball hoop hung from the garage, solar panels covered the roof, and a wraparound porch hugged the large house.

I don't belong here. We can't even afford to fix the dent in Pa's truck.

As she got out, Cali sped over, bringing her citrus lemon scent with her. "Princess Rae, can you help me with the groceries?"

As Raelyn grabbed the multiple grocery bags, they banged against the convertible. On the porch, someone in army cargo pants stood with his back toward Raelyn, his dark hand holding a thick book relaxed at his side.

A boy—no, a man who looked carved out of stone shifted his weight and turned Raelyn's way.

Oh my god. It's him!

Raelyn stumbled up the stairs, tripped, and flew through the air. The bags and their contents scattered to the porch.

Mr. Rugged-Guy reacted quickly, catching Raelyn in his warm arms. She breathed in his scent.

Mmmm. Fresh laundry from the dryer—clean and warm.

A jolt of electricity shot through her veins. His minty breath gently blew into her face, their noses only inches apart like he dipped her for a dance.

Breathe. Just breathe.

Cali walked out of the house and took in the fairytale scene gone awry. "What the—?" She pulled Raelyn from his grasp. "Hey, newbie. I won't be able to take you anywhere if you're gonna fall everywhere. First the skateboard, now it's a s'mores massacre," she joked, then pointed at them both. "Kody, this is Raelyn. Rae, meet my big brother."

"Kody." A tingling sensation ran over her lips when she said his name.

His face was hard and focused, but his deep gaze told a different story—an adventure? Raelyn bit her lip.

Kiss me. End my misery.

Windchimes jingled in the breeze, and Kody nodded toward the house. "You two go in. I'll get these bags." He crouched to pick up the marshmallows and graham crackers spread around the porch.

"Thank you." Raelyn glanced behind her. "Um, later, can I ask you something?"

He barely moved a muscle, but she caught his slight nod.

Cali froze. "What are you two whispering about?"

Kody waved her off.

Raelyn stared at him for a moment, then followed Cali through the wide front door. The fragrance of fresh flowers blossomed from the entrance into the open living room. She approached the mantelpiece full of photo frames and red roses. The largest picture depicted what seemed to be Mr. and Mrs. Walsh and two brothers, all wrapping loving arms around Cali, as if she were the center of their worlds.

Kody's not smiling in any of these pictures.

He walked in with bags over his forearm, creating little line indents on his bronze skin. Without effort, he snatched the basketball from the top of the tall bookshelf.

Cali nodded to the ball. "Are you playing with Dad?"

He tensed. "No. Walter's ... working late."

"Walter? His name is Dad, weirdo." Cali waved her hand. "We have *far* more important things to do than dribble that stupid ball around. Why are guys so obsessed with balls?" Cali kept rambling, jumping from one topic to the next as Raelyn used all her power to not stare at Kody.

Cali said, "... I got a sensational job at an ancient record store. I swear it's the last one on the continent. I listen to different styles all day, and when customers ask questions, I actually know what I'm talking about."

"Can I visit sometime?"

"Of course! They have open mic Thursdays. Come then. I bet you one and a half seesaws that I'm gonna be discovered before graduation. Where do *you* work?"

"Hopefully at Oak Library," said Raelyn.

Almost through the door frame, Kody turned quick. "You like reading?"

Raelyn rolled in her lips and nodded.

"We'll have to swap books. I'd love to hear your thoughts on some of these." He pointed to a stack of seven thick books.

As he walked out, Kody's stance almost filled the door frame.

"That's your brother?"

"Yup. Kody. He's the only brother who flushes the toilet, so I gotta give him a little credit." Cali brushed her fingertips over the artistic flower arrangement on the coffee table, then swooped across the room. "Come on. I'll give you an out-of-this-world tour." She skipped up each step with endless energy.

Raelyn tiptoed after her as if a grenade might suddenly explode at her feet. "You don't have a basement, right?"

Cali giggled. "Are you afraid of the boogeyman?"

"I don't like being underground."

There were five bedrooms, all partially opened except for one. One door had two door knobs, one six inches above the typical location.

Raelyn pointed. "What's that?"

"Oh. Since Kody's so tall, Coop thought it would be funny to add that."

Raelyn took a gander across the hall inside Kody's room. Pieces of a chess game sat atop the dresser, a long ironing board rested against the corner, and his bed showed not one wrinkle.

"Are both your brothers older than you?"

"Coop is twenty-three. He already wants to settle down and will only ask out a girl if he sees a possibility of marriage. Like my parents. They're like two bookends, always holding everything in place.

"And the *other* brother?" Raelyn looked out the window at the basketball hoop.

"Kody? Don't get me started on him." Cali ping-ponged around her room, full of spunk. "He turns twenty in the summer, but he acts like he's forty. All Kody does is read or box. He's super boring."

Raelyn stifled a giggle.

"But still, anyone who dates Kody has to go through ME first."

Off-limits, got it.

Raelyn didn't need to discover new books with the universe's hottest man, or taste his lips. There was no reason to want to teach him how to take pictures with her new camera or learn how to throw a better punch. She would never again imagine him shirtless. Because friendship was more important, and there was a good chance that Cali was her best chance of surviving senior year in a new school.

Cali danced on her toes in place. "Kody's the first one I told that I'm bi."

"When did you know?" asked Raelyn, hoping to move the conversation topic away from her drop-dead-gorgeous brother.

"Probably when I was thirteen. Kody accepts me for me. He knew some of my crushes when I was a sophomore. But goose eggs and pumpkins, my brother should never date anyone."

"What do you mean?"

Cali stuck her hip out and put a finger to her chin. "You know stone statues?"

Raelyn nodded.

"The artists chisel bits off of stone to form something beautiful." Cali waited a beat. "Well, someone would have to slam a sledgehammer to break the stone that Kody is made of."

Raelyn scrunched her nose. "Why is he like that?"

Cali shrugged. "I dunno. Something shifted in him the second half of senior year. But I guess he's always been kind of like that. My Kody will save the world one day, or work in the CIA, or he's Batman. I'm just saying, once, Kody fought a thunderstorm on a cold night and won."

Raelyn smiled.

Cali kicked a pile of her dirty clothes to the wall, and her fingers tapped a chord on the keyboard by her queen size bed. Two guitars rested by the bay window, and an upside-down hamper posed as a drum. Glossy posters from Beyonce to The Rolling Stones plastered her walls.

The name Calipescia adorned a small African statue. "Grandma gave me that one. Calipescia is my full name. A lot of people can't pronounce it." Cali quickened her words, her voice tense. "Did you know some kids say I'm not Black enough because of my big house and my pool in the back? Some kids say I'm too Black because of my skin color. Is there only one way to be me? It's exhausting."

"Oh, um." Raelyn sucked in her breath. "I know we just met, but can you ever tell me if I say the wrong thing about race? Or kick me if I'm ever stupid."

"I'm always on board with kicking people, but you'll have to put some effort into learning on your own. It isn't my job to teach you."

Raelyn nodded.

A woman probably ten years older than Pa knocked on the door, an ambrosial scent of plants floating in her wake. "Calipescia, did you find a new friend again?" The woman smiled; her deep dimples danced on her cheeks.

"This is my mom." Cali curtsied. "She's a badass lawyer."

"Hi. I'm Raelyn." She peeked outside Cali's curtain to see teens walking around the side of the house.

Cali's doorbell rang. "Ooooh, s'mores time!" She flew down the stairs, gripping her guitar in one hand. "Rae, it's for you," echoed down Cali's hall.

"Huh?" She joined them on the front porch to see Mason holding one of her many journals in one hand and his walking cane in the other.

"I'll leave you two alone." Cali winked.

Mason held up her journal. "You forgot this in our literature class."

"Oh, thanks." Raelyn clutched it to her chest, then glanced behind Mason, where Kody finished a layup.

Mason's slender frame shifted when he placed the sunglasses up on his blond hair, revealing his blue eyes filmed with a glossy layer. "I didn't read it, I swear," he joked.

"Thanks for bringing it."

"It seems like you're blossoming. The new school thing doesn't seem to bother you."

Raelyn smiled. "Blossoming?"

"I have a word of the week calendar." Mason flashed a smile that would make any girl swoon. But the sight of the man dribbling behind him stole her attention.

Mason blurted out. "Can we hang out sometime?"

Warmth crept up her neck. Red blotches were probably forming, but that wouldn't matter with Mason.

"Aren't you dating Natalie?"

"No, no, no." His blond hair and big smile completely fit the mold of his student council president status.

She couldn't help but peek behind him again at Kody. "Well, Pa probably won't let me date."

"I'll try to convince him." Mason inched closer. "May I?" He held out his hand, palm up.

She placed her fingertips in his palm. Mason grazed each nook and cranny between her fingers, studying the length of her nails and even measuring the circumference of her wrist. But the touch of his soft hands didn't fit, like two wrong puzzle pieces forced together.

"You're cute," he said.

Raelyn laughed. "Thanks. You too."

"You have to say that."

"I do not."

An autumn breeze dropped a red leaf into her hair. Raelyn picked it out and turned the leaf over, no holes. She pressed it flat between two pages in her journal.

The neighbor had a campfire lit across the yard, where a comforting scent of burning leaves trailed to her nose. She became hypnotized by the orange flickers swirling in the fire, creating a nightmare of Ma being blown to bits by a bomb.

A dribbling sound echoed from the driveway. The campfire light danced along the outline of Kody's raw muscular form.

Raelyn looked straight into Kody's perfect eyes and a felt a spark singe its way deep into her soul, but she ignored it and stepped around Mason. "I'll meet up with you later. I gotta throw this stuff in my truck."

Mason smiled. "Okay. I'll save you a seat out back by the campfire."

"Okay." Raelyn marched up to Kody. "Hey, soldier."

Kody rolled in his lips and nodded without a word.

"Tomorrow, can I take you someplace so I can ask you some questions?"

"Not now?" He seemed to have a hint of mischievousness under the surface.

"No, Cali's waiting in your backyard for me."

The sunset's rays bounced off his glistening skin as he moved the basketball from one hand to the other. Kody cleared his throat and backed away. "Sure. I'll make sure Cali finds a good place for us three tomorrow."

Unable to read his expression, Raelyn gulped. She'd have to pretend with all her might to deny the strong draw toward him.

It's not a date.

8

KODY

THE NEXT NIGHT, OPAL'S Cocktail Lounge smelled of fresh tobacco and old leather.

Maybe I can avoid the questions Raelyn wants to ask me.

Trailing behind, Kody couldn't help eyeing Raelyn's curvy hips compared to her petite frame. Before they had left the house together, Raelyn had spilled soda on her shirt. When Cali found her a new one, she just happened to throw Raelyn one of Kody's old Cubs shirts. Kody's body betrayed him, throbbing at the sight of her in his clothes. His eyes unwrapped the shirt that looked like a dress covering her slender body. It almost reached her knees and had a tear in the side, revealing her hip bone. Time stood still.

What is she doing to me?

Each time a new civilian entered the bar, the bell jangled over the door. Three men entered holding balloons and prizes from the county fair games outside. They scuffled across the floor, flirting with anyone with breasts.

Amateurs. They'll end up just like Walter.

Earlier, his father's pleading look before they left didn't halt Kody's plans to expose him and his cheating ways, but Raelyn's attendance had interfered. Walter's actions had brought poison into their family. Years ago, he had sworn to Kody it was the last time, but recent lipstick smears on his collar proved otherwise.

I need to tell Mom.

Kody's chest constricted as his brows creased. Would he smile more often if he had never walked in on Walter and that woman after his State Championship? That moment had destroyed the perception of his hero.

Suddenly, Kody noticed his ex, Ivy, standing in the corner, seemingly unaware of his presence. With her swinging pendulum of mood swings, she could be a ticking time bomb.

Raelyn would make a better partner than Ivy.

He shook his head, trying to erase the thought. But what drew him to Raelyn even more than her looks were her sweet demeanor and intellect. He never should've told Mr. Bell that he would stay away from his daughter; it was impossible. When she completed homework at his parents' place earlier, Kody made an excuse to sit near Raelyn by saying he needed a specific lamp for his crossword puzzle. He must've sounded crazy. She kept asking about his books, but he'd shut her down with one-word responses. It didn't matter. Her curiosity got the better of her, and she'd reel him into a discussion. The way she argued was sweeter than his grandma's pie.

On the drive there, she had briefly mentioned little bits of her life, like how much she loved her part-time job at the library, the trails she used to hike in her hometown, and when she took her first photograph. He had listened in silence. Reading between the lines, Kody could easily tell that her entire life's purpose seemed geared toward pleasing her father and winning his affection.

Mr. Bell wouldn't approve of me. There's no point in complicating her life.

Kody sighed and approached the pool table. A sense of security encompassed him when he grabbed one of the pool sticks, like the weapon he had used in martial arts. He aimed for the cue ball and shot toward the left corner pocket, but it veered to the right. Kody focused on Raelyn's amber eyes that had completely ruined his concentration.

As Cali sang Ariana Grande's "Into You" on stage, Raelyn's deep gaze showed him that she had the potential to coax him into anything she wanted. Her sun-kissed neck begged for his lips.

"Want to share some fries?" Her mild southern accent eased the heaviness in his mind while she read the meal choices aloud as her fingertips combed the brown hair that fell to her waist.

"Nah, I can eat three plates on my own."

Raelyn grinned, whispering, "Greedy man."

Cali bounced over and yanked on Kody's wrists. "Join me on stage, bro."

"No."

Cali rolled her eyes. "You're no fun."

"Let's keep it that way."

"Oh, wait. The band's taking a break. I'm gonna go get the singer's number and see if I can audition."

Raelyn's legs fidgeted under the high-top table. She bit her nail and quietly asked, "So, I've been researching daggers and rose symbols. In the army, have you ever seen similar symbols?"

"Kody, is that you?" Ivy's high voice rang clear behind him.

He didn't turn, knowing exactly who stood behind him. "Here you go." Stiff as cardboard, he offered the pool stick behind his back to Ivy, who let it fall to the floor with a loud clatter.

Ivy squeaked. "Excuse me? Are you avoiding me?"

He turned reluctantly. Her hoop earrings stuck in her blond hair. It brought back memories of when her jewelry used to lie on his dresser at two in the morning. Ivy lifted her chin closer to his.

"Nice to see you." He nodded and picked up the pool stick. "Sorry about that. I didn't know you had your hands full."

Ivy pushed a cart of art. "You remember the shop I wanted to start? This bar lets me sell stuff here on Fridays." Her sexuality swirled around him like a tornado. Ivy took his hands and placed them on her waist. "You still owe me." Her sweet, sugary smile didn't tug on his heart anymore.

"What do you mean?" He kept his eyes on Raelyn, who was acting unaware of Ivy's presence by watching Cali on stage.

"You owe me a real present. I spent hours making that scrapbook of us for our anniversary." Ivy pouted her lip innocently. "You didn't get me anything."

"What do you want from me? We're not together anymore."

She massaged his palm with her thumb. "Wanna come over tonight?"

"No." Kody dropped his hands, hoping the sharp crackling of billiard balls striking one another didn't allow Raelyn to hear their conversation.

"You're still afraid of PDA? You can fight in a war, but you can't hold my hand. Why are you always so afraid?"

"I'm not afraid."

"Sure you are. Otherwise, when we were dating, you would've opened up to me about … anything."

Ivy leaned against the pool table, tapping her finger to the beat of Cali's song. "Girl's got pipes. Want to dance?"

He glanced at Raelyn, who was ordering drinks. "I'm going to head back. I'm here with—"

"Your sister? I know. I see her. Come on, you never want to play."

"Life isn't a game," Kody's stern voice silenced her.

Ivy stepped back, then followed his gaze to Raelyn. "Oh. She's cute."

He jolted as if ice ran down his spine.

She spun around and walked to Raelyn. "Hey there. You're out a bit late. Past your curfew?"

Raelyn walked toward them. Her thin lips rose, and cute crinkles formed at her amber eyes. Her fingertips grazed a canvas painting in the art display, one depicting flat-topped mesas and golden canyons in the background.

Ivy's eyes sparkled at the possibility of a sale, and in an animated voice, she began the theatrics. "Ah, you like that one?

Raelyn tilted her head. "Yes. Most people assume the desert is empty and lifeless, but it's home to millions of creatures. People and animals have adapted to life in the desert since the beginning of time. Dust. Everything originates from dust."

Kody held back a grin. Despite wanting to wrap his arm around the back of her waist, he held his position.

Raelyn fiddled with the strap of her satchel. "How much?"

"Thirty." Ivy dropped her voice low in a flat tone.

"Oh, never mind, that's a lot." When Raelyn swooshed around, she left an intoxicating coconut lotion scent in her trail.

Kody pulled out his wallet. "I'll get it for you."

Ivy's jaw dropped.

Raelyn's cheeks turned red. "Oh, no, it's okay. I got it." She handed over the money, emptying her wallet.

She likes to be independent. Got it.

Ivy narrowed her eyes and opened a jewelry box showing various colors reflecting and flashing light from the neon sign. "How about this jewel? It's a beautiful jawhara."

"Excuse me?" asked Raelyn.

"Jawhara." She said it slowly, pronouncing the word with a stressed "o" like "Joe" and emphasis on the first syllable. "It means jewel."

"Quick. What rhymes with Jawhara?" Raelyn pulled out the pen from her bun. "Yo momma?"

Kody held back a laugh.

Raelyn scribbled words on her hand.

"Are you getting anything else or not?" Ivy asked.

Raelyn looked up. "Those earrings are awesome." She pointed to a pair of ruby red gems wrapped in a thin gold chain. "They match a necklace my Ma used to wear."

"I could buy you a pair," Kody said quietly.

Ivy eyed Raelyn. "Are you two together?"

Raelyn smoothed her silky hair. "Does it matter?"

Kody couldn't help himself. He slid his hand around Raelyn's back, onto her waist, and brought her in closer.

Ivy snapped the jewelry box shut. "I'm closed!" She walked away.

Kody relaxed and exhaled as Raelyn walked back to their table. He cleared his throat as he scooted his chair in. "Cali's pretty talented, isn't she?"

Raelyn zipped and unzipped her satchel repetitively. "That was your ex, wasn't it?" She crossed and uncrossed her legs under the table, bumping against his knee. "How long were you together?"

"A year."

She finally turned, her amber eyes melting his insides, and her pupils doubled in size. "Do you have anyone now?"

Better to stay a lone wolf.

"No." Kody's eyebrow rose. "So, where did you move from?"

Raelyn slid the saltshaker to the right, caught it just short of the table's edge, then sent it sliding into her left palm. "Ash Mountain."

Why does that sound familiar?

Raelyn giggled and gestured. "You brought a book to karaoke?"

The book, *A Vision of Hope for Our Time* by Desmond Tutu, was wedged between his arm and side.

"You brought your journal." He moved to the edge of his seat, aware of his knee inches from hers.

Raelyn fidgeted with a straw wrapper, absorbed completely, as if trying to tie a wireman's knot. He imagined her delicate fingers wrapped around his—no he couldn't imagine that.

"So, what's going on with your parents?" She scrunched her nose and eyed him.

Kody froze. "Nothing. They're fine."

Cali hollered, "Did ya see me on stage? That was ridiculously scrumpti-licious, if I do say so myself," she weaved between the restaurant tables. "That guy over there is a music producer. I got his card!"

Kody sipped his drink, then said, "Be careful of scammers."

Cali rolled her eyes. "You have so much faith in me."

When he leaned back, the metal chair sloped into his back under his shoulder blade. Cali gave a detailed play-by-play of her set on stage. Every so often—when Cali paused to breathe—Kody latched on to the twinkle in Raelyn's eyes.

". . . I still need to find a drummer for my band." Cali spun the sugar packet on the table. "Oh Mason's cousin knows how!" Cali plunked her elbow on the table, placing her chin in her forearms and leaned forward. "Rae, did Mason ask you out yet? I'll get you that first kiss if it's the *LAST* thing I do." She stood and used a straw as a sword. "I make an oath to defeat all the obstacles in my way for our quest of lip-on-lip action."

"Cali!" Raelyn turned scarlet. "We're not seven!"

"Look who's talking Ms. Never-Been-Kissed at sevenTEEN."

"First kiss?"

Kody stretched his arm up and linked his fingers behind his head.

Raelyn clamped her eyes shut, squeezing them hard.

Cali took a sip. "Yeah, there was this Matt, but he's a butthead. So, Mason's the target now. I give Raelyn two weeks before—"

"I'm gonna run to the restroom." Raelyn fled quicker than a soldier from a grenade.

Kody's eyes betrayed him as her shape bounced away. Watching her leave his side gave him a different feeling compared to Ivy's departure. The two women were opposites. Raelyn seemed to have a bigger heart than anyone he had met, full of a caring nature.

Kody tapped his sister's hand. "When Raelyn gets back, we're leaving. If we stay another two minutes, you'll jump back on stage."

Kody all but stood at attention when Raelyn returned. The large shirt she wore fell limp, revealing her shoulder speckled in tan freckles—freckles he wanted to taste.

Just one kiss—then I'll move on.

His smartwatch beeped, indicating a quick pulse acceleration. He looked around for danger, but the scene remained stable.

"What was that sound?" Cali hounded him playfully. "Are we being followed? Are you wearing a wire? Are we being recorded?"

He focused on breathing deeply, mentally counting to ten repeatedly to soothe his racing mind. "It means time to go."

He'd be gone in a few days. Next year, Raelyn would have a boyfriend and be a freshman in college. She wouldn't wait for him, so there was no reason to get his hopes up.

Outside, he could hear distant squeals from the roller coasters at the county fair behind the bar. Car horns honked in the distance, and cigarette smell crept up from behind the karaoke bar.

"You didn't get to ask me your questions," Kody said.

"You're right. Let's meet tomorrow." Raelyn's smile was as cute and radiant as ever, shining in the inky blackness of the night.

This was his chance. Kody moved closer.

Her first kiss.

His heart thumped hard as he fixated on her amber eyes. Her partially parted lips were begging him closer. Raelyn looked up at him.

A noise exploded above them, causing Raelyn to jump and grab his hand. Fireworks freckled the sky with blasts like gunshots.

Soon, I'll be six thousand miles away, loading my weapon.

Kody dropped his hand from hers and crossed his arms.

Duty first. There is no option for someone in my life, no matter how intoxicating.

Raelyn's glittery eyes turned to ice. She opened her mouth and closed it again. He knew that look: disappointment.

Kody looked away. "Tomorrow, I don't have much time. I'll need to pack."

She walked across the parking lot, angrily mumbling something under her breath.

Kody memorized each of Raelyn's curves in case he never saw her again.

9

RAELYN

After school the next day, Raelyn read Cali's note with doodled flowers on the edges:

> If you have any ounce of humanity, I'm begging you, dearest, pretty please with a cherry on top, meet me at my house after theater club, or else I'll start my senior prank ideas early. Believe me, no one wants to see that mess.

Raelyn smiled. She had wanted to investigate the warehouse from Ma's map again, but Cali needed her. As she drove into the Walsh's driveway, a cop car followed her again.

Are you kidding me?

She made sure to use her turning signal at each light, but her hands started shaking. Once she turned into the Walsh's neighborhood, it disappeared again.

So strange.

The sun illuminated the path as the boom of a ball pounding on the pavement echoed off the house. Kody wore a fitted Cubs shirt, basketball shorts, and sneakers. When he shot a three-pointer, his muscles tightened, making her breath slip away for a moment and her stomach flutter.

Don't look at him.

She couldn't help it. When Raelyn shuffled past, she looked straight into his perfect eyes.

No. His eyes are the worst ... toad eyes. Poison eyes.

Last night, Kody had softened in her presence and finally brought down his wall. They had two hours' worth of deep discussions before karaoke about all his books, then at the bar, she could feel the heated tension between them sky rocket when his ex showed up.

She only had a few days left with him and needed to savor the opportunity. Her first kiss with a man like him would be completely unforgettable, not even comparable. She laughed at the thought of sabotaging any future relationship by starting out with "the perfect one." Everyone else would just be a disappointment after Kody.

I can do it now. I'll take charge, just march up to him, grab the basketball, and wrap my hand around his neck, and ...

A black car zoomed up the driveway, causing Raelyn to jump as if a spider had crawled over her wrist. Was it the mystery cop? Kody's jaw set tight as he stared the car down as its door swung open wide. A titan of a man stepped out with a small bald spot at the crown of his head, but his short buzz cut disguised it. Their father, Walter, eased his way toward the house. His work shirt was untucked, and the buttons didn't match up to the proper holes. A pink smudge was smeared on his collar. Walter met eyes with Kody and then dropped his gaze to the ground. Kody's fist curled into a ball. Raelyn glanced between the two before his father disappeared inside.

She concentrated on the smudge on her white sneaker. She asked Kody, "Is there anything you want to talk about?"

"Nope." Kody fixated on a cardinal chirping from a branch.

"Do you ever answer in more than one syllable?"

"Yup." He shot a basket, swishing the ball through the net and stormed into the house, leaving her standing alone, wishing with every ounce of her body that she could hug him and ease his worries.

Inside the house, Raelyn smelled a strong cinnamon scent as if it was sprinkled over every surface. She hesitantly slid onto the barstool, tapping her pen to the sound of the giant ticking clock.

Kody poured water into a crystal-clear glass. The ice crackled inside as the water sloshed over the cubes, but he didn't spill a drop over the rim. He raised it to his full lips, and Raelyn couldn't help but watch his large Adam's apple rise and fall in his broad neck as he swallowed.

Kody pointed to Raelyn's journal and turned it over, studying the cover. "Does that hold your deepest secrets?"

The butterflies in her stomach went on overdrive. If only he knew the most recent journal entry about him.

"Nope. Notes about my mother's article." She whisked it away into her satchel.

His brow raised. A verging smile halfway appeared but didn't permit his full amusement to show.

"What are the articles about?"

Raelyn took a deep breath. She worked up the courage and informed Kody about Ma's trunk at her old house, how Pa kept the true cause of Ma's death a secret for so long, her assumptions that the map had to do with the article Ma wrote for work, and her guess that Ma was somehow involved with the military if she was investigating that warehouse. Kody listened intently, but his face remained stone-like.

He slid a barstool closer to her. "So, what would a dagger symbol have to do with Joanna's work?"

"I don't know. There are rose symbols on the map. It got to be a secret coded language."

Kody smiled. "Can I read the sand tunnel article she wrote?"

Raelyn clicked a few buttons on her phone. "Oh, it's not listed under her name anymore. That's weird. I have a framed copy at home I can show you sometime."

"I'm deploying soon." He dropped his gaze and went silent, then grabbed a crossword puzzle from the counter.

"Right. But you must know more about—" Her words faded while watching him scribble, all Raelyn wanted was to skim her fingertips over the veins of his forearm. She had to move away from him; any distraction at all was required or she'd likely set herself up for heartbreak. Raelyn scooted away and started scrubbing some dirty plates.

Kody tapped his pencil to the newspaper. "Could you please help me with a nine-letter word for … adorable?"

Raelyn paused. "Endearing?"

"Mhhmm." He reached over and quieted the beeps, then put pencil to paper again. "So, are you going to Tuzlicci over New Years?"

"Pa probably won't let me." Raelyn squeezed soap into a pot. "What's your role in the army?"

"Infantry. Mainly, we will walk around in the desert and drink a lot of water." He tapped the counter. "They send us first to secure locations and complete patrols. Everyone else is our legs."

Her insides fluttered. "And you like infantry?"

"It's where I belong. I'm hoping for a promotion soon."

Raelyn nodded and stared out the window. She cleared her throat. "Do you work with army guys who can look up detailed information on people?"

He ignored her question. "I'm gonna go wash up for dinner. Are you staying?"

Raelyn held her breath for a moment.

Is he hoping that I stay?

"I'll ask Cali what she wants when she gets here," she said.

Kody's brow rose. "What do *you* want?"

"I want you to tell me why I have to keep the chart in the warehouse a secret."

"We'll talk later." He hurried up the stairs.

Raelyn turned her calculus page, then bit her nails. Unable to focus with him so close, she pushed her homework aside and grabbed her journal. With an army green pen, her hand fluttered across the page, scrawling a new poem.

Before, I had no seat at the round table.
Insecure, hesitant, not at all able.
My heart shows love words scribbled on a page
Passages on paper rip open my cage

Screw this! I'm totally able. I can find the answers.

An idea sparked in Raelyn's mind. She tip-toed up the stairs and into Kody's room. The shower was still running in the connected bathroom, so she had to hurry. Raelyn searched for his phone, hoping she would find pictures of the chart they found or any clues of what had gotten him so flustered at the warehouse. His phone sat on his nightstand, begging for Raelyn. She rolled in her lips and held her breath, grasping it quickly with shaky hands. The screen was unlocked and lit up with a new message. Raelyn swiped her finger to ignore it and opened his photo album. A gasp escaped her lips. A handful of nude pictures of Ivy, his ex from the karaoke bar, were plastered and saved in his photo album.

"What are you doing?" Kody's voice was low and calm behind her.

Raelyn jumped and dropped the phone to his floor. She turned fast to the sight of Kody glistening in front of her. A towel was wrapped around his waist and water droplets dripped down his chest. Her heart hammered in her chest.

"Uh, nothing. Sorry." She couldn't peel her eyes away from his sculpted muscles and the 'V' shape leading lower, under his towel.

"Why are you going through my phone?" He pointed to the floor.

"Um." Raelyn cemented to the spot as he approached her.

His brows tightened. "I told you we'd talk about the chart later."

"I'm sorry." She wasn't sure how she managed to form the words, hypnotized by his body.

When Kody bent down to pick up the phone, the towel unraveled in slow motion and fell off his waist. He grabbed it mid-air, but she still got a good look—at everything.

Holy hell!

Raelyn sucked in a deep breath and bolted past him out his door. Her heart pounded and heat overtook her body.

I need to get out of here!

All at once, the circus came crashing through the door as Cali stormed through inside, in her wake a strong lemony scent. "So, Mr. Dinglebutt for English class didn't gimme extra credit." Cali rolled her eyes. "What's the difference between "accept" and "except" anyway? But no worries, the next test is take-home. Did Kody annoy you? His tough-guy face is ridiculous. I can't count all the times he acts so serious when his wheels are just turning up here." She pointed to her head. "I swear he's not mean. I'll make him be nice to you."

Raelyn shook her head. "He was fine, but I need to go. Now!"

"No way. You're staying. Our dinner tonight is a rare Walsh reunion since Kody leaves soon."

She crossed her fingers and prayed to some random deity that Kody would stay in his room all night. "Where's your mom? I can see if she wants me to start cooking."

"I'm the cook." Kody's voice surprised her again.

Raelyn jumped, not knowing Kody had snuck down so quickly. Kody stood like a column of stone with his arms strained across his chest, looking out the window. His eyes moved from one direction to another, probing, watching everything from a distance, in jeans and a white button-up shirt. But all she could envision was the part of his body that would forever be imprinted on her mind.

She stood next to him, staring out at the sunset. Raelyn breathed in a waft of his cologne and sighed deeply. It mixed well with the fresh scent of pressed cotton, making her want to curl into him. "I'm sorry I went through your phone."

"It's fine," he said matter-of-fact, but his eyes showed concern.

What's he nervous about?

He looked over. "Just so you know, I'm not with Ivy anymore."

Raelyn raised both hands. "Hey, you don't need to explain. I'm really sorry." Her insides squirmed when he closed in on the sliver of space between them, thinking he was moving in for a kiss after all.

But Kody went to open the fridge. His veins surged in his thick forearms under the rolled-up sleeves.

After cooking together, the aroma of steak filled the air. Raelyn stood by the oversized round table, placed her hands in her pockets, and shifted her weight from one foot to the other. Shoes trampled against the hardwood floor like a stampede. Presumably, the oldest brother, Coop charged into the kitchen. He didn't resemble Kody's sharp features. He was a little under six feet, with a natural afro that made him look taller. He jumped on Kody's back, making them both flash bright smiles.

If only I could capture Kody's smile on film …

Cali turned on music, "I Will Wait for You" by Mumford & Sons. Soon, the kitchen was full after Wanda and Walter joined. Raelyn noticed how Kody continually turned his back toward Walter. The spacious table could fit twelve, so Raelyn laughed when Cali shuffled their two chairs closer, forcing her to eat right-handed. Kody claimed the chair across from her.

New life goal: don't choke during the meal. Well, Kody giving me mouth-to-mouth wouldn't be so bad.

The red juices from the steak made her mouth water, and the steam flowing off the broccoli caused her to lick her lips. Waffle fries were piled high. When the first savory fry hit her tongue, she moaned. Raelyn clamped a hand over her mouth fast and met Kody's eyes, which sparkled with interest.

Wanda asked, "Where's the salt?"

When Kody stood to grab it, a loud clunk knocked into the side of the table.

Coop looked up. "Are you carrying your Glock now? At home?"

"No, it's just my belt." Kody lifted his shirt to display only his belt buckle. At the memory of what she had already seen below those rock-hard abs, Raelyn almost spit a fry out her nose but disguised it as a sneeze.

Cali threw a napkin at Kody. "Stupid guns! I'm gonna convince Kody to drop out of the army. Or at least not re-enlist."

"I love my job. I can't see myself doing anything else." Kody stuffed a big bite in his mouth.

"I like steak. It doesn't mean I'm turning into a cow," said Cali.

"They need a soldier like Kody," grunted Walter. It was the first time Raelyn had heard their father speak. When he looked back down to his plate, his bald spot reflected a bit of light from the lamp.

Kody's fork stabbed his broccoli, and his other hand curled and uncurled as if he was squeezing an imaginary stress ball.

Wanda scratched her nose, changing the subject. "Raelyn, dear, what do you plan on majoring in?"

Cali answered for her. "Creative Writing, right? From all your poems? Rae quotes dead philosophy guys at lunch. Who knew that would get all the boys' attention? Mason's in love already, adoring Rae's deep intellectual shit."

In a whisper, eyes glued to the floor, she protested, "No, Cali's messing around. I don't date."

Coop pointed at his hole-less jeans and button-up shirt. "Well, I DO date. I don't dress this nice for you people. I'm seeing Meisha tonight."

Cali creased her forehead. "Any girl who's dating one of my brothers needs to go through me first." She turned to Kody. "Got that? I'll be the inspector. Only the best of the best for you two."

"Roger that." Kody's striking smile belonged on the front of a magazine.

And his penetrating eyes belong in the bedroom.

Raelyn's eyes widened at her thoughts. She had to leave and do homework in her room—alone.

A knock rapped on the door.

"I'll get it!" Cali hopped up faster than a kangaroo.

When she returned, a serious soldier about Pa's age walked in. His shoulders were pinned back with perfect posture, a scar crossed over his chin, and his nametag showed "Snyder" on his fatigues. Kody immediately tensed and stood at attention.

"At ease, Walsh." Snyder shook Walter's hand and smiled. His charming voice sounded like it was made for a radio career. "I'm sorry to barge in on your family dinner. I make it a habit to meet my teams' family before deployment. That way, I can put faces to names. The closer our relationship is, the stronger the team will fight to remain safe."

The room was silent, everyone waiting, as if each person had a dozen questions but unsure what the protocol was. Raelyn studied Kody; his energy had completely switched.

Kody broke the tension with his deep voice. "Would you like some steak?"

"No, thank you. I won't be here long. Can you introduce me to everyone, please?"

Cali sped over as if floating on air. "I'm Cali! If you know of anyone single and ready to mingle—"

"Cali!" Kody cut her off.

Sergeant Snyder laughed. "Unfortunately, the army isn't a dating service."

Everyone seemed to relax a bit.

Raelyn met Snyder's gaze for the first time when he asked, "And who is this?"

She opened her mouth to answer, but Kody cleared his throat loudly and cut her off too. "Sergeant, let me show you my father's cigars in his study."

Why wouldn't Kody let me answer?

Behind Snyder's back, Kody gave her a quick head shake. She put her hands on her hips, ready to speak up, when Kody, Coop, and Walter led his Sergeant down the hall. Wanda and Cali talked about her theater club as the three of them cleaned up the dishes, but Raelyn couldn't focus on their conversation. The smell of cigars drifted from the hallway.

Is Kody ashamed of me? Is that why he silenced me?

The doorbell rang, making Wanda laugh. "Goodness, we're popular tonight." She raised her soapy hands from the sink. "Can you get that, dear?"

When Raelyn answered the door, Yohaan, her neighbor who had gifted her cookies a few days ago, stood on the porch in his police uniform. This time, there was no smile spread across his face.

"William wants you home."

Rage boiled in her blood, but she took a deep breath. "Why is he sending you to fetch me?"

"Apparently, you didn't answer your phone when he called."

She stuck out her hip to the side. "So, a cop's job is to track down every teenager who is busy with homework?"

Yohaan smirked. "Listen, no hard feelings. I'm just doing him a favor. And I need to put the tracking app back on your phone."

Raelyn crossed her arms. "Excuse me? Is that legal?"

"Do you want to see me every day? Just make your old man happy so we don't have to do this again." He held out his hand.

She pulled her phone out of her pocket, noticed five missed voicemails, and laid it in Yohaan's palm.

After a few clicks, he sighed. "There. Done. Now drive on home, miss."

"This is ridiculous. It's only seven o'clock."

Yohaan lowered his chin. "Please."

"Have you been following me after school?"

Yohaan didn't respond but nodded to Wanda across the room.

She joined Raelyn. "Is everything okay?"

"Yes, ma'am."

Raelyn huffed just as the three men came from out of the study. Kody's body language was as tight as a rubber band ready to snap, and his eyes flickered around the room as if the walls were on fire.

What did they talk about?

Raelyn moved to the side as Snyder walked past her and out the front door. He scanned Yohaan. "What's going on out here?"

Kody moved between her and Snyder. "I'll walk you out." He took her by the arm softly.

Snyder shifted his feet and smiled, but the way his lips crept up his face resembled a dying worm still trying to crawl. Raelyn lifted an eyebrow as Kody's grip around her arm tightened.

While basically dragging her to her truck, Kody whispered, "Do your homework at your place until I'm deployed."

A lump formed in her throat. "What? Why?"

He paused and wouldn't meet her eyes as he ushered her into the front seat. "Listen, I agreed to stay with my parents during this time before deployment to get as much quality time with my family. You're disrupting that and you went through my phone. It's disrespectful."

Raelyn's jaw dropped. "Okay. Yeah. You won't see me again."

He turned without saying goodbye. "Good."

A huge weight bore down on her chest, and she struggled to gather enough air.

Raelyn's gaze followed Kody's back as he put more distance between them. She glanced to the porch, where Snyder and Yohaan stood. They were both watching her.

10

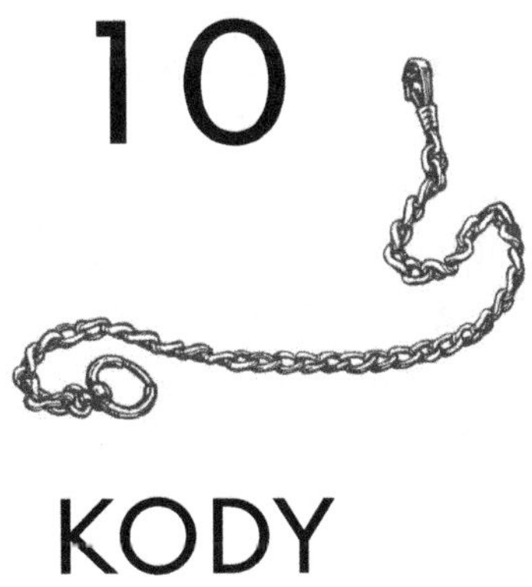

KODY

A WEEK LATER, IN the Forward Operating Base in Tahil, Kody towered over his buddy in the narrow hallway. After the jet lag had ceased, Kody had grown accustomed to life in the desert location quickly. Luckily, he shared a double room with his best friend, Huffman, and all his duties had been boring and uneventful. In the army, that was always a good thing.

While walking through the base halls, Kody shook his head at the thought of not sharing a proper goodbye with Raelyn. She deserved better. Yet he was relieved she hadn't returned to his house since the dinner when Snyder showed up.

Thinking back, Kody still couldn't quite figure out what Snyder was trying to communicate while smoking the cigars with Walter and Coop. He kept talking about sacrifices in order to ensure the best thing for the team—a similar speech to the one he gave during that odd meeting in his office. But there was a layer of cryptic messaging under his tone. Other officers only offered positive comments about Snyder, and Walter and Coop seemed impressed by the man, but Kody wasn't so sure anymore.

Kody had checked with his other teammates, and they denied anyone coming to meet their families. The way Snyder had eyed Raelyn put Kody on edge. Something wasn't right. During the rest of his break, Kody hadn't dared to leave his parents' house even to exercise, just in case Snyder had returned.

Why had Snyder asked me not to follow orders?

On the way to a briefing meeting, Kody asked, "Huffman, what was it you wanted to show me?"

Huffman reached into his pocket. "I got something on patrol. I bet it's worth a whole lot. The gold and red—"

When Huffman brought his hand out of his pocket, it showed an envelope. "Oh, I forgot about this." He opened the latest letter from his fiancée and stopped mid-stride under a flickering fluorescent light. His eyes lit brightly, and a smile overwhelmed his face.

"I'm having a son."

Terrifying. I could never have a kid.

"Congrats, man." Kody nodded with an ever so slight grin.

Dabbott rounded the corner and jumped on his back, squealing. "Big Papa!" Like always, her lotion radiated fresh oranges and her cornrows were pulled tight at the base of her neck.

But their chatter slowed down as they approached the debriefing room. Sergeant Snyder cleared his throat and rubbed his scarred chin. "Today should be a piece of cake. We're hosting a leader engagement meeting where town issues will be discussed in the large conference room. A team will guard inside the room. Walsh, you're in the north corner. Huffman, east. Dabbott, south corner. Daniels, you're in the west. There's another security team around the exterior."

Snyder widened his stance and continued, "Once you're stationed, three local men will enter. Your charges are two town leaders. They'll each have one security man on his team. The highest priority is the leader. As usual, they'll be instructed to unload their weapons prior to entering the facility.

The Battalion's staff, including Lieutenant Meadows and I, will sit across from them. The meeting may last two hours."

Snyder stared straight at Kody. "If a problem arises, your *orders* are to immediately take down the threat."

Kody lowered his head and clenched his jaw.

Snyder told me not to follow orders. Did that mean not to shoot a hostile?

"Strap on your body armor and helmets," said Snyder.

Kody nodded to his teammates and followed Snyder into the large meeting room. It reminded him of his old high school's basketball court—same size, white walls, high windows, smudged floors. He and his comrades stationed at each of the four corners.

One long table sat where half court would be, and instead of jerseys, the two sides wore white flowing robes or army camo. At his station, his weapon was loaded at duty rest, safety on, finger off the trigger.

The local men entered with solemn looks, but the minute Snyder turned on his charm, their faces lit up. Snyder kept glancing up to the window. Kody followed his gaze. Nothing.

Huffman stood to his right, focusing on the meeting. Dabbott was across the room. She was short but powerful, grasping her heavy rifle. Kody kept his eyes and ears sharp, but his gut squirmed.

As the minutes ticked on for an hour, Kody couldn't help but smile to himself at the memory of Raelyn's face when his towel had accidentally dropped in front of her.

If only I had more time with her.

The interpreter relayed information like a tennis ball, out of Kody's ear shot, but the tone of the language spoken in the middle of the room increased in hostility.

He heard yelling outside the windows.

Muscles knotted at the hinges of his jaw. A shadow moved across the exterior of the high window—a bird? Tires screeched outside. Kody glanced at each of his teammates as they tensed their grips on their rifles.

Voices rose in the middle of the room. Chairs tumbled back as the seated men bolted to their feet. Kody's muscles stiffened.

A door flew open and slammed into the wall. Confusion whirled like a tornado through the room. Kody positioned his weapon as a man stormed inside, shouting. Kody didn't have a clear shot at him without risking injury to an officer. Static buzzed on his personal radio, distracting Kody for only a moment.

The local security guard pulled out a pistol. Kody pulled the trigger. Two bullets pierced the guard's chest, then he dropped.

The loud growl of an explosion outside shook the walls. Two men smashed through the high windows, swinging on ropes and carrying AK-47s. All the soldiers aimed for the intruders—except Kody. His eyes and weapon locked in on Snyder.

Snyder's weapon remained idle at his side. Kody watched him drop the marble box in the local leader's pocket. There was screaming and shouting as bullets ripped through the room. Kody's comrades tightened up, but he remained at his location, keeping the back door in his peripheral vision. His heart pounded.

More shots fired. Daniels slumped to the floor. Kody took cover on the ground. Sweat dripped down Kody's forehead. He fired two more shots at a hostile, who sank in a crumpled heap. A bullet hit the wall where Kody stood seconds before. He ducked his head to the floor, remaining flat. Snyder shouted something.

Silence. Kody looked up.

Is it over?

The remaining threats stood in his sightline, under American control. Snyder pressed his pistol against a hostile's back.

The radio static dissipated, and Lieutenant Meadows reported, "All clear. The risks have been identified and neutralized."

Huffman lay motionless. Kody's shoulder went numb from the weight of his rifle.

Lieutenant Meadows started a roll call, but Kody sprinted to Daniels sprawled on the ground, arriving before the tactical combat casualty care team. Kody pressed two fingers to Daniels's wrist. Splattered blood covered his pale neck. No pulse.

Damn it.

His glossy eyes were frozen on the ceiling. Kody stepped over the body and ran to Huffman, where a medic had cut through the side of his uniform, revealing blood gushing over his dark skin. The medic put pressure on his underarm wound.

On the count of three, they mounted Huffman, who reached out to Kody and groaned, onto a gurney.

Without skipping a beat, Kody slowed his panting and said, "It's okay. You'll have a heroic story for your son someday." The medic wheeled Huffman away.

In a daze, Kody walked around the camp aimlessly. For an hour, he replayed the scene in his mind. What could he have done differently? Which person did Snyder order him to *not* shoot? What was his plan? Why did the hostiles attack? Why did Snyder give the leader the marble box? Were they working together? There were too many secrets. Eventually, Kody sat on a curb outside the medic center.

Lieutenant Meadows approached with a pained expression. "You saved lives today."

Kody took shallow breaths and opened his mouth, but no words came out.

"Walk with me to your med check."

Kody followed, only half-listening as Lieutenant Meadows prattled on. "The security guard that interrupted the meeting was an insurgent, along with the men who ambushed the room. Another hostile was outside the building. We suffered two casualties."

Kody's knees weakened.

"These guys had a bigger plan. Without your reflexes, who knows where we would be? I'll make sure to put you in for a Bronze Star for your quick response today. You did a good job taking that man down so fast."

"Who was the other casualty on our side?" Kody braced his arm against the wall.

Meadows paused. "Private Huffman."

No …

Kody bowed his head. A sudden numbness overtook his chest.

Meadows swung Huffman's old pocket watch in the air. "He left this for you."

Kody recognized it from the first day he met Huffman during training. His grandpa had passed it down to his father, both who served in the army too.

Why wouldn't Huffman pass this on to his son?

He must not want his son to serve—to save him from the same fate. Kody held it to his ear, and the faint tick tock of the sound reminded him what was important in life.

A tightness formed in his throat, and he held back tears.

"You'll have a few minutes alone until the After-Action Review." His Lieutenant clicked the door shut behind him.

Kody pushed his knuckles to his forehead. The room started to spin, and acid rose in his throat. He dropped to the floor in the empty room and closed his eyes, but the scene ran on repeat in his mind. He tried to drown it out by doing push-up after push-up. Up. Down. Up. Down.

I need to figure out why Snyder gave the leader that marble box.

11

RAELYN

MONDAY MORNING, RAELYN BOUNCED on the bumpy bus ride to their field trip at The Oak Museum of Art. She winced as her butt slammed against the ripped-up seat. The strong smell of exhaust fumes made her nauseous. An earbud amplified a hip hop song she didn't recognize from Cali's shared playlist, but Raelyn blocked out the tunes in order to plan a time to go visit the warehouse again.

Cali poked her and pulled the earphone out. "So, I was doing my homework earlier. Do you know the difference between a kadole and a leemron?"

"No."

"Okay, good, 'cause I made it up." Cali plucked the grape-colored pen from Raelyn's messy hair bun and doodled on her wrist. "Who should I set you up with?" Cali smiled. "Mason is the obvious choice, but there's Drew. He's sweet and shy, so you two would get along. Do you like Mason?"

"He's … nice."

Cali smirked. "Pathetic answer. You know he joined photography club for you."

"Yeah." Raelyn scrunched her nose. "Anywho, I dare you to ask Breanna to the winter formal."

"Can't. I already asked Dustin."

"Who? But you like Breanna."

Cali shrugged.

Needing fresh air at the thought of dating, Raelyn opened the old bus window. The only good thing about Kody pushing her away was the record-breaking twelve poems she had written in a week about her mixed feelings. He didn't need to be so cold with his last words to her. And he had intentionally saved those pictures of his ex.

Cali was right about Kody not being relationship material.

Cali stopped mid-story and asked Raelyn, "What's your biggest fear?"

Raelyn shuddered. "Being underground."

"Spooky!" Cali slapped her knees. "Oh! I have the best question. What do you want more than anything?"

Raelyn sat and fumbled through her satchel, then pulled out a crinkled picture of their family at Disney World from when Raelyn was four. "You're going to laugh at me."

Cali zipped her lips.

Raelyn paused as the bus jostled them to the side. Out the dirty window, her gaze settled on the blue sky, the same shade as Ma's bright eyes—the only physical trait they didn't share.

Raelyn sighed. "I want to feel completely and totally loved by someone. Anyone. A love that will never be taken away."

Cali stopped moving for a millisecond. "Whoa. Deep. But you have your pa and me."

The bus made Raelyn bounce in her seat. "Pa doesn't love me. Not really. He works, then is out in the yard all evening. Never spends any time with me.

How can that be love? That's why I miss Ma so much. The way she looked at me. That love. I want it back."

"What happened to her?"

"Ma was blown up."

Cali placed her hand on Raelyn's knee. "What?"

"A terrorist attack. Pa lied to me about it for years."

There was silence for a moment.

Raelyn drew a heart on her journal's cover. When she looked out the bus window, a cop car drove in the lane next to them. She quickly brushed away the thought that it was the same cop as before. Squinting, she tried to catch the license plate number but couldn't see it before the car turned.

Raelyn patted Cali's knee. "So, what's your darkest secret?"

Cali tugged on the frays of her ripped jeans to widen the hole in the left knee. "I pretend a lot. Everyone sees me as the positive girl who will lift their spirits. I can't ever be sad or scared."

"Isn't it a gift to be able to make others happy?"

Cali attempted a Yoda accent. "A curse, every gift has, young one."

"Ah, so wise." Raelyn laughed and held out her pinky. "Promise me to be upfront even if what you're feeling is negative. Deal?"

"Deal shmeal." Cali wrapped her pinky around Raelyn's.

"Mason told Dustin, who texted Breanna, who told me that he wants to sit by you on the bus ride back from the museum. Would you date Mason if he asks?"

"What about Natalie?"

"He doesn't like her. What do *you* want?"

I want Kody.

"I want to see the photography wing at this museum."

"There you go, changing the subject again."

Raelyn chewed the inside of her lip at the thought of Kody. He wouldn't be good for her. Once he returned to Oak City, a year away, if she wanted to date him it'd probably feel like pulling teeth to convince him to go out with her. And then after forcing him into a situation, she'd probably spend years investing her energy in asking him to be more vulnerable. Raelyn wouldn't ever feel loved by someone who had the same habits as Pa, someone who put up walls. It would be better to choose a partner who was genuinely interested in being with her.

"Yeah, I might date Mason."

The bus pulled up, and the senior class hooted and skipped off into the downtown streets. Raelyn took a deep breath. The temperatures were lowering as each day passed. Natalie leaned against the side of the museum, holding a pack of cigarettes to her mouth. She caught one between her teeth and pulled it out. At the same time, Cali was playing around by smacking Breanna's rear while the tour guide herded them into the museum like cattle.

Classmates idled in front of historical masterpieces. The tour guide stated, "And to our left is the contemporary photography exhibit …"

What I've been waiting for!

She gripped the camera hanging around her neck tightly, an extension of her body, like another limb. Raelyn stood on her tip toes and lifted her chin, then leveraged her palm off the top of someone's shoulder to see. A sign read "Renovations." She groaned.

The tour guide rambled and flocked the rest of the class through the narrow halls.

I can break the rules once more.

As the class disappeared, Raelyn dipped below the cautionary tape. The entire exhibit displayed desert scenes. A few photographs grabbed her attention, especially ones with the sunlight reflecting off the golden sand. She peeked around the corner at more artwork.

The face of a woman in a black and white photograph pulled her closer like a magnet. A prickling sensation overwhelmed her body. With each step her heart rate quickened. The photograph called to her. When she stood a foot from the image, Raelyn covered her mouth with both hands and her stomach flipped.

The 20x30 photograph illustrated a woman who seemed unaware of the camera pointed at her. She was on her knees, showing a group of children a handful of sand that sifted between her fingers. She moved her eyes around the photograph, up to the woman›s face. A gasp shocked her system. Raelyn stared into the eyes of her mother.

That's Ma. It can't be. But that's her face. Those are her eyes.

Raelyn's head spun. She released the oxygen from her lungs. Looking closer to the etchings on the plaque, she gasped and dropped her journal to the floor.

The date on the plaque indicated the photograph was taken only six months ago. It felt like a bolt of electricity ran through her muscles and shocked her brain.

Is Ma alive?

Raelyn's world churned. She sunk to the ground, tilted her head back, and drank in the mystery. Seconds, minutes, lifetimes ticked away. The room closed in around her, dissolving into nothingness.

An unknown number of minutes later, Cali held a juice box to Raelyn's lips and was apparently in the middle of a dramatic story when Raelyn's attention snapped back into focus.

"... so we were in the pottery section of the museum, but you had disappeared like Houdini. It took me four thousand days to find you. I thought you died in the bathroom, but no, you were sitting on the floor, worshiping some lady in a random picture like she was a goddess. How'd you get in there? It was all taped off. I dragged you out, the heroine that I am." At this point in the story, Cali had leaped up and started acting it out.

"Earth to Rae!" Cali waved in front of her face. "Can you transform out of your super serious librarian alter-ego? Your lips aren't purple anymore, so I saved your life." She snapped in front of her eyes again. "Rae?"

Ancient Egyptian sphynx statues surrounded them, but Raelyn stared across the hall to the photography exhibit.

Was I dreaming?

Cali jumped up and down. "So, what actually happened? Did Mason ask you out in the photography wing? Is that why you freaked out? Did you say no and then he turned awful? I can smack him around a little for you." She flexed to show off her muscles.

Raelyn leaned back against the cold wall. "Hold on one second." She hugged her knees to her chest and wrote a poem in her journal with a mulberry pen.

Interpret emotions designed by art
Old camera captures secrets to impart
Listen close my dear, how old is your soul?
Whispers of the artist will only know

As she told Cali about the photograph, her worries lightened bit by bit as she described all the details. Her tale stretched through the time it took three tour guides to pass by. Cali's mouth dropped at all the right parts of the story.

"I was too stunned to write the name of the photographer. But I wrote the name of the photograph in here."

Cali leaned over her shoulder and read the title out loud. "*J's Joy*." Her eyes bulged wide. "Like, Joanna's Joy?"

Raelyn paced the pristine white floor. "What on earth do I do next?"

"Here, I'll research online." Cali pulled out her phone and clicked and swiped ferociously. Her eyes grew. "Oh my! Some of these sites show a completely different kind of joy." Cali laughed. "Wanna see?"

Raelyn covered her eyes and looked away. "No way."

"Oh, wait, here's something. This one looks like the picture you described. Is this it?" Cali shoved the phone in her face. "Open your eyes. It's not porn."

Raelyn looked. "Yeah, it's similar, but this one's in color. The picture in the other hall was black and white." She inched closer. Her fingertip put extra pressure on the screen, causing her to accidentally zoom in.

"Oh my god!" Raelyn jumped, smacking Cali's face with her elbow in the process. Her heel caught on Cali's shoe and Raelyn tumbled onto the floor.

"Ow! Jeez. What the—?" Cali covered her eye with one hand.

Raelyn grabbed the phone again. "It's Ma's necklace!"

"Huh?" Cali leaned over her shoulder.

"Look, I wouldn't have missed that before. The necklace wasn't in the photograph at the museum. It must've fallen off between these two pictures. It's Ma's. Pa gave that to her when they got married."

"Are you sure that's the same necklace?" Cali cringed.

Raelyn's heart leaped. "Yeah! It's a thin gold chain and a large ruby stone."

Cali pointed. "At the bottom of the website page it says "Tahil." Do you think that's the photographer's name?"

Raelyn stopped. "That doesn't sound right." She looked around the hall. Their teachers would surely notice their absence by now.

Cali hopped in place. "Let's put in your contact info on this inquiry page. Someone probably has a listing of who took the pictures, right? What's your cell number?"

Raelyn typed in her cell and pushed submit. "This is all so strange."

Her phone chimed. "It's a text from an unknown number." She glanced at Cali.

"What's it say?"

Raelyn turned the phone and showed Cali.

he sell jawhara soon. he want power. help us. hurry.

"Let's call the number back." Raelyn hit the button to put it on speakerphone.

"The number you have dialed is not in service," said an animated voice.

Cali dropped her shoulders. "Cherry gumballs. Someone's playing a prank."

"No, something about that word sounds familiar. Jawhara."

Cali waved at the air. "It's definitely Mason's way of asking you out. Boys are all insane. Let's come back to the museum after school. We can ask a tour guide for more info."

"No, now." Raelyn pulled her up and glanced at the clock.

Quickly, they darted across the hallway. Cali set off at a sprint, not checking behind her. Panting at the end of the hall, they made their way to the photography exhibit to find one wall freshly painted. Raelyn marched to where the photograph hung an hour before. The spot was empty.

Cali flaunted her hips at a young employee, "Hey, big fella."

Raelyn palmed her forehead.

The guy looked around then pointed to himself, blushing. "Me?"

"Yes, you, my knight in shining armor. Do you know where the photograph in the corner went? The one of the lady and all those happy kids?"

"No, I'm sorry, miss. They took that one down. I bet it's in the cleaning station in the basement. Or another museum may have purchased the piece."

"Look at you, all knowledgeable. Can you take me to the basement to kill my curiosity?"

He shook his head. "Sorry, miss. That's beyond my pay grade."

Cali smiled and made her eyebrows dance. "I know what our plans are for tonight." She hummed the tune to *Inspector Gadget*'s theme song.

This is the worst idea of my life.

At midnight, one streetlamp flickered behind the dumpsters of the art museum. Graffiti lined the back wall, and the stale stench of old beer filled her nostrils. Raelyn and Cali crouched in a bush, dressed all in black. Despite the Wonder Woman mask that Cali bought from the dollar store and made Raelyn wear, she still tugged one of Kody's Cubs hats low over her eyes.

Cali imitated the sound of a creepy violin, alternating moments of sharp, then quiet stirring sounds. "Do you wanna call it off?"

"No. I *have* to learn more about my mom. Even if it kills me."

"I need that in writing." Cali sprinted toward the side of the brick building. Raelyn tried to move forward, but her leg was glued to the soil. She picked up rocks and threw them after Cali's feet to get her attention but missed and hit a low window to the basement. The glass shattered.

Cali whirled around. "What the hell are you doing?"

"I can't go in a basement! It's underground!"

Cali jogged back, grabbing Raelyn's wrist. "I can't hold your hand the whole time. Do you wanna find out about your ma or not?"

"Yes. But I can't–"

"Yes, you can." Cali held both her hands on the side of Raelyn's face. "What's the purpose?"

"Learn about Ma."

"What's your goal?"

"Find the photographer's name."

"Let's go." Cali's mask covered her smile, but Raelyn could see the sparkle in her eyes. She crept toward the small, low window the rock crashed through.

Cali squatted, pulling a screwdriver from her fanny pack, and broke the rest of the window. She swept the remaining glass with the screwdriver before maneuvering her arm to flip the lock. Raelyn's curvy hips squeezed through, barely.

It's not underground. It's just a normal room. Everything's fine.

She dropped into the basement smelling of cleaning chemicals. Water dripped from a distance, making a steady plinking noise. The ventilation creaked. At each abandoned room, chills shook her shoulders. Eerily, the lights flickered but didn't plunge them into total darkness—yet. Raelyn's phone flashlight illuminated piles of art stacked in bubble wrap.

We won't have enough time.

A giant sign right above read "Renaissance." They were in the wrong room. Raelyn turned the squeaky door handle to reveal a long hallway with countless doors that led out of sight. Anyone could lurk undetected behind a corner. The headlights of an approaching car shone into the window near the ceiling illuminating a "Photography" sign.

Raelyn dashed in the shadows of the corridor. Scanning the contents of the new room, her breathing accelerated.

I found it!

The photograph of Ma lay right in front of her.

Raelyn snapped a quick picture of the artwork and flipped the portrait over to check the back for the photographer's name.

"Where's the plaque?"

No response. She turned. "Cali?" Raelyn whispered but got no response. Her eyes darted around. She was alone.

High heel clicks echoed in the long corridor. She froze, glancing in each corner. Shivers crept up her arms.

No other exits.

Sweat formed on her palms and the back of her neck. Her heart pounded under her ribs, threatening to break free and reveal her location. The footsteps faded away. Raelyn's hands ransacked through nearby boxes. Bubble wrap concealed dozens of art pieces. Raelyn slashed packages with her nails until she found the plaque labeled "J's Joy."

The photographer's name was Emme O'Reilly. A door groaned behind her. Raelyn spun, but no one was there. Her breathing quickened. The footsteps clattered again, accelerating in pace and increasing in volume.

Raelyn turned the handle and peeked around the door and into the darkness beyond. Racing back across the hall, she stacked boxes into a pyramid under the broken window with her shaking fingers. In her haste, all the boxes toppled over. Footsteps thundered closer. She whipped her head around.

Cali rushed over. "Effin' fireballs. They're coming!"

The hallway light flared brightly. Cali leaped on a cabinet a few feet away and heaved her body through the window, grunting.

"Stop!" shouted a female voice.

Raelyn's arms shook.

Cali already waited outside above her. "Come on!"

Raelyn scaled a table and sprang onto the cabinet. It crashed down. The pursuers stumbled over the spilled boxes, tripping. She had more time to aim for the window again. Pulling herself to the window at the last moment, the razor-sharp glass from the broken window offered another hazard. Cali dragged Raelyn out onto the pavement. A sharpness sliced through her forearm. Blood trickled down her elbow.

A flashlight bounced around the back corner of the museum. Raelyn froze again. Cali pulled her and dashed to the car. A second flashlight danced in the dark, moving closer and closer. A third. Raelyn tripped on a rock, skidding across the concrete.

"Get up!" Cali grabbed Raelyn's waist and threw her headfirst in the passenger seat, slamming the door and sprinting around the front. Tires squealed, and they sped out of the parking lot.

Minutes later, on a calm street, the girls looked at each other, wide-eyed. Raelyn locked her door with her trembling hands, and Cali burst out laughing.

"I can't believe we did that!" Raelyn held her hand to her pumping chest.

"I need to find this O'Reilly photographer."

Who do I know that could find information about people?

She looked at the image on her phone once more. In the portrait, a circle of laughing children surrounded a lady in the sand with an old spiral shaped tower in the background. Eight of the kids had skin features like the locals and wore torn rags. One boy on the side had wavy blond hair. He was the only one staring straight into the camera, trying to communicate something with his blue eyes.

12

KODY

On the jogging track at the Tahil base, Kody jogged in place while Dabbott bent to the pavement to retie her shoes, still somehow radiating her fresh orangey lotion scent. As desert sand blew into her face, she glanced at Kody. "I met with the chaplain. Did you?"

"No." Kody started jogging away.

"Oh, don't worry about me or anything. I'll catch up," Dabbott shouted after him.

Moments later, her footsteps caught up and kept a steady pace behind him.

"I know what you're feeling," Dabbott said.

No. She can't understand. It's my fault those soldiers died.

Her breath struggled as she said. "You didn't do anything wrong, Walsh."

Kody's feet rhythmically pounded the pavement. Despite the sand blowing in his face, he found relief in the exercise, allowing his thoughts to finally fade away.

After only five miles running together, his phone pinged. He silenced his music and saw an email from Raelyn. Kody stopped in his tracks, accidentally tripping Dabbott, who collided and fell backward. Kody reached down to help her while reading.

"I hope you have some good books at your camp, or base, or is it post? I'd never ask for help unless it's important ... Do you or an army friend have access to files on people? If I wanted to find records about Joanna Bell. I found a portrait in a museum that looks like her. There are two pictures attached to this email. The pictures were taken six months ago. It can't be her. I mean, it's not possible. Right?"

Kody typed: "I know what it's like to lose someone."

His thumb hovered over the "Send" button, but he deleted the message instead.

There's no point in trying to form anything deeper with Raelyn.

He rotated his phone, bringing it closer to his face, squinting at the photograph Raelyn sent, studying the details. The image seemed zoomed-in. Instantly, Kody recognized the old spiral tower in the background only twenty miles away. No one could miss that building, it stood out for looking like an upside-down waffle ice cream cone, except flat across the rooftop.

Dabbott looked at Kody, her face looking tired. "Did you get the same message? Meadows wants to see us. Now."

The hinges of Meadows's office door creaked with rust. Kody's shoulders extended to the full width of the door frame.

Lieutenant Meadows sat calmly behind his desk. "I know it's your day off, but we have your new team assignment. Privates Quincy and Peterson are an attachment from the Brigade Headquarters. Walsh is team lead on this one. Routine patrol. There'll be two other vehicles and twelve men."

Dabbott swayed. "Sir, I don't think I can go."

"Why?"

She turned, vomiting in the nearby trash.

Kody recoiled back. "You okay?"

She gave a thumbs up and waved him off.

"Walsh, you take the two new soldiers," said Meadows.

Kody grabbed his equipment, mulling over the information Raelyn provided.

I can help her and not become attached.

On patrol, Kody controlled the panels aboard the Armored Troop Vehicle, heading straight toward the city of Haavij that housed the spiraled building from the picture. A disgruntled man in a long robe threw trash at them, but around the next bend, a young girl offered water to the soldiers in gratitude for the military's extra aid.

Atop the tank, the new guy, Peterson, kept randomly swearing into the headset over the roar of the engines. Tattoos crawled up his long arms when he rolled up his sleeves.

Kody began, "Peterson—"

"Call me Phoenix."

"No."

Peterson chuckled as he pulled out a postcard from his pocket and studied it. "So, you like to be formal? I bet you like rules too?"

Kody took in the new guy. He looked like a lifeguard, ripped muscles with highlighted surfer hair he'd have to shave off soon. More tattoos inched out on his lower neck whenever his uniform shifted.

The other new guy, Private Quincy, blocked his beady gray eyes and pale face speckled in red freckles from the swirling sand.

A young woman tripped to her knees on the street. Kody jumped down from the tank and helped her up. He sensed Quincy and Peterson's penetrating glares on his back. As the tank slowly followed, he walked faster and discreetly showed the museum picture to men on the streets in Haavij.

"Know her?" Kody asked them in his limited broken Arabic.

A few shook their heads, and most avoided eye contact. He turned the corner to a small produce market and looked at the tower in person. It was over seven stories tall. The ancient, ruin-looking structure didn't blend into the shops lining each side of the street. One bar with a chipped red door stood out from the rest as a drunken man stumbled out.

Kody angled himself to the exact position of where the photographer must have stood. There seemed to be a rose garden at the base of the spiraled building, and trellises too, but surely no one could live inside that ancient building. It must be crumbling apart. Kody kneeled in the same spot as the woman from the photograph. He dropped and brushed his hand over the thin layer of sand.

Is she Raelyn's mom?

He sighed. There was no point in chasing a dead woman's shadow. Kody checked in on how Dabbott was feeling and sent her Raelyn's photographs to ask for help. His phone pinged upon the receipt of a new message. Expecting Dabbott, Kody's brow raised when he saw that the message came from an unknown number.

Find the woman in that picture. Break the stone. I need her.

Who is this?

Text here when you've gained possession of the woman and the stone.
You've got three weeks.

Kody shook his head in confusion. No one else had seen the picture other than Dabbott. But Kody would trust her with his life. A villager he showed the picture to must have gotten his phone number.

Who sent me this message?

13

RAELYN

WINTER SETTLED IN OAK City. Frigid air iced Raelyn's lungs as she opened the frosted glass door to Cali's backyard, letting Bear roam through the snow-globe-like scene. Raelyn's boots left tracks in the blanket of white. A flurry of red cardinal feathers fluttered about before landing back down on the soil.

Her boots slipped on the ice, and she flailed her arms in the air until she grasped onto the back of a cold lawn chair. Shivering, Raelyn unwrapped the sweatshirt hanging around her waist and threaded her arms through the sleeves. She pulled the neckline of her shirt tighter to her cheeks. Each cold breath she sucked in stung sharply in her lungs.

Raelyn caught flakes on her fingertip only to have them vanish in an instant. *Why does love disappear the same way?*

"Let's go inside, Bear."

Raelyn climbed the stairs and laid next to Cali on the bed with an abundance of food-shaped pillows surrounding her every limb, a donut pillow, a pancake pillow, a cupcake pillow to name a few. Raelyn sat next to her and reread the photographer's response for the twelfth time.

Good afternoon Raelyn,
Thanks for reaching out. Yes, I am the photographer of "J's Joy." Unfortunately, that piece is no longer available at that museum. How can I be of service? I'll be out of town in Europe for a few months, so I may not be able to respond right away.
Emme O'Reilly.

Raelyn looked at the ceiling. "What should we write back?"

The Disney World photo stuck out from Raelyn's journal.

Cali snatched it. "The woman in the museum picture looks like your Ma in this picture, but it's too hard to tell for sure. Let's send a copy of this to Emme."

"Good idea. See, Ma's wearing that necklace." Raelyn leaned in. "At Disney World, Ma wanted to ride all the roller coasters, but I was too short. Pa followed us around without a care in the world. I sat on Ma's shoulders during the fireworks display. You know, the one they do over the castle. It was like a painting in the sky, like huge roses bursting to life. That was the first and only time I saw Ma cry."

"You must be like her, then."

"How do you mean?"

"You never cry."

Raelyn quieted.

All my tears left when Ma died.

Cali tilted her head. "Ask Emme if she recognizes your ma. Here, write what I say."

"I can do it." Raelyn scrunched her nose and read the last line of the email out loud, "I'll be traveling to Tuzlicci soon. Can we meet and talk?"

She pushed send, sighed and tossed her phone into her satchel.

Cali jumped up and dug in her chaotic closet, pulling out more pillows, pinching them between her fingers like crab claws. She catapulted her pillow, whacking Raelyn straight in the ear. Raelyn's return attempt missed her target and hit Bear instead, who raised one eyebrow and slumped his head back down. Raelyn laughed and made a new list in her journal.

Reasons Why I Love Cali:

- Binge eats chips with me
- Cries every time a pet dies in a movie
- Fantasizes about her future platinum album
- Analyzes any interaction with Breanna to the smallest detail
- Makes me pet her hairy legs ... only on Sundays
- She literally jingles when she walks because of that charm bracelet
- Texts me when I'm in the same room

Cali tossed over an envelope from her fanny pack. "This is from my brother." She inched closer to Raelyn's face so the tips of their noses touched. "Is there something you're not telling me?"

"Nah."

"I think Kody likes you too."

Raelyn opened her mouth but didn't speak.

"But Kody is a challenging person. I'm not sure what's best for him right now."

Raelyn ignored her. Just like the blanket she was sitting on, if she pulled on one loose piece, the whole thing would come completely undone. Before risking unraveling herself, she needed to determine if she really wanted Kody and all the difficulties that would come with him in the packaged deal.

She pulled out his gift. "Tickets for the movie *Creed* at Oak Theater. The last movie I saw at a theater, the couple lived happily ever after. Hollywood is so frustrating, falsely portraying entertainment as reality."

"Leave it to my bestie to go and make things so serious."

"Reality is Ma being blown up on the other side of the world and Pa, who abandoned me emotionally. Now *that* makes a good film."

"You forgot the best friend who becomes the main character and saves the day."

"You know, some things *can* be serious."

Cali pulled out nail polish colors from her drawer and picked vivid pink. "I hate that Kody's enlisted. I don't hear from him much. He's glued to his work. I miss him. Every day, you know?" She blew on her nails. "Kody may have a military connection to help learn about Joanna, but I'm not gonna ask him. He's got too much on his plate."

Crap. Cali will hate me when she finds out I already asked Kody for help.

"I bet your pa knows more. Have you made up with him yet?"

"I don't know. The last month has been weird. He grounded me for checking out the warehouse."

"Don't forget him sending that cop to my house to check on you."

Raelyn snorted. "Yeah, and tracking my phone. Now, I'm avoiding him too, so it all feels worse. The distance between us this time seems different than past arguments. He's been working double shifts. Convenient, huh?"

"You know, he may not be the only one who pushes people away."

"What's that supposed to mean?"

"Nothing," said Cali.

Raelyn plucked a pen from her ponytail and pulled her journal from under a pillow. She wrote a new list.

- In fourth grade, Pa packed me a lunch every day, with a note on the sandwich.
- He leaves my slippers on the bottom step in winter so my bare feet don't touch the frigid hardwood floor
- Pa knew I needed Bear
- He moved away from everything he knows to give me better extracurriculars

Raelyn sighed. "I could forgive him and go back to the way it was, or I could leave."

Cali's head snapped up. "Leave? Where would you go?"

"Aunt Aubree's." Her phone buzzed. "Speak of the devil. I bet that's Pa."

"He's the devil now?" Cali laughed.

Raelyn's mouth dropped. "It's from that untraceable number. A second message."

Cali crawled over fast. "What's it say?"

Raelyn showed her.

help jawhara. he want all the power. hurry or he hurt your brother

Cali's brother? Kody? No ...

Raelyn leaped up, making Cali's mattress creak. "My neighbor, Yohaan, is a cop. He can help."

"No. It's probably a scam. The cops won't care about this." Cali scratched her head.

"None of this makes sense. It's probably from the museum security."

"Nah. If the museum wanted to catch us for breaking and entering, there'd be some other way of tracking us down.

"Jawhara ..." Raelyn tapped her pen on her leg. "Why do I know that word?"

"Maybe you're saying it wrong. Pronounce it like this, *Joe*-ha-rah."

"Ivy!"

"Kody's ex?"

Raelyn spoke quickly. "At karaoke night, she said jawhara means jewel or gem or stone or something. Why would anyone care about a missing jewel?"

"So, these messages are from some girl who sells jewelry and wants to get back with Kody? She's jealous or something?"

"How could it be from Ivy?" Raelyn shook away the images of Ivy's nude pictures on Kody's phone. "She doesn't have my number."

"I have her number. Let's call." Cali pushed a few buttons and waited, rolling her eyes as it kept ringing. "Ugh, voicemail."

"I wish we could text the messenger back. It won't go through, see?" Raelyn showed how she tried to reply. "It's blocked."

"Numbers can be configured to reject texts." Cali swiped her phone. "Wait! Maybe it's because we responded to that website. They may have push notifications. Let me put in my cell number and see if they respond." Cali kept clicking her phone. "Wait. The website is gone. There's no results."

Raelyn stared at her friend. "It just ... disappeared?"

"Yeah."

She paused. "I'm gonna go home."

Cali glanced at the clock. "What? Now?"

Raelyn shoved her belongings in her backpack. "Yeah. After I fix things with Pa, he will tell me and I'll get all the answers."

"Don't forget to have him sign the permission slip to Tuzlicci."

Raelyn pushed down the corner of a note to Pa on his bathroom mirror. The scent of toothpaste overwhelmed her senses.

I genuinely want to apologize
No need to blame, you're not the bad guy
Unstable ground shifts at my feet
What I knew to be true turned obsolete
Striving for clarity on how to be brave
The answers washed away in just one wave

She walked to the living room and threw logs in the burning fireplace, bringing back childhood memories of Ma and opening presents under the tree. The scent of pine needles floated in the air. Red ornaments hanging from their Douglas Fir reminded Raelyn of all the times Pa laid on his back in the snowy mountains, after strenuously sawing down a tree.

Pa's a good dad—keeps me safe and fed. He works steady hours and built my new bedroom furniture by hand.

Pa's voice echoed from down the hall. "Hun, Scrabble?"

He must've seen my note.

"You know it's midnight, right?" But any time he offered to spend with her was what she always wanted—strained or not. "Yeah, okay."

She joined him in the living room, where a cinnamon scent wafted through the air from a candle. A spoon clanked against his favorite mug as she stirred a cup of sweet tea he set next to her.

He scattered the game pieces over their table. She reordered her scrabble pieces on the plaque, then placed the word "frog." He added two tiles, then blew onto the surface of his tea, changing the shape of the misty steam in the air. Raelyn shook the tiles in her hand and placed three more. Bear readjusted and lay over her feet, warming her. Rearranging the letters on his Scrabble tray, Pa lengthened her last word by one tile.

"What do you want for breakfast tomorrow?" she asked.

Pa flipped over tiles from the side pile in silence, then rearranged the letters, spelling out "FORGIVENESS."

Her heart skipped a beat. Meeting his misty eyes, she knocked the board over as she leaped across the table and into her father's arms.

"I'm so sorry, hun. I want you to be happy and safe. I shouldn't have kept the information about how your Ma died from you."

When he wrapped his arms around her, the comfort of his lumber smell eased her muscles into tranquility. She let herself fall into her father's embrace. His tears rolled off his cheek onto her shoulder.

"I'm sorry, Pa. I've been so mean to you."

He stopped her. "No. It's okay. I'll be better. I'm sorry."

Her voice cracked. "I'm sorry."

"No, *I'm* sorry." He pulled away, then Bear joined, licking at the salty tears dripping down his face.

They both laughed.

"Bear makes everything better, doesn't he?" She sighed.

Pa nodded. "Things will be different from now on." Pa spurted upright. "Actually, I have something for you. Wait here."

He sped to his room and back, returning with a paper in his hand.

"Your ma wrote this for you to open on your eighteenth birthday. It's a little early, but here. This doesn't belong to me." He placed a worn envelope on the table.

Raelyn read aloud with shaking fingers.

My Raelyn,

Hey, munchkin. You're 18! Well, not really. Today, you're still just five. I wonder what you look like now. Still have your long hair? As I write this, your whole hand is wrapped around just one of my fingers. I cherish these tender moments alone together.

You're the best daughter I could imagine. If you ever question that, take a moment and look around. You already have everything you need. XOXO

One tear slid down her cheek. She couldn't remember the last time she cried and didn't even try to wipe her tear away.

Raelyn smiled faintly. "Thank you." She held the letter to her chest and took a deep breath.

The corner of a small, shiny image poked out from the envelope. A sonogram.

A gentle grin spread across her face as she examined her own shape inside her mother's womb.

This bond, this connection. It's all I want.

Pa exhaled slowly. "I'm glad you like it. Ma loved you. But, hun, there's more. Read the back."

Raelyn flipped it over:

Now, you'll need to share my time with a little brother. It's crazy to think he will be 12 when you read this.

You're an adult now, so you'll have your own life and priorities. But promise me to still help your brother. Protect him. Use your gifts to guide him. Support him like Pa and I have been there for you all these years. Love, Ma

Raelyn gasped. The date on the sonogram wasn't her birth year.

Baby Boy Bell

2004

Gestation: 18 weeks

12 oz

Raelyn clapped her hands over her mouth. The sonogram dropped to the floor. A sharp pain tightened in her chest.

What? Ma and Pa were gonna have a son?

The puzzle pieces of her youth snapped into place. She closed her eyes and swept herself back in time when she had to rise on her tippy toes to reach the door handle. After Ma's funeral, little Raelyn stood in pink pajamas, clutching her unicorn. She had peeked around the corner in her Aunt Aubree's hallway. Pa had spoken from the darkness. "Please, keep her. I could handle a boy—I'd know what to do. But she's too much for me to handle." Heavy circles underlined Pa's eyes. Little Raelyn backed away slowly, dropping her unicorn on the ground, and tucked herself into bed.

She had not lost one parent, but both. Pa had always wanted his son.

I can't give him that. I'm a burden.

Her heart thudded in her chest. "Did you give me up to Aunt Aubree?"

"I didn't think you'd react like this." Pa covered his face with one hand. "When your Ma died, I didn't know what I was doing with you. She was always such a good mom. Your first word was "momma." You only wanted to be held by her when you got hurt or really any time at all." He moved closer. "I couldn't do it alone. I didn't know your favorite fruit or how to braid your hair. I couldn't get anything right. A week after the funeral, I asked your Aunt Aubree to raise you."

Raelyn gasped for air and stabbed the air with a stiff finger toward the sonogram. "But you wanted him? You wanted a boy so badly you kept his sonogram?"

He picked the sonogram up off the ground. "Please calm down."

Her bottom lip trembled. She opened her mouth, but words wouldn't come.

"It was so long ago. Why does it matter anymore?" Pa wouldn't meet her eyes.

"I can't believe I forgave you. You didn't want me." Her feet cemented into the floor. "You wanted him."

"Of course I wanted you." His shoulders dropped. "Joanna miscarried. I wanted to forget losing him, but she wouldn't let me. I know I've had years to get rid of the sonogram, but after time passed, I never had the courage to." Agony lived in his small wrinkles.

Raelyn screamed. "You can't push things away because you don't want to deal with them." She froze for a moment and lowered her voice. "Well, I guess you can. You pushed me away. You stopped teaching me about hunting and trucks years ago."

"No—" Pa moved toward her, his arms extended for a hug, but she jumped back and shook her head.

"Next year, I'll go to college far away! You won't have anyone to pull you down anymore."

She wondered why she had to hide in the shadows of a boy who never saw the light of day. Her pain erupted in nonsensical screams. She hurled every object she could grasp in his direction—pillows, shoes, dog toys.

"You never wanted me!"

His eyes widened. "That's not true."

She ran to her room and stared at the meaningless dresser Pa had built her years ago. With her pen, she stabbed the picture of them on a hike together, slicing through it like a dagger. A knock sounded at her door, and a cold emptiness seeped into her veins.

"Please." He tapped on her door again.

She flung it open. "You were never there for me when I needed you." Raelyn stormed out of the room. Bear's head lifted from his pillow in the corner of the hallway.

Things will never be the same again.

She scrambled desperately, shoving her camera, toiletries, and journal into her backpack, then snapping to Bear.

Pa chased them outside. "Where are you going?"

A lump formed in her throat. "Why does it matter? You never talk to me when I'm here."

"I'm trying my best. My job is to keep you safe."

She glared back at him, heat rising in her face. "Your job is to love me!"

Pa stepped back, and his face turned white as a ghost. "What? How could you say that I don't—?"

"I'm going abroad."

"Hun, calm down. Don't act like a child."

She turned on him. "Excuse me? Even when I was eight, I could never be a child!" Her voice rose. "I had to cook for you when I was eight! Eight! Because you just sat in that same chair staring at pictures of Ma. No one helped me with my homework! Do you want to know why?"

Pa reached out his hand. "That's not true—"

"I had to figure it all out for myself because you spent all your time reading Ma's old journal articles over and over. You wasted years of my childhood. I had to step up to keep food in our pantry."

"Raelyn, that's not what happened."

She swallowed hard and jumped in her truck. "Don't call me a child! I never had the chance to miss Ma." She grabbed a form from her dashboard. "Sign this. If you don't, I'm moving in with Aubree. She said she'd sign it."

"What is it?" He ripped the seal in a straight line.

Raelyn spat out, "A permission slip for the senior class trip for Tuzlicci next week. We leave the day after Christmas."

"No. You can't go overseas." Pa folded his arms and set his lips straight.

Raelyn stretched the truth. "They'll accept Aubree's signature if I'm living with her as my primary caregiver. I already collected the forms from the school office to change my permanent address."

I don't want to live at Aunt Aubree's.

He shook his head. "But Aubree lives an hour away from your school."

"You'll get what you always wished, to pawn me off. I'll find a new school."

He leaned back onto an oak tree trunk. "You've already looked into all these options?" Pa pulled on the chain connected to his compass and gripped the metal in his palm.

She handed over a pen from her messy bun. "Sign it."

"If you travel to Tuzlicci, I'm going with you."

"No. The chaperones are already set." Her voice was solid. "What would Ma have done if she were here? If you want to prove your love, sign it."

He hovered the pen over the paper, then signed his name.

Her penmanship was so different than his. Pa wasn't forced to keep so many secrets from her. He had the choice of opening up. But for now, she'd let it rest since he signed the form. At least she had one victory on her side. She'd get the rest of her answers later. Even if it wasn't the one that truly mattered. Raelyn would ask Pa more after she returned in the New Year.

Raelyn took her keys out of the ignition and sniffed. "Pa, what would you have named my brother?"

He was choked up with a pained expression when he said, "Liam."

14

KODY

A BULLET HADN'T PIERCED through a Hesco at the Tahil base yet, and hopefully, none would during Kody's next gate duty. He peered over the desert landscape during another afternoon jog with Dabbott. They circled the same mile route for the fifth time. Guards were posted every three hundred meters by the razor wires and twenty-foot walls of interlocking sandbags. Running near the front gate, he ducked under the heavy cables that prevented trucks from entering. Kody's body ran like a machine, efficient and unrelenting.

His mind whirled as they rounded the lot. Another message came in.

I doubt Wanda would want to receive the same news as Huffman's mother. Get the stone. You have two weeks.

It has to be an administrative soldier, but what motive would they have? If I ask intelligence to look up the number, they'll probably say the POG used a burner phone.

Kody kept running, allowing the exercise to drain his concern. "Dabbott, did you show the picture of that woman by the spiraled building to anyone?" Kody's voice turned harsh as his footsteps pounded on the gritty sand.

"No. Why?"

I have to trust Dabbott. She's all I have.

Kody stopped abruptly.

"Thank god. Are we done?" Dabbott collapsed in the dirt. "Is running all you've been doing?"

Kody frowned. "I've needed some space recently. But you keep following me on these runs."

"You're not the only one missing Huffman. He was my friend too."

Kody stretched in place. Without a tree to hold on to like back at home, he balanced on one foot.

Sand swirled into her face as Dabbott put her hand on Kody's back. "Listen, the chaplain has helped me. He would—"

"No. It's almost time for your shift. I'll walk with you."

He inhaled the desert air as they approached the Ammunition Holding Area for her evening guard duty. They positioned themselves outside the entrance to guard the equipment inside. The desert wind whipped sand against his face, stinging the only skin not covered by his uniform or gloves.

"I need to learn more about the name Zohaib."

Dabbott's forehead wrinkled. "Ask civilians in Tahil."

"No, the last time I asked around, someone sent that text message I told you about. The one from the blocked number."

"What did it say again?" asked Dabbott.

"Find that woman. Break the stone. I need her. Text here when you've gained possession."

"It's a fluke."

Kody ignored her. "Some villager I showed the picture to must know who this woman is and then reported me. But who? And why is she important?"

An officer passed in front of them, silencing the soldiers' conversation and forcing them to stand at attention.

After the officer passed, Dabbott spoke. "Someone knows the lady in the picture. Let's ask Sergeant Snyder—"

Kody's body stiffened. "No!"

She shrugged. "Okay, that's clearly out. Why?"

He spoke slowly. "A few months ago, I found a chart with a list of names, and it linked Snyder to Zohaib. I need to figure out how they're connected."

Kody tried to remember the rest of the list from the warehouse chart, but his mind reeled around the image of Raelyn's electric amber eyes. Despite the many distractions within his platoon, his focus lay six thousand miles west. What was she doing right now?

Dabbott crossed her arms. "So, our intel could help Snyder."

"I don't trust him." Kody clenched his jaw.

"Why? There's no reason ..." Dabbott trailed off when Kody glared.

Kody glanced around before saying, "Snyder extorted me."

Dabbott's jaw dropped. "When? How?"

"Right before Huffman died." Kody dropped his head. "Sergeant Snyder might be involved with the hostiles who attacked."

Dabbott's eyes widened. "Walsh ... that's a *big* accusation."

"Snyder told me not to follow orders. Our orders were to take down any threat that day. He must've meant for me to allow the hostiles to take over. But if I didn't react, you could've died too."

Dabbott kicked the side of the building. "Shit!"

A loud tank rumbled by, pausing their conversation. Kody tilted his head back and stared at the stars sprinkling the sky. A hawk or some bird soared silently. His mom once told him certain animals were considered omens of events to come, relaying messages of luck or warning. Was the bird sending him a signal? Some mysterious person was threatening his life. He had to protect himself.

Kody tapped on the edge of the building. "I need to find answers. Do you know anything about Snyder's son?"

Dabbott shrugged. "The teenager he's in the market with sometimes? The one with wavy blond hair? I've only seen the back of him."

"No, I meant the tee-ball kid. In Snyder's office, there are pictures of the boy at practice. He's young, seven or so, brown hair."

She looked in the distance. "I thought he had an older kid, about thirteen."

"Are you sure the one who visits him is his son?"

Dabbott's eyes grew more tired the longer they talked. "I don't know. I never saw his face. Why does this matter?"

"If we had leverage on Sergeant Snyder, we'd have a leg up."

"Good guys don't blackmail." Seeing Kody's face, she frowned. "You can't be serious?"

Kody's shoulders relaxed. "Yeah, you're right." He clapped his hands together. "Okay, have a good shift. I'm gonna go talk to Meadows and try to trade my R and R with another soldier."

"Why?"

"My sister will be in Tuzlicci soon. I want to try and see her. I'll talk to ya later." Kody jogged to the office building.

Maybe Raelyn will be in Tuzlicci too.

He passed by the med center building, hoping he'd never be a patient in there, when, all of a sudden, Private Peterson stepped from around the corner, cutting him off.

"Let's go. You're needed in room B14," Peterson said.

Kody tried to move around him, but Peterson stuck his arm out.

"I know we haven't seen eye to eye, but I found that woman." Peterson's grin twisted.

Kody stiffened. "Tell me more."

"Follow me."

Kody's forehead wrinkled, and he hesitated before following. Peterson snaked him through back hallways and beckoned him into a small office room. Kody paused but walked through the door. The room was empty except for one chair and a desk. Kody's gut tightened.

Peterson shoved him inside in a fury, attacking Kody.

Kody rammed his fist into Peterson's jaw. But his elbow pounded on Kody's shoulder, making him keel over backward.

Peterson turned and narrowed his eyes. "What did you do with the women?"

"What are you talking about?" Kody threw a punch, but Peterson tackled him, taking out his legs.

A blow to the ribs stole his breath. He smashed into the wall. Pain ripped through his back, and Kody thudded to the floor. His hip bone met concrete.

Peterson shook his head "You're not as macho as you think, man. Stop fighting."

Kody rose and held his fist in front of his face. But Private Quincy jumped out from the shadows and slammed Kody into the door. Two trained soldiers against one. He froze when Quincy pulled out a gun. The pressure of the cold barrel pressed against his temple.

"We know what you're up to," threatened Quincy.

"Don't shoot him," Peterson commanded Quincy.

Kody controlled his breathing, glaring him down.

Peterson rocketed a blow to Kody's gut. "What did you do to those two women?"

Groaning, Kody hunched over as a distraction. He knocked the gun out of Quincy's hand and hit Peterson in the face—one, two, three times. Peterson stumbled back into a desk, blood rushing from his nose. Kody grabbed Peterson's head and pushed it. His knee collided with the man's smug face, and Peterson fell.

Kody licked blood from his lips.

"What the hell?" Kody bellowed, kicking the weapon away. He turned.

Quincy held up a phone, his beady gray eyes taunted him. "Smile for the camera, Walsh." He snarled. "I can edit this. You initiated the attack. Now, we own you. Do what we say, or no more promotions for little Kody."

That video could get me kicked out.

A sharp pressure clamped on his temples, and his surroundings faded away to a blur. His jaw dropped. Everything he had worked for could be swiped away. His future would be obliterated. He stared at the bloodied carpet and broken desk.

If Quincy and Peterson were doing something shady, others were involved. They couldn't manage alone. Kody considered that a tech or a supply soldier had helped. The Criminal Investigation Division would fry them if found out. No commander wanted investigators sniffing around. An air conditioner clicked on from the vent.

"What do you want?" Kody growled.

Peterson covered his bloody face with one hand. "I'll ask you one more time. Where are the two women?"

Kody growled. "I don't know what you're talking about. Delete the video."

"No. You have two days to return those women, or Meadows sees the footage."

Kody paused before he asked, "Was it you who sent me the threats?"

Peterson glared. "What are you talking about?"

15

RAELYN

At the New Year's Eve dance in Tuzlicci, a flowery scent spread throughout the hotel's rooftop garden. Atop a hill, the view could've been plastered on the cover of a postcard. Raelyn moved to the roof's edge. Below, vines climbed the buildings and cream-colored awnings. The setting tangerine sun cast perfect lighting of the town square, so she snapped shots of the slight bend of the brick bell tower and the sprouting red roses lining café windows.

A man in all black paced below by the outdoor market. He seemed to be the same size as the guy she thought may have been following her during a tour earlier that week. But of course, it was just her imagination.

Technicolor lights bounced around from the hotel's interior reception room. Raelyn's cranberry-colored dress flapped on her thigh with each swooshing step back to Cali as the DJ played "Shut up and Dance with Me" by Walk the Moon.

"Come on. I've seen you dance in your PJs at home to Michael Jackson." Cali pulled Raelyn onto the dance floor, spinning her friend. Her lemon lotion was laid on thick for that dance, but Raelyn basked in her best friend's citrusy scent. It was better than the smell of all the sweaty boys dancing around. Raelyn's dress flew up fast, so she shot arms down to flatten it, but not before her lace underwear was viewable by the entire class.

"Cute panties!" Cali swung like a trapeze artist from one side of the floor to the other, then formed a circle of students for history's greatest dance-off. Mason chopped through the air with his cane, showing off his dance-karate moves. Music blared, but after the embarrassing underwear reveal, Raelyn stood as frozen as an ice sculpture.

"We glow like angels together, darling," Cali said in a British accent, batting her eyes under a sparkling tiara that matched her short, white dress. She jaunted a little shoulder shimmy and nodded slightly to Breanna. "Never have I ever made out in Tuzlicci."

Raelyn smiled, shaking a finger at her.

"You know Mason would've agreed to be your date. Why didn't you ask him?"

Because I want Kody.

"Because I can't dance."

When couples paired together for a slow song, Raelyn pulled Cali through the huge arched doorway to the garden.

Raelyn pouted her lips. "I can't believe we fly back home tomorrow."

"Oh, cheetahs and monkeys! I didn't tell you? Mom got permission to supervise us when all the other students return home."

"So, we have more time in Tuzlicci?"

"Yeah, since Kody's here, she said we could visit a few cities with him so we're not stuck to her work schedule. We'll meet up with my mom in a few days."

"Kody?" Raelyn's head snapped to meet Cali's eyes.

Cali clapped her hands together, making her charm bracelet jingle. "O-M-G, Rae, I'm stoked to see him again."

"How has this not been brought up?" Raelyn's chest constricted. "He's gonna be here?"

"I told you that. You're always daydreaming."

Raelyn approached the marble face of an ancient statue on the garden's fountain and skimmed her fingertips across its cheek. What was this man's story? Did he fight for his country like Kody? Shades of rose and plums highlighted the sky from their balcony view. The breeze struck her face as he gazed at the wildflower fields in the distance.

Cali's voice rang out. "Come dance!"

"I can't. I need to see if that Emme photographer emailed me yet."

"I got this." In a few quick clicks on the phone, Cali typed:

Mrs. O'Reilly - Stop ignoring me! I need your answers about Joanna Bell! Remember me?! I'm not going anywhere! I'll be expecting your response in two hours!

Raelyn blew a loose strand of hair out of her line of vision as she tried to see what Cali wrote. "Hey! You can't send that!" She deleted the message and started again.

Mrs. O'Reilly,
I'm your biggest fan, and I'd love to meet you for an article I'm writing for the Oak City Times. Can you meet in Tuzlicci tomorrow?
Yours Truly, Kathy Ferriwinkle

"Ferriwinkle?" Cali snorted a laugh.

"Nothing else has worked. Maybe a fake name will."

A cloud of cigarette smoke puffed out from around a trellis of the rooftop garden, and Natalie's voice whispered, "Raelyn would fit in better if she moved back to the mountain. And that dress, ugh."

Raelyn looked down at her dress. A lump caught in her throat.

Natalie coughed. "And I'd never come without a date. How pathetic." She rounded the bend with a cluster of girls, and her eyes grew like a balloon.

Cali's brow furrowed. "Natalie, you don't have to be a bitch because Mason would rather be with Raelyn than you." Cali threw that saucy smile of hers, and then turned her back.

"I d-didn't m-mean—" Natalie flicked the cigarette into the bushes.

But Cali guided Raelyn away to the shadows. "She's just jealous."

Raelyn twirled the hem of her dress around her finger. "I'm gonna go to that café downstairs."

"Want me to come with you?" Cali's eyes drifted back to Breanna smashing the dance floor to pieces.

Raelyn shook her head, knowing Cali wanted to spend more time with Breanna since they just became an official couple.

"You look pheno-pickle. Next dance, you'll have a date, and we'll rent a limo, and Justin Timberlake will sing to us all night. Wait! JT will be your date. Unless you have someone else in mind?"

"Nope. I'll be happy with some Justin Timberlake. Though, he's like forty years old. That's Pa's age. Eww."

Cali giggled and skipped away barefoot.

The music faded as Raelyn left the dance, taking the elevator downstairs.

Raelyn stepped onto the cobblestone street, breathing in the foreign air. A chalk artist on her hands and knees colored in a gorgeous drawing on the street that would be washed away in a week's time.

Stucco peeled from the side of a café, revealing chunks of exposed brick. Raelyn tugged on her updo to let it fall loose to her waist, and with the back of her hand she wiped off the makeup Cali had drawn on. She pressed her fingertip to the café's glass window of desserts and tried to keep her mouth from drooling at the cheesecake options. Her stomach grumbled.

A man inside the rustic pizzeria waved her in. Raelyn plopped onto an old metal chair and fumbled through her translation app but ended up pointing to the cheesecake she liked through the glass case. The man mimed a chef's kiss with his fingers and smiled.

While waiting, she pulled out one of her journals from her satchel and reached back to pluck a pen from her messy bun, forgetting her hair was down. A pen that matched her dress stuck out of her satchel. The tip clicked repetitively under her thumb as her thoughts trailed to the dance. She blotted the page with a sea of ruby ink.

Meet me where cliffsides sings a harmony
History echoes a tune from memory
Meet me where the map changes to crystal blue
Feathered arrow points to a central clue

Someone tapped her shoulder. Raelyn snapped her journal shut and whipped around. Her arm knocked over the vase of red roses from the bar, causing a loud clatter.

"Whoops. Sorry. Let me get that." She looked up into Kody's soulful eyes.

Shivers rattled her spine, and words failed her.

"Buongiorno." Kody's bold eyes bore into her soul. Her whole body fought her mind about whether to stay put or finally crush her lips against his. He had a fresh, clean smell like a shirt flapping in the summer breeze on a clothesline.

The waiter chose that exact moment to deliver her extra-large slice of cheesecake. She dropped her head so her hair shielded her cheeks, most likely the same shade as the strawberry topping on her dessert. In the reflection of the cheesecake glass, her slender reflection was dwarfed, swallowed by his tall, wide frame.

Kody pointed to an empty corner booth. His chest filled his shirt when he held his arm out to let her pass. She lingered to breathe in his sharp aftershave. As she scooted into the booth, the leathery cushion stuck to her thighs. His knees hit hers under the table before he readjusted.

Raelyn couldn't help but glance at the curves of his muscles, imagining wrapping both hands around his biceps. Her fingertips probably wouldn't be able to touch.

He laid both his hands on the table, as if an open invitation. "I haven't received your report on the books I lent you." He confidently took her hands in his.

Her breath hitched. "I didn't want to bother you."

When his rare grin showed itself, a light came from deep within that beamed through his eyes and spread to every part of his face. "You're never a bother. Sorry for what I said before I was deployed."

She pulled her hands away. "So, then why say those things?"

"I'm sorry. Let's forget about it." He looked off in the distance. "So … have you been busy with your journals? What's in there anyway?"

"Mostly poems.

Kody sat back. "When did you start writing?"

When I was about ten. My poetry stemmed from a need to connect with Ma. I thought I would learn more about her if I tried her hobbies. But over time, poetry evolved into a natural rhythm.

His eyes seared through her. "Would you read one for me?"

"It's personal." She quieted and turned her head away. "If I share my poetry with you, it's like giving you a piece of me. You go back to the base in a few days. So, I can't."

He looked away.

Her throat went dry. "Um, I should probably go. I need to cyber stalk a photographer." Raelyn pushed back on the chair legs.

Kody leaned forward. "So, did you like the movie, *Creed*?"

She paused for a beat. "Oh! Yes, thank you for those tickets. That was so sweet of you." She tried to read him, but his eyes never matched the rest of his face. "I'd take *that* actor to the dance."

Kody smirked. "Oh, would you? Do you have a type?"

"What do you mean?"

Kody leaned back and cleared his throat. He paused and narrowed his eyes as if unsure if he should go on.

"What is it?"

"How do you feel about your best friend being Black?"

What if I say the wrong thing?

"Oh." She fidgeted. "We haven't really talked about it. I learned about the term color blind—I thought I didn't see color before. Race never mattered." She paused and stirred her straw. "I may have been looking at it wrong. To be color blind would be to deny who she is."

He nodded.

"But it's confusing. I don't want to treat Cali differently than other friends. Sometimes, I'm afraid I'm going to mess it all up. And then there's *you*—"

Kody arched his eyebrow. "Me?"

Raelyn's cheeks warmed and she fumbled, "I don't want to put her family in a bad position if I say the wrong thing and make a situation worse.

His hard features shifted to softness. "Speaking of color ..." Kody leaned forward. "Red may be my new favorite."

She glanced down at her dress, realizing she showed more cleavage by leaning forward, so she straightened fast just as a waiter came by. Ice crackled against the water he poured from the pitcher.

Kody stretched out, putting both hands behind his head. "We'll have limoncello and the biggest pizza you make."

She smiled. "You're going to eat all of that?"

"I share."

"You didn't want to share fries with me at that karaoke bar."

There it is, that devilish grin.

Kody gulped down the chilled drink but held her eyes. "Topping?"

She smiled while tying her straw wrapper into little knots. "I like lots of sausage."

Kody choked on his water mid-laugh.

"Oh, I meant..."

"Forget it. So, how was the dance?" He held out the space between his words like a sweet, seductive torture skill. Pieces of herself became lost, disappearing into his gaze.

Just as the chef tossed pizza crust into the air near the back oven, someone walked into their table, causing Raelyn to jump and clutch her heart.

Mason? Of all the times for him to show up.

"Are you okay?" Two male voices asked the same question, but only one voice sliced into her soul.

"You scared me, Mason."

Mason gripped his cane. "Sorry. Cali said you might be down here. I had a little trouble finding it."

She squirmed in her seat. "This is Kody."

Mason frowned. The booth table shifted slightly when Kody stood out of respect. Despite almost being the same height, Mason looked half Kody's weight. After he seemed to realize they wouldn't shake hands, Kody sat back down.

Mason moved forward. "You left the dance."

"Yeah, I was hungry." Raelyn glanced at Kody. His eyes had lost their spark.

"I didn't get a chance to compliment your dress." Mason held out his hand. "May I feel?"

"Uh. Okay." Raelyn stood and held out the fabric to Mason's hand.

His face turned a shade of brick red. "Satin? Pretty."

Kody sat upright and stared into his glass as if he were studying the cracks in his ice cube. The tension in the air was as tight as her dress was on her body. The waiter dropped off the plate of hot, gooey pizza, making her mouth water.

Mason put his back to Kody. "Smells like you got your food. Do you want me to walk you back to your room?"

"Why?" Her head twisted around. "Is this town dangerous?" For a moment, she thought about the man in black who was probably just a figment of her imagination.

Kody shook his head silently.

Mason smiled. "We could eat in your room."

Raelyn gently tapped Mason's hand, then pulled away. "Thanks, but I'm gonna stay. Maybe we can share notes on the cathedral tour sometime?"

Mason lit up. "Okay! Hug?" He held his arms out. Raelyn looked at Kody, who guzzled down his ice water and leaned back in the chair again. She allowed Mason to wrap his arms around her before he walked away. A big sigh left her lips, but when she turned her attention back to Kody, an invisible wall masked his face.

Is he jealous? Bored?

"Mason likes you," Kody said.

Raelyn scrunched her nose but wouldn't meet his eye. "Nah, he's just being nice." She playfully pushed her hand against Kody's firm chest, resisting the urge to keep her hand there a moment longer.

When the first cheesy bite of pizza hit her tongue, she moaned.

Kody's eyes widened, and the twinkle returned. His sparkling white teeth had a spec of tomato on them.

Raelyn smiled. "You've got something on your teeth."

"I like it there." He didn't try to swipe it away but grinned bigger.

She laughed and touched his forearm. Unsure how long she could acceptably keep her fingertips on his skin, Raelyn bravely traced the vein running from his inner elbow to his wrist. The heat on his skin gave her goosebumps. He licked his lips, making Raelyn avert her eyes to the roses on the café's windowsill.

Kody laid his other hand on top of hers, sandwiching her fingers between his warm skin. "Can I take you to your next dance?"

Raelyn's heart tumbled into chaotic spasms. Her words dried up in her throat.

Is he joking?

She leaned forward and sipped some water. The freezing liquid flowed down her throat. "Don't make promises you can't keep."

He pulled away and dropped his gaze.

Raelyn's stomach twisted into tense knots. "Sorry, it's just that Pa lied to me about a lot of things recently. I don't want my friends to disappoint me too."

"Right, we're friends." Kody cleared his throat. "What did your Pa lie about?"

"Everything. He and Ma were going to have another baby. A little boy."

"So, you're upset because he didn't tell you, or because you didn't want a brother?"

"I've always wanted a brother, but I'm most upset because that baby was an important part of Ma's life I never knew about, which makes her a stranger. I can't tolerate that thought." Her eyes watered, but tears refused to fall. "What's worse is, Pa didn't want me. All these years, I assumed I was a burden to him. It seems I was right." Her cheeks burned, and a lump rose in her throat.

How will my relationship with Pa ever get better?

"I doubt he thinks that. What would Joanna say?"

"Probably something along the lines of there being two sides to every story." Raelyn took another bite and said quietly, "I just can't believe he never told me."

Kody took a deep breath. "So, you hate secrets?"

Raelyn nodded.

She ripped tiny pieces of her pizza crust and nibbled. In silence, he shoveled in piece after piece of pizza.

After more conversation, he signed his name on the receipt. "Ready to go?"

Kody held the front door open. Fiddling with the strap on her satchel, she started moseying up the cobblestone hill.

In the silence between them, she stared up at the crisp array of stars. Different constellations shone than what she was used to. The stars blossomed in the darkness, and the crescent moon waltzed over the sea down the hill in the distance. She plucked a red rose from a bush and propped it behind her ear.

Kody pushed a thumb in his pocket and offered his elbow. "Can I walk you up?"

Raelyn gulped hard and took his arm, moving closer. "I can take care of myself, thank you very much."

"Even with all the evil villains in this quaint town?" He grinned.

"Yes, sir."

Kody pushed his sleeves higher over his biceps, his features blending into the night. "Let me see some of your self-defense."

Raelyn laughed. "Now?"

"Yup. Face me."

Locked under his spell, she said, "Anytime now, soldier."

He reached out, clutching her wrist. "If I grab your wrist on this side, lift your hand up like you're holding a mirror to your face. Take my wrist with your other hand and rotate." He moved her arms. "Good. Now use your hip."

"But you're so big."

He frowned. "It doesn't matter."

"And if some guy grabs me on the opposite side?" She wrapped her hand around his wrist.

"Pretend you're playing foosball." He maneuvered away. "Squeeze and twist. Then, kick him in the crotch."

She laughed. "What if he comes at me from behind?"

Silhouetted against the moon, he said, "Then we need a second date to cover that."

Raelyn wrinkled her nose. "This isn't a date."

"Okay."

Faint music played from the alleyway. They stood next to the pizzeria, and she leaned against the wall while the voice of Dan Stevens sang "Evermore" from a speaker. After listening to the first few lines, she bit her bottom lip and became hyperaware of Kody's breathing. She matched each of her inhales with his, their chests rising and falling in unison. The hairs on her arms stood on end.

Kody moved toward her, pinning her between his body and the wall. The energy circulating between them was too much for her to handle. Holding her breath seemed like the only option. Kody tucked a loose strand of her hair behind her ear and leaned toward her lips.

"Raelyn!" Wanda's voice echoed from the hotel lobby entrance, making her jump. "Dear? Are you down there? It's almost midnight."

Kody whispered, "Raelyn ..."

Every time he said her name, shivers worked their way down her whole body, but she couldn't kiss him at midnight on New Year's Eve—that was too big of a deal. It wouldn't just be a kiss, but a new beginning. She could see the strong column of his throat work as he seemed to be thinking hard about something. Raelyn had to find something else to focus on, so she asked, "Can you do me a favor?"

His hungry eyes locked on hers. "What do you need?"

16

KODY

On New Year's day, after all the other seniors flew back to Oak City, Kody trailed after Raelyn and Cali wherever they wanted to explore. While dragging his boots along the cobblestone at markets and shops, he tried to honor Raelyn's request of the favor she had asked the night before—to find a photographer, Emme O'Reilly—but didn't have much luck.

Eventually, Cali led them to the base of the cliff, only a few feet from the pounding waves crashing into the rocks.

"I've made a discovery! Get me a flag." Cali rushed to claim an abandoned, rock-covered beach just outside Tuzlicci. She immediately stripped down to the swimsuit under her clothes and tickled Raelyn until she did the same and revealed her one-piece red swimsuit hugging all her curves.

Kody peeled his eyes off her form and stared through the transparent water on the white-pebbled beach. His heels sank unevenly into the wet sand as he soaked up the rays. Facing the horizon, he watched Raelyn snap a picture, then point her camera at him.

He had better reception on his phone there than he had all day. Quickly, Kody researched information about Emme O'Reilly's career and tried to determine where she might be staying. A message distracted his pursuits.

You have one day. Find Jawhara. Break the stone.
Or Cali goes up in flames.

Kody's fist clenched.

No one in Tahil knows where Cali is. She's safe here.

Regardless, if this guy laid one finger on Cali, there was no way Kody would be able to contain himself.

Kody's attention flickered back to Raelyn splashing in the waves. Tiny curls formed where the loose strands of her hair were damp. If Joanna was the lady in the museum picture and was somehow alive, there must be something good that kept her from returning to Raelyn.

Raelyn skipped rocks by the sea. Joining her, Kody picked up a soft stone and threw it twice as far as hers, but the ripples hers made looked more poetic.

"Can I teach you how I shoot?"

Raelyn looked over. "Like a gun? How did an airline allow you to bring a gun on board?"

Kody dug into his backpack. "Same as anyone else. Locked case in a checked bag."

"Okay. You think it's safe?"

He pointed to a tree. "That's the target. Watch my arms and posture."

"Isn't this illegal?"

He shrugged. "Probably. There's no one around."

She smirked. "I thought you always followed the rules. I can't figure you out."

Kody steadied his feet shoulder-width apart. The easy squeeze of the trigger with the pad of his finger came naturally, and the familiar scent after a shot wafted in the air. The bullet pierced the bark. When Kody turned the weapon over to Raelyn, her innocent face absorbed the sun's light as she tilted her head to the side. He stepped closer, correcting the awkward angle at which she held the gun, and steadied her hand.

"Aim and shoot."

Raelyn squeezed the trigger. The crack of the bullet permeated the air, sharp and crisp. She jerked back from the gun's powerful kick, but the bullet successfully lodged an inch above his in the trunk's center. She grinned.

"Not bad for a recruit," Kody commended her, matching her bright smile.

She smoothed the tangles from her windblown hair; the compulsion to kiss her flowed through his veins.

"I wonder how bad it hurts?" She grimaced.

"Being shot?" He put the safety on. "I wouldn't know. Hopefully, I never will."

She turned back to the beach, and without looking up, she wrapped both hands around his forearm as they walked.

Arriving at their backpacks, they each looked around for Cali, who was off in the distance by the shoreline. Kody stooped down to the sand and propped himself up on one elbow. He wanted to put his other arm under Raelyn's head like a pillow but gave her space. It didn't matter; Raelyn curled into him.

"It's chilly," she whispered.

The slant of her collarbone framed perfectly by her swimsuit evoked fantasies of where his lips might explore one day. Kody cleared his throat and used every ounce of energy to take his eyes off her.

"I told you about Pa. Tell me about your relationship with your parents," she said.

"My mom is full of fire and strength, like Cali. She's a proud woman, intelligent, and she raised us well. If I ever had a daughter … never mind."

"And your dad?"

"I refuse to be like Walter. I don't like a lot of choices he made."

"I only see good in you."

Kody grunted. "Naw, Good people don't kill others. I've been trained to be a weapon. Being the strongest person in the room is how everyone sees me."

"I bet when you taught me self-defense, it's because you think I'm weak?" Raelyn's velvet voice drifted toward him through the sound of the waves crashing on the shore.

Kody held back a grin. "And how did you come to that conclusion?"

"You treat me like a damsel in distress." She rolled away from him a bit.

"How?"

"You open doors for me. You paid for my dessert. I can take care of myself." She crossed her arms, never once breaking her stare.

Kody ached to feel her rosy lips. "You don't need someone to take care of you, but that doesn't change the fact that I want to."

She froze. "Don't say things like that."

"So you don't want anyone to take care of you? I bet you think that if you have to rely on someone, then you're weak."

"You don't know me." Her chin moved in his direction. This time, he couldn't deny the hungry look in her honey eyes.

Kody couldn't resist Raelyn any longer or deny his interest. With two days left, he had to take advantage of their time. He held his breath, inches away from those lips.

A vespa's horn blurted out, cracking through the air like a whip. When she turned toward the source of the sound, the coconut lotion on her neck wafted to his nose. Then, she moved away—the moment lost.

Cali pranced over and unfurled a map. "Let's find a hostel. My feet are gonna start squealing like a piglet." She swirled her finger in the air, then placed it down at random. "That's where we're going."

Kody grunted. "Okay, then. Nothing can go wrong there."

Cali skipped ahead.

"So … if you can find me the photographer, I'll owe you a favor. What would you want?" Raelyn asked.

"When Mason asks you out, turn him down."

Their hostel down an alley was lined with trash. Kody lifted the bottom of his shirt over his nose and breathed through the fabric. A figure darted behind the dumpster around the corner.

"What was that?" Raelyn twisted, looking further down the alley.

"Probably a buffalo," said Cali.

"A harmless homeless man," said Kody.

The sunset stained the clouds red, framing the ocean as the day slid into the quickening evening.

At check-in, the man handed over keys and pointed up. "Fourth floor. No elevator."

Once in their shared co-ed room with ten bunk beds, Cali leaped on a top bunk and Kody's backpack landed on the lower bed with a *thunk*. On the balcony, Raelyn's camera's strap flapped in the wind as she snapped pictures from the fourth floor.

A solo guitarist played a slow tune in the street below, but a series of connected flat rooftops blocked him from view. Raelyn pointed her camera at the clotheslines tied across the alley, all connected to adjacent balconies. Clothes dangled across the line, swinging gently high over the street. A bird landed on the rope, making it sag a bit, before flying off.

"Any award-winning pictures?" Kody slid closer to her, his finger brushing against her side.

The sunset made her skin glow when she leaned over a little to show him her photos. When he laid eyes on his favorite image, Kody put his hand out to stop her and squinted in for a closer look.

In the image, a mother and daughter sat in front of a fountain. The mother was fixated on her daughter, passing the girl a plump balloon. The petite girl reached out for the dangling string, but her longing eyes focused on a stone well. This second of separation caused the balloon to hover between them, frozen in place between the two, only moments before it drifted away, forever out of reach.

"Some of the guys on base have told a story about a fountain like this. The well offers magic with each sip, a choice between immortality and love. Which would you choose?"

"Easy. Love," she said.

If only Kody could capture Raelyn's sweetness in a bottle, seal it tight with a lid, and take it with him to the base.

He cleared his throat. "Are you good at everything?"

"Photography isn't hard. Let me show you." Raelyn placed the camera in his big hands. "Look around at what you find most inspirational. Aim and shoot."

He pointed the lens straight at her face. Raelyn gently pushed the camera down and looked at him, moving closer. Kody's heart rate spiked. She rose higher on her tiptoes.

"Wild pirates! This is tangy!" Cali's voice broke the spell from inside the hostel room. Raelyn hopped away from his side just before Cali joined them on the balcony.

"I thought you went to brush your teeth?" Raelyn giggled.

Cali nodded. "I did, but gelato tastes *so* much better than toothpaste. Who wants my sticky fingers?" Cali stuck her hands in Kody's face. "I'm so sticky! Lemon gelato is my favorite today. I bet I'll have a new favorite tomorrow."

Tomorrow. I have to kiss Raelyn tomorrow.

Turning away, he read a new text from his friend, Private Dabbott. It read:

The Zohaib leader guy takes teen girls away from their families.

Hours later, Kody woke in his hostel bed, coughing and rubbing his eyes to confusing flashes of dancing red light.

Heat. Why is it so hot?

Thick smoke burned his throat.

A crackle popped to his right. His head snapped in the direction. His sheets twisted around his ankles, nearly tripping him. He bolted out of bed.

Kody jostled Cali, roaring, "Fire!" He pulled on her arm, bringing Cali to her feet. "Let's go!"

"What?" Cali turned groggily.

Raelyn coughed, but he couldn't see her through thick smoke. A crash boomed behind him, making Cali shriek.

"Where are you?" Raelyn's small voice was nearby.

"This way!" Kody squinted, then tossed all three of their backpacks on at once.

He touched the door with the back of his forearm, cringing. Heat seared through his flesh. Pain scorched his skin.

"The balcony!" Kody shouted.

"What about the door?" Raelyn squeaked.

"Blocked!" Kody commanded. "Come here!"

He pushed them down to bend low. Sweat dripped off his forehead. Coughing, he ripped open the window. Smoke flew out, stinging his eyes. He glanced in each direction. They were too high. A lone red-headed man stood on the cobblestone below, his hands in his pockets.

"Help!" Kody yelled.

The man turned behind a corner of a pizzeria restaurant.

What the hell?

Kody straddled the window ledge and tossed their backpacks far below to the cobblestone. The flames steadily approached from behind.

His eye darted to the left. "I'll throw you to that balcony. You'll pull yourself over the edge."

"What!" Raelyn clasped her hands over her mouth.

"Okay." Cali bent her knees slightly. "I'm ready!"

Below was only open air, then solid ground.

If she falls, she dies.

Kody wrapped his hands around his sister's waist and heaved. A grunt exploded from deep in his throat as he tossed Cali through the air. She latched on to the other railing and pulled herself over. She was okay.

Quickly, he turned to Raelyn, holding out his arms.

"I can't do that!" Raelyn backed up.

"You have to!" He pulled her closer. "Keep your eyes open."

Kody wrapped one arm around her waist and, in a swift motion, flung her into the air. Screaming, she reached her hands out and grasped the ledge.

Cali hauled Raelyn over the rail, and they landed with a thump on the balcony. Kody stood on the ledge, took a deep breath, and jumped. Whizzing through the air, he dropped too fast. But his fingers barely latched onto the bottom rail. His muscles strained, but his grip slipped. He squeezed and gritted his teeth. Panting, he pulled himself up. Fire sparked out the window, sending showers of red onto the pavement. It blazed in a rampage, devouring the side wall of the hostel.

Cali hugged him close, coughing. "We have to get down!"

Kody glanced in every direction. He saw a guy who looked identical to Quincy forty feet below—short and stocky, with flaming red hair.

"Help!" Kody waved, but the man turned and disappeared into the shadows. He swore under his breath and pointed. "That clothesline rope, we'll scale above the alley to that window."

Raelyn shook her head. Kody tugged hard on the clothesline draped between the two balconies, testing its strength.

Flames busted out from the window of the hostel room they had exited.

"Kody! What do we do?" Cali started crying.

He lifted Raelyn to the rope. "Hands first. Wrap your knees and ankles around the rope. Keep moving. Don't stop."

Raelyn left the balcony, suspended over the cobblestone. She had to make it to the other side. There were no other options. The temperature behind him rose.

"Let me go now!" Cali moved further from the burning window.

"No!" He restrained his sister. "The rope may only hold one at a time."

Raelyn's piercing scream filled the air. He whipped around. She hung by her legs. Raelyn's fingertips pointed straight to the ground.

Kody's gut wrench from dread. He climbed out onto the clothesline, praying it'd carry them both. He pulled himself halfway across. Cali screamed behind him.

Kody froze between the two. His gaze jerked to where Cali stood. There was a loud snap and the entire balcony dropped a foot. He kept going on the rope, reaching Raelyn in seconds. Squeezing his knees together around the rope, he pulled her clammy hands back up. He resituated and hung by his hands.

"Grab on to me!" Kody commanded.

Raelyn wrapped her legs around his waist.

"Slide down, then drop to that rooftop." His muscles strained. The roar of flames grew. Raelyn lowered herself, using Kody's body like a ladder. She slipped, but his foot caught under her armpit. He groaned, holding both their weight with sweaty hands. Raelyn dropped to the other rooftop, further from the fire.

Cali screeched as her platform dropped another foot. Crackling flames and the sound of splitting wood came from within the smoke.

Fire sirens echoed in the distance. Kody swung on the clothesline all the way to Cali. He dropped onto the unsteady balcony, but his weight sent it crashing. His arms wrapped around Cali as she screamed. Their balcony collided with one below.

"Jump!" Kody heaved Cali from the cracked balcony to the lower one.

It had an escape ladder. He unlatched the clasp, letting it tumble down to the cobblestone below with a loud bang. Heat poured out of the hostel.

"Hurry! You go first." Kody shouted.

Cali wasted no time, swinging her body down the metal until finally standing on solid ground.

She's safe.

Kody scaled down and landed with a thud. He ran over to where Raelyn dangled her legs from the side of the roof. Black smoke exploded out a nearby window.

Kody looked up twenty feet high to Raelyn. "Jump to me. I'll catch you!" He shouted, bracing himself.

"On the count of three!" Kody hollered. "One!"

Raelyn shook her head above. "No!"

"Two."

"I can't!" Her grip tightened on the side of the roof.

"Three!"

Raelyn let go, and her scream soared through the smoky air. She smacked hard against him, and they tumbled on the hard cobblestone. Her small body fit perfectly in his arms as her head curled into his chest.

She's okay.

"Where's Cali?" she asked.

"Behind me on the ground," said Kody, panting.

"But where?" Raelyn's head swiveled.

He rolled over. Cali stood leaning against the outside of a shop, her eyes on the stars. But behind her in the dark alleyway, a shadowy figure approached, reaching his arm out as if to snatch her. Panic took over.

"CALI!" Kody bellowed, raising himself up and rolling Raelyn to the ground.

He sprinted to her. Fire trucks pulled up, blocking access to her. He ran around the side of the giant red engine. Cali was alone. Kody reached her side and stared down the dark alleyway. Quincy's gray, beady eyes glared back before he disappeared behind a corner.

17

RAELYN

Hours later, Raelyn followed in silence as Cali sauntered ahead. In a daze, she tried to focus on the cliffsides in the distance and the sunrise bouncing off the rooftops in the small town. Vibrant burgundy popped out from its sister shades, drenching the morning sky, but she could only think of the flames.

"There's a winery ahead. I'm gonna go see when they open," said Cali.

Raelyn raised her hands. "Wait! Are we in the twilight zone or something? Can we talk about what happened?" She glanced between them. "How are we not hurt?"

Cali let out her breath. "I told you Kody could save the world."

"We almost died. Why are y'all not freaking out?" asked Raelyn.

"We're safe. Everything's okay." Kody looked off into the distance as if trying to hide the anger she could see under the surface.

"Did you both lose too much oxygen to your brain or something?"

Cali huffed, crossed her arms, and walked faster down the winding path. Raelyn stared after her friend.

Kody avoided Raelyn's gaze. "There was probably a loose wire, and the hostel didn't meet code guidelines. The firemen controlled the flames. It's over."

He's worried about something else. What is it?

"So, just like that, we're fine and move on?" Raelyn asked.

"Yes." Kody wrapped his arm around her shoulder. He nodded to the menu shown outside the entrance to a winery. "Which would you try? Sangiovese or Primitivo?"

"I don't drink."

Cali's eyes grew wide. "Wait, Kody, are you limping?"

"I'm fine." He waved her attention forward.

Cali squared off her jaw. "The winery won't open for hours."

Kody nodded. "Good. No need to drink your emotions."

"Excuse me! At least I *have* emotions."

Kody didn't flinch and stared down his sister. "Do you have something to say?"

"Yeah. Don't act like you don't give a damn about my friend when you clearly do."

Raelyn backed up.

No, no, no. Don't put me in the middle.

"Stop being so dramatic, Cali," said Kody.

Cali's jaw dropped. "Fine. I'll be the cheery one that everyone wants. I thought you understood me. I guess not."

"That's not fair." Kody crossed his arms.

Silence.

Cali's hands shook.

Wait. She's scared.

"You're hiding what you're actually upset about, aren't you?" Raelyn moved in for a hug. "It's okay to be afraid."

A tear dropped from Cali's eyes, and her voice shook. "I—I didn't say I was scared."

"The fire was bad. It's okay to be upset." Raelyn tightened her hold on her best friend.

Cali's chest rose and fell harder. "You both almost fell. And—" Her sudden sobs drenched Raelyn's shirt.

While Cali cried into Raelyn's shoulder, she couldn't help but wonder if the fire was an accident. And who did Kody yell at in the alleyway? Why did he chase after the stranger? Something didn't add up. Raelyn wondered if she needed to be more worried about the messages she had received after going to that museum. But, surely, no one would commit arson and attempt murder just because she was looking into Ma's past. Kody had remained too calm during their escape from the flames for there to have been any real danger.

Everything's okay.

Eventually, Cali pulled away. "I got it all out. I'm okay."

Kody stepped forward. "You sure?"

"Yeah." Cali gave him a hug and smiled. "Thanks for saving my life—again."

Kody grinned. "Just doing my job."

"You *did* save our lives. I'd be dead if it weren't for you."

"Do you need a minute too?" He locked eyes with Raelyn.

"I'm fine."

Am I, though?

They walked and walked and walked and walked some more. Thoughts consumed Raelyn's attention. Even if he wouldn't admit it, Kody had clearly seen someone in the alley before the fire trucks showed up. Who was it? Were they in danger? The scent of saltwater hit her nose before the sound of waves crashing on the shore. Hours passed enjoying the scenery. Cali sighed loudly.

Kody looked at his sister. "Bored already?"

"Did you bring a dictionary?" asked Cali.

He smiled and reached behind him. "Yup, let me pull it out of my—"

"I don't know the meaning of the word bored. I need to look it up."

Kody threw back his head and laughed, a deep rolling sound stirred from within.

If I could only capture the sound of his laughter in a colorful photograph.

Cali jumped on Kody's back and pointed to the boulders projecting out onto the sea. "Giddy-up." She stole him away in a flash.

When Raelyn sat, the stone curb dug into her butt. From afar, Kody playfully feigned pushing Cali into the ocean.

Cali grabbed a handful of berries from a bush and dropped into the prone position, yelling, "Attack!" as she hurled fistfuls of fruit as ammunition at Kody.

Raelyn couldn't help but smile.

We almost died. I have to learn more about Ma before it's too late.

Kody covered his face, then returned a handful of berries. Shrieking, Cali jumped behind a boat stand and spewed more smashed red gunk. A murder scene unfolded before them, with more red splattered on them than on a wounded soldier.

Wounded soldier. I can't even think about that.

They turned toward her, and she looked down, pretending to write in her journal. For a moment, the only sound was the water lapping onto shore.

Raelyn took out her phone and saw that a voicemail was awaiting her. She played it three times, each repetition increasing her heart rate.

A giddy voice on the other line said, "Ms. Ferriwinkle, I apologize for not getting back to you sooner. I hope our paths cross before you return to Oak City. Let me know when your flight leaves, and I'll check my schedule."

The photographer is here!

On a return call, miraculously, Emme picked up and agreed to meet at church Duomo Nicola for an interview, only half a mile away. Cringing from her poor decision but unable to wait any longer, Raelyn texted Cali quick and rushed off without further explanation.

I'll be right back. They won't care.

During her brisk walk, Raelyn couldn't stop thinking about how this photographer may have seen Ma about eight months ago. She approached a bewitching cathedral. A short woman with pixie-cut hair and a large camera dangling from her neck tilted her head when they locked eyes.

I can do this.

"Emme O'Reilly?" Raelyn asked.

"You can't be Kathy Ferriwinkle. You're too young."

Raelyn's hands shook. "I'm actually a photography student. I wanted to meet you and learn more."

Emme tilted her head and grinned. "Well, you've got guts." She glanced at her watch. "I'll chat for a few minutes. The cathedral is a great idea. Good photo ops. There's a great garden I can show you."

"Thank you so much."

They walked through the front entrance. Treasures reflecting in the mosaics stopped the hands of time.

"Show me what you've got," said Emme.

Barely able to take her eyes from the frescoes, Raelyn pulled up the image of her last photograph onto the display.

"No. I don't care about the finished product. Show me your process. How do you capture what you shoot?"

Raelyn twirled the strap of her camera. "Oh. I just aim and shoot."

Emme shook her head. "It's never that simple. What do you take pictures of the most?"

"It used to be sunsets, rivers, or roses."

"And now?" Emme smiled.

"Eye contact." Raelyn thought for a moment, then said, "You know, when someone glances up, there's a single second before they have the chance to change their facial expression. I try to capture that moment."

Emme asked. "So, what is the theme you're trying to grasp?"

"I don't know."

"Close your eyes and imagine your favorite shot."

Raelyn closed her eyes and pictured Kody's smile when he didn't know she was watching. "Authenticity."

"Why is that your favorite?"

Raelyn sighed. "I'm connected to what's real, something deep."

"Maybe connection is your motivation."

Raelyn's mind whirled and she struggled to contain herself. Her heart beat faster.

Of course! Connection—with Ma. Pa. Cali. Kody.

Flustered, she moved forward to this Emme stranger, asking, "What if I never find the connection I'm looking for?"

"You're doing fine for a beginner, many usually don't even—"

Unable to pretend any longer, Raelyn jerked her head up. "What do you know about Joanna Bell?"

"Excuse me?" Emme lurched backward.

"Joanna Bell."

"I don't know any Joanna." Emme walked away through a sunken iron gate into the garden.

"Who's Zohaib?" Raelyn followed her.

Emme quickened her pace and spoke over her shoulder. "I'm sorry, I don't have answers for you."

Raelyn pressed on. "Who else was in the desert when you took that picture?"

"Ugh! I don't have to tell you any of this!"

"Please!"

Emme turned, pushing against the spot between her eyebrows. "The woman in "J's Joy" wasn't allowed to speak with me."

She looks like she's lying.

Emme continued, "She was there with a man about her age, good looking, tall, white, broad shouldered." She weaved through a maze of gravel paths spiked with flowers.

"Do you know his name?"

"I think it started with an 's' or 'z.'"

Raelyn's lips quivered. "Do you know why the museum took down the photo?

"They were mad that a duplicate photo was discovered online. It was a polaroid I gave to a boy in the desert. It hurt the museum's credibility." Emme threw up her hands. "'J's Joy' isn't worth this mess. I need to go."

"Why did you name the piece that?"

"Her son seemed to be her complete joy."

Raelyn's heart skyrocketed. "What?"

"The way she looked at that boy, she had to be his mother. I'll never forget his face. Her joy was all wrapped up in his smile."

"Are you sure they were related?"

"Well, no."

Raelyn's shoulders dropped as Emme started taking pictures of the garden with her own camera in silence.

Raelyn stepped closer. "Did you see where they went afterward?"

Emme hid behind her camera. "No. You may be searching for a shadow."

"What was she like? The woman you photographed."

Emme lowered her chin. "She wasn't someone I'd ever want to mess with." She paused. "I'm sorry that I can't help you more. Please, don't contact me again. I need to go." Emme's silhouette faded into the doorway's shadows.

"Wait! What does J stand for?"

Only the wind responded.

With a big sigh, Raelyn pulled out her phone to call Cali. She had ten missed voicemails.

Crap!

Raelyn dialed Cali's number as she ran back to the beach. She picked up on the first ring.

"Rae! Where are you? What the hell?"

"I'm two minutes away. I'm fine." Raelyn rushed faster through the trail.

"Kody is burstin' like popcorn! Hurry!"

The dirt turned to sand under her cowboy boots, making her sink with each step.

Kody's shape raced toward her with the bright horizon behind him. His face seemed strangled with horror until he met her gaze; then, his body softened. But still, he sprinted closer, faster, until they were face to face.

Both panting, he stopped abruptly and held out his hands. "Where were you?"

"I went to meet the photographer."

He shook his head and yelled, "Without telling anyone?"

Tears formed behind her eyes. "I—I sent Cali a message."

Kody's voice rose. "Use your head! You're in the middle of a foreign country, and we were victims of arson last night. Someone is trying to—"

Her heart rate spiked. "You think that fire was started on purpose?"

"What if something happened to you?" He seemed to choke on his words.

Raelyn grabbed his hands and stroked the inside of his wrists. "I'm sorry."

Kody wrapped his arms around Raelyn, hugging her tight. Pressed against his chest, she breathed in his scent.

Cali joined. "You two okay?"

They broke apart fast. "Yup," Raelyn mumbled.

She wanted to tell them about what the photographer had said but was unsure if they'd just get mad again because of her disappearance, so Raelyn kept quiet.

Cali pointed. "Uh, anyway, the hostel owner told me about a tiny grotto under this mountain. The boats have to squeeze into a gap under the cliff-side." She slapped her thigh. "Call me a cricket and shiver me timbers, matey. Adventure awaits! And I want my own boat."

Raelyn stopped in place. "Wait. Does a grotto mean underground?"

Kody shook his head. "Not really. It's like a cave in the water. I'll be there with you. Look, the dock is right there."

When they walked closer, the sound of the water softly lapping along the shore seemed to pull away any tension from her muscles and ease them into the waves. The dock creaked underfoot. Three small canoes were tied to the pier with two guides leaning against a cooler.

Kody pulled euros from his wallet and paid the guide, threw their back-packs in the boat, then held out his hand to help Raelyn step into the boat. Kody wedged himself in at the end of the canoe and gestured for her to sit close. "Lean your back against me."

Raelyn inhaled sharply and sloped her back onto his shirt, feeling his hard chest against her shoulder blades. She relaxed into his body. A craving she'd never experienced before arose from down deep, a longing to belong to Kody.

I could melt into him.

Raelyn managed to squeak, "Am I squishing you?"

Kody laughed fully, joy seeming to erupt from his belly, then commanded. "Onward, good sir!" He waved to Cali, who was in her own boat.

"The water is freezing!" Cali hollered before drifting out of earshot.

Raelyn gripped on the sides until her knuckles turned white. Unfortunately, ocean wind blew her hair into a tangled mess while the boat swayed along, but Kody didn't seem to mind the strands whipping his face.

Kody pried her fingers from the sides of the boat, resting them in his. Her pulse spiked. The fresh scent of his breath blew gently in the wind: mint.

The guide said, "Only one boat has smashed into the cliffside rocks. Legend has it that ghosts haunt the cove. The ghosts are matchmakers, pairing one couple in a special boat with the gift of love."

Her breath quickened at the thought of dying from smashing into the side.

The sun's warm rays on Raelyn's cheeks contrasted with the frigid waters splashing over the sides. She shivered, but Kody's solid arms wrapped around her waist, warming her.

Inches from her ear, he whispered, "I've got you," and pulled her in close.

She could feel his breath on her neck as the tiny entrance to the grotto came into focus as their guide paddled hard, shouting for them to hold on. Raelyn braced herself for impact against the cliff walls, and Kody's muscles tightened around her as the boat slid through the narrow cave opening in one smooth swoop.

The rocking subsided, and the boat slowed. Raelyn gasped at the color of the water below her. They glided on liquid light in a sweet pool of a heavenly blue. Giant stalactites hung from the cavern's ceiling like crystals from a chandelier. Raelyn tasted the thick moisture in the air.

Magical spirits had to exist in beautiful nature like this. The deep pull to something bigger than her life was why she enjoyed photography, but only so much could be captured on film; the rest had to be experienced first-hand instead of hiding behind the lens. A thrill of hope tingled her senses.

Everything about Kody made her feel alive. She wanted to drink him in every day and become completely inebriated on him.

If a flawless moment exists, it's now. This is it.

Kody's arms wrapped around her despite the calm waters. Her heart raced wildly. Raelyn angled her neck back, held her lips below Kody's, and waited. They gazed into each other's heat-filled eyes.

He gently brushed his lips against hers. She held her breath.

Slowly, Kody leaned down to seal her first kiss. His lips were buttery soft. His sweet tenderness sent passion surging through Raelyn's veins. Kody's movements were tender, but she could sense his restraint, as if he wouldn't be able to hold back much longer. Raelyn took over and kissed him harder, wanting to merge fully with him. His hands tightened around her body, cradling her close. She would've kept going if he hadn't pulled back for a breath.

While Kody rested his forehead against hers, she locked her hands around his neck.

"Again," she whispered, tugging him closer.

Kody traced soothing circles at the base of her spine while his lips hovered over hers. Then he kissed her.

All her worries left, the pool swallowing them into the depths below. At first, their tongues explored with hesitancy that quickly escalated to absolute need. It felt as though she'd never be able to breathe again without him by her side. He bit her lip slightly. She gasped and wanted to ravage all of him at once.

Raelyn glanced up to see his reaction, and his eyes were already focused on her. She couldn't hide her smile if her life depended on it. Leaning deeply into the comfort of his chest, she sighed. "Do you think my camera will be ruined if I take pictures?"

"You should definitely take pictures." Kody's voice was softer, and when he leaned forward, he kissed her shoulder softly. His arms enveloped her frame as he rummaged through their bags.

She snapped pictures of the gorgeous blue. Greed overwhelmed her. She wanted more of him and to stay in that cave for eternity, but they glided out of the cavern, back into sunlight and calmer waters.

"We survived!" Cali yelled from her own boat meters away, barely audible.

At the pier, Kody extended his hand as she climbed out of the boat. When she stepped on solid ground, he gripped her hand more tightly, locking into place with hers, the missing puzzle piece. Raelyn's heartbeat went on overdrive.

Cali caught their entwined fingers, and her eyes twinkled, but for once, she didn't say a word.

"Here, take my sweatshirt. You must be freezing." Kody dug through his backpack and flopped the hole of his sweatshirt over her head.

She drowned in the excess fabric. "Thank you."

On the pier, she stepped closer to him. "Do you think we could talk more when you return to your base?"

Kody caressed behind her neck. "Yes."

"Really? You do?"

"I want to know everything about you. We can work it out. I'll find a signal to email twice a week."

We could have a chance.

She smiled and scooted closer. "Okay. I'll send you one of my poems."

"I'd like that."

"And you'll visit me when you come back?"

"You'll be my first stop."

"Promise?"

Kody paused. "Yes, I —"

She expected to find his warm eyes from the grotto, but his stony expression had returned as his phone chimed. He looked down and fixated on a new message alert on his phone.

"I have to go," he said and backed away, letting her hands drop from his.

Her heart grew heavy. "What? Right now?"

""Work emergency." Kody pointed to Cali. "You two go meet up with Mom."

She threw her hands in the air. "You're leaving at this very second?"

"Yes." He wouldn't meet Raelyn's eyes. "I'm sorry."

Without another word, Kody turned and jogged off, creating a giant hole in Raelyn's heart.

18

KODY

A WEEK LATER, ON a routine evening patrol atop the M-ATV in Tahil, Kody peered into the endless tan desert, like concrete coated in dust.

His fist clenched at the memory of Raelyn's confused face on that pier. Kody flipped open his phone and reread the threatening message that made him abandon the girls.

I heard you had a sizzling trip. Get back to base now.
Or your girls may suffer more trauma.

Quincy had gone AWOL, never returning from his leave, and Kody had no proof that it was him who set the fire. He had to leave to keep everyone safe.

I shouldn't have agreed to email Raelyn so often.

But the taste of coconut would forever be intertwined with the memory of her soft mouth. The bliss of their time in Tuzlicci competed with the confusion clustered in his mind. He could easily forget about Raelyn and live without her warmth. Kody had survived nineteen years without her. He could tolerate a life without her smile or the image of wrapping his hands around her waist. It didn't matter that he fell asleep to the memory of their kiss each night.

She's no different than any other girl. Her sweet demeanor doesn't have any effect on me.

Kody reread Raelyn's message that he had been avoiding.

Hi, soldier. Thanks for the grotto, and the beach. What book did you start?

He slowly typed out:

Too busy at work. Tell Cali I won't make her graduation.

His thumb hovered over the send button as he stared out into the distance.

She deserves better than me.

Dabbott's soft hand nudged him.

Kody looked down again. The message had sent when she brushed against him.

"Shit!" He sighed.

Kody checked his pocket watch. "Peterson, do you know if Quincy traveled to Tuzlicci recently?"

"I don't know. I'm not his babysitter," Peterson barked. "Orders from the base. We need to stop a civil disagreement in town."

Dabbott questioned, "At nineteen-hundred hours? Since when do our orders come from you?"

"They're from Sergeant Snyder." Peterson glared. "We've got maps, contingency plans, medical evacuation routes, and communications all set."

Kody's nails dug deep into his palm. With that video footage, Peterson owned him. Kody had no other choice but to sabotage their routine patrol for whatever Peterson seemed to be scheming.

Lying through his teeth, Kody avoided eye contact with Dabbott. "Yup, go ahead and do what he says. Meadows told me. I forgot to inform you."

"Roger that," said Dabbott, trusting fully.

Peterson nodded to Kody and took the place of the top gunner. The clanking of the tank's tracks against the road rumbled like a bulldozer as they rolled. Kody chugged a sip of copper-tasting water from his canteen bottle but spit it out over the side of the tank. Ever since Huffman died, he connected the copper smell to that of blood and charred flesh.

The streets didn't hold a soul—no sign of a village dispute. The entire town seemed abandoned. The hairs stood up on the back of Kody's neck as if the desert cacti needles shot out of his skin.

A swish of light flickered in the distance, and Kody squinted, leaning forward. The darkness transformed into a flurry of chaos. Bullets pelted an old shop with a long line of holes.

"Ambush!" Kody yelled.

"Contact!" Dabbott screamed a second later.

"North!" Kody readied his rifle, but the targets were too far off. There was a sniper on a rooftop.

"One hundred meters."

Bullets ricocheted off the tank in loud pings. A window shattered behind them. The M240 repelled the attackers. The noise pounded against Kody's eardrums.

Over the team radio, Kody heard, "Dig in and lay down suppressive fire. Where's our assault element?"

Hollers and clangs rang around him.

Peterson fell. Blood poured out of his upper leg.

Shit!

Quickly, Kody ripped off a chunk of his sleeve and wrapped it tight around Peterson's leg. "Keep pressure on it."

A woman's scream pierced the night air, and Kody's head whipped around.

"Dabbott, take over the machine gun." Kody jumped off the tank with a thud.

"Death before dismount!" yelled Dabbott.

Kody yelled as dust whirled through the air. "Then get on the machine gun."

He looked up. Peterson had already manned the top gunner position despite his injury.

"I'm coming with you!" Dabbott shouted.

Kody turned and ran toward the strangled scream as bullets whizzed by. He flinched and kept his eyes peeled for explosives. The continued screaming came from a run-down house.

The door swung open from the other side, and a white woman yelled, "Help!" in an American accent as she crouched and brushed away a layer of dirt, revealing a cellar door.

"Stay flat!" Kody pushed her to the ground, then heaved open the cellar latch. A man's body was sprawled on the floor, and the air smelled of feces. Gripping the side, he dropped down.

Chains restrained two women's wrists. One was gagged with a cloth. Kody ripped through the fabric, and the woman gasped for air, tears rolling down her cheek. Matted hair clung to her face. He rummaged through his backpack and grabbed a set of bolt cutters. Kody snapped the first chain, and she rubbed her wrists, stuttering in Arabic. He pushed hard on the bolt cutters, squeezing with all his might, but the other chain wouldn't break.

"We need to go!" Dabbott wailed above.

Kody kneeled, allowing the one woman to step onto his knee. Dabbott lay flat on her stomach and pulled her out of the cellar as Kody pushed from below. Shouts escalated outside. The woman pleaded in Arabic, trapped in chains with tears streaming her face. She pulled on the chains. Kody wrapped both hands around the shackles, dug in his heels into the dirt, and hauled, groaning.

Stuck!

"Walsh! Now!" Dabbott hollered.

"I'm not leaving her!" Kody screamed. Bullets tore through walls above.

He pulled harder. His palms bled from the pressure. The uninjured American jumped down and helped pull. Finally, the chain burst.

The prisoner tried to use the dirt wall for support but fell, shaking. Kody lifted her from the ground and over his head to Dabbott. He turned to help up the American, looking for her long, brown mane, but she had vanished.

Kody shone a flashlight. It was a tunnel. The American had disappeared. He yelled to Dabbott, "Go!"

"Not without you!" Dabbott hollered, reaching down.

"Damn it!" Kody grabbed Dabbott's hands. He hung midair, unable to kick off anything. A grenade exploded outside. Dabbott grunted, barely lifting Kody out of the cellar. Both panting, they lay on the dirt ground.

After a quick breath, they jumped up. Kody curled the injured woman over his shoulder and carried her across the room. He held his rifle with one hand.

"Come on!" Kody motioned for them to follow. Shots flew through the solitary window. Voices blustered on the other side of the door. The smell of spent cartridges whipped through the air for a moment until the wind shifted. Kody focused on controlling his breathing.

A grenade rolled where the cellar door lay open.

"Move!" Kody yelled, then jumped out of the way before the explosion busted the walls and roof. The mortar cracked, showering stones over their heads. Shattered rock sprayed onto his helmet. The women covered their heads with their arms.

"Blocked!" yelled Dabbott from a pile of rubble.

The engine of the tank rolled further away. The voices disappeared, but shadows darted. He froze. Footsteps shuffled outside their only exit.

"I'm out," Dabbott whispered behind him.

"We have to move!" Kody led them forward. Pointing his rifle, he aimed and shot. One hostile fell. Two. Three.

A shot thundered across the street in an echo. Sharp pain scorched at his bicep. His arm felt weak. He looked down. A bullet had pierced his skin and was lodged inside. Pain devoured him.

Ignore it.

He herded the women toward the tank, then squeezed his trigger again. Four more hostiles fell. They had no cover. Bullets soared through the air. His vision whirled at the chaotic scene as sounds and sights blurred into one. The pain increased. One of the prisoners tripped over a body. Kody hoisted her to her feet, still clutching the other woman over his shoulder.

His eyes were peeled for threats. The empty town lay in shambles. Arriving at the tank, he lifted the women to safety. The pain grew intolerable. He dropped to the gravel. Blood dripped down his arm, and his vision turned cloudy.

"You were shot?" Dabbott's steady voice faded in and out. "Hold on!"

Kody's eyes snapped open.

Where am I?

Wind rushed in from the outside of the aircraft hangar, causing sand to stick to his lips. The roar of a jet engine nearby made him bolt upright in the unfamiliar bed. Wincing from the sudden movement, he glanced at the bandage climbing up his left shoulder.

Kody shouted to whoever was nearby. "Get Lieutenant Meadows. Please."

A beautiful woman with arched eyebrows, pouty lips, and brown skin turned and smiled at him from the foot of his bed, rolling him closer to the plane. "You like my dad, huh? He's busy right now. My name's Xeera."

Lieutenant Meadows's daughter?

"You're okay. The doctor will be right back." She wore a backpack, and her thick black braids, adorned with beads, were fastened into a bun.

Snyder's voice crept behind him like a sneaky snake. "Leave, miss. You're done here."

Xeera gave Snyder a look that seemed to burn holes into him before she marched away. Unease inched up Kody's spine. Without a weapon to protect himself, he was vulnerable. Not even a medical tool was within reach since his hospital bed was marooned in the giant aircraft hangar.

Snyder glared and rubbed his scarred chin. "I don't like how this makes me look. Sure, you took down six guys by yourself, but it's a disaster out there. What the hell happened?"

Images of the night flashed in Kody's mind, but he didn't respond.

"Did you see anything of interest?" Snyder stood near his pillow.

Kody's lips pulled into a tight line.

Snyder applied unnecessary pressure as he patted the spot above the bullet wound. Kody clenched his teeth in pain.

"Nothing to report that'll help our team?"

Kody looked away.

"I see." Snyder released his grip and looked in the direction where a blond boy stood by the back door. "You're going back to the States for a month of rehab. If your memories change, contact me." He turned away and, over his shoulder, said, "You're not cut out to be a soldier. I don't see you making any sacrifices."

Fuck you.

Kody's gaze lingered on Snyder's wedding ring, then spoke in a low voice. "Is that your son?"

Snyder whipped around quickly. "Excuse me?"

Kody nodded to a boy in the distance. "I bet he wants to be like you."

The Sergeant's demeanor transformed before his eyes. "He's been practicing at the shooting range." Snyder's face warmed for a moment. "You should see him." He smiled proudly, in a way Kody hadn't seen before.

He cares about the kid. I can use that.

"Training him to take over and look for Zohaib?" asked Kody.

In an instant, Snyder's slimy eyes returned. "Watch yourself."

Kody pushed up and swung his legs over the side of the bed. A sudden flare of pain in his bicep made him suck in air through clenched teeth. Standing inches away from Snyder, he looked down at him and whispered, "Your son ..." He pointed. "My family. They're the very reason we do what we do, aren't they?"

Snyder's eyes grew wide. "Stay away from Liam!" He marched away, leaving Kody to sway on his heels.

Xeera returned. She eased Kody back into the bed and rested her hand on his thigh. "Easy there, soldier."

Kody sighed, laying back down. He waited for Snyder's frame to disappear before asking, "Is Dabbott okay?"

"The other soldiers are all alive and accounted for. Your brachial artery was hit. Luckily, no broken bones. When you were on the Blackhawk, the medic team controlled and stopped the bleeding, but you had extensive blood loss before they got to you. There's no infection so far." She sat close to him on the bed.

"How do you know all that?" Kody could see down her blouse when she leaned closer to pick a hair off his bandage.

Look away.

Xeera winked. "I'm pre-med in the National Guard. When I visit my dad here, I shadow the medic team." When she smiled, the whites of her teeth matched the clean, white paint of the wall. "You may have some shrapnel souvenirs sewn into your arm for the rest of your life. But they got the bullet out."

He sighed. "So, I'm flying back to Oak City?"

"We've got three upcoming flights, some transfers, then back to your Fort via the C-17."

"Us?"

"You, Peterson, and me."

"Does my family know?"

"I think your mom does."

Cali and Raelyn can't find out that I got shot.

Dabbott appeared out of thin air, arriving at his bedside, along with her fresh orangey scent. "Walsh, how are you holding up?"

"I'm fine." Kody shook her hand with his good arm, then lowered his voice. "What about the three women?"

Her brows were tight as she scanned the large hanger. "Two are safe and accounted for."

"The third never returned from that tunnel?" Kody rubbed his temples, creating pain from his movements.

"Right. Two are with the medics, and intel will speak to them in a few days."

Dabbott nodded to a bed holding Peterson being wheeled past by the flight personnel. "I informed Meadows how you saved Peterson's life." She forced a smile. "Walsh, they're loading up. I won't see you for a while. Stay safe."

Xeera moved between them. "I'll take care of him at rehab."

Kody waved to Dabbott as the medics wheeled him away. The sharp pain making him bare his teeth over every crack in the pavement as they boarded the plane. Peterson groaned next to him.

Kody looked at Xeera. "Where is your accent from?"

She winked. "Once we're back, I can tell you all about myself … at my apartment."

Kody's eyes flickered to her hand resting on his leg.
Her apartment?
Raelyn's smile rushed through his mind, but he pushed it away.
Raelyn will be much better off without me.

19

RAELYN

A MONTH LATER, YELLOW already coated Raelyn's cowboy boots as she walked through her yard with Bear. A tingling sensation crept up her nose, and she sneezed from the early arrival of spring pollen.

Her phone chirped. Kody hadn't responded to any of her messages for a month. She knew the possibility of finding someone to really connect with was too good to be true. Kody proved her fear accurate.

If I don't have Ma, I have no one.

She scrolled on her phone to read the message.

Jawhara is gone. Help.

Raelyn sighed in confusion. She had assumed these people wouldn't contact her again since so much time had passed since the last message. She tightened the plaid shirt that hung around her waist. At this point, the anonymous messenger seemed like a never-ending prank.

But from who?

And on a separate note, Raelyn had no leads to finding out more information about Ma. Calling her old journalism office had been a waste of time since they couldn't relinquish any confidential files.

A car pulled into her driveway and Mason stepped out of the passenger seat with fast food and milkshakes in hand-again.

Mason wouldn't leave me in a foreign country.

Raelyn rushed forward. "Do you need help?"

"I don't have my cane. Just tell me if Bear steps in front of me." Mason laughed. "I brought dinner."

She inhaled, and her mouth immediately watered at the smell of a greasy, drippy cheeseburger inside that bag. Her stomach rumbled. "Follow my voice. We can sit on the front porch."

"Did you have any luck finding information about the word jawhara since the last time we talked?"

"Yeah. When I used a different email to contact the O'Reilly photographer, she ended up telling me that the title of the photograph, 'J's Joy,' stood for 'Jawhara's Joy.'" Raelyn dropped her forehead into her hand. "So I guess it really is someone's name. Is Ma's name Jawhara now? I'm still confused because whoever is sending me these prank messages couldn't have known about the photographer's information. It doesn't make sense."

Mason nodded and sat. "I did find one article of a Battalion Commander Stephano Zohaib, but I doubt this guy is the Zohaib you talked about. He has run so many charity events in Iraq, a big hero over there."

She tied her straw wrapper into little knots. Mayonnaise dripped out of her burger and onto the sidewalk, which Bear eagerly licked up. Raelyn covered her mouth with her hand as she chewed and talked at the same time but realized Mason wouldn't be able to tell, so she just let herself be a slob.

Mason's voice was always so tender. "You seem a little distracted these days. Stressed?"

"I just have a lot on my mind."

They chowed down as the birds tweeted and Bear begged for food at their feet. She sucked on the straw, but the milkshake was too thick, so she took off the top and used her straw as a spoon. The grainy, chocolatey taste lingered on her tongue.

Mason put his hand on her knee, his first real initiation at making a move in the last few weeks. "What are you thinking?"

"Nothing."

Raelyn's phone rang. "Cali? You only text. What's wrong?"

"Kody's home."

"What? You said his tour was another nine months. It's only been one month since we saw him."

"There's more." Cali's voice was full of concern. "Rae, unfortunately, Kody has a girlfriend. But she's the worst."

Raelyn ignored the rest and swallowed hard while staring at the grass swaying gently by her cowboy boots. Her brain knew that Bear and Mason were probably making noise around her, but it felt like the entire world stopped—except for those pieces of grass. In a daze, she hung up the phone, numb to everything.

"You okay?" Mason frowned.

"Yeah. Everything's fine."

He put a hand on her knee. "The thing about being blind is that I rely on my hearing more. You like Kody don't you?"

Raelyn choked back tears, unable to answer. He inched away, which only made everything worse.

Mason sighed. "I'm gonna call for my ride to come pick me up. We can study another day."

Raelyn couldn't wait any longer. She stormed inside, batting tears from her eyes.

A girlfriend? It's not possible.

Just after Bear slid in behind her, Raelyn slammed the door to her room. A framed picture she took in Tuzlicci of her and Kody that hung on a hook crashed to her desk and knocked her pen collection across the old carpet. A burning pain stabbed through her chest, like it was on fire. She pressed her hand over her heart as she slid down the wall. Bear nestled in beside her and rested his head on her leg, not taking his pleading eyes off his owner. He inched closer, nuzzling her hand until she petted him.

At least I'll always have Bear.

A cranberry-colored pen lay by her foot. She grabbed it and filled a journal page with passion.

Some days, I wish I didn't care.
If I could send out a heavenly prayer,
I'd wish you didn't affect me so much
Because I'm leaning on a broken crutch.
Your choice rips my joints out of socket,
But a piece of me stays in your pocket

Her breath caught in her throat.

Why do I care so much? I couldn't possibly love him. Oh my god, that's it! I do love him, don't I? No, I can't.

The song playing from the speaker on her desk switched to "You Needed Me," and Rihanna's voice distracted her and sent her spiraling for a moment.

"Did you hear me?" asked Pa from the hallway.

She exhaled and shoved her journal under her pillow. "What?"

Pa peeked his head through the crack of her door. "Oh! What's wrong?" He walked in her room.

Raelyn wiped her nose with the side of her arm. "How did you know you were in love with Ma?" The tightness in her chest ached as if a mountain sat on top of her body.

He rubbed his beard with one hand. "Well, in college, we had a psychology class together. I didn't think Joanna would notice me. She was out of my league. The professor assigned us together for a group project. We were studying by a pond on campus. Joanna chatted my ear off as I took in her every word. Then, she spontaneously stood and chased the ducks like a madwoman. She flapped her arms in the air when they took off. That was it. I knew I was in love."

Raelyn curled her knees into her chest.

"That didn't answer your question, did it?"

She sniffed. "Not really."

He kneeled in front of her. "Are you worried about me, hun? I can't give up on life like I did before. I have to try to date, someday."

Raelyn took a deep breath. Through the window, a pair of geese flew in harmony across the brilliant blue sky. "I want you to be happy, Pa."

Pa had been in a much better mood for the last month. All the issues between her and Pa seemed to have magically disappeared while she was at Tuzlicci, as if starting on a clean slate. They must have switched roles. Now, Raelyn was the somber one dragging her feet around between school and shifts at the library.

"You still don't look satisfied." Pa rubbed the spot where his wedding ring used to lie.

"How do I know if *I'm* in love, though?"

Pa's eyes widened as he stepped back. "You?" He shifted his weight between each foot. "Well, there's no easy way to tell. I bet for some people, it's like a river. It starts slow and speeds up when the current takes over."

She sighed. "Really, Pa? A river metaphor."

"Hun, why do you ask?" His words were hesitant and full of worry.

"I don't want to be in love. Not if it hurts like this." She pulled a quilt over her shoulders.

"You don't think he will feel the same way?" Pa sighed. "Is it Mason?"

She buried her face between her knees. She needed someone who would understand heartbreak, and a woman. She needed Ma. Cali had admitted to never being in love. Wanda was sweet, but she couldn't replace the connection Raelyn longed for. There was no one to talk to.

Pa wouldn't ever fully understand her, but at least he was more attentive to her since they'd moved. But why did they move in the first place? If she couldn't have Kody, then all her time and energy had to be put toward finding out why they left Ash Mountain. The torn piece of paper she saw under Pa's desk in the farmhouse study couldn't have been junk mail. She had never seen a red envelope before.

"Pa, what is 'J's file?'"

He froze. "What do you mean?"

"Does 'J' mean Joanna? What is on Ma's file?"

Pa shook his head. "I'm not sure what you mean. I'll be right back. I need to grab something from my room."

Bear growled next to her.

"You're hungry, aren't ya?" Raelyn took a deep breath and led Bear to the kitchen. Upon looking around, refocusing on her surroundings, Raelyn immediately backed up against the wall in shock and scanned the room.

What the hell?

Their kitchen and living room lay in shambles. Someone had broken in, opened every cabinet and drawer, threw the blankets on the floor, and flipped over the coffee table. A single large kitchen knife was stuck in the middle of their counter.

Raelyn grabbed a broomstick that had been resting along the wall. Her knuckles wrapped tightly around the shaft and raised it like a sword. She heard her voice shake when she screamed, "Pa!"

He came around the corner in a hurry. "What is it, hun?"

When he scanned the room, Pa's body went rigid, and he quickly yanked Raelyn close to him. He searched around the corners for any intruder. The criminal hadn't stuck around. Pa kicked their belongings across the floor. "Go to Cali's."

She looked up. His emerald eyes were iced over. "Who did this?"

"I'll call Yohaan. Leave to Cali's. Quickly!"

Raelyn held on to his large hand tightly. "When was someone in here? I've been outside."

Pa faced Raelyn and put both his hands on her shoulders. "Look at me. Please don't stop anywhere. Keep your phone on. Go straight to Cali's."

"Pa, I'm scared." Raelyn's hands shook when she clutched her keys from her pocket.

She peered outside his window, getting an eerie feeling of someone watching them from the street. Raelyn drove her truck down the road, past the blossoming, pink, cotton-candy trees in the spring sun, but nothing in her life felt like sugary gumdrops or candy. In fact, everything was falling apart.

At least Bear could keep Pa safe. Yohaan's police squad would probably find fingerprints on something. But the guy didn't seem to take anything.

The Walsh's driveway was full—Walter's black car, Wanda's silver one, Cali's white convertible, and two Jeeps.

Crap. Kody can't see me.

Raelyn parked on the street and walked quickly up the grass. An eerie feeling of someone watching her made the hairs on her arms stand on end. She kept looking behind her but saw no one. The sun hadn't fully set yet, so Kody's broad figure standing under the basketball hoop was clearly visible. Thankfully, he had his back toward her with his phone up to his ear.

Raelyn tried to tiptoe around him to the back door but could still hear his phone conversation.

Kody chuckled quietly. "No, I can't tonight, man. I've got a date with Xeera. She keeps me busy all night."

Raelyn's eyes began watering, but she held them back. Every fiber of her being wanted to shove, punch, smack, and hit Kody for payback of tearing her heart in half. How could he not care? Was he just using her in Tuzlicci? Her boot crunched on leaves, and Kody turned and met Raelyn's gaze.

"Shit! I gotta go, man." Kody hung up, his face full of an emotion she hadn't witnessed on him before. Regret?

Despite her fear of being stalked and anger at Kody's new relationships, she still had half a mind to trace the new slight black beard with her fingertip, over his solid jaw line. A gray t-shirt tightly hugged his chest and shoulders. Raelyn's lips tingled until she noticed a white bandage wrapped around his upper arm.

What happened to him?

Raelyn stepped around Kody.

"Raelyn—" His deep voice felt like a warm blanket wrapped around her full body, completely consuming her.

She didn't bother turning but marched inside without a word. Cali pranced to welcome her and pulled her straight up to her room. "Are you okay?"

Telling Cali about the break-in wouldn't do any good, so she kept the information to herself. There wasn't any point in scaring her friend.

"Yup, never better," Raelyn mumbled.

"Do you want to talk about my horrible brother?"

Raelyn clicked her tongue. "Nooooooo, I was thinking … I need a change. Can you dye my hair?"

"Abso-frickin'-lutely. Turtle shells and pumpkin shakes! Are you serious? I have a whole stash in my cabinet waiting for you. Who do you want to look like?"

"Ma."

"Then let's do a few shades darker. But you're gonna need three boxes for your length." Cali moved toward her bathroom and crouched to reach under the cabinet for all the boxed dye.

Raelyn continually checked her phone for any updates from Pa and sat silently in the chair as Cali told her stories about her cousin who would be arriving that night for a visit while she dyed Raelyn's hair.

One—or fifty—hours later, Raelyn hopped into the bath to wash out the dye. A bubble refused to pop as Raelyn placed her toe just outside the sphere. Fruity scents enveloped the small room.

Who would break into my house? Why? How could Kody have a girlfriend? Did our kiss mean nothing to him? Will Mason ever speak to me again? At least I have Cali. Why does this dye smell so awful?

When finished, she wrapped a towel around her breasts. Fierce whispers echoed from the hallway. Between the small crack of the door, Raelyn saw Cali put a finger to her lips to silence whomever stood further down the hall.

Kody's voice came muffled from behind the corner.

Raelyn's heart skipped a beat.

I can't face him.

"You need to leave." Cali crossed her arms.

"I need to talk to her." He moved forward, into Raelyn's sightline.

"You played my best friend."

Kody's posture sagged. "Xeera understands my job and knows the limitations of what I can give in a relationship."

"BS! You didn't even try!" Cali pointed a finger in his face.

He narrowed his eyes. "What do you expect, fairy tales and happily ever after? That's not real life." Kody raised his hands.

Cali whispered, "Whatever. I'm gonna go talk to Mom downstairs."

Kody stood in the hallway, tightening and relaxing his fists; then, his eyes met hers through the crack.

Raelyn pushed the door open and pointed to his bandage. "What happened to your arm?"

"I'm okay." His eyes absorbed her as she stood enveloped in only a towel. "Cali wants me to leave. What do you want?" The way he phrased it seemed like a purposeful loaded question.

Raelyn folded her arms tight. "What I want doesn't matter to you. You made that perfectly clear after—"

Kody moved so close she could feel his body heat. "What do *you* want?"

I want you, all of you, to myself. Your strength. Your determination. Your mind. Your eyes. Give yourself to me.

She bit her lip. "Nothing."

He sighed, then nodded to her wet hair. "Changing things up?"

She shrugged. "Being my old self hasn't been working well for me."

"You don't need to change for anyone." Kody turned to leave but then sighed and backed up toward her. "Actually, I need to ask you something."

A lump formed in her throat.

The warmth in his eyes that she had grown accustomed to in Tuzlicci had disappeared. Kody's stern, cold face returned. "Why did you move away from Ash Mountain?"

Raelyn tilted her head. "That's a random question."

"Just wondering. We've talked about so much, but not that."

She tapped her toe along the baseboard of the hallway. "I'm not sure. My dad freaked out one day. Something my grandma said must've upset him. That was a weird day. I'll never forget it, though. September twenty-third."

Kody's vein throbbed in his forehead. "September twenty-third?"

"Yeah. Why?"

"I need to think." He walked away.

Raelyn sighed and returned to Cali's slob of a room.

While looking at the beanbag where Bear usually slept when he was there, Raelyn wished she could run her hands through his soft fur to make herself feel better. But Pa needed Bear tonight more than she did.

Cali hiccupped as she joined her. "Kudos. Whatever you said to Kody has got him more riled up than a chicken on caffeine. His veins were about to bust outta his forehead. Well done." In front of the mirror, Cali applied burgundy lipstick. "My cousin's coming over later. You haven't met this one."

"I know, you told me." Raelyn puckered and applied deep berry and blotted a perfect kiss on a tissue. "Can you put darker eyeshadow on me?"

"Girl! What has gotten into you?" Cali smiled while a rerun of the show *Friends* played in the background. She smacked her lips in front of the mirror. "Breanna's brother is throwing a party tonight. Why don't we go? You don't have to drink. It's all about the dancing."

"I'm not supposed to leave your place tonight."

"Why?"

Raelyn scrunched her nose. "Nothing." If she didn't talk about the break-in, it would disappear from her mind.

When Raelyn walked into the Walsh kitchen, she checked to make sure Kody had left. The scent of chicken fumed the air.

Wanda spoke to a woman in mid-conversation. With a lighter brown skin tone, she didn't look much like Cali or Kody but must be their cousin. She looked a little older than Kody and was a few inches taller than Cali, with toned arms under her fitted navy dress.

Wanda leaned in for a hug. "Hi, Raelyn. Your hair looks wonderful."

"Thank you." Raelyn retrieved silverware then asked the new girl, "So, were you close to Cali and Kody when you were younger?"

Confused glances met her gaze from around the kitchen.

Raelyn cleared her throat and tried to clarify. "I mean, y'all have spent so much time together. Did you and Cali fight or get along?"

"Um … in Tahil City—"

Raelyn smiled. "Oh! You're in the army too?"

Kody entered the back door, wiping the dirt from his shoes, holding a lilac purse.

Raelyn met his eyes, but they were flat, a spark missing, as if she were a hat rack in a corner. Her breathing quickened, and her face flushed.

Cali rambled on about theater club while they all filled plates and sat at the table. Raelyn tried not to think of the burglary or the handsome man across from her or the way her heart pounded a million beats per second whenever she thought his gaze landed on her from the corner of her eyes.

In attempts to get her mind off of Kody's intense energy, Raelyn blurted out, "So, I don't have any cousins. Tell me what it's like."

The room stood still.

"I'm confused. Whose cousin?" On the table, the woman laced her hand into Kody's.

Raelyn cemented to her spot.

Is this Xeera?

Raelyn desperately wanted to take her gaze off their hands but couldn't. All she could imagine was Kody's hands touching this girl, sharing himself with her. A sour taste rose up her throat and Raelyn had to swallow the vomit down inconspicuously.

Xeera said, "I haven't met Kody's cousins yet. I mean, I barely see him as it is with our work schedules. Apparently, I pick men like my father, committed to their work to a fault."

Her words sent a fire crackling within Raelyn.

Xeera laughed. "But I'll see more of him soon since we're moving in together."

The feeling of a knife slicing through Raelyn's stomach sent her gulping for air. Simultaneously, Kody looked up sharply, as if a trap door fell out from under him.

Cali coughed, choking on her bite. After regaining her exposure, she exclaimed, "you two met, like, a minute ago!"

Xeera barreled on. "Wanda, would you like to help me pick out new furniture tomorrow? We're donating both of our beds and buying a new one together."

Raelyn scooted her chair out, rushing from the kitchen like she was escaping a fire. "Excuse me." She hid on the other side of the wall and placed her shaking hands over her heart.

Xeera said, "Who was that girl anyway? She's a little jumpy."

"Don't worry about her." Kody's voice was quiet.

Raelyn sank to the floor. His words ripped out her heart. A hollowness seeped into her—a hole so large it threatened to swallow her completely. She remained hunched by the bottom step of the stairs until Cali pulled her elbow with a piece of cake in hand. “Come on. Chocolate fixes everything.”

In Cali’s room, Raelyn fiddled with a blanket on the bed. She slumped onto the cold floor and lay in the fetal position, silently begged for tears to flow, but her eyes stayed dry. “Say Something” played through the speakers with artists A Great Big World and Christina Aguilera. Piles of rocks mounded on her heart, and tears collected behind her eyes as she listened to the lyrics.

Cali bit into the cake. “Rae, I didn’t know you liked him *this* much. I don’t know why he’s with Xeera. I’m sorry.”

“I’m not feeling well. I’m going to head home.”

She’d rather face an armed attacker in her home than be around Kody a moment longer.

“Thanks for dyeing my hair.” Raelyn gathered her satchel.

“I’ll show you how to scale down the pergola so you don’t have to pass by the kitchen.” Cali opened her window.

She used her heels to dig into the slope of the roof and gripped the shingles tightly.

Kody knocked at Cali’s door. “Where is she?”

Cali stomped on her brother’s foot.

He didn’t flinch.

“We’re doing … womanly things. Get out.”

“I swear, I never asked Xeera to move in with me. I don’t know why she said that. It’s not a serious relationship.”

Out on the rooftop, a scream built inside Raelyn’s chest.

“I need to talk to Raelyn,” he said.

Cali crossed her arms. “I’ll pass along your message.”

“The information I have doesn’t concern you.” Kody lifted the comforter and dropped down to look under Cali’s bed.”

“Who does it concern?”

“William Bell,” Kody said.

“What?” Raelyn poked her head from outside the window.

“Raelyn!” Kody rushed forward. “Get down from there. You could fall.”

“I’m not made of porcelain,” said Raelyn.

“Fine. I may have a lead about the museum photograph,” Kody said.

Cali whirled to Raelyn, anger taking over her face. "You got my brother involved? If you thought this was all legit from the beginning, how could you possibly put my brother in danger? Tell me! How?"

"Calipescia, be nice!" Kody shot his sister a glance. "It's not like I was shot because of Raelyn."

Raelyn gasped, staring at Cali. "He was shot, and you didn't tell me?"

"Excuse me? You didn't tell me that you went behind my back and put his safety in jeopardy!"

He sighed, wrapping his sister in a hug. "I'm fine. It's healed. You know my philosophy. I don't tell you about the dangers. That way, you don't have to worry."

He pulled away when Cali calmed and reached for Raelyn. "Come inside!"

"No!" she screamed, surprised by her own volume.

"Fine." Kody squeezed his eyes shut and pushed his fingers against both temples. Drawing out each word, he said, "Please tell me your old address wasn't 222 Golden Street in Ash Mountain."

Her heart rate sped. "Yeah. It was. How do you know that?"

Kody tried to hide a cringed look. "I had an assignment to that house."

"What does that even mean?" Her foot slipped on the shingles as rage singed at her core. "More secrets! You know what, Kody? You don't have to worry about becoming like Walter in the future. You're already a liar, *just* like him."

Cali shot a dagger look at her. "Where did that come from? You're insulting my family and putting them in danger. You're so selfish!"

Raelyn dug in her satchel for her journal, flipped to the bookmark, and tore out a page. Behind her best friend's head, she caught a glimpse of the photo frame Cali nailed together in art class as a wood project. The frame outlined the two of them mid-laugh at the county fair. Raelyn had ordered a deep-fried Oreo, and the powdered sugar made her sneeze right when she clicked the selfie.

"Here. I wrote you a damn poem. But you can throw it out." She crumpled the paper into a ball and threw it in the window, then scaled down the side of the gutter without waiting for either of them to respond.

Forget them.

20

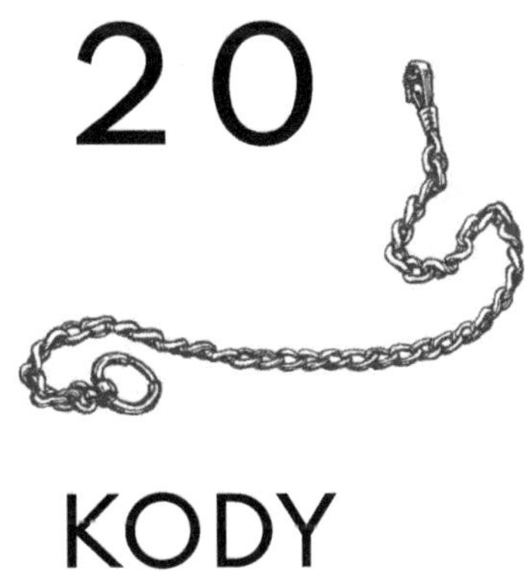

KODY

PACING THE DOWNSTAIRS HALLWAY, Kody's mind whirled with possibilities.

I should chase after Raelyn and tell her about the red envelope. But I'd have nothing to say. I don't know what was inside.

Why had he sabotaged his chance with Raelyn? She deserved better than what he could offer. Every day for the last month in rehab he had considered calling Raelyn, but what could he say?

Sorry for abandoning you in Italy. Sorry for having a girlfriend. Sorry that she's not you.

Indulging in his new nervous habit, Kody palmed his pocket watch but winced from the sudden movement. Luckily, his arm didn't need further surgery, but recovery had become his new full-time job.

His phone buzzed.

Please be Raelyn.

Instead, a message from a new unknown number flashed across the screen.

You keep failing. Watch your back.

The threatening messages had stopped after he had left Tuzlicci. Kody had thought it was over.

Mom walked over slowly. "Can I talk to you for a minute?"

"Yup." Kody retreated to the back of the study and put a pencil to the crossword puzzle on the desk. He wanted to be fully present for Mom but couldn't get his mind off of Raelyn's expression before she scaled off their roof.

Mom and Coop followed. Upon seeing their faces, Kody shot upright. "What's wrong?"

"Your father—"

Kody tapped the keys in his pocket. "Is he okay? I can go get Walter."

Mom gave a sideways look. "Why do you call him Walter?"

This is it. I have to tell them.

Kody sat again, leaning back against the fluffy cushion. "I don't trust him anymore."

She laid her hand on his. "You know, don't you?"

Kody took a deep breath. "Mom, he's been cheating on you for years. I didn't know what to do. Then it seemed like I waited too long. What could I say? I'm sorry."

Mom tapped his hand. "It's okay. Coop told me a few months ago."

Kody met his big brother's eyes and wrapped his fingers around his pocket watch, squeezing until the metal absorbed his worries.

Coop stepped forward. "What's done is done. We need to focus on Mom and Cali."

"What do you need?" Kody asked.

"I'd like his stuff out of this house after we tell Cali. I've needed these months to figure out if I can live with this and have a future with your father or not."

Kody hugged her. "And you can't?"

She shook her head.

"Okay. When do we tell Cali?" asked Kody.

Mom moved away. "Tomorrow, but she's not the one I'm worried about. It makes sense that you knew. Your relationships have probably been influenced by this. You don't trust yourself in a commitment, do you?"

He cleared his throat.

"You're not Walter. Please, listen to me. You never choose someone who is good for you. Instead, you date women you don't have to talk deeply with, someone who stays on the surface." She patted his shoulder. "Just promise me you'll think about it."

I already know.

"Love you, Mom."

She kissed the top of his head. "Love you too."

After Mom and Coop left, he let his mind drift into another world.

I did this to myself. I should've chosen Raelyn.

He joined Cali and Xeera in the kitchen, where they were washing dishes.

"We should go shopping! Sisters are the best, aren't they?" Xeera hugged Cali awkwardly, then kept cleaning the plates.

"I wouldn't know," mumbled Cali.

"Someday soon, you will." Xeera flashed her ring finger.

Cali widened her eyes at Kody behind Xeera's back as his girlfriend whispered, "I'll wear that silky thing you like later."

Kody cleared his throat. "Xeera, can I talk to you in my room, please?"

Xeera winked, "Mhm."

As he ushered her in his room, Xeera slowly clicked the lock into place, then ran her hand under his shirt, edging her long nail along his spine.

He rubbed the slight beard that had formed. "We need to talk."

She silenced him with a kiss.

His dick immediately hardened as Xeera knocked pillows off the bed. "We can't do this right now."

"I should tie you up again." She winked. "I know some wicked knots."

Xeera's clever comments and sly gestures didn't make up for the fact that, in bed with her, night after night, images of Raelyn flashed through his mind.

Kody's phone rang. "What do you need, Walter?" Kody asked as Xeera massaged his ear lobe.

His dad sighed on the other end. "Is that the way to greet your old man?"

The creaks of the old leather chair at Walter's office gave away his location.

While Xeera ran her hands under his shirt, Kody lowered his voice on the phone. "Mom knows."

Walter was silent for a while. "Listen to me, son. Your mother and I haven't been good for a while. Talia was there for me when your mother wasn't."

"She was my calculus teacher!"

Walter's smile bounced off his words. "One day, you won't judge me so much. You and I are more alike than you'd admit."

"No. We are not the same. I'll *never* cheat. You're wrong." Kody growled. "Why did you call?" He glanced at the dark sky out the window, trying to focus on anything other than where Xeera's hands were caressing his body. Kody backed away, but she cornered him. He watched as Xeera kneeled in front of him and unzipped his pants. Kody gulped as Xeera pulled down his briefs. Unable to say more, he shook his head at her but she wouldn't stop.

He was about to hang up when Walter said, "Cali's friend … what's her name?" Papers ruffled in the background.

Kody's muscles tensed as he pushed the phone harder to his ear and whispered, "Raelyn?" His body clenched from Xeera's mouth on his skin.

Walter cleared his throat. "Yes, Raelyn. Her father, William, invited me over for poker last night. He asked a bunch of questions about our law firm and said he needed some help investigating something. The guy sounded a bit paranoid."

Kody tried to focus on what Walter said as Xeera's hands explored below his waist. He rolled his lips in and braced himself against the wall. Just as her tongue began exploring, Kody let out the breath he was holding. Shaking his head, Kody gently pulled Xeera to her feet and zipped back up.

Xeera sat on his bed and crossed her arms.

His father's tone went formal again. "I told William you'd help him find answers. Legally, my hands are tied, but soldiers in the army …"

Silence. Kody would have thought Walter had hung up if not for the shallow breathing on the other end. "Son?"

Kody's body tense. "Don't call me that."

"You'll always be my son."

Kody ground his teeth together and hung up.

"What was that about? You've never stopped me before." Xeera pouted.

"We need to break up."

Xeera jumped to her feet from his bed. "What?"

"I don't want this. I don't want us."

"You're breaking up with me? No! No! I don't think so! I'm breaking up with *you*!"

He moved quietly to the other side of the room, hoping his family wouldn't hear her rising voice.

Xeera yelled like a boot camp drill sergeant. "This is over! You never take me anywhere, damn it!" She shoved her keys so hard into her purse it looked as if she might rip the seams. "All you do is work and read."

He leaned against the wall.

I can change for Raelyn.

Xeera spun on her heels and glared. "You don't talk to me about anything. Your answers are always one syllable. Am I not worth a real conversation?"

Kody stayed silent.

"You're not fully present. You're in another world half the time." She marched across the room and laced her shoes.

He glanced out the window.

Where's Raelyn right now? I should've chased after her.

Xeera stomped. "You even talk to yourself but don't talk to me. How am I supposed to have a relationship with an asshole like that?"

Kody stood perfectly still and finally spoke. "You're right."

For a moment, her face showed hope, and her eyes lit up.

"We don't see eye-to-eye on many things. It won't work."

"Goodbye, Kody." She picked up her purse and walked into the hall. He didn't follow but heard stomping down the stairs and the front door slam shut.

Sighing with relief, he covered his face with his hands and collapsed onto the bed.

I never should've dated Xeera.

Coop walked in. "It had to be done."

"That sucked."

"Now, what do you want?"

Without an exchange of words needed, Kody shook his brother's hand and rushed outside to his Jeep. He brought his phone up and called Raelyn. A phone rang from the bushes.

Cali came up behind him. "She must've dropped it during her Jamie Bond exit! Girl power!" Cali exclaimed. "Wait, no, I'm mad at her." She crossed her arms.

Kody crouched, picking up Raelyn's phone from the ground. He read a message that flashed across the screen.

If Zohaib find jawhara first, he will kill her. he want all power.

Kody's vision blurred. "We need to talk to Raelyn." He held the phone up for Cali to see.

Cali rolled her eyes. "Oh, another one of those. Great."

Kody's gaze snapped to meet his sister's. "What do you mean, *another* one?"

"This is the third. The first said something about tracing Raelyn's phone or knowing where she lives and them selling some jewel. The second one said we need to help, or they would hurt someone's brother."

Kody's voice boomed. "How could you not have told me this?"

"It's a prank, right? We haven't heard from them in a month."

"No, it's not a prank." He took a breath. "Let's go. We need to find Raelyn."

Cali huffed. "No! She needs to apologize to me first." She stormed inside.

"Fine!" Kody jumped in his Jeep and flew down his drive, almost crashing into a cop car at the bottom. He slammed on the breaks and looked in the mirror. Raelyn's cop neighbor stepped out, waving, and jogged over to Kody's window with concern on his face.

As he rolled down his window, Kody's body felt numb from fear. "What's wrong?"

"Where's Raelyn? The tracker says she's here."

"You track her phone?"

"It's necessary."

Kody handed over Raelyn's phone from the passenger seat. "Why?"

"Is she inside?"

"No. She left about an hour ago."

His eyes widened. "Where to?"

"I thought she went home."

Yohaan scrunched up his face. "No, she can't go home."

"Tell me what's going on."

Yohaan glanced around the yard. "This afternoon, someone broke into the Bell's house and left a threat. I'm surprised she didn't tell you. She was there when it happened."

Kody's heart drummed faster. "What?"

"We're investigating."

Kody looked at Yohaan. "Can you go talk to my mom inside? She's a lawyer and may be able to help." He said it just to get rid of the guy. If someone had broken into the Bell's home, there wasn't one person he could trust. Kody switched gears and thought of the places she could be. The library was the best bet.

A text buzzed from Cali.

Guess you went after Rae anyway. Since I'm such a great sister, I'll tell you where she is. Under one condition—never see Xeera again."

He typed out, "Deal" fast and waited. Ellipses popped up and disappeared. Cali's text came in slowly.

Kody punched the steering wheel. "Come on!"

"My girlfriend, Breanna, has a brother at State. He is throwing a frat party. Apparently, Raelyn is there."

He pushed the limits of his Jeep around tight turns in the neighborhood then onto a busy street without slowing at the stop signs. At a stoplight, a Cadillac turned behind him. Kody turned right. The Cadillac followed.

The car stayed on his tail. Kody glanced in the side mirror.

What the hell?

The other car's tinted windows blocked any view of the driver. Kody's hand turned clammy on the steering wheel. He turned his Jeep right; the car behind him turned right. Adrenaline flooded his system. He sped up, but the car continued to trail him through each intersection, staying on his tail.

His knuckles tightened around the steering wheel. Kody revved his engine, flooring his Jeep onto the highway ramp to merge. Stepping heavily on the pedal, he reached ninety miles per hour.

He looked in the rear-view, the guy wouldn't let up.

110 miles per hour.

The car swerved around a van behind him.

120 miles per hour.

The Jeep couldn't handle much more. Kody soared off the next exit, and the car followed. He pulled into a restaurant parking lot and jumped out of his Jeep. Hand on gun. The Cadillac didn't pull in. He peered around the side of other vehicles. The car had disappeared.

Who's following me? Why?

Bending over and holding his knees, Kody breathed out all the air he had been holding in since the exit.

What do they want?

21

RAELYN

Blaring music escaped the frat house and blocked the opportunity for any decent conversation outside on the dark lawn. Raelyn chugged another solo cup of god-knows-what. Breanna leaned against Raelyn's truck, chatting with Natalie. At least Breanna hadn't asked any questions when Raelyn randomly showed up at her house asking to hang out. It was the only address she remembered without her phone. As she took another large swig, the same thought repeated in her mind.

I have no one.

Breanna barely knew her, and she was the only person left in Raelyn's life. If it was up to her, she'd light the frat house on fire and let her life go down in flames. The wind howled and echoed between the empty hollows of the tree trunks. Raelyn stared at the black sky dusted with stars, then tripped on the stairs into the house. She walked through tendrils of cigarette smoke and waved her hand in front of her face, coughing.

Giggling, Breanna pulled her through the front door. "Raelyn, you look so different with all that makeup. At least four years older."

Thumping music of "Gun In My Hand" by Dorothy competed with voices chanting, "TONY! TONY!" from the keg in the corner. They squeezed between bodies in a humid room as a girl with only one set of fake eyelashes attached banged into Raelyn. Nearby, posters advertising college clubs hung from dirty walls. One showed smiling, filthy athletes swinging over an obstacle course of mud pits. Her thoughts traveled back to that morning months before, when Kody taught her how to throw a punch.

He'd be a good trainer for a mud run race.

Raelyn gripped the solo cup in her hand tighter.

"We should've hung out like this all year!" Breanna chugged from her red solo cup. "Want another beer?"

Raelyn made a sour face. "No. What's in that cooler?"

"Jungle juice. A mix of everything."

Raelyn scooped out red slush with a solo cup, spilling liquid on her forearm in the process. She licked it off, and pineapple was the first thing she could taste. Raelyn didn't know anything about alcohol to know what the other flavors could've been.

Breanna teetered in her stilettos. "Look, Mason's here!"

Raelyn sipped the jungle juice despite the room already swaying. She couldn't feel her lips but started smacking them together, making popping sounds.

Next to his friends, Mason teetered like a boxing bag being shoved between bodies, so Raelyn went over and guided him out of the crowd.

"Thank you," he said without a smile.

Breanna giggled. "O-M-G, when you guys become a couple, your names could be May and Rae. MayRae, get it?" Breanna chugged another drink with an arm around Raelyn's neck, moving the two closer together.

"You two okay?" asked Mason.

"We're great!" Raelyn hollered over the music. "Dance with me."

Freedom strummed in Raelyn's bones as she moved her body to the rhythm. The room turned to a haze of colors and a swirl of sounds. Her hands wandered around Mason's belt line; then she wrapped her arms around Mason's neck, pulling him close.

"You really like me, Mason?" She rose on her tiptoes.

He nodded.

"What are you gonna do about it?"

Mason kissed her. And she let him. But Mason tasted wrong. His touch was wrong. His lips were all wrong. His smell was wrong. Bodies bumped into her.

"Come here," said Raelyn as she led Mason through the jumping mass of college students, down a hallway, and into an empty room.

"Where are you taking me?" Mason asked. She could hear him better, but her ears pounded.

Raelyn pulled him inside and pinned Mason against the wall, pushing her body against his.

"Raelyn, you're drunk." Mason tried to lower her wandering hands to the side.

She ran her hand through his thick hair.

"How many drinks have you had?"

"One outside, two with Breanna, then that one guy got us—"

"I can't."

Raelyn pulled her shirt over her head and pulled his hand to her chest. "Do you want me or not?"

Mason ran his fingertips over her skin. "Oh, god."

She placed his hand on the clasp of her bra. As he unclipped it with one twitch, the padded lace fell to the floor. His hands explored her body fast. She moved closer despite his cold skin on her breast. His fingers pinched her nipple, a sensation she hadn't felt before, making her gasp.

Someone pounded on the door. "Raelyn?"

Raelyn covered her breasts with her arms, knowing that deep voice from her dreams.

Where's my shirt?

As she dropped to the floor, the door handle turned. Her fingers landed in goo. Grimacing, her stomach revolted from questionable smells. Raelyn brushed the floor, scurrying to feel cotton. Dim light from the hallway cast on the floor as the door opened. On her hands and knees, she saw her shirt by Mason's shoes, and crawled forward fast, but it was too late.

Looming like a giant above, Kody peered down at her on the ground—shirtless—kneeling in front of Mason.

Kody's eyes widened and locked on her bare chest. "Are you okay?"

On the ground, Raelyn shoved her arms through her sleeves as Kody looked away and Mason cleared his throat. She pulled her hair out from inside the shirt, letting it tumble down her back.

She staggered upward, surprised by the sudden loss of balance. "I'm fiiiiiine."

Kody's voice rose as he glared at Mason. "She's drunk?"

Mason raised both hands. Kody's momentary stillness resembled a stealthy panther about to strike. He charged forward, grabbing a fistful of Mason's red polo shirt, and pushed him against the wall.

"Stop!" Raelyn yelled. "Mason's blind. He didn't see anything."

"That doesn't matter. He sees you in other ways." The hot blaze of Kody's eyes erupted like a volcano. "Did he hurt you?"

"No." Raelyn tried to stand tall but swayed into the wall.

She stepped forward and laced her small fingers with Mason's. Glancing at their hands, Kody wore an entire funeral on his face. Her insides exploded with passion for the man standing fractured in front of her.

Kody's gaze looked straight through her. "We're leaving. Get your stuff."

Mason whispered, "My cousin has a dorm you can stay in if you don't want to leave with him."

"Get outta here, kid," Kody growled.

Mason grabbed his cane leaning against the door and pointed it at Kody. "No! You come in here commanding the room like she owes you something." Mason moved to Raelyn. "I need to tell you something."

The room spun slightly, but she tried to give Mason her attention, despite the chaos enfolding. "What?"

He rubbed his hand over the back of his neck and whispered, "Can we talk somewhere, alone?"

"Um, just tell me. What is it?"

"I can't wait any longer for this. I've been meaning to …" Mason rolled in his lips then took a deep breath. "I'm in love with you."

Raelyn's heart spasmed.

Kody dropped his chin. "We don't have time for this. I need to get you to a safe place."

Raelyn shot him a look. "Be patient! For once, just wait!"

Kody lifted Raelyn over his shoulder and carried her down the hallway. A few college students stared and pointed, mouthing words to each other over the loud music as he rushed down the corridor.

"Are you crazy? Put me down!" Her fists slammed his back as Mason's questioning voice faded under the music.

Kody kept storming through the hallway and Raelyn continued to thrash her body over his shoulder. He finally set her on the floor, and she turned down a different hallway, darting away.

"Raelyn!"

She didn't slow and squeezed through couples making out in the hallway. One girl loosely swung a full cup at her side, which Raelyn grabbed and chugged in a few seconds. Shaking her head, she wiped her mouth with the back of her hand, and continued to march down the long hall.

I can't face Mason right now.

A beefy-looking guy with dark blond hair watched her. He reminded Raelyn of a surfer who won a pullup contest at her most recent beach trip. His tight shirt showed off his broad shoulders, and obvious military dog tags looped around his neck. She felt like she was teetering on the edge of a cliff, the universe daring her to jump into the abyss. Raelyn smiled when he nodded, but Kody's eyes flashed through her mind.

No. I'm done with Kody.

The stranger confidently walked forward and leaned in close. She kissed his cheek without a blink, then pulled away.

"That was unexpected." His blue—no, green eyes sparkled as he said, "Follow me."

She held out her hand. A little smirk snuck on his lips as he laced his fingers in hers. Turning, he led her down a long hallway. The frat house was less crowded the further they walked, but the light faded too. Had she been down that way earlier? He opened a door to a large closet.

"Do you want me to leave this cracked open?" He gestured toward the door.

"No." She closed the door behind her. "Privacy is better."

He started to say more, but Raelyn crushed her mouth to his. He kissed her back, not hesitant like Mason, not warm like Kody, but hard and urgent. His hand found Raelyn's waist and moved up her back. He took one wrist and pinned her against the wall.

What am I doing?

But she kissed him again. His tongue hypnotized her mouth.

Someone wants me.

His lips were thinner than Kody's but just as in control. The guy's other hand roamed her outer thigh. A moment offered itself to her as a gift. She could take advantage of the situation to experience something new. Before she could change her mind, Raelyn guided his hand to her short's zipper. He pulled away for a minute and cocked his head to the side. Raelyn stared him down as she shimmied down her shorts to her knees and guided his hand to the warm spot between her legs.

The guy's eyes turned to fire as he slipped his finger on the other side of the cotton, skimming her skin where no man had ever touched. She bit her lip and went in for another kiss but he arched his head back a bit. "No. I want to see your face." His tingling touch teased her, making her legs slightly shake.

Raelyn's heart rate doubled as the grip of his other hand tightened around her wrist. "More," she said.

His Adam's apple rose and fell noticeably as one finger slid inside her. She gasped.

The guy's eyes widened. "Damn!" He circled around, giving her new sensations.

The rest of her body stiffened as she could only focus on the blissful feeling of his touch. She closed her eyes and dropped her head back. "More."

He stopped. "Only if you open your eyes."

Raelyn locked her eyes on his again, unable to tell if they were blue or green. But it didn't matter, because the room seemed to fade away when he slid another finger inside and moved faster. Her mouth clamped shut in a tight line right as a soft moan escaped her lips and her legs shook harder. She tried to speak but couldn't. The perfection of his swirling motion sent her senses spinning. He pinned her against the wall harder, moving in a perfect rhythm with his hand. She reached up and brought his face to hers again, devouring his kisses.

The added stimulation was too much to tolerate. Panting, all at once, her insides felt like a tsunami wave of pressure combusted into a million sparks of fireworks. The intensity exploded all at once. Then the waves eventually faded away. Her body went limp as he withdrew, a big devil smile across his face.

I want more of him.

Raelyn, still panting, whispered, "What do you want?"

"What are you offering?" The handsome stranger raised his brow.

After the fog of ecstasy passed over, the realization of the potential danger she had put herself in immediately slapped her into reality. She stepped back. "I have mace, you know."

He smiled. "It makes sense why Walsh likes you. You're adorable."

"You know Kody?" She clenched her jaw. "Who *are* you?"

"My name is Private Peterson." His features hardened. "We don't have much time."

"What are you talking about?" All of a sudden she felt foolish for being alone with a stranger.

Voices mumbled from the other side of the door in the hallway.

"Raelyn, focus. I need to tell you some information."

How does he know my name?

Raelyn backed up. "Why did you kiss me?"

"You're hot and we both wanted it. Simple as that." He held out both hands softly. "Listen, give me two minutes. I have information about Joanna Bell."

Raelyn's head whipped to meet his gaze. "What? Is this some joke?"

"I have reason to believe Joanna Bell was captured by a man named Zohaib."

Her jaw dropped and the music from the hallway faded away to nothingness.

He spoke slowly. "Do you recognize that name?"

That name was on the back of the map. On my phone. Which I don't have.

"How would you know anything about my mom? Is she still alive?" asked Raelyn.

"Listen. Walsh's probably tearing down the entire house looking for you. I need you to put this tracker on him." When he reached inside his pocket a postcard dropped to the floor. He handed over a small, circular, pin-looking, device.

"Why?"

"Don't trust Walsh. He's working for Zohaib."

Raelyn's mouth dropped, and her heart thundered in her chest.

"You're in danger."

Her stomach tightened, and a sour taste reached her mouth. She turned to the side, emptying her stomach onto the floor.

"Water?" Without hesitation, he pulled a water bottle from his cargo pants.

The water tasted like droplets from heaven. Raelyn ripped open a gum wrapper that the guy handed over from his other magical pocket.

He repeated. "You're in danger."

She looked straight into Peterson's eyes, and said, "Kody would never hurt me," but tears formed behind her lids.

"I just saw you kicking and screaming over his shoulder."

Her tone turned sharp. "You've been watching me?"

"I've been keeping a close eye on Walsh. My duty is to protect. You need to stay away from him." Peterson's voice rose.

"How do you know Kody?"

"He was on my team." His voice quieted.

Her head pounded, so she massaged her temples with two fingers. "Why aren't you in the desert?"

"I was shot on the same night he was."

"Did *you* shoot my Kody?" Raelyn shoved his chest with both hands.

He didn't flinch. "No. I took a bribe to do another man's dirty work which got us both shot. Place the tracker on Walsh, and have a friend take you home."

Raelyn's eyes narrowed. "I can't trust you."

"But you can kiss me?" Private Peterson smirked and grabbed his wallet. "Take my military ID if you want proof. I've got to go, Ms. Bell. You'll hear from me soon. And whatever you do, don't be alone with Walsh." He rushed down the hallway.

Raelyn read the name, 'Phoenix Peterson' on the card and yelled after him. "You didn't answer me! Is Joanna Bell still alive?"

22

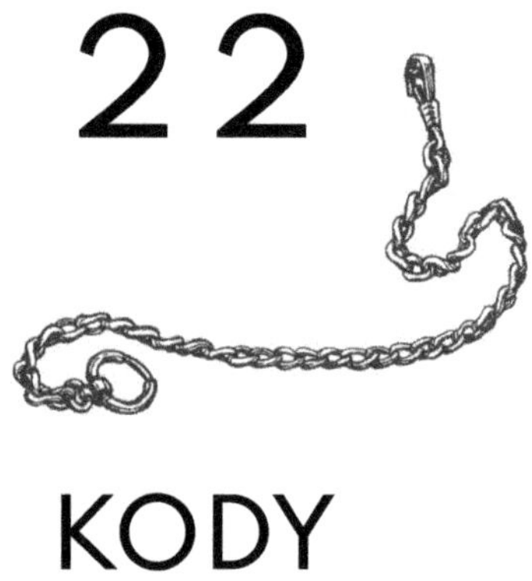

KODY

The foul smell of stale beer was coated into each inch of the frat house. Kody ducked into every room, searching for Raelyn. He pounded on doors and pulled every short brunette from the clutches of their unsuspecting frat guy. "Close" by Nick Jonas started playing from down the hall.

His heart hammered in his chest. Beads of sweat fell from his forehead as he stormed down the long hall. Suddenly, he saw Raelyn hunched against the stained wall. She had her head buried in her arms over crossed knees. His love for her stretched into every fiber of his being, taking his breath away.

I love her …

Her eyes were watering. Each tear she held back counted for one of his mistakes. Regret consumed him. Kody longed to take her pain away, erase the last month from existence, and just start over in the grotto cave.

He worked his jaw loose and blew out a long breath, trying to forget their fight. Kody kneeled next to her. Raelyn looked past him. He glanced at her shaking hands. There were bruises on her wrist.

I'll kill that Mason kid.

"Are you okay?" Kody asked.

"I need Cali." Raelyn's voice trembled.

He sighed. "Okay. She's at home."

Just hug her.

Raelyn lifted herself from the ground. "She didn't come?" The gaze of her doughy eyes sent heat across his skin.

"No." Kody held out his hand. "Come on. It's getting crowded in here."

But his breath caught in his throat when she refused his hand. Kody angled Raelyn's waist to the door, but when she stiffened at his touch, he removed his hand.

Outside, Breanna ran up. "Cali's pissed. She heard you came to a party without her."

Raelyn sighed. "I suck."

Breanna smiled. "The only thing I hear you've been sucking is—"

"Don't finish that sentence." Kody stared her down.

"What?" Raelyn eyes flitted between the two.

"Natalie heard you were with Mason, so she started a rumor that you were with three guys tonight. I don't think you'll have the same reputation at school on Monday."

The moonlight made her skin glow as Raelyn buried her face in her hands.

"It'll be fine." Breanna hugged her.

"Don't squeeze so tight. I'll hurl again. I'm gonna go home." Raelyn swiped her phone from Kody's palm. "Where's Mason? I can go to his cousin's dorm."

She doesn't want to be near me.

Kody's jaw clenched. "I have my Jeep."

Placing both hands on her hips, Raelyn narrowed her eyes. "I don't belong to you. I'm not yours."

He stepped back. Her glare shredded him to pieces. Music blared, Lady Gaga's song, "Perfect Illusion," and more bodies filled the front lawn.

"Fine, I'll get Mason. He's better for you anyway."

"Better for me? Better than what? I have no relationship to compare it to, thanks to you." Raelyn screamed, and her face turned red. "Why are you here? Go home to Xeera. She's picking out your bed! You chose her!"

"I broke up with her," Kody said coolly and crossed his arms.

Raelyn gulped and moved across the narrow neighborhood street. She shouted across as if they were worlds apart. "Well, you should go make up with her. You and I would never work."

He tossed his hands up in the air. "Stop pushing me away."

"If we tried to be together, you'd leave me!"

A car passed between them, blocking his view of her for a moment too long.

Her pitch rose so high he could barely understand her words. "You'll leave me for work. Just like you left me on that pier."

He clenched his fists into tight balls, trying to stay calm. "If we tried to be together, you'd resent me for not talking to you enough and accuse me of sleeping with Dabbott or something."

She stared. "Who? So, there's *another* girl on your mind? *More* women who can give you what you want. I'm not one of them."

Kody dropped his shoulders. He could see through her accusations now.

She's just as afraid as I am.

He stepped forward and softened his tone. "You don't need to *give* me anything."

Raelyn's chest rose and fell fast. He only wanted to hug her, but then she asked, "When were you at my farmhouse?"

He didn't blink. "September twenty-third. The same day your pa made you leave."

Her bottom lip dropped, and she dashed down the street. "It's true then I can't trust you."

Mason yelled to Kody. "If you touch her, I'm calling the cops on you."

Kody switched his attention back to the road, but Raelyn had disappeared. He sprinted down the street, his heart beating frantically. Kody curled his fists and pumped his arms up the steep hill and spotted her again. Raelyn was struggling at the top but she didn't stop. She didn't slow. Kody gained on her. Ahead, she almost tumbled. They neared a red-light intersection.

A car!

"Stop!" Kody yelled.

Raelyn looked over her shoulder, but she didn't slow as the car approached fast.

"Stop!" Kody screamed, closing in on her.

She stopped. "What!" Her glare looked like clouds before a storm.

Kody took her wrist and switched their positions so he was between her and the intersection. The car sped by. Kody studied her face as she panted, which seesawed between disappointment and venomed rage.

"Why does everyone keep secrets from me?" she screamed louder than he thought possible.

"What are you upset about? Xeera, or your farmhouse?"

Her liquid eyes looked through him as if he were invisible.

"Raelyn, you and I … We weren't ever officially together."

"Obviously."

"Please, look at me," he begged.

"I can't." Raelyn's eyes turned icy cold, freezing an impression on his soul. "I can't ever see you again."

Her words sliced sharper than any knife.

Kody whispered. "That's not possible."

"Why?"

"Because I love you." A ton of weight immediately lifted from his shoulders.

Raelyn's jaw dropped slightly. "No, you don't."

Kody moved closer. "Yes. I love how you correct crooked pictures in public places."

Raelyn backed up. "I do that?"

He lowered his voice. "I love the way you always knot straw wrappers."

She crossed her arms and looked down. "Well, they're just sitting there."

Kody couldn't contain his slight smile. "I love that you cuddle with five pillows when you watch a movie with Cali. I love how you take care of Bear."

Silence. She started walking back to the frat house. Kody gave her space but followed, keeping his eyes alert for anyone watching them. An eerie feeling that they were being followed haunted him. When the biggest threats seemed to be crickets, he swallowed hard and let his mind wander.

Does she love me too?

The lights and music from the frat house grew stronger. Breanna and Mason waited by the front gate. Before they rejoined her friends, Kody hustled faster to Raelyn's side and whispered, "I do. I love you."

Raelyn jumped away. "Stop lying to me!"

Kody's insides were being ripped out.

Breanna laid a hand on Raelyn's shoulder. "Rae, it's been a rough night. Let's get outta here. You'll be asleep in your bed before you know it."

"She can't go home." Kody stated.

Raelyn's glare was so sharp it almost made Kody stagger back. Sirens squealed into the night, and lights flashed, sending college students running from the frat house in all directions.

Kody fiddled with the pocket watch with his fingertips as he approached Mason. "Have you had anything to drink?"

Mason shook his head.

"Please convince Raelyn to stay here. I need to talk to the police."

Mason chuckled. "They're here to arrest you."

"No, they're not." Kody confidently walked toward Yohaan, hoping the cop had more answers about the break-in. He didn't dare look over at Raelyn's expression over his shoulder.

She didn't say it back. She doesn't love me.

23

RAELYN

DESPITE HER CLOSED BEDROOM window, the air smelled of barbecue and smoke. Lying flat on her bed, like roadkill, Raelyn glanced at her phone for the tenth time in an hour. No new messages showed up. It had been six horrible days of hell without contact from Cali or Kody.

Of course I love him. Why didn't I say it back?

She threw the tracking device in the air and caught it in her palm, then flipped it over and inspected it closely—again.

Raelyn talked to the pin device Phoenix Peterson gave her. "Hello in there. Can you see me? Can you hear me? Invisible soldier, you're the only one who cares about me."

Raelyn pulled the covers over her head, blocking out the sunset's rays creeping through her window. A slit of light came through the crack under her blanket.

Bear pawed outside her bedroom door. Rolling out of bed and crawling across the carpeted floor, she cracked the door open for him before getting back under the covers. She shoved her pillow into her face and made screaming sounds like a dying rodent into the fluffy cotton.

Why did I push Kody away?

Happiness was in front of her, and she knew she had been prioritizing the past over a future with Kody.

I could've told him I love him. I did this to myself.

Teardrops smudged the paper as she plucked a pen from her messy bun and wrote in gray ink.

Ready to breathe the soft one awake
Lay down my armor and shield that were fake
Ready to be consumed by wonder
Embrace my strength and rise from slumber

She grabbed the tracker device from Peterson and threw it into the trash.

I know what I want.

Laughs escalated outside her bedroom window. Pa flipped hot dogs with Yohaan on the grill. Raelyn's mouth watered, but she refused to join them. She grabbed her keys and ruffled Bear's fur and kissed his forehead. "I'm going to figure it all out, Bear."

Bear barked.

"You want to help me fix everything?" She grinned. No matter how bad life got, Bear was always there for her.

"Okay, come on, boy." Raelyn marched outside to her truck. The scent of freshly cut grass filled the air. Her keys jingled against the plaid shirt around her waist.

"Where are you going?" Pa waved his spatula.

"Work."

Pa pulled on the chain connected to his compass and gripped the metal in his palm. "Since when are libraries open Saturday nights?"

She stopped, realizing Kody always made the same movement with his pocket watch. "Pa, what else was in the red envelope at our farmhouse?"

His face turned the same color as the envelope. "What?"

Raelyn said coolly, "What was in it?"

Pa stared up at the sunset, gloomy from the approaching storm. "Please stop asking."

Her chest tightened as she hopped into the truck. "Why did we leave?"

Moving closer from the grill, Pa swung his spatula. "Stop!" His eyes were made of icicles as he glared her down.

"No!" Raelyn closed her truck door. "And I'm taking Bear."

She slapped her thigh, and he bounded after her.

I know exactly where I'm going.

"Wide Awake" played like an anthem, and Katy Perry sang the perfect lyrics for what she was thinking.

The rain-slick asphalt reflected the flickering street lights lining the two-lane road that stretched ahead like a ribbon. Thirty miles down a highway, in a small studio, a soldier she could share her future with unknowingly awaited her arrival. She rolled her truck's windows down despite the menacing clouds lurking in the distance. Bear curled into a ball in the passenger seat.

I can do this.

Trees whipped by her peripheral vision. Raelyn's skin tingled with electricity at her plan as she accelerated, sudden clarity flowing within her veins. Her eyes bounced between the truck's clock and the road. Pavement whizzed by. She'd be there in a few minutes.

Raelyn took a deep breath and called Cali, unwilling to be at odds with her best friend any longer. Because of the approaching storm, she put her phone on speaker.

"Finally! Bananas and cockroaches! I hate being your enemy. Let's make up." Cali's voice rang clear.

Raelyn smiled. "I'm sorry about what I said earlier. I was wrong for going behind your back."

"No, I'm sorry. I should've told you Kody was shot."

"It's okay." Raelyn sighed. "I suck."

"The only thing I hear you've been sucking is—"

"Cali!"

"Is it true?"

"No." But Raelyn pictured Phoenix's smile and eyes from that night.

A car honked.

Raelyn spoke louder. "Have you ever wished you had a sister to talk to or share with after some big milestone event?"

"Not really. I have my mom." Cali dropped her voice. "Oh, I see what you're saying."

In the driver's seat, Raelyn resituated her breasts in her red push-up bra, one she'd never worn before. "Cali, you're like a sister to me. But I can't share everything with you, and I don't have Ma to talk with."

"Is there something you want to share now?"

Raelyn's mind switch over as she imagined Kody's hands on her, potentially moving lower on her stomach. "No, I'm good."

"It's okay if you have a few secrets to yourself."

Cali continued, "But I can always be your person. I'm the one who helped you set up those backdrops for your photography and stood in line for two hours to get that book signed. I'm the one who shoved ingredients into jars for that bake sale and twisted a hundred tin tops on until my fingers fell off. I know you wish your ma was here, but I've been here."

"You're right." Raelyn sighed.

"I'm your person, girl. I'll always stand by your side."

Raelyn smiled.

"I'm there for you 'til the day I—"

"Don't say that." Raelyn cut her off. "You'll live forever."

Cali laughed. "Actually, I have a poem for you."

"Really?"

"Shhh, you're ruining my dramatic moment. Like sturdy stems of a vine. We will always be intertwined. Two hearts to endure any weather. Ropes twisted by adventures together. Extra hands to beat down a wall. Catch and raise me when I fall."

Raelyn smiled. "I meant it when I wrote it, and I still mean it now."

"I love it!"

The rain came down harder, and Raelyn squinted to find the apartment building. "I gotta go." She was grateful Mrs. Walsh had handed over Kody's address without questions.

"See ya later, alligator."

The silver moonlight glistened over the trees that lined the road like proud chess pieces. Inhaling sharply, she hung up and parked outside an apartment building that was three stories tall, beige, and brick.

Bear licked her face as she rolled her window down. The plinking of raindrops bouncing off the sidewalk sang like a melody until the thrum of a neighboring car rolled next to her. A Cadillac crushed the grass flat. The reflection of the headlights in her mirror made her realize she hadn't put any makeup on that day.

Oh well. This is me.

A door on the first floor opened, and someone's wide frame blocked light from shining through. A security guard manned the entrance? He shifted in a way where the light illuminated his face. It was Kody. They locked eyes, and he smiled first, hesitant but genuine. Kody jogged out, not taking his gaze off of her.

Raelyn looked up at him nervously. "So, you don't actually live inside the fort's walls?"

"Affirmative. There are some singles outside the Fort. Let's get you out of the rain."

She shielded her head with her hands and stepped around a puddle. Bear frolicked as if he was trying to keep his paws dry.

They walked in silence through his hallway, but a flash of intensity crossed Kody's face. His energy already had a tingling effect on her until she saw a piece of paper flapping on his front door. Raelyn pulled it off. "What's this?"

Kody snatched the note from her grip and shoved it in his pocket. "Just for work."

She raised an eyebrow as he opened his door for her. It could be a note from Xeera. Was it an omen to flee as fast as possible? Any deceit in a relationship was poison.

Raelyn backed away into the hallway. "I shouldn't be here."

His words sped out. "Please stay."

Raelyn shifted her weight on the other foot, twiddling her fingers on the strap of her satchel. "Okay, I'll come in." She walked inside his studio. The first thing she saw was his king size bed that claimed the space, and a shudder went through her body as she tried to block out the images of his body in the sheets. A full bookshelf stood on the side. The rain pitter-pattered against his window almost as fast as her heart beat in her chest. Raelyn's hair dripped water droplets onto his tile floor. She bit her lip. "Sorry. I can clean that."

"It's fine." He dropped a hand towel on the floor and mopped the puddle with his foot.

"So," she said slowly as her eyes outlined his sculpted shoulders, "why did you break up with Xeera?" Placing her satchel on his tiny kitchen counter, she walked closer. Her pens rolled out and across the surface. When one fell over the side, Kody gracefully caught it in midair and gently stuck it in her hair.

"We weren't a good fit." He shrugged.

She ran her fingers over the wood of his oak bookshelf. Raelyn fiddled with chess pieces on his bookshelf as Bear sniffed around the room.

"Go ahead and help yourself to some of those books," he said.

Her fingers traced the spines. "Any of them? How about this one?" She could feel his gaze on her back.

"Yup."

"How about this one?" Raelyn bent over to the bottom shelf, pulling out *Stride Toward Freedom* by MLK Jr.

In a serious tone, Kody said, "What's mine is yours. You can have them all."

She grabbed seven thick books but dropped half of them in the process. He walked over and kneeled to help. They grabbed the last one at the same time, and she looked directly into his rich eyes. A kaleidoscope came to mind. Whenever she had looked into the abstract colors shifting, she'd always assumed what the distorted image's true shape was, only to be surprised when stepping back to look from a new vantage point.

Raelyn sighed when recalling all their deep discussions the first week they met when she was supposed to be doing homework with Cali. Things were easier then, when Kody was off limits and unavailable overseas for a year. But now, Cali showed she didn't care about them being together, and he would be near Oak City indefinitely.

Kody held out his hand, lifting her up. "Raelyn, why are you here?"

She wanted to know if he actually loved her. Without alcohol in her system or fear from a burglary or toxic energy about Xeera, she could truly study his eyes and know if he spoke the truth. But, she couldn't ask him to repeat those words unless she could say them back.

I do love him.

Kody studied her.

"I deserve a better apology. You left me in Tuzlicci. You told me you'd email me. You lied."

"I'm sorry," he said softly, moving forward.

"Actions speak louder than words." She put her hands on her hips.

"What do you need from me?"

Everything. All of you.

Raelyn scrunched up her nose. "I registered for a mud run obstacle course. I was hoping you could train me."

Kody smiled. "Now?"

"It's muddy. Seems perfect."

"And you'll forgive me? If we go on a run?"

Raelyn thought about what exactly she would be forgiving him for. He hadn't cheated on her with Xeera since they had never established a relationship. However, he still made a commitment to talk. What exactly was she upset about—the fact that she couldn't trust him? Or was it something else entirely? Was it because of what Phoenix warned her about?

Now that she knew Kody had been to her farmhouse, there was a possibility that he may have been the ultimate cause of her world turning upside down. If she asked, would he even give a straight answer or sidestep the topic?

She bit the inside of her cheek. "Did you deliver a red envelope to my farmhouse?"

He sighed. "Yes."

"Did you know what message was inside?"

"No, I promise. And I didn't know you lived there."

She crossed her ankles over one another. "Is there anything else? Anything at all?"

He paused. "No."

Why did he hesitate?

Raelyn nodded. "I want to be your friend, but I also need to trust you."

"A friend? Nothing more?"

She bit her lip. The possible ramifications of going after what she wanted had the potential to shred her soul into even smaller bits. But the more she learned about his charm, ambition, drive, and intellect, the harder it was to stay away. Raelyn knew she was changing and could no longer predict her actions around the man who held her heart in his pocket.

She smiled. "Maybe I'll decide on our run."

Kody smirked and peeled off his shirt. "I'm ready. But you're in a dress."

"Okay. Turn around so I can change quickly," she said, gesturing a twirl with her finger.

"There's a bathroom right …" He silenced himself and turned away. She pulled off her dress. Standing in red lingerie, she took a deep breath.

Raelyn reached her hand forward to tap on his shoulder, but spotted a picture of him with his army friends on base, holding giant guns. Even if she put herself out there, Kody lived a life with a high risk of never returning to her.

I'm gonna get heartbroken.

She froze and muttered nonsense to herself, then threw on her sports bra and yoga pants from her satchel.

"You good?" Kody asked.

"Yup. All set. Let's leave Bear here. He doesn't like the rain."

Kody turned and plopped his Cubs cap on her head, then tossed her damp dress in his dryer.

He led her outside and started his running app. "We'll do one mile and see where you're at."

Raelyn watched the rain bounce off his bare back, reminding her of his glistening body after his shower months ago. Her shoes thudded clumsily against the wet pavement.

As each minute ticked by, her pace slowed.

Cold mud splashed her legs as she panted behind him, focusing on his muscles coated in droplets. Finally, he stopped. Drenched, she hunched over, placing her hands on her mud-splattered knees.

"Big, steady breaths," he said, not the least bit winded. "Good start. Need me to carry you in?" He smiled.

She held out a middle finger, unable to speak. Kody laughed. She couldn't help but smile in between gasping grunts. She wished she could photograph Kody in this exact moment without changing anything.

I love him so much.

They stood, soaked, staring at each other in the dark. Goosebumps instantly formed on her forearms, so she rubbed her hands together. He wrapped one arm around her. The scent of rain mixed with his hot skin.

"Let's get you dry." Moving into the hallway, he took his Cubs hat from her head and shook it out, flicking droplets to the ground.

Back inside his studio, Bear was asleep on the couch. Kody closed the door behind her and stared into her eyes. He wrapped his arms around her waist and leaned down. His soft breath whispered in her ear. "Raelyn. I really do love you."

Raelyn caressed his chest, fingers curling over his heart. All the sensations she felt in Tuzlicci came rushing back. In an instant, her future became clear, and she could no longer fight it. She needed him in her life like she needed air.

Her heart rammed against her chest ferociously. She couldn't hold back any longer and tugged his neck down until their lips met, which sent sparks throughout her entire being. Her fingertips traced his warm skin over his muscular back, making her want more of him. She moaned softly between kisses.

Kody lifted her and placed her on his counter without breaking their kiss. Her heart raced on overdrive as his hands glided over her skin, tracing over her curves and pausing at her chest. Kody took off her wet sports bra and dropped it to the floor in a soppy mess. As he buried one hand in her thick hair and the other cupped her breast, his tongue swirled hers. Nothing had ever felt so good, and she knew that, in the morning, she'd no longer be wondering what her first time would feel like.

Her nails dug into his back, and she wrapped her legs around his hips, pulling him closer. Her thumb traced the edge of his drenched cargo pants.

He shuddered and twisted away. "Let's slow down."

Raelyn's mouth dropped.

He walked to his drawer in his soggy sneakers and threw on a dry shirt. "Do you want one?"

"No. Come back over here. And get out of your wet clothes."

Kody licked his lips and stared at her bare breasts but shook his head and turned around, mumbling nonsense to the wall. He tossed her a dry t-shirt over his shoulder, which she let fall to the floor. Kody turned, his jaw set firm, and clasped his hands behind his back, but his soulful eyes told her everything she needed to know.

He wants this too.

Willing to play by his rules for just a bit, Raelyn dropped down from the counter. "Hungry? I can make you something," she said, twiddling with the wooden spoon on the counter.

"You're going to cook for me? Half-naked?"

"Have something else in mind?" Baiting him, Raelyn moved behind him and pressed her bare chest against his back lightly. She wrapped her arms around his waist so her hands covered his chest and moved in small circles, feeling his hard pecs under his shirt. Her heart rate spiked.

I can do this.

Kody pressed his palm against his forehead as he turned. "Raelyn—"

Her breasts rose as she tied her hair into a loose bun. "Can you give me a massage?"

Nodding slowly, he released a deep breath. One leg at a time, Raelyn unrolled her yoga pants from her legs. She watched him take her in. Kody's chest rose and fell rapidly. She slipped off her panties, revealing all her curves, then bent over to move a pile of pillows.

"Christ, Raelyn." His deep voice vibrated in her bones. "You're … gorgeous."

She smiled and walked toward his bed.

His eyes narrowed while he closed the space between them. "Lie down."

Raelyn lay face down on her stomach. Her heart thumped wildly in the stillness. "Kody …"

"Mhm?" His hands massaged her lower back, skimming down her spine. His face was so close behind her that his breath warmed her neck.

"Do you remember the first time we met?" Raelyn asked.

He deepened the pressure. "Yes." His voice cracked slightly as his palms wrapped around more than half her frame.

"What did you think of me that first day?" She breathed in his aftershave scent from his pillow.

"I was drawn to your curiosity and determination."

She moaned softly from his touch and raised her hips involuntarily.

A soft growl escaped from his mouth. "Turn over." He didn't wait for her response but quickly rolled her flat on her back.

The size of his shoulders and arms at this angle shocked her. Her hands roamed his body. "Take this off." She pulled at his pant pockets.

"No way. My clothes are staying *on*." Kody's eyes searched every inch of her.

He's torturing me.

Kody kissed her deeply. Raelyn responded by kissing his shoulders as if she'd never leave him, and she kissed his lips like a promise. Guiding his hand to her inner thigh, she let out a small gasp as his fingertips started moving in slow motion, spinning her body out of control. A lump formed in her throat.

His eyes widened. "Raelyn." His breathing became audible. "We have to stop …" But he cut himself off and positioned himself over her. As his fingers continued massaging lower and lower, he moved his lips to her collar bone, trailing down her nipples, her stomach, and right when he was about to move lower, she grabbed his shoulders and pulled him up to meet his gaze.

"I want to be with you."

"Me too, but not yet." Kody pressed his lips to hers again and again.

A knock came from the front door. Bear barked, and Kody hurtled back swiftly, peeling himself off the bed. "I have to get that."

Raelyn gulped as he checked through the peep hole, then opened the door. A package sat on his front stoop. Kody squatted, turning it over.

"That's weird."

She grabbed a pillow to cover herself and curled into a ball. "What?"

"The return label is from Private Dabbott in Tahil." Stepping back inside, he ripped through the thick tape. While he fumbled through bubble wrap, a sloppy note slipped out. He caught it in midair and read, "'I found this taped under Huffman's old bunk. I think it's what he found in the desert. Have you heard of Storm Force?'"

She searched his face for any clues of his thoughts. "Storm Force? That sounds like a cartoon name."

Kody sunk into his couch on the other side of the room and rummaged inside the foam peanuts, finding a small bag. Upon seeing the contents inside, his mouth dropped open.

He pulled out a gold chain necklace with a large, ruby-colored stone in the center. Thunder and lightning shocked the sky. He dangled the jewelry in the air.

Raelyn's body tightened. "Is this a joke?"

"This looks like the necklace in the photograph from the museum." His face was inscrutable as he stood.

"Yes. It looks the same as Ma's. Why did Dabbott have one? Wait, do you think—?" She stared at the red gemstone, starting to hyperventilate.

He rushed over to her and lay his hand on her thigh. "Raelyn, breathe."

"Does your friend know where the necklace came from?" She pulled the blankets from his bed, wrapping them around her naked body.

"All I have is this note about my buddy."

"Can you ask her to look into it more?"

"Do you think this is actually Joanna's?" Kody passed the necklace over.

She nodded, shaking, then clutched it tightly in her palm. It was heavier than she expected. Ma never took it off. Raelyn had never held the full weight in her hand.

"There's a high chance nothing will come of this." He stood, starting to pace.

"I don't want to put your job in jeopardy." Raelyn stood and followed with the blanket wrapped around her.

"I can take care of myself." Kody moved to his computer on his desk and typed a quick email. He placed his large hand on hers, guiding her to the send button. "You may not like what Dabbott finds. This is your call."

Her heart flipped inside her chest.

What'll happen if I push send? What'll happen if I don't?

Clenching her teeth, she firmly pressed her finger down on the send button.

"Thank you." Raelyn lowered her eyes.

The vibe had completely shifted. Backing away, she quickly retrieved her dress from the spinning dryer in silence, still clutching what may be Ma's necklace in one hand. The bathroom door gently clicked closed behind her. She leaned her forehead on his mirror. After splashing water on her face, she put her dress back on and rejoined him, but the energy in the room had been sucked dry. After folding his blankets in silence, she picked up her sopping workout clothes from the floor.

He didn't look at her. "I can put those in the dryer too."

"No. I'm gonna go." Raelyn grabbed her satchel.

"You can stay."

Raelyn stared at her feet.

He lifted her chin. "You don't need to have sex with me for me to love you. I just don't think we're ready yet."

"Right. Okay." Her cheeks flushed. "Come on, Bear."

Kody sighed. "Here. Wear my jacket. It's still drizzling."

"Thanks. Can I keep this?" She clutched the necklace to her heart.

"Of course."

Raelyn rushed outside, guiding Bear to her truck.

Ma is dead … isn't she?

The stone from the old necklace hadn't lost its sparkle, and the gold chain still shone brightly under the moonlight.

As she drove toward the highway, the raindrops rushed past the window. The windshield wiper squeaked, wiping droplets away. Raelyn didn't know what she was more upset about—Ma's necklace magically appearing or Kody's rejection.

Suddenly, the tires spun on the slick pavement, and the steering wheel trembled in her hands. Her seatbelt locked, tearing the breath from her chest. The Chevy swerved across the line, spinning wildly onto the shoulder. She pushed Bear against the passenger seat with one arm and slammed her brakes. The branch of a tree crashed through the side window. Glass shattered over her forearm.

Frozen, she stared out into the rain, unable to process what happened. The radio still hummed the song "Heartbeat" by Carrie Underwood, but the lyrics all blended together in a haze.

What happened?

Raelyn rotated her neck, making sure she had full range. Shards cascaded from her hair. She peeled her clenched fingers one by one off the steering wheel before centering her hands on her shaky legs.

"You okay, Bear?" She petted the dog, whose tongue stuck out from the side of his mouth like he had just been on a joyous roller coaster ride.

Coughing from the fumes of burnt rubber, she glanced at her hand.

Ma's necklace!

It was gone.

Trembling, Raelyn frantically dug under the seats, groping side to side. A thin, cold chain brushed against her finger. She grabbed it and blew off crumbs stuck to the side of the stone. Placing the necklace over her head for the very first time, she skimmed the gold chain with her fingers.

Thunder boomed as she inspected the damage—one shattered window. Raindrops streamed through the window, wetting her face and making her teeth chatter. She grabbed at her phone; her finger hovered over Kody's name.

I must've looked so desperate.

Raelyn shook her head then sent him her predicament and location. A strange heat ran along her arm. Bear whined. Looking down, she watched a thin streak of bright red blood spread against her forearm. She pulled a roll of gauze out of the glove box and wrapped the small cut. Shivering, Raelyn reached back on the floor. Once she slid her arms through the extra-long sleeves of Kody's jacket, she closed her eyes and sighed.

Soon, Kody's Jeep rolled to a stop behind her. Goosebumps popped on her arms. His headlights pointed directly at her, illuminating his powerful frame as he walked toward her. Hail bounced off his broad shoulders like bullets deflecting from a metal shield. Watching him scrutinize the scene in only a moment, she bit her bottom lip as his pace quickened to a jog.

Kody stuck his head through her window. His eyes widened. "Are you okay?"

Her insecurities, confusion, and complex web of emotions tore apart when he reached in, his hand brushing hers.

"I got a small cut. I took care of it." She pulled her injured arm behind her back.

He opened her door and swiftly scooped her into his arms, carrying her to his Jeep's passenger seat. Bear followed; thankfully, he didn't have a scrape on him. Jogging around the front, Kody jumped in, looking over her frantically. "Where are you hurt?"

"I'm okay."

He swiped the water off his face and moved closer. "Let me see."

She crossed her arms, the sleeves hanging past her fingertips. "I'm fine."

"Let someone else help you for once." He tried to disguise his grin, but the corner of his lips rose slightly.

As she narrowed her eyes, he rolled off the jacket from her shoulder and took her arm in his large hand. She didn't pull away but cast her sight to the mud on her shoes. Kody lifted her chin with one finger, forcing her to look at his deep eyes. "Everything will be okay."

His confidence sent shivers through her core. Did he even know what he was promising? What exactly did he think would be okay? Their non-relationship? Raelyn knew she had just messed her chances of dating him up further by trying to jump him at his apartment. Or was Kody referring to the fact that everything in the world would magically be fixed now that she was in possession of Ma's necklace? Or was Kody trying to tell her that everything will be okay in regards to who broke into her house? What exactly would be okay?

Kody unwrapped her bandage, inspected her cut, then nodded and rewrapped it. Neither moved their hands off each other.

"Tell me what you're thinking," she demanded.

Kody leaned back and took a deep breath. "Will you be my girlfriend?"

Every inkling of doubt was swept away in one question. He'd never have to ask twice, but she could at least make him sweat for a minute.

She bit her lip. "Kody, you really want a relationship with me? Because you can't just dip your toes in. You have to be completely invested. Is that what you truly want?"

"I'm sure. I want you."

A new frenzy started in her body when he smiled. Heat singed her neck beckoning her to lean closer, to smell him, touch him, and taste him.

Raelyn scrunched her nose. "Why?"

He kissed her softly. "I can't imagine my life without you."

Raelyn pulled away. "Really?"

"Really." Kody pulled his full lips into a perfect pout. "Please?"

A little squeak left her lips as she smiled, then wrapped her hands around his neck. "Only if you teach me how to play chess."

"Deal."

He moved in again, sealing their lips while tucking a damp piece of hair behind her ear. Kody held her tighter. "Listen …"

She stared into his brown eyes.

"There's one more thing," he said.

"What?"

He sucked in a deep breath and blew it out slowly. "I got a response from Dabbott already."

The words paralyzed her.

"Your ma may be alive."

24

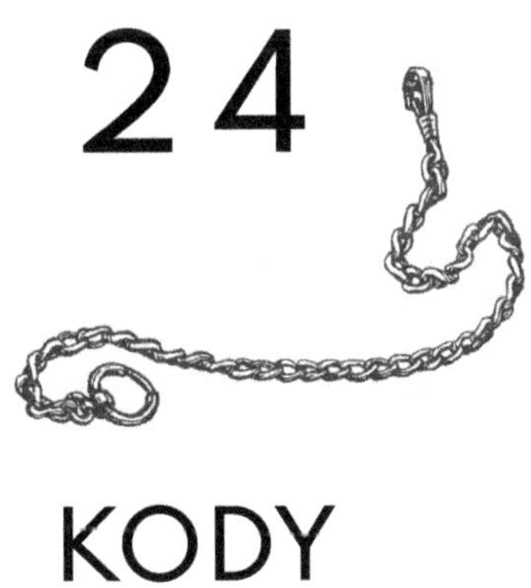

KODY

In his Jeep, Kody watched Raelyn's amber eyes dart to the necklace in her hand as the rain turned to drizzle outside.

Bear fell asleep in the back seat as Raelyn moved closer. "Why do you think Ma may be alive?"

"Dabbott thinks she saw the woman from the picture."

"Where?"

Shit. I need to protect Raelyn from pain.

Kody couldn't tell her that Dabbott believed the woman in the museum picture was the same as the American who disappeared into the tunnels the night of the ambush. Joanna was probably a prisoner by now.

Kody looked away. "I don't know."

Her eyes were wide and wild, full of uncertainty. "I have to do something."

He wrapped her shaking hands in his. "Dabbott will look into it. There's nothing else to do."

"I can't sit here and wait! I'll fly to the desert."

"It's hostile territory. We have to wait for help," he stressed, tucking a loose strand of her hair behind her ear. He could almost see the neurons in her brain rapidly firing, so he gave her space and time to process. Kody could ease one of her worries. "Raelyn, about earlier …" Kody said her name like a smooth caress.

Understanding lit in her eyes as she climbed on top of him in the driver's seat, making him immediately hard. Raelyn could be his candle in the darkness, someone who shone bright enough to guide him.

She pressed her lips to his, then whispered, "It's okay."

He reveled in her coconut scent as her soothing hands touched his neck. "You know I do want to sleep with you, right? But let's just wait a little bit."

A menacing wind blew up the road when another pair of headlights appeared in the darkness.

Raelyn scrambled off his lap. "If Pa found my location on my phone again, he couldn't have gotten here so quickly."

Gathering himself, he adjusted the rear-view mirror.

Kody instantly recognized the Cadillac as the one that had followed him. Private Peterson stepped out, slammed his door, and charged toward the Jeep with his slight limp.

"Stay here." Kody's forearm brushed the side of his jeans. In his rush to help Raelyn, he had forgotten his gun at his apartment.

Shit!

Kody reached in the back of his Jeep and grabbed a bat. He jumped out and hit the door's lock button.

"What's going on, Peterson?" Kody growled.

"Why do you have her?" Peterson roared.

Kody stormed down the side of the road with a baseball bat dangling from his right hand. "Who?"

"Raelyn. I'm taking her home. Stay out of my way, and you won't get hurt."

Kody's fists clenched. "How do you know Raelyn?"

"Let her go." Peterson pushed him.

Kody slammed his foot hard into Peterson's bad leg, making him stumble.

A door shut behind him.

"Get back in my Jeep!" Without turning, Kody yelled to Raelyn, but she rushed between him and Peterson.

"Watch out!" Kody hollered as Peterson regained his footing on the gravel, moving toward her fast.

But nothing happened the way Kody expected.

Peterson gently moved Raelyn behind his back, shielding her from him. Kody froze. "What's going on?"

"Wait." Raelyn sidestepped, trying to maneuver around Peterson, but he held her back.

Kody screamed. "Let go of her! Now!"

"I won't let you mess with this girl, too."

What's he talking about?

Kody charged and pushed his bat against the spot where the bullet had hit his leg during the ambush. Peterson's knees hit the pavement.

Raelyn jumped in front of Peterson. "No! Kody, stop!" She pulled out Peterson's ID card.

"Why do you have that?" asked Kody.

Raelyn held both her hands up. "We all need to talk."

Peterson limped out and reached for her wrist. "Let's go."

"No, Peterson. Explain yourself this time." She stood by Kody.

"This time? How do you know each other?" Kody glanced between them. "Why don't you think my girlfriend is safe with me?"

"Ah, I guess I missed my chance." Peterson winked.

Bear barked from the open Jeep window.

Kody looked at Raelyn. "What is he talking about?"

"We kissed. But it doesn't matter."

Focus. Breathe. I can't hurt Peterson in front of her.

To calm himself, Kody zeroed in on the faint drizzle that ran from his own temple and slowly trailed down his jawline to his chin. He loosened his fists. "What do you need, babe?"

Raelyn's eyes softened. "I need to know why Peterson warned me to stay away from you."

Peterson didn't hesitate. "Walsh will hurt you. Just like the other women."

Kody sent another murderous glare. "Me? You jumped me for no reason in Tahil. You've threatened and blackmailed me. What was so important to you that we had to go into that village?"

Peterson spat. "The ambush wasn't my fault. I was shot too!"

"I have no reason to trust you."

"I know what you did, Walsh!" Peterson hollered.

Kody's stomach turned.

Is he talking about me stealing the marble box or that it was my fault that Huffman died?

"I don't know what you're talking about," said Kody.

"Are you loyal to Sergeant Snyder or no?"

Kody stared him down and spoke slowly. "He's my senior, so I'll do whatever he orders."

Peterson grinned. "I can see it in your eyes. You hate the guy too. But why?"

Kody stood silent. He had to get Peterson to talk before releasing all his information.

Peterson continued, "Snyder told the team that your buddy, Huffman, had kidnapped some teen girls from the village to have some fun and that those girls never returned home. The word is that you took over for Huffman after he passed away. Every time a local girl went missing from the village—that was you."

Raelyn gasped.

Kody gripped the bat harder. "Huffman never did anything like that."

"But you did?"

Kody's eyes narrowed. "No."

Peterson circled around him as the rain came down harder. "Sergeant Snyder said you'd deny it. The girls stopped disappearing since you've been back in Oak City. How convenient." He paused. "Snyder also said you wouldn't make any sacrifices for your career or your team."

"I bet he did." Kody's voice rose. "You want honesty? Snyder is a complete ass. If you're close with him, then I have every reason to pummel you with this." He lifted the bat.

Raelyn stepped closer and meshed their hips together. Behind their backs, she slowly massaged his inner wrist with her thumb.

She knows what I need.

"I'll be calm," Kody whispered to her, taking a deep breath and counting the circles she traced.

"Yeah, I fuckin' hate Snyder. But I never thought you'd say that." Peterson studied him until his mouth hung open, then finally asked, "So, you really didn't abduct any girls?"

Kody stretched both hands wide in the air. "No."

Peterson put a finger in the air before asking, "And you know for a fact that Huffman didn't?"

"Correct."

Peterson calmly sat on the curb, straightening his bad leg. "Then why did Sergeant Snyder say all that?"

All of a sudden, the wind in the rainstorm shifted. The guy's body language and expressions softened, completely at ease, as if his safety weren't at risk at all and his only agenda was to put the missing pieces of the puzzle together.

He's not here to hurt us.

Kody let the bat clatter to the pavement. "Snyder must've blamed Huffman and me to cover for someone?"

Peterson dropped his head in both hands. "Who? If it's not you, I have to start all over."

"I can help."

"Listen, Walsh, you saved my life. I would've bled out. If you're telling the truth and aren't with Snyder, then I owe you and need to make it right." Peterson took a deep breath. "The night of the ambush, I was supposed to meet a civilian and take the file. I don't know how you managed to get ahold of it, but I need it back."

"What file?"

"Hold up! Don't you have it?"

"I don't *have* anything." Kody tossed his hands in the air.

"I swear, ever since we got back to Oak City, things aren't adding up. I overheard Sergeant Snyder on a call in his office this morning. He definitely told someone that you have the file."

"Snyder is *here*? At our Fort?"

"Yeah. Since a week ago."

He thought about the knife stuck into Raelyn's kitchen counter that Yohaan described and the fire in Tuzlicci. What would be next?

I shouldn't leave Raelyn alone.

Kody wrapped his arm around her shivering shoulders. "Raelyn, can you go check on Bear since the Jeep is running?"

When she spun around, her wet hair sprinkled drops everywhere.

Peterson raised a brow. "Getting rid of her? You have intel, don't you?"

Kody pulled a crumpled paper from his pocket. "This was taped to my door." As he angled the paper toward the streetlight, sloppy handwriting showed.

Tape the file to the bottom of your welcome mat tonight or someone dies this time.

It has to be from Snyder. What file does he want?

Suddenly, Bear jumped out of the open door of the Jeep and started running behind Peterson's car. Another vehicle was pulling over.

Kody glanced at Peterson. "Did you tell anyone we were here?"

His eyes grew. "No. You?"

Kody picked up the bat just as Raelyn whizzed by him chasing Bear.

"Raelyn!" Kody rushed after. Out of the car's tinted window, a gun protruded. Kody ran faster. "Raelyn!"

"Bear!" Raelyn yelled.

The dog jumped at the stranger's arm, biting down hard. A bullet shot straight up into the sky. Kody reached Raelyn and tackled her into a puddle. The guy twisted and turned his arm, trying to shake Bear off. But the dog latched on hard.

"Bear! No!" Raelyn screamed from under his body.

The man went in reverse fast, throwing the pup in the middle of the street. Another car zoomed by and smashed right into Bear's side, sending him thudding hard several feet. The gunned man zoomed off.

Raelyn squirmed out from under Kody and raced to Bear, who lay unmoving on the side of the road.

The pain in her voice was too much to hear. "No!"

His heart drummed hard.

Raelyn crouched down. Her whole body shook. Bear lay flat on the pavement. Her pup's chest rose and fell fast. He tried to stand up but weakly collapsed to the ground in a heap.

"It's okay." Raelyn gasped and cradled Bear's head in her lap. "He needs a vet!"

Bear's breaths were heavy and labored. She ruffled his small ears gently as a tear fell. "It's okay."

25

RAELYN

MINUTES SEEMED LIKE HOURS. Raelyn stood frozen like a statue in the vet waiting room, staring at the same smudge of paint on the wall. Her phone whirred repetitively from Kody, who Pa had shunned from their presence. But she couldn't move. It was as if the smudge on the wall held her together.

It'll be okay. Bear will be okay.

Memories flooded back at such a rapid pace, and she couldn't think straight.

Suddenly, Raelyn was six again, sitting on a log pile by the back red barn. Pa's truck pulled up on the grass, and a bunch of round puppy heads peeked out from the passenger window. Raelyn waited patiently, holding Grandma's hand as her foot wiggled in her shoe. A bunch of golden retrievers flopped out of the truck. Five pups sprinted around the farm like lunatics, a tangled mass of paws and tails, but Bear lifted his small nose and trotted right over to her side.

I belong with Bear.

The vet entered.

Raelyn stood, wringing her hands together. "He'll be okay, right?"

The vet shook his head and spoke slowly. "Mr. Bell, can I speak to you in the hall please?"

Pa's voice croaked, "Okay."

"Pa?" Tears ran down her cheeks. She couldn't stop them. Raelyn ran over and swiped Pa's wallet from his pocket fast and flipped it open, looking for any credit card. She could pay Pa back, but she had to give the vet all their money to save Bear. Only cash lay inside, not one credit card.

Raelyn backed herself against the wall, shaking her head. Her body felt numb, so when she rushed through the vet's back door to the lab, her legs almost gave out. Bear lay motionless on a metal table. Seeing him helpless was like someone ripping her throat out of her neck.

"I'm sorry, Bear," she said. The tightness in her chest wouldn't go away. She held his chin in her hands. Bear thumped his tail twice but didn't even try to lick her. She leaned over the table, tears running down her face, and stroked his soft fur, lovingly, gently.

"It's okay. I'm here." She let the tears fall, burying her nose in his neck.

I can't lose him. I'll do anything.

Pa walked in, placing his hand on her shoulder. "The vet said there's nothing they can do."

"You must have medicine or something to save him." Her breathing quickened.

The vet didn't respond.

Her eyes darted to Pa. "I'll take a year off before college and stay home with him all day and nurse him back to health."

Pa bent over and softly whispered in her ear. "It's time to say goodbye."

"I can work here as a tech for free to pay off the bills."

"It's not about the money, hun."

"They can do surgery! We can find a specialist."

"Hun—"

Raelyn covered her body over him like a protective blanket. "No! I can't. He's always there for me. No matter what. Bear never gets mad at me."

Pa reached out his hands.

She held his paw in her hand. "No! Bear's never upset with me. He loves me so much. Every day, every minute without question, Bear is by my side! He's the only one."

Pa gulped and cried with her. "It's time."

"Why! It's not fair. He's a good boy! Bear did everything right."

Bear tilted his head and gazed at her.

She took a deep breath, though the rolling tears down her cheek kept flowing. "It's okay, boy."

Pa's face was pained and tight when he patted Bear's head and kissed the dog's nose. "Thank you. I'm forever grateful that you took care of my girl." He nodded to the vet.

All Raelyn wanted to do was scream, but her body surged with shattering grief. Her world crashed down around her as she caressed his fur in slow smooth circles and spoke soothingly to her first friend.

"If I knew yesterday was our last walk together, I never would've stopped."

Bear met her eyes, and her sobs escalated.

"If I knew it was our last time wrestling on the carpet, I would've played for hours and given you extra treats." Bear placed his paw over her hand when she said treats. She couldn't help but cry and smile at the same time.

"I can't let you go." Her head pounded. "You're such a good boy. Those men are bad. You don't deserve this. Remember our hikes? And when we caught fish? How can I go on without you?" She couldn't stifle her weeping but held Bear's gaze.

He knows.

Bear told her it was okay to let him go. "Pa, Bear knows. He's telling me it's okay. But how can I?"

The vet prepared.

Pa hugged her tightly, but it could never be tight enough. Nothing could prevent the pain about to cascade down on her like an avalanche. Teardrops ran from the corner of Raelyn's eyes, across her cheeks, and down her neck. "Bear, remember the barn?" She petted him softly. "Remember when we used to fall asleep on that haystack? You used to keep me warm." She sniffed. "It's my turn to keep you warm when you fall asleep this time. I love you so much, Bear."

She held his heavy chin in her hand and kissed him on the forehead. As the vet finished, Bear's eyes closed for the final time, and Raelyn's heart shattered wide open.

As soon as the sun rose, Pa drove them west to Ash Mountain. Raelyn clutched the small urn of Bear's ashes in her lap as the mountains grew larger on the horizon. Her long hair blew in the breeze when she rolled the window down further. She breathed in the earthy scent of the woods.

Home

Raelyn's spirit belonged in those hills.

Pa sighed. "I'm sorry."

She jumped a little at the sound of his voice. Neither had spoken for hours.

"For what?" Her voice was flat.

"Bear would've lived longer if we'd stayed out here."

"Pa, I'm allowed to be sad. It hurts, but questioning the past won't bring him back."

Pa pulled into the empty lot of their favorite hiking trail near the river. They sighed at the same time and shared a weak smile before opening the truck doors.

She clutched the urn under her armpit. "Can you give me ten minutes alone and then meet me up there."

"Okay, hun."

She rambled up the steep, sloped trail. The vast, dense forest was filled with fluttering red cardinals. The wind whistled through the branches, and an eagle soared above. Green surrounded them in a canopy as she imagined Bear by her heels. On the way up, her boots knocked loose stones, which rolled down the mountain behind her. Every few minutes, she would've sworn she saw a hooded figure in the distance behind a line of trees, but it must've just been a deer.

It's not fair. First Ma. Now Bear.

She had previously thought that the love Ma enveloped her in could never be replaced. But, the whole time she had Bear—who took over her job. And she might never feel that love again. Life only took good things away. There was no point. No one could love her like Ma or Bear.

Raelyn marched over to a bush sprinkled in red roses. In raw rage, she tore each off their stems. Red painted her skin as she crushed the petals in her hands.

When Raelyn reached for more roses, a thorn slightly stabbed into her wrist. She ignored it, picked up a stick, and slashed it through the air until it hit bark, slamming it over and over against the tree's trunk until the stick snapped in two, the pieces falling to the ground at her feet. She stomped both feet on the stick and screamed. Raelyn picked up a pile of pebbles in her cut-up hand and hurled them down the mountainside. The rocks scattered and ricocheted off other stones. She did it again and again until sweat dripped from her temples and her shoulder was sore. Screaming, Raelyn dropped to her knees, breathing heavily.

She let herself cry. "Ma, why aren't you here?" Her tears soaked her face and dripped down into the dirt. She tilted her head to the treetops and screamed into the green of the forest. "I'm broken! Fix me!"

The wind answered by brushing her face and reminding her of Ma's letter that said, '*You already have everything you need.*'

Wrong. I have no one. You're gone. I'm lost.

Her tears soaked a hole through the top corner of the page.

Atop Ash Mountain, Raelyn hung her feet off the canyon's edge. Oak trees stuck out from all angles of the land like candles on a cake, and purple flowers sprinkled the soil as decoration. The horizon met the sky in peach and fire shades. With a deep inhale, she closed her eyes to a breeze tickling her face. Ma's voice whispered lullabies in the wind.

Do I have everything I need?

As the wind softly whizzed through her hair, she closed her eyes and thought about the times Pa helped her climb up a giant pile of boulders. When she looked out from the top, little Raelyn had felt like she was on top of the world. Little did she know they had only been twenty feet high. Pa had created an imaginative world full of knights on horses and mysterious, locked away treasure. And Raelyn remembered looking into Pa's eyes knowing she already had all the treasure she'd ever need.

A deep breath caught in her throat as she realized how wrong she had been. She closed her eyes.

I have love. Pa. Now Kody and Cali. I have everything I need. It'll all be okay.

Pa's heavy footsteps came up behind her. "Has it been ten minutes?"

Raelyn laughed and wiped away a tear. "Only six and a half."

"Well, I missed you."

She tilted her head. "Why don't I feel that more?"

"What do you mean?"

"Sometimes I don't feel loved or missed by you."

"Well, hun. I've always loved you, and I always will. No one can convince you of that but yourself."

She sighed. "You're right. It was never your fault. I'm the one who needs to change."

"I love you the way you are." Pa sat next to her and smiled, but it was sad and forced. "So, want to bury the urn?"

"No. I'm terrified of underground. I don't want Bear down there."

"Why does it scare you so much?"

She sighed. "During Ma's funeral, that box ... that coffin ... I couldn't stand the thought of being trapped underground for eternity, because ..." She gestured over the valleys. "Because look at this beauty. No one should have to be separated from this. Bear deserves to fly free in the wind. But I guess she was never down there. You never told me they didn't return a body."

"You were so little, hun." He wrapped his arm around her. "So, what do you want to do with Bear?"

She nodded to the canoe rental station they had used a hundred times. "Time for a ride. Bear always wanted to join us on the river. Now, he can." She breathed in the familiar smell of the woods, river and fish, immersing herself in nature like old times.

Pa walked over to the small canoe rental stand. For the first time, Raelyn noticed a small cabin tucked behind the trees behind them. She watched quietly as Pa paid for a canoe by inserting coins in a slot like a parking meter which automatically released a canoe from its lock. He lugged it over, creating a line in the dirt. When he stepped in, the canoe rocked in the water. "Let's go."

Raelyn pushed off the side of the bank, and a chunk of clay wedged under her fingernails. She reached over the side of the boat and dipped her fingertips in the crisp water, washing away the clay in one sweep. The sun warmed the back of her ears. As she paddled on the river, the canoe rocked, and the small splashes doused her boots. Green leaves hung over the river, playing with the breeze, refusing to surrender their part of the sky.

He nodded and took a breath. "Ready?"

Together, they scattered Bear's ashes in the river. Pa left the last scoop for her. If she let the tears come, they'd never stop. But she wasn't only crying for Bear. Looking over at Pa, she realized how much support he had always given her. Why was she so set on searching for love from her dead mother when Pa had been there for her all along?

I have everything I need already.

"I just thought of some poem lines."

"Can I hear it?"

"With a love this powerful, the nightmare of losing you rocks me to my core. Can't trade a life for a life. But, if possible, I would give up mine to save yours."

Pa smiled. "Bear would've loved it."

"I know. But it was about you. Promise you'll always be here?"

"Hun …" His voice low, Pa laid his hand on hers.

"I couldn't bear it." She looked away. "Promise me."

He sighed. "I promise. And all this time, I thought you hated me." Pa nudged her.

"I've never hated you." She tilted her head. "Well, maybe one percent."

Pa chuckled. "When it's my time, I'd want to be buried right at the summit of Ash Mountain. Right by the little cabin I used to take you and your Ma to."

"Don't say things like that."

"No one lives forever."

"You can."

Pa flexed his bicep.

She laughed. "Stop making me smile."

"But your smile is perfect. Just like your Ma's."

So few pictures remained of Ma. It was hard to see her smile clearly anymore. The face of the woman in the museum photograph had a different quality in her expressions than Raelyn recalled from long ago. If it was Ma in that desert, she had changed.

What happened to her?

Raelyn started rowing again. "Do you ever wish Ma could come back?"

"All the time. But I stayed in a ghost land far too long. I need to move on."

"Pa, the map you didn't want me looking at, it led to that warehouse. There was a name listed, Zohaib."

"Hun, I don't think—"

Near the fork ahead, the mild rapids ahead rushed by rougher than usual. Another canoer paddled parallel to them, his fisherman's hat low, blocking his eyes. Raelyn tensed and waved her arm for the guy to move. The man lowered his hat over his eyes and stuck the paddle deep, as if trying to hold his position.

What the—?

Their canoe bucked. Pa missed their turn. She paddled hard but met resistance, as if she were digging a grave. She stroked one, two, left, right.

Snap.

The paddle blade broke and rushed away down the current. The canoe shot toward the rougher path.

She clutched onto the side of the canoe hard. Pa yelled something from behind, but his voice trailed into the wind. The canoe tipped sideways and collided into sharp rocks. Raelyn shrieked and tumbled out.

"Raelyn!" Pa plunged into the water after her.

The cold water stabbed like daggers, and the current forced Raelyn to the spiraling waters. Fighting the ravenous current with all her might, she was helpless as the waters sucked her away. Her lungs ripped with pain.

Swimming harder, Raelyn panted between the white rapids. She crashed into a boulder. Pa's arms wrapped around her and lifted her on top of the rock. The raging waves battered him below the surface.

"Pa!"

He disappeared from view.

"Pa!"

Nothing.

Where is he?

A fear stronger than the force of the deadliest current rushed through her veins.

"Pa!" Her throat burned from screaming. "Come back!"

Complete isolation suffocated her, strangling Raelyn's neck. It had been too long.

He surfaced and gasped for air. She jumped in and gripped his back, pulling him to shore as hard as she could. She kicked desperately. One foot away.

Pa pushed her close to a branch jutting over the water. She clung to a limb on the side. Raelyn crawled away from the water, coughing, but turned back, reaching for Pa. Using all her strength, she tried to heave him up onto the dirt. Raelyn ripped a tear in his shirt while grabbing at the fabric. He sprawled on the soil, panting.

Flat on his back, Pa laid his hand on his daughter's forearm. They were alive.

"Are you okay?" Pa panted.

She nodded and coughed.

He interlaced his fingers between hers, then said, "I love you."

Why can't I say it back? What's wrong with me?

For a few minutes, they laid there stretched out like starfish, staring up at the puffy clouds. The dirt under elbows itched her wet skin as her panting slowly subsided into calm breaths.

"You're okay." Pa leaned over, kissing the top of Raelyn's head.

She couldn't respond yet.

He sat up, a pillar of strength before her as he pointed in the distance. "Remember Lake Emerald? Your ma and I used to take you to climb trees."

She slowly managed to sit, sore and soaked. "Yeah, me and Amy used to have contests of how high we could go. I always lost."

"Once, your sneaker got stuck on a branch. You tried to yank it free but then hung upside down from one foot."

"Sounds like me."

"What am I gonna do when you go to college?" He stared at the sky. "You'll visit me every weekend?"

She rolled her eyes, smiling. "Pa! No way! Once a month is the max!"

He nudged her side. "You're killing your old man."

She smiled and rung out her soaking hair and started walking back down the path. “I need to go to the barn and leave Bear’s collar in the loft.” She wobbled on a rock, and he caught her before she fell. Her soles of her shoes squished, full of puddles.

The sun dried them off on the hike back down before it lowered itself behind the mountains. Raelyn hummed a tune. She never sang until Cali came into her life. Her best friend had more spunk than cookies had sugar. The move was a blessing, maybe this was her final goodbye to her past—no need to return.

Back in the truck, Pa turned the keys and joked, “Should I get out my GPS?”

She smiled. “You’ve never used one before, and you say that *now*, when we’re four minutes from home—I mean, the house. Does someone live there now?”

“Yes. Your grandma Viola bought it from me and rents it out.”

Her eyes widened. “Really? It still belongs in the family?”

“Yes.”

She spoke slowly. “And you didn’t tell me because … you wanted to keep me safe?”

He turned on his blinker to pass a John Deere tractor. “Yes. Because I love you.”

She sighed. “I love you too, Pa.”

A tear rolled down his face.

“What’s wrong?”

“That’s the first time you’ve said that since your ma died.”

“Really? That’s a long time.” She gently rested her forehead against the truck window. “All I’ve wanted for years was to feel loved. Instead, I pushed it away.”

She thought about Kody professing his love to her, multiple times. Why hadn’t she said it back?

I’m afraid.

Just last night on the highway made it plenty clear that some evil guy was threatening her boyfriend for information. He could get hurt or shot again at any moment. She thought back to the river and the man who was in the canoe.

“Pa? Did you see that guy block our path on the river?”

“Yeah.” Pa pulled in behind the red barn. “Look, home sweet home.”

She shook the image from her mind and grabbed her camera. Raelyn snapped pictures of her old farmhouse.

"Sshh!" He pressed his finger to his lips, smiling. "We're trespassing."

"It's Grandma's property. What's she gonna do? Arrest us?"

"Obviously, you don't know your grandma very well."

She laughed while stepping over a pile of leaves. "Can I do this alone?"

He nodded. "I'll give you five minutes."

"Does that mean four and a half?" She rolled her eyes and rushed toward the barn, jumping when the automatic light flipped on. Raelyn climbed up, recalling the last time she'd been in the barn. So much had changed, but Bear's spirit resonated strong, wagging his tail by her ankles.

The floorboards of the loft creaked. She didn't need to pull on the rusty latch; the door was already open and the large trunk sat in the same place inside the closet-like space. Raelyn loosened a floorboard by kicking it with the heel of her boot. She kneeled, pried the end up, and slipped the collar underneath for safe keeping.

"Ouch." A paper sliced into her finger. Grimacing, she withdrew her hand quickly.

Raelyn pulled harder on the floorboard, snapping a chunk off. Sharp edges of wood lined the little hole. She sprawled on her stomach, reaching at an odd angle.

"I got it, Bear!" Raelyn pushed herself up, grasping crinkled papers, then spoke into the wind that flew through the barn and rustled the papers. "Bear, it's Ma's handwriting."

She could hear his sharp excited bark asking what it said.

I'll show you one day, boy. Wait for me.

Raelyn unfolded the papers frayed with age. Flattening them out, she saw that they listed names and addresses in English, then many lines of another language she couldn't read.

The top of one read,

SAFEHOUSES

She gathered the papers and grabbed the canvas image of Ma with a line of women in the desert, then rushed out to Pa's truck. He wasn't there. The back door of the farmhouse was open. Raelyn tiptoed in, her boots creaking in the same spot it had all her life.

"Pa?"

"In here." Pa's voice came from the study.

Grandma hadn't changed the decor, but Raelyn did see her purse sitting on the kitchen counter. Raelyn dug inside quickly and pulled out a credit card, hoping Grandma wouldn't need it or notice for a while. Somehow, Pa had managed to pay in cash for everything since they'd moved. She had only noticed it recently but decided not to question him on it. But Raelyn wouldn't be able to purchase an airline ticket to Tahil with cash. She pocketed the credit card fast and joined Pa in the study.

Whispering, Raelyn said, "I thought you said we'd get in trouble."

"Maybe I like adventure today."

She held up her hands. "Look what I found in the loft."

Pa frowned and stared at the antique desk, no longer full of messy papers. "I'm surprised there wasn't more."

Raelyn held her breath for a moment, hoping she and Pa could work together to solve the remaining pending questions.

"Pa, I think Ma is still alive."

He looked toward the lacy curtains. "Hun—please don't."

"Months ago, a soldier found this in a village about twenty minutes from where Ma was working when the attack happened." Raelyn dug in her satchel and pulled out Ma's necklace, swinging it in the air by the gold chain. "The soldier found her necklace!"

Pa's jaw dropped. She slowly set the stone in his hand, but he let it slide it through his fingers. It clunked to the desk.

Pa shook his head. "No—no—it can't be. That could be anyone's."

"Look me in my eyes and tell me that you're a hundred percent certain this isn't hers." She collected it, the heavy gem swaying from her fingertips. "A soldier Kody works with even thinks she saw Ma."

He grunted a fake laugh. "How could someone know what Joanna looks like?"

Raelyn held up a picture on her phone of Ma from the museum, surrounded by children, laughing in the desert.

Pa's hand moved on its own to bring it closer. "She's older, with wrinkles around her eyes. How?"

"The photographer took this picture less than a year ago."

He pushed himself back. "No. No."

"Look, she's wearing the necklace." Raelyn zoomed in.

Pa recoiled against the chimney, his chest rising heavily. His mouth opened, but he was speechless.

She smiled. "We could finally bring Ma home."

He covered his face with his hands.

"Pa? Let's go get Ma. We can buy two tickets. I'll wait to start college for a semester."

He shook his head.

Tears formed in her eyes. "What? Why! We don't need more proof. She's right there!"

He stared out the window at the oak tree in their old yard, the one with the rope swing dangling. "When you were a baby, your ma ached for a career. If I had been a more supportive partner in raising you, she might not have felt so trapped. Joanna wouldn't have returned to work at all."

Raelyn hugged him. "No one could've known what was going to happen."

"I knew she was barely hanging on here at home. She went back to the desert for an assignment when you were four or five."

She turned the canvas around, displaying the line of women in hijabs. "This one?"

Pa briefly glanced at it and nodded, then set it aside. He took both Raelyn's hands in his. "Listen to me. I didn't want Joanna to keep traveling, so I asked her for another baby. I hoped that if she were pregnant again, she'd stay home. But we lost him. It's all my fault."

"Pa, that's probably not how she saw it. She wouldn't blame you."

His face was red. "Don't you see what I'm trying to tell you? I pushed her away. If a soldier saw her—if your ma is alive—she's choosing to not come home. It means she's purposefully staying away."

Raelyn dropped her hands from his, shaking her head. "No."

"I'll try to help you, but I don't think you'll like what we find. If we go over there and she's happy with some guy, that will crush you. It'll crush me. It'll destroy us."

"I'm stronger than you think." She gulped hard. "What if Ma apologized, would you take her back?"

"Of course, hun." Pa hugged her in close. "Forgiveness if the only option, Family always forgives. There's no need to hold onto anger. It only poisons the water."

Raelyn raised her chin, her voice calm. "I'm flying over there—soon."

He nodded. "Okay. I'll come with you."

26

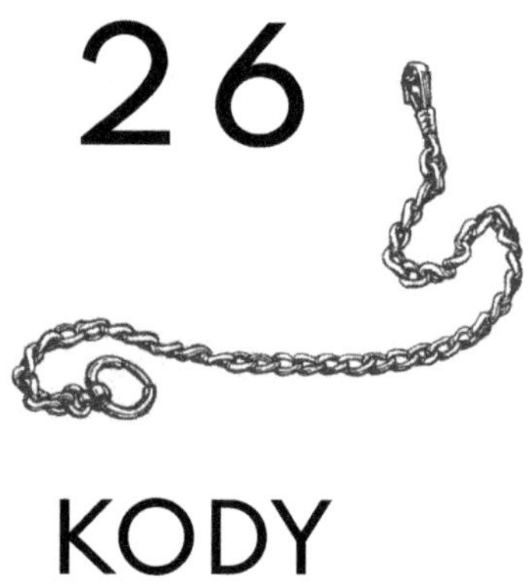

KODY

A FEW WEEKS LATER, limbs spread like a starfish on his comforter, Kody groaned, stretching his sore arm after a workout. Exercising outside in April temperatures was easy compared to the desert temperatures he'd have to tolerate if he were still deployed, but he could still only do half as many pushups as usual.

My arm will never be the same again.

His phone purred on his nightstand. It'd probably be Cali with more news. Apparently, Walter and his new fiancé were expecting a little girl at the end of the summer. Kody couldn't tolerate any human under the age of thirteen and used all options to escape any type of encounter with children.

Or maybe it was Raelyn texting him. They'd been talking nonstop, learning about each other. At this point, he could probably win the highest prize money on a game show about Raelyn Bell. If a host asked him any question, he'd know the answer, ranging from her favorite character in the novels she read, to what foods she was allergic to, what she thought about global warming, and how she organized her sock drawer. The miraculous part wasn't the information that he had accumulated, but that he had been reciprocal and told her just as much information about himself.

In anticipation of hearing what else he could learn about her, Kody pushed himself up and curled his bare toes over the smooth, hardwood floor. His hands curled into fists when he read.

"You didn't get me Jawhara. So, I'll take your girl today. She's a fine replacement."

Kody kicked in the bottom of the nightstand with his heel, denting the wood.

What the hell am I supposed to do?

Weeks had passed without much information. He and Peterson had been in constant communication trying to figure out who wanted the file and what was on it. Yohaan had a surveillance team on Raelyn, without her knowing, when she was at school and work. The only time she wasn't watched was when she was in transition driving between locations. Raelyn hadn't received any more messages, and it seemed obvious from the grammar used that it wasn't the same sender who had been threatening Kody.

He rushed to his computer to send Lieutenant Meadows and Yohaan an update of this more recent threat. Whoever had threatened Cali about going up in flames definitely wasn't bluffing. So, Kody had to treat this threat on Raelyn's life as legit.

Tap. Tap. Tap.

Kody jumped. Someone knocked on his door again. He peeked through the hole and sighed. Quickly, Kody opened the door, scanned the hall, and pulled Raelyn into the room.

"Hey, babe." He kissed her forehead.

She surveyed his face. "You okay?"

He closed the door fast and locked it. "I am when you're with me."

"What's with the new cameras out there?" Raelyn pointed.

Kody kissed her hand and rubbed it in his. "Protocol."

"But none of the other doors have it."

He smiled. "When did you start noticing details?" Wrapping his arms around her waist, he moved her away from the windows and kissed her. "I missed you."

"I missed you too. But why are you so tense?" Raelyn reached up and rubbed his shoulders.

"Dabbott found more intel. The two women we saved from the cellar are still in US possession." He paused. "Apparently, they had been sold as slaves to Zohaib's mansion."

"How awful. Why would they admit to this information, though? The Zohaib guy would come after them if he found out, right?"

Kody paced the room, glancing out the window every few seconds. "Those three women witnesses have been granted transportation to the States in return for their compliance."

"Three?" She sat on his bed and kicked off her cowboy boots. "You said there were two."

Kody cringed at the realization of his slip. "One didn't make it to the tank on the night I was shot."

Raelyn unwrapped the blue plaid shirt from her waist and tossed it on his sheets. "What happened to her?"

Kody cleared his throat. "I lost consciousness. The other two believe she was trying to return to Zohaib."

Raelyn's jaw dropped. "Why would a slave return?

He shook his head and said slowly. "Babe, I need you to take a deep breath."

"What?"

He locked in on her eyes. "That slave may be your ma."

Raelyn choked on her spit, turning red, before she forced out, "What? What happened to her?"

Kody eyed her carefully, trying to read her mind. "Dabbott is trying to infiltrate."

She stood and started fanning herself. "So, Ma could be in some villain's mansion?"

"It's a possibility," he said, nodding.

"What can I do?"

"Nothing. I need to keep you safe."

"I have to help her." Raelyn groaned. "I'm going over there!"

Kody blocked her exit. "Give me six months."

"No!" She tapped her foot.

"Wait until graduation." His eyes were desperate.

"No. If you won't help me, I'll do it myself." Raelyn started researching flights from Oak City to Tahil on her phone. She still had Grandma's credit card in her satchel.

Kody rubbed the stubble on his chin. There was no way she'd back down. He couldn't let her go over to hostile territory alone. A trip would risk breaking army rules, and an officer may even consider him AWOL.

I can convince William to travel with Raelyn—at least she'd be safe that way.

But her father had no military training. What if he put her in more danger without realizing it? William's emotions were involved with Joanna too, and that made them both vulnerable for countless mistakes.

Kody lowered her phone. "I'll go with you. Give me three weeks."

"Two."

"Fine." He fingered the strap of her tank top, edging it over her shoulder.

"Hey!" She wriggled away.

"My lips want your skin." He leaped after her, grinning.

She squealed, circling around his kitchen table, and grabbed a spatula, ducking down behind the counter.

He lowered his voice, teasing, "Lady Rapunzel outwits her evil suitor with a giant plastic spatula."

"Warning! I'm armed!"

He laughed. "Oh yeah? Got some potatoes back there to hurl at me?"

"There's no way you can stop me!"

"Not true. You need to open this birthday present."

She came from around the counter and rose on her tip-toes, kissing him again. He smiled, placing one hand below her butt and lifting her up. She squealed.

With his good arm, he pulled out a pair of earrings with swirling ruby precious stones. "Sorry it's a few days late."

"These are just like Ma's necklace."

He smiled, and she returned it.

Raelyn winked. "You know what I really want for my birthday, soldier."

He pinned her against the wall, pressing his lips against her neck. She moaned. With intent, he sat on a kitchen chair, positioning her atop his lap. His heart raced.

This is it. Her first time.

She slid each of his shirt buttons through the fabric slits as he hardened under her. Raelyn licked his ear, and he shivered. When Kody pulled her in more tightly with his hands on her lower back, he grazed his lips on her neck. She tried a little bite, and he groaned.

She laughed, but her joy didn't drown out the noise of his front door knob twisting. He whirled around. A ruffling sound swished from the hallway.

"Get in the bathroom," Kody commanded.

"What?"

A loud thud knocked. "Walsh!"

Kody recognized Snyder's snarling voice. His heart juddered. He put his finger to his lips and scooped her up silently, taking her into his small bathroom.

Thud. Thud. Thud.

"Walsh!" The angry voice wouldn't let up.

He lifted her into the bathtub. "Stay low. Don't come out until I get you!"

"Kody?" Her eyes grew wide before he closed the shower curtain.

Snyder continued to pound outside. "Walsh! I won't be ignored!"

He glanced at his locked gun safe across the room.

No time.

More banging followed. Kody gripped the pocket knife from his beltloop and palmed it behind his back before swinging open the door. "Yes?" Kody looked down at Snyder.

"I have updates." Snyder shifted his stance, narrowing his eyes at Kody's unbuttoned shirt.

"I'll swing by your office," said Kody. He didn't budge when Snyder moved forward.

"We'll talk now." Snyder reached up and angled the camera away while keeping his eyes glued on Kody. "You don't seem to understand."

I understand. The man is here to take Raelyn.

Quickly, Snyder closed the small gap between them, pressing his thumb hard against the spot where Kody was shot long enough for him to fall back. Kody grunted in pain. Snyder pushed his way inside and started looking around. Kody stayed between him and the bathroom.

"You have the file I need." Snyder sifted through drawers. "Give it to me, and you'll still keep your current title and honor—and girl."

He'd hand over any file in a heart beat to save Raelyn, but it wasn't an option. The man had wrong information. Kody clenched his jaw but forced a softer tone. "How about we go take a walk? You can let me know how I can help you."

"None of this would've happened if you were smart enough to listen to me. How hard is it to *not* shoot someone?"

Kody stood still as a statue, rubbing the cold pocket knife behind his back until the metal warmed.

I did my job.

Snyder almost growled as he said, "I had a plan! Everything I've been working for has been stripped away."

"What are you working for? Let's talk it out."

"You're a pathetic soldier." Snyder snickered, but then his lips straightened. "You couldn't even make any sacrifices to find Jawhara."

It's been Snyder all along.

Kody kept a straight face. "Why did you pick me to help you?"

"I had to choose a weakling like you who cares way too much about his people. So, how's Cali–?"

Kody stepped forward and clenched his fists. "Don't you *ever* speak of my family. If you want a damn stone, go find it yourself."

"Don't act clueless." Snyder shoved his phone in Kody's face, showing the museum photograph.

Kody stepped back, confusion overwhelming him.

He wants the necklace?

Snyder slammed his fist on the kitchen counter. "Where's her necklace?"

Kody tried to visualize Raelyn's outfit from minutes ago.

Is Raelyn wearing the necklace now?

All he could imagine were her scared eyes. Beads of sweat formed on his forehead. "I don't know. If I hear anything, I'll let you know." Kody gestured Snyder to the front door.

"I know you have it."

"Why would I want some random woman's jewelry? She probably got it from her husband or something. Go find *him*." Kody realized his mistake immediately. His gut flipped.

If that woman truly is Joanna, I can't lead Snyder to threaten William.

But Kody didn't expect the next words that spat out of Snyder's mouth.

"I *am* her husband."

Kody released the breath he had been holding in.

So, the woman can't be Joanna. All of Raelyn's searching has amounted to nothing. She'll be devastated.

Kody gestured Snyder to the hall. "Then let's go ask your wife."

"I can't!" Snyder kicked over the kitchen chair. The wooden leg snapped into two pieces and rolled across the floor, toward the bathroom door.

Kody clenched his jaw. "Why?"

"She—she ran off. Who does she think she is? I gave her everything."

If I act like I care, he'll give more answers.

Kody softened his face. "I can help you form a team, and we'll find her. Let's talk about it outside."

"No. That's what Quincy said, that worthless piece of shit. That useless moron better not set foot in my army again."

Kody waited to see if he'd spill more information.

"It doesn't matter. I'll find that slut and kill her myself."

Kody's back muscles tightened. "What? You'd kill your wife?"

"She tried to leave me!" Snyder paced, and Kody only caught a few of his words. "… damn mountain man … fuck him!"

Kody leaned forward. "What did you say?"

"Nothing. I never cared about that slut."

"If you don't love her, why do you care? Leave her be."

Snyder paced. "Because she's made a fool of me. She has been working against me for years. Sabotaging my plans. And all the proof is on that necklace."

"Okay, let's go to the office and think of a plan of where it could be."

Snyder went off on a tangent, mumbling to himself while pacing. "I thought she served her purpose by giving me a son, a boy I could train and pass down my plans to." Snyder's lips curled into a sneer. "But she's a liar! After everything I did for her, Liam isn't mine after all. I'm not his biological father."

Kody recalled the tall, blond boy in the aircraft hangar the day he had been shot and transported out.

Snyder's face turned soft for a moment. "That bitch tricked me for years."

Kody took a deep breath. "Slow down. Why are you telling me this?"

"This is all your fault, Walsh. I lost everything because of you. If you'd chosen the right side and done as you were told, she'd still be with me. All my planning has been swiped away by your carelessness." He pounded a fist into his palm. "If you don't give me the necklace, then it doesn't matter what I tell you. You won't be talking to anyone after today. And what I do to you, your girlfriend will feel double. Then, I'll pass her around after I'm done with her."

Kody's chest squeezed tight, and his insides lurched. He didn't wait for Snyder to turn his back, didn't bother looking for an opening. He ran full force right into his stomach, crashing with him to the floor. They rolled on the kitchen floor, scrambling limbs knocking into the legs of the table. The pocket knife flew out of his hand and rolled across the floor.

Snyder pinned Kody, his knees on his chest, pushing him down with his body weight. Snyder punched him square in the nose. "Give me the necklace!"

Kody covered his face with both hands as warm blood rushed down his cheek. Twisting and turning didn't work. Snyder wrapped both hands around Kody's neck.

I can't breathe.

"Give me the necklace!"

The bathroom door creaked open.

No! Go back.

Kody's strength faded. Raelyn ran out. There was a loud bang, and Raelyn screamed.

27

RAELYN

Raelyn thrust open Kody's apartment door, and it banged loudly against the wall. She screamed at the top of her lungs until her throat was raw. From nearby apartment doors, soldiers spread around her like wildfire, rushing toward her bloodcurdling sounds. Men surrounded her from all angles.

"What's wrong, miss?" A man with a round face rushed to her side.

All she could do was point to where Snyder was strangling her boyfriend, pushing down on his throat. Kody fought, trying to shove Snyder off.

Soldiers drew their guns and rushed in. They alternated who to point them at.

"What's going on?" one shouted.

Three charged forward, knocking Snyder over and binding his hands behind his back.

Kody gasped for air, rolling to his side. Blood trickled from Kody's face, and he lay panting. Sobs erupted from Raelyn's mouth as she collapsed to the floor.

Kody croaked in cracked syllables, nodding to a soldier. "Take her somewhere safe. Anywhere."

The soldier moved toward Raelyn, but she quickly crawled to Kody. "I'm not going anywhere!"

The room moved in a haze. She couldn't focus on the words being said. Three soldiers kept Snyder's wrists behind his back. Raelyn stared at the man who had almost killed Kody, like her brain etched a mug shot to haunt her nightmares. He looked a couple of years older than Pa and a couple of inches shorter. He was stocky, had beige skin, a wide nose, a scar under his chin, and a shaved head.

"Let me go. That's an order," Snyder yelled.

The men hesitated, glancing around.

"Don't let him go." Kody tried to stand, teetering to the side. "I have multiple cameras that should've caught everything on tape." He finally had something to put away the guy messing with his entire life.

"Roger that. You want a medic?" a soldier asked.

They dragged Snyder out of sight.

Kody's voice cracked as he answered, "No. I'm fine." He gathered the soldier's contact information and sent the hidden camera footage to him from the ap on his phone. The soldier nodded and walked out, clicking the door shut slowly.

Raelyn jumped to the kitchen, poured a glass of water, and handed it over. "You need a doctor!"

Kody shook his head, rubbing his throat. He gulped water, took a deep breath, and sighed.

She clutched the necklace under her shirt, pressing it tightly in her palm.

"That guy almost killed you." Tears fell. "What do we do? What's going to happen? Will he come back?"

"No. You're safe. Snyder's got a lot of explaining to do. It's his word against half a dozen witnesses." He turned toward her. "He's in custody. It's all over." Kody lifted her chin and kissed her lips.

"You almost died."

"I'm fine. Snyder will most likely get kicked out of the army. We won't have to deal with him again."

"I should've given him Ma's necklace."

Kody shook his head. "You did nothing wrong. But listen, I don't think that's Joanna's necklace. I'm sorry. Snyder said he's married to that woman."

"Oh. So, this is just someone else's?"

"I think so. Are you okay?" His forehead creased in seriousness.

"Yeah." She sighed. "It's a pretty big coincidence. They look so much alike."

Kody stroked her hair. "Do you want to talk about it?"

"Not right now. Rest your throat."

He cuddled her in close. "I never want to put you in danger."

She said, "I'm not the one who matters. I can't lose you."

He wiped away a tear running down her face. "Okay. Then we both become immortal. I mean, there was that magical fountain in Tuzlicci." He glanced down at the red blood splotches on his white t-shirt.

"Oh, Kody. Let me help." Her heart drummed against her chest while looking at his cuts. "I'll take care of you. Go sit."

On the way past his stereo, she turned the knobs, and a slow beat pulsed in the air. She swiped bandages from under his sink and gently tended to his cuts. What if Snyder came back for him?

I can't lose Kody.

He lifted her chin. "I'm okay." He kissed her forehead, lingering long enough to take a breath before standing. "I'm gonna wash off."

From the corner of her eye, she watched him peel off his shirt; the muscles in his back flexed on display for a few moments. A cinnamon-scented candle sat next to a couple of lighters on his counter. She lit a flame, the heat flickering around her fingers.

Once she heard the shower running, she quickly searched for plane tickets from Oak City to Tahil.

Kody's wrong. It has to be Ma. There's no other option.

Her teachers would have to understand her missing a few weeks of classes. She pulled out the credit card she had stolen from Grandma's purse, then hovered her finger over the "Purchase One" button. Cali would understand if Raelyn missed her solo performance at graduation.

Kody would have to understand her need to go over to the desert and bring Ma home. Raelyn took a deep breath and pushed the "Confirm Ticket" button.

Pa would have to forgive her for traveling alone. She knew he didn't truly want to hunt for Ma in a foreign land since he didn't think anything good would come of it. Hopefully, she wouldn't come home empty-handed.

Plucking a maroon pen from her messy bun, she wrote the thoughts floating in her mind in looped cursive.

Take me as I am, in this sacred space
Where love can heal, and music slows the pace
A moment of time to ponder your face
Synchronized movements of endless embrace

Raelyn knew she would stay with Kody long-term, taking the good and the bad, the challenges and the risks. Beyonce's "Halo" played while Kody walked out of the bathroom with a towel wrapped around his waist. Her lingering stare absorbed a water droplet as it eased down his bare chest.

She glanced at his stern face. "Have you been thinking hard? I do my best thinking in the shower."

Kody ran his hand over his head. "Raelyn, listen. My life and my job—our relationship won't be an easy ride. I'll get deployed again, and the danger won't go away."

She placed down her journal. "I'm not going anywhere." Rising from the couch, she glided toward Kody and wrapped her arms around his toweled waist. Her fingertips tapped the rhythm of the song on his lower back.

His forehead creased, and he was about to speak. Raelyn put her finger to his lips, making him smile softly. She held his chin between her thumb and finger and kissed his thick lips.

Kody sighed. "You'll stay with me?"

He may never be truly safe again.

Looking into his eyes, the years of trying to mend her splintered heart faded away. She smiled, nodding. "Always."

"Even when I'm away?"

She ever so slightly tilted her chin down and whispered, "Kody, I love you."

He smiled, and she kissed the stubble from his chin to his ears.

"I love you too, babe. Always." Kody took a deep breath and straightened his back before hesitantly asking, "Will you go to prom with me?"

She tapped her chin. "Only if I can wear gold like Belle. You can be my Beast."

His belly laugh echoed around his room. "Is that what you want?"

Raelyn looked up into his gaze. "I want to be with you—now."

His intense eyes turned to fire, and he bent to trail his lips along the line of her neck. Raelyn unwrapped his towel and let it drop to the floor, looking down at his entire body. Her eyes widened at the sight of his girth, pointed straight at her. She stifled a gasp and knew her cheeks were flushing.

She guided him to sit on his bed. Shimmying out of her shorts, she tugged her long t-shirt lower in an attempt to cover her upper thighs.

"Don't hide. You're beautiful."

She pulled on the side of her red panties nervously. "Your favorite color."

"They're perfect." He gently placed his hands on the back of her thighs, right under her cheeks, bringing her closer.

She kissed him softly and tossed each leg around his waist. A deep hum escaped from his throat. Raelyn brushed her lips along the muscled curve of his shoulder, and goosebumps formed where his skin touched hers.

"I'm yours," he whispered and reached behind her neck, loosening her hair tie so her thick locks tumbled over her back.

Raelyn bit her lip. "Maybe I should go for a jog," she teased and scooted off his lap across the room.

He smiled ear-to-ear. "Do you know what you do to me?" He held out his hands. "Come here."

For once, Raelyn didn't have to work hard to decipher Kody's face. She smiled. "Make me."

Kody let out a little growl, rushed across the room, and pinned her against the wall with his body. With one finger, he skimmed her hipbone, stretching the red cotton away from her skin with his thumb. He pulled her underwear down, letting them fall to her ankles. Kody scooped her up in his arms and tossed her on the bed.

The threshold of her willpower to tease him faded away. Sliding his hands up her body, he gathered her shirt, and she took a deep breath and pulled it off. Her mind swirled into nothingness, making all fears and worries fade away. All she cared about was him.

Wrapping her own arms around his back, she kissed him deeply, pouring all her love into that kiss, trying to show him she would be going nowhere without him. Kody brought her breast to his mouth, kissing everywhere but the pointy tips. Raelyn's back arched for more. Her heart rate sped up, and shivers covered her body as she laid naked against his pillows.

Kody's gaze trailed her entire body. "Damn. Look at you."

Her hair probably covered his white sheets. When she leaned up, nibbling his neck, his throat vibrated under her lips as his deep voice asked, "What do you want?"

Her breath quickened fast in anticipation. "I want you."

Kody locked eyes on her. "Are you sure?"

On her back, Raelyn gulped. "Yes."

This is it.

Her heart pounded.

From his drawer, Kody pulled out a condom and rolled it on. She blew out a long, deep sigh at the reality of the situation unfolding in front of her. Tilting her head at the sight of his muscular body, she licked her lips, which seemed to send him in another frenzy. His brown eyes turned savage.

He took a shuddered breath and moved closer. "You're killin' me."

Her hands rose and lingered on his hard chest, outlining the divots of his abs. She let her fingers wrap around his sizcable length.

Kody's rugged eyes never left hers. "Holy hell," he rasped when her hand stroked him slowly. Their deep, passionate kiss let their tongues move in rhythm with one another. Craving him, she guided Kody's hand between her legs, and he circled gently, his thumb massaging the perfect spot.

When Kody increased his finger's pressure and speed, Raelyn began panting. The deep, guttural sounds he made while he watched surged an electric pulse through her veins.

"Oh my god," Raelyn whimpered, and her head dropped back as she stared at the ceiling. Her heart thundered in her chest. "I can't wait any longer."

"Now?" He cradled the back of her head with one hand.

She bit her lip and nodded.

"Look at me."

Raelyn locked onto his piercing brown eyes.

In one fluid motion, Kody smoothly slid inside. A long moan purred from her throat as she felt his hardness fill her. Heat soared through her body, and her shoulders gently shook. He touched places within her she didn't know existed. Starting shallow, he stroked gently, and the sensation of bliss poured over her like a fountain. His movements were like a slow wave until she finally embraced all of Kody.

He held steady, allowing her to adjust to the feeling. "You okay?"

Unable to speak through the pleasure and overstimulation, she only nodded. The depths of his eyes bore into her soul, combining them into one. His skilled hands claimed every inch of her, sending her into a flood of disbelief that anything could feel so whole and real.

The bed springs grinded under them as the candle burned lower and lower. Their bodies continued to waltz across the sheets as the shadows of the flickering light danced on the wall.

Kody pumped slightly harder while he held her hips down and studied her face. Raelyn's eyes kept rolling to the back of her head, but when she could keep them open, his deep gaze was still fixated on her. His body was gorgeous, putting her in an overwhelming trance as he continued to work his magic sliding in and out.

He grunted, and his voice turned husky. "I can't hold off much longer."

Raelyn naturally grabbed the bed post with her hands behind her head and squeezed herself around his thickness, feeling every inch. Her heartbeat raced as she watched all his muscles bulge. Kody's neck, shoulders, chest, and arms filled with veins ready to pop. His thrusts were intoxicating, making her pant hard.

She clenched tighter. Kody cried out as every muscle in his body flexed and convulsed above her. He collapsed, their chests heaving together.

Raelyn couldn't stop smiling as he brushed his fingertips over her oversensitive skin, making her shiver. His lips found her breast as he rolled next to her, sending a quiver from head to toe.

Raelyn turned on her side, stared into his perfect brown eyes, and kissed the tip of his nose. "You're mine," Kody whispered as his fingers worked their way between her legs—again.

I can't ever lose him.

28

KODY

Kody stepped out of the limo, buttoning the coat of his navy tux, and patted his pocket watch through the layer of expensive fabric. He strutted across Marble Street with scarlet roses in one hand, trying to shake the image of the last ten perfect nights with Raelyn. He was completely addicted to her, in every possibly way. Kody started tapping his other hand on his hip but stopped himself as he stepped onto their porch.

Not a time for nerves.

When he knocked, no dog barked. William answered the door.

"Good evening, sir." He held out his hand to shake. "Can we talk out here for a minute?"

"Well, okay. Raelyn's almost ready, though. She wants me to take pictures of y'all on the lawn." William kept the door open behind him, fanning his face in May's humid air.

He seems much more relaxed.

Kody swallowed, straightened his tie, and got right to the point. "I'm sorry Raelyn missed her curfew the other night. You can blame me."

William's forehead crunched. "I do."

A picture of the quaint farmhouse with lacy curtains blowing through an open window hung on the wall.

Kody pointed. "Sir, can I see your compass?"

William unlatched it and handed it over. "If you break that, we'll have a problem. Joanna gave it to me as a wedding present over eighteen years ago."

I need to ask him now.

There wasn't even an opportunity to talk to Walter about relationships when he was younger. On the night he caught Walter cheating, Kody knew he'd never take advice from that man again. Without knowing William well, Kody still needed to go out on a limb and get some guidance from a man in his life with experience.

"Sir, how long did you know Joanna before you proposed?"

William crossed his arms. "You can't be serious?"

Kody held his gaze and planted both feet firmly in a wide stance.

William scratched his beard. "I never proposed. We eloped. I was twenty-one and knew her for about six months."

Kody nodded slowly. "And you knew that you could vow an eternity to her?"

William waited a beat. "Yes." Then, his eyebrows scrunched together. "What are you getting at?"

His heart raced, but he focused on his steady breath. "I want you to know how serious I am about your daughter."

William shifted his weight. "Are you asking me permission to marry her?"

"No, sir. I respect you, but one day, that'll be her choice."

Yohaan's cop car passed by their house, and he waved out the open window. Neither of the men on the porch moved a muscle. Kody heard Yohaan's chuckle before he rolled the window back up.

The wind tousled William's thick hair. "Raelyn still needs to figure out what she wants in this world."

Kody lowered his chin. "I'll be alongside her each step of the way."

"Can you manage your career and this relationship?"

"If I can't give her what she needs, I'll find another job."

William's eyes widened. "You'd quit the army for her?"

"I'd do anything for her, sir." Kody straightened his stance and tugged on his tux jacket. "And at this point, I need to come clean with what Raelyn and I have been doing together."

"Excuse me?"

He sighed. "Listen, a colleague and I are investigating what happened to Joanna."

"Don't start this again."

"Let me explain."

William kicked the dirt halfheartedly. "I already agreed to fly over there with her, to search for Joanna. But, it's a bad idea."

"I agree with you, sir. Tomorrow, I think we should go to the police with all the information we have so far. I don't think we found Joanna, but there are other women in danger."

"It can't be Joanna." William nodded.

Raelyn once told a story of how William threw his wedding ring into the prairie in Ash Mountain. How could someone give up on love like that? Kody would always fight to stay with Raelyn. If anything happened to her, he'd search to the end of the earth until his dying day to find out the truth instead of giving up like William.

William put up a hand. "Hold on. Here comes Raelyn."

"Pa?" Raelyn's angelic voice came from inside.

Raelyn glided like a swan around the corner, and Kody's jaw dropped at the sight of her silky, gold dress fit snugly around her curves.

She blushed slightly as she moved to his side, then interlaced her fingers through his. A beautiful ear-to-ear smile stretched across Raelyn's face. "Hey, you two." Raelyn glanced between them. "Is … everything okay?"

"Yes." Kody used all his effort to not scan her body again in front of William.

"You look beautiful, hun." William hugged her, but she didn't let go of Kody's hand as she leaned in.

Raelyn's cheeks turned pink. "Oh, wait! My shoes!" She pointed to the floor. "I can't reach."

"I got it, babe." Kody kneeled. "Hold on to me." He slipped them on one at a time, then rose and dared to meet William's eyes that lasered into him. The man cocked his head to the side.

William shook his hand again—harder this time, with intent. "Take care of her. Keep her safe."

Kody nodded. "Always."

"I'm serious."

"I know."

Raelyn waved between their intense eye contact. "Uh, hello. I'm right here."

William shook his hand tightly. "I'm looking forward to getting to you know you better, son." William looked at his daughter, and his voice cracked. "Well, this is it. The moment I've dreaded."

She smiled. "Pa, it's not *that* bad."

William sighed and held both of her hands in his. "Prom is a perfect mother-daughter moment. Joanna should be here."

"Father-daughter moments are pretty great too." She kissed his cheek.

Under the sunset, Raelyn leaned against an oak tree, stunningly beautiful with half her long hair curled down and the other half partially up in a high bun. They posed for pictures with the green oaks setting the backdrop. A soft, golden glow gleamed on her skin.

William handed Kody the camera and stood proudly by his daughter. After Kody lowered the lens, he curiously watched William's loving gaze follow Raelyn's movement toward the limo. William held her hand a moment longer until he finally let go.

What is that like? To love a daughter that much?

She turned back and kissed William's cheek. "Bye, Pa."

Her heels added three inches to her height, bringing her closer to his lips, which he'd have to wait to kiss until they were outside of William's view.

Inside the limo, it smelled like leather. Kody looked down at his phone, checking the current footage from his newly installed security system, and rechecked the alarm through the app.

Kody said, "Didn't I tell you that I'd take you to your next dance?"

"I didn't believe you for a second."

"Your dress is perfect." Kody scanned her curves under the golden V-neck. He brushed back a strand of hair that had dropped from her pin.

Raelyn's scarlet lips brushed against his neck. "I should've had Cali do my hair. Where is she going to meet us?"

"You get me excited and then talk about my sister." He smiled between kisses. "What am I going to do with you?"

"We have forever to learn."

He could feel his forehead tighten. "I'll give you forever and a day."

She kissed his neck again, sending shivers down his spine. Between breaths, her body melted into his. His arms folded around her, drawing her closer, as he angled Raelyn's head back and kissed her forehead. Kody's finger skimmed her collarbone, brushing against Joanna's necklace.

Kody laughed. "We're doing prom backward."

She snuggled into his chest. "Then get my mind on something else. If that's possible."

He laughed. "How can you want more? I mean, after every night just this week, you've kind of broken my body."

She shrugged and tickled his thigh. "I'm addicted to you."

Kody smiled. "Okay, okay. This will distract you." He gently moved her hand away. "I have an update on those two women at the Embassy. The ones Dabbott and I saved from the cellar."

Her eyes widened. "And?"

"They aren't holding back info anymore. Dabbott's team confirmed that they referred to the third woman as Jawhara."

Raelyn's eyes widened as she stood, making her head hit the limo's ceiling. "The photographer said that was the name of the lady in the picture. And whoever sent me those messages kept using that word. Ma must've changed her name to Jawhara."

"Babe, I don't think Joanna is Jawhara. She and Snyder have been married a long time."

Raelyn rubbed her thumb along the jewel. "Wait, then why did one of those messages say that he will sell Jawhara soon? Would someone really sell Ma?"

"Well, whether it's her or no, we asked the incorrect question earlier. She didn't want to return to the mansion for something. Jawhara wanted to return *for someone*—a boy."

29

RAELYN

THE SUNSET CHANGED FROM flamingo to sangria to plum as Raelyn walked through the hotel's grand entrance. Kody pushed the glass door open with one arm as the other hugged her waist. Inside, the chandeliers provided a Hollywood effect, making her shimmering gold dress sparkle when she looked down. A grand marble staircase that would've put a princess castle to shame led down to a large lobby.

Cali rushed over with an entire entourage trailing behind. She looked them up and down. "Seriously? Beauty and the Beast? You're wearing gold and navy." Cali beamed, dragging her train. She wore a black mermaid gown with the shoulder straps draping over onto her arms. "Come to the bathroom. I need to fix my lipstick."

Raelyn glanced back at Kody, who moved toward the wall with a slight grin. Following, she pulled a hair off the back of Cali's dress. Probably Breanna's.

In one giant breath, Cali said, "The DJ is great. The decorations are subpar, but who cares? Breanna looks yummy. I wish she could have a guy roommate freshman year. But everything's all perfect and whatnot." Cali shifted. "You, my peanut butter cookie, belong on the cover of a magazine."

"Thanks. You too." Raelyn curtsied in front of the mirror.

They stared at each other in silence for a beat, then sighed at the same time. Giggling, Raelyn held out her pinky, Cali shook it and placed her forehead against Raelyn's. "Nothing will change next year. We'll still be besties."

Cali was her rock. While thinking of everything they had been through together during senior year, a single tear streaked down Raelyn's cheek, wetting her makeup.

"None of that. Not tonight. Our hot dates are waiting! Well, mine is hot. Yours smells." Cali laughed then yo-yo-ed across the bathroom in front of the mirrors.

They went back out and parted through the sea of teachers to the dance floor. Kody seemed to be scanning the room for threats, as if prom was full of trained assassins in each corner, before joining them, standing like a statue amid the sweaty teens. Raelyn looked up and kissed his thick lips.

Finally, a slow song.

Rhianna's "Stay" played, prompting Kody to cradle her hand in his for a dance. His steady hand wrapped around her back as he guided them. Kody was light on his feet, swaying her around with more ease than she assumed possible.

"Jeez! When did you learn how to dance?"

"Boxing."

She scrunched her nose. "Well, I memorized all your moves, so I know your plans ahead of time."

Kody laughed.

Someone interrupted, guiding Mason over to them. He cleared his throat. "Hey, can I dance with her once?"

Kody looked from him to Raelyn. "That's not my call to make."

She nodded.

Kody marched to the double door entrance and positioned himself as if on duty. Smiling to herself, she jumped at the touch of Mason's hands on her waist. His energy didn't compare to Kody's; the fire wasn't lit.

The last time he was this close was at the frat party.

"Sorry if I bump into someone." Mason smiled.

"It's fine. That's my style every day."

"Are you two official?" Mason asked, holding her closer.

Her body stiffened, but she took a deep breath. "Yes." Raelyn could feel his breath on her neck.

Mason softly raised his hand by her throat, asking, "May I touch your dress?"

Her breath stitched. "Okay."

Mason gently ran his fingertips along her collarbone, to the shoulder strap, and down the V-neck hem line lower. She tilted her head and watched his facial expressions, wondering what life would be like without vision. Mason deserved so much better than how she treated him.

"I'm sorry if I hurt your feelings before, Mason."

"It's fine. I mean, it's not, but—" He froze. "Your necklace."

"What?"

He pulled his hand back. "Sorry, I think I made your necklace come apart." He held the large ruby stone in his hand separate from the gold chain.

"Oh." She sensed Kody's silent presence behind her.

Mason placed the necklace in her palm, then turned it over and kissed her hand. "You'll be at my graduation party this summer?"

"Definitely." She stared at her hand as he walked away.

Kody's arm wrapped around her waist behind her. "You okay?"

"I thought he was going to kiss me."

"Me too. That wouldn't have been my best moment." Kody walked her to the side of the banquet room.

"Jealous?"

"Let's call it … something else."

We can make it. I'll always have Kody.

Raelyn inspected Ma's necklace in a jangled mess in her palm, attempting to thread the chain back through. She squinted as her fingers fidgeted with the clasp. "Did I break it? I can't get a hold on it. This corner seems loose."

"Let me see." Kody held it up to the light. "Wait, the necklace seems to be a locket. There's a tiny hook here." He stopped himself and gaped at it. "I'm so stupid!"

"What?" Raelyn stared at him.

Kody's eyes lit up. "Break the stone! How did I not notice this before?"

"What does 'break the stone' mean?" Raelyn desperately tried to open the clasp of Ma's necklace, flipping it with her thumb. Her hands started to shake.

Kody leaned over her shoulder. "That command was in a message I got."

Raelyn bolted to a hallway. The walls were hung with the same uninspired artwork that lined the hotel's lobby, and the thumping of the bass from prom vibrated the floors.

"You're blocking my light." Raelyn eased him away. "It's stuck." She shook the necklace next to her ear, and something small rattled inside.

"We need to break it!" Kody swiped it from her grasp.

"No way! It's all I have left of Ma!" Raelyn grabbed his wrist.

His voice was unrecognizably wild when he said, "What Snyder wants must be inside there."

She bit her lip. "What do you mean?"

Kody stared at her. "He kept asking for a file."

Raelyn held out her hand for the necklace.

Cali jogged over barefoot, her stilettos in one hand and a few beads from her braids in the other. "What's up?"

Raelyn gulped. "Apparently, I gotta break the stone."

"Great!" Cali looked around. "Wait, what stone? Let's find a sledgehammer!"

"No, this one."

"Your Ma's? No way! That's your everything."

Raelyn sighed. "No. You two are my everything."

Cali tilted her head to the side, and Kody held back a smile. Raelyn took a deep breath, kissed the gem, and then held it to her heart tight. She smashed the stone against the wall, showering ruby pieces like raining blood. The impact only made the corner shatter. She rammed it again and again until more and more red rained like cascaded glitter.

Finally, a tiny thumb drive fell to the floor. She swiped it, inspecting each angle, and picked up the largest salvageable chunks of Ma's necklace and chain. "Something was in there!"

"The file!" Kody's eyes grew. "We need to see what's on there. But the computers here in the hotel aren't safe to use."

"Library?" asked Raelyn.

"All closed." Kody paced.

"Phoenix could help."

Kody gave her a sideways look. "Who?'

"Peterson!" Raelyn gestured wildly. "Call him!"

Cali pulled Raelyn aside. "Are you okay? What are you thinking?"

"I'm so confused. Snyder needs a file inside Ma's necklace? Why? And Ma might have been one of the women Kody saved from that cellar, which means she was a prisoner? Why would Snyder want a prisoner's necklace?" Raelyn stared at the broken stone in her hand. "I feel like I'm missing some big piece of information."

"I don't know, Rae." Cali winced. "It's a lot." Raelyn caught Cali and Kody exchanging skeptical glances.

Kody pulled off his tux jacket and laid it over his shoulder, untucked his shirt, and rolled up his sleeves. "Peterson will be here in less than ten minutes. His computer is secure. I'll get a room for privacy." He walked toward the front counter and took out his wallet.

Raelyn held out her pinky to her friend. "I don't want to ruin your prom, Cali. You're the Prom Queen. Do you want to go back in?"

Cali latched Raelyn's pinky. "I'm not leaving you."

They bunched their long dresses in their hands. As they approached Kody, a team of cops stormed through the front doors.

Kody grabbed the key cards from the counter and rushed the girls into the elevator. "Come on."

"Was that Yohaan?" Raelyn looked at him. "Why would he be here?"

"We don't have time to find out," Kody said as the elevator doors shut out the sounds of prom.

They sped down the silent hotel hall, as if in another world from the pumping bass below. Inside the hotel room, Raelyn bit the side of her manicured nail and stared at the alarm clock as it flicked to the next minute. Kody peered out the window, unmoving, and Cali paced, making popping noises with her lips.

Pop. Pop. Pop.

Then came *Clunk. Clunk. Clunk.*

Raelyn jumped at the knock on the door. Kody put his finger to his lips and motioned for her and Cali to stay in the back corner behind the bed. He peeked through the hole, and his shoulders noticeably dropped.

Kody opened the door. "Hey, Peterson."

Phoenix's smile sent a shiver down Raelyn's spine. She couldn't deny his attractiveness as his gaze pierced through her, showing a mix between claiming ownership over her and a protective friend.

What is he all about?

Phoenix limped in. "Sugarplum, if you chose me, I'd at least get you a king size bed." He grinned at Kody. "Really, Walsh? From the skills Raelyn showed me, she deserves better than this."

"Shut up!" Kody growled.

Phoenix eyed Raelyn. "Are you okay?"

"She's fine." Kody's fists curled.

"I wasn't asking you."

Raelyn jumped forward and laid her hand on Phoenix's chest. "Phoenix, are you here to help us or not?"

He looked down to her hand lingering, which she swiftly pulled away. "Yeah, I'll help *you*. Anytime." When Phoenix set up his laptop on the desk, a postcard slid out from the keyboard.

"What's this?" She picked it up and glanced at an image of the Egyptian pyramids.

Phoenix held out his hand. "A place I want to visit someday. Maybe you can come with."

"Let's get to work." Raelyn snatched the memory stick, and for a moment, only the hum of a laptop was heard.

This could give me all the answers.

Her heart slammed against her ribcage as she inched closer to the computer. Feeling her mouth dry, she remembered to breathe before inserting the drive with a click.

"It's going to take a minute," Kody said as he threw his navy tux coat on the bed and unbuttoned his shirt.

Raelyn straightened out his white shirt and brushed her hands over his shoulders.

He kneeled in front of her. "Don't move. He sliced his knife through Raelyn's gold prom dress above her knees.

"What are you doing?" She gasped and placed her hand on his back for support.

He glanced at Phoenix, who followed and kneeled in front of Cali's black dress, cutting it shorter too.

"Easy there, soldier!" Her eyes opened wide. "Kody, is this necessary? Mom paid two hundred dollars for this dress." Cali looked down and put her hands on her hips. "Careful!"

Kody frowned. "Just in case you have to run."

"Run? From who?"

"Just a gut feeling."

Phoenix limped over, handing Kody a bulletproof vest. "Time to party?"

Kody took it. "Hey, man. Did you bring any boots for me?"

"No. You didn't give me much time." Phoenix lifted the second vest. "I only have one more. Who wears this one?"

Kody froze. His face hardened as his eyes darted between Cali and Raelyn. Phoenix handed it to Raelyn.

Raelyn pushed it away. "We don't need these. We're just in a hotel room, on a computer."

Immediately, Kody handed his over. "Here, Cali, wear mine."

Raelyn looked up. "Who would shoot at us?"

"We don't know what's on that file. There are tons of cops downstairs." Kody pulled her in tight and kissed her forehead. He whispered in her ear, "I love you," then tightened her vest with a confident tug.

"You're being dramatic." Raelyn scrunched her nose.

"Nothing bad is gonna happen." She rose on her tiptoes and softly brushed her lips to his. His cologne was different than his usual scent.

Kody moved back to the laptop and started reading. "A bunch of these files are in Arabic. We'll have to figure that part out later. But here's a list that may help."

Raelyn squinted as they all leaned in behind her.

"It looks like that list of names I saw at the warehouse," Kody said as he scrolled down. "I assumed the arrows meant subordinate and officer. But I don't think that's right."

Cali rattled off ideas. "Code names? Addresses?"

"I don't think so. These are dates—wait no, forms of currency." Kody leaned out of the way so she could see.

Phoenix spoke up. "This one has women's pictures."

Raelyn's heart raced wildly. "What if it's what Ma found when she was working as a journalist?" She spoke slowly. "Sand Tunnels Disguise Secrets."

"The most recent file is a video from April last year," said Phoenix.

"Play it." Raelyn reached forward to click start.

Kody grabbed the laptop and lifted it over his head. "Are you sure you want to see this? This could be anything. I don't want you to see someone being abused or—"

"Play it!" she and Cali yelled at the same time.

Without another word, Kody put the computer down and started the video. A woman appeared on the screen. The same woman from Emme O'Reilly's portrait. The same woman in the Disney photograph. The same woman who tended to Raelyn's skinned knees.

It's Ma.

A fresh scratch across Ma's cheek oozed blood, and a bruise covered her forehead. Raelyn pushed Kody out of the way. The air in the room stood still as the woman spoke frantically with a determined expression.

"This is one of two critical drives. Today is April seventh, at fourteen hundred hours. We are an underground group that works together against Storm Force. They capture, enslave, and sell women."

The woman in the video ducked, and there were screeching voices in the background for a moment, then silence. Her head popped back into view.

"Today, two more girls were abducted. One was sold off, and the other goes to auction tomorrow. These files hold some of the evidence needed to take Zohaib down.

"I've been safe until recently. But something has changed. Snyder is threatening to sell me. He's brainwashing my son and putting weapons in his hands. I need to find us a way out to a safehouse. There are two facilities that may have information of our location. The first may be at 35.1415N and 79.0080W. If anyone finds this …

The woman paused.

Raelyn held her breath, and Kody rested his hand on her shoulder. Tears blurred her vision.

The woman continued. "My name is Joanna Bell. Please get this to my husband, William Bell. And tell Raelyn I love her."

Static cut out the video.

The room spun as Raelyn's legs gave out. Kody steadied her.

Raelyn buried her face into Kody's chest, focusing on his warmth. "Ma's alive," she mumbled.

"That was recorded almost a year ago." Kody spoke cautiously. "A lot could've happened since then."

Raelyn wiped away her tears. "Dabbott saw her in that cellar this past January."

Kody took a deep breath, about to speak, but Raelyn played the video a second then a third time as the others watched her silently.

"If Ma had a son, then that could be the boy the photographer mentioned. A son would be another reason to keep her in the desert," she rambled. "The lady in the cellar wanted to return for her son. Ma wouldn't leave without him. She wouldn't put him in jeopardy. Ma wouldn't put me in danger either."

Kody cleared his throat. "Raelyn? Does the name Liam mean anything to you?"

Raelyn clasped her hand to her mouth and nodded. "Where did you hear that name?"

"I thought it was Snyder's son. But when he attacked me, Snyder said Liam wasn't his biological son."

Raelyn stumbled to the side. "Oh my god! I have a brother. Liam is Pa's son." With new determination, she slipped out of her heels. "Those numbers on the video are coordinates right? Where do they lead?"

Kody paused and glanced at Phoenix. "The warehouse."

"What?" Raelyn turned fast. "You mean the place where we met?"

Kody nodded.

"I'm going! Now!" She swiped the gun Phoenix brought, which was laying on the table, and ran out the door, sprinting down the hotel hallway.

The heavy, bulletproof vest weighed her down and strained her breathing. She raced by a loud buzzing of a vacuum that smelled of burning trash stuck inside the tubes. Her bare feet left imprints in the carpet. She slipped past the cleaning lady and out the stairwell. With each quick step down, the increased, bass-driven music from prom thrummed the walls. She glanced up the stairwell.

Why isn't Kody chasing me?

When Raelyn reached the bottom, a giant red warning confronted her:

EMERGENCY EXIT
Alarm will sound!

She tucked her chin to her chest, closed her eyes, and pushed forward.

No alarm.

Raelyn rushed outside into the darkness at the back of the hotel. Crickets chirped. Flashing blue lights of a cop car reflected off a window and approached her. Raelyn crossed her arms over the vest to cover the gun. Cali's head popped out from the driver's seat of a stolen squad car, her eyes wide with excitement. "Get in! Let's go!"

Raelyn's mouth dropped. She ran to the other side of the car, hopped in, then stared at her best friend. "How did you beat me?"

"I'm a frickin magical unicorn!" Cali flipped a switch and turned off the flashing lights. "We can do this!"

Raelyn's heart raced.

There's no turning back now.

Both girls slumped as low as they could as Cali pulled away from the hotel and onto the street and accelerated through each yellow light.

"How did you steal a cop car?"

"Quiet!" Cali glanced in the rear-view mirror, then pushed harder on the gas, merging onto a highway. "Hurry! Get the directions to the warehouse."

Raelyn glanced in the side mirror to the sight of an empty street. "How did you—?"

"Shh! Tell me which way to go!"

Raelyn's GPS lit up, and her fingers shook. "Get off in seven exits."

Cali turned on the siren and floored it.

Raelyn grasped the handle above. "Where's Kody?"

Cali didn't answer but jutted her chin forward and swerved around other cars.

We're gonna die!

Raelyn held her breath as the squad car zoomed off the exit and screeched on a right turn to a smaller road. "I've been here before. It's a few blocks that way." She pointed.

Night surrounded them like a heavy curtain. A tall warehouse dominated the sky in the distance. It looked completely different in the shadows compared to that morning when she met Kody. Cali turned off the siren again but didn't slow down. The car bumped and jostled them as she flew up onto a small field covered in graves and long weeds. The tires stuck and spun in the muck, unable to move further. Bats circled near the one flickering lamp post.

"Are you kidding me? There's effing bats!" Cali's eyes widened. "It looks like a dungeon from medieval times. We're going in *there*?"

"No, just me." Raelyn jumped out and wrapped Ma's bare golden chain around her fingers like a figure eight. "Stay here."

"I hate everything about this." Cali reached to her ankle and unstrapped her stilettos. "Want my shoes?"

"No, I'm faster without heels."

Cali nodded to the gun. "Please don't use that."

Raelyn gripped it and put it behind her back. "I won't need it. Everything will be okay. No one is here. I just need to find Ma's location. It's in that warehouse somewhere."

I'll be okay.

Raelyn turned her gaze to the sky, where the dark, stone warehouse crept toward the clouds. She hustled up the steep hill, panting. With every passing second, her heart pounded.

She'd been there before but didn't remember much about the layout of the warehouse. The black gate at the bottom creaked open with the slightest push. While climbing, she glanced at a crow that had landed on the far corner that had crumbled into rubble. She tiptoed carefully over pebbles and stubbly grass that pricked her bare feet. At the top of the hill, a parked truck came into view.

Pa's truck?

She jogged closer. The driver's door was angled slightly open. Squinting under the silver crescent moon, Raelyn looked inside.

"Pa? Are you in there?"

The truck was empty. The journal she'd gifted him lay open on the front seat. She flipped through the pages with her thumb, full of Pa's chicken scratch.

What is all this?

She went back to the beginning. A poem she had written before and forgot to rip out of her journal claimed the first page in spotty red ink.

Wandering through tunnels with withering walls
Chilled bones exposed like skeleton breath
Extinguished flame reveals the ghost of these halls
Questioning how to defeat one's death

Between the next pages, a familiar red envelope was tucked inside. She recalled seeing it on the floor of the study in Ash Mountain. A piece of crunkled up paper stuck out. Raelyn pulled it out. Two torn pieces were taped together, showing.

Give me J's file, or I take your girl tomorrow.

Her lips went pale, and her eyes rounded before reading the rest below.

A threat? Is this why we left Ash Mountain? Pa was protecting me.

Her heart slammed against her chest as she skimmed Pa's notes, showing his plans dating back to the day they left Ash Mountain. She flipped page after page of Pa's thoughts and investigation, all marked with different colored pens that arrowed to other charts and lists. A tingling crawled up her spine.

Why is Pa here tonight, though?

Pa's phone laid on the floor of the truck. She bent down and read a text to him.

Thought you could hide? Meet me at 35.1415N and 79.0080W at midnight or Liam dies.

Liam? Wait! No!

Pa was in danger, and now her little brother needed her help. And they were both there, right in front of her. She had to forget about Ma. Raelyn slammed shut the journal and quickly sludged through fresh footprints etched in mud. Approaching the opened steel door, she hesitated.

Who could be in there?

She slowly pushed a door of the warehouse open with her shoulder. A trail of mud markings crossed through the gym room that smelled of cleaning chemicals, reminding her of the locker room at school. Her gaze flickered to the place she first saw Kody. Beads of sweat dripped from her temple and splattered onto her bare feet.

A second door was across the room. Last time she was here, Kody's eyes distracted her and she hadn't noticed that door.

I should go back to Cali and call for help.

Raelyn shook her head and rushed forward. She turned the metal knob slowly. When it squeaked on old hinges, she opened it as far as she dared and slipped through the narrow opening, into a hallway painted with graffiti. It immediately smelled of mold. Her gun knocked against the wooden frame and snapped the door shut. With trembling hands, Raelyn turned and tried to turn the knob.

Locked.

She was trapped on the other side. The only option was to move forward. Raelyn whipped out her phone and brought up the saved pictures of Ma's old map. Only 8% battery.

Damn it.

The map routes showed an entrance to an underground tunnel system with an entrance down the hallway. She wanted to sprint down the dimly lit corridor but could barely see the floor. Little pebbles poked into her toes.

"Hello?" Her soft voice echoed against the walls. A tall silhouette made her jump. Her breathing accelerated. She squinted. It was only a dummy, possibly one used for sparring. Moonlight shone through a window, lighting a circular door on the floor, like a cellar entrance. A metal latch with chipped paint stuck out.

She checked her phone. The symbol on the latch matched the one on the map, a rose. Raelyn twisted the lever. A loud *clunk* rang out when she lifted the hatch, and flying dust caused her to sneeze. Eerie silence surrounded her.

Where's Pa?

Raelyn crouched, and the smell of mildew assaulted her nostrils. Cold air creeped up. Her old phone didn't have a bright flashlight, but it was better than nothing. A spiral metal staircase that descended into dark depths made her skin crawl.

No! Not underground!

7% battery.

Raelyn couldn't see the bottom. Her heart raced, and she became lightheaded.

I can do this.

She tightened her grip on Ma's gold chain for support. Climbing down, her foot almost slipped on the mud-covered rung, but she caught herself. The ladder felt icy to her touch. With each step, the temperature dropped. Once she finally hit the floor, water trickled over her bare toes. The stale air sent shivers down her spine.

"Hello? Liam?"

Her own shaky voice echoed back.

Two tunnels split off, left and right.

6% battery.

Worn graffiti painted the walls, and the same symbol as on the latch was above the tunnel on the left. She followed the rose to the end of the long hall. Eerie silence held the air around her.

5% battery.

Keep moving. Keep moving.

The pathways in front and behind her were both completely dark. Something slimy slithered on top of her foot. She jumped. A hissing sound grew louder. Raelyn hopped from foot to foot on the grimy, cold, muddy floor. The noise crept closer, and she pointed the gun at the ground, dropping the remains of Ma's necklace. The hissing stopped. She didn't dare crawl to find the necklace, but left it behind, for good.

Water drops plunked down, and she jogged in the direction of the noise. Her feet splashed through inches of frigid water. It grew deeper as she ran, up to her ankles. A soft light appeared in the distance. As she raced forward, it grew brighter. Raelyn shifted the heavy gun in her hands.

The light gleamed stronger. She hurried, laboring to breathe, a cramp pinching her side. Raelyn rubbed her hands together and blew her breath on her fingertips. Slowly, she walked up five stone steps to a room.

Dim light flickered from candles bouncing shadows over a giant library room. A spiderweb-filled chandelier hung from the ceiling. Thousands of dusty books filled shelves, and a ladder on wheels seemed to lead up to a loft platform above with old wooden beams.

She raised the gun higher and stepped out of the tunnel. A loud clank sounded behind her as a metal door slammed from the floor to the ceiling, not allowing her to leave.

It's a trap!

A voice that sounded like a hiss of a serpent reverberated from somewhere. "Oh, be my guest."

She whipped around and stared at the man who had tried to choke Kody weeks ago—Snyder.

Her heart thumped hard.

"Raelyn! Don't move!" Pa rushed toward her out of the shadows, butSnyder's scarred hand shoved Pa to the side. Pa lost his footing and dropped through a covered trap, landing with a loud crack. He screamed out.

"Pa!" Raelyn dropped to her knees and peered over the side of the hole.

Laying on his pinned arm, he yelled, "Aah!" His breath was visible in the cold air. A bulge stuck out through Pa's shirt, but he propped himself up with his other arm slowly.

"I'll help you out!"

Pa shrieked. "No! He's armed! Watch out!"

Raelyn bolted to her feet. She glanced at the floor, then up at Snyder, who held her gun casually. He paced the outer rim of the hole.

"Let my kids leave!" yelled Pa from below.

Kids? Plural?

Snyder stared at Raelyn but pointed the gun straight at Pa. "If you say a word, I shoot him. Understand?"

Raelyn stepped forward and balled her hands into fists. "Why did you threaten us?"

He racked a round and pulled the trigger, making a hole a foot above Pa's head.

Pa ducked.

Raelyn screamed.

Snyder hissed. "I said silence!" He rushed forward, inches from her face. "Jawhara tried to leave me for you two? Pathetic."

Raelyn's heart pounded. Snyder backed her into a wall and unbuckled her bulletproof vest. She kneed him in the crotch, hard, but solid plastic hit her bone.

He winked. "Nice try," he said, lifted the vest off her, and threw it to the ground in a loud thump. His stance widened, and his face slid into an insincere smile. Snyder's strong thighs wedged her legs between his, trapping her between his solid frame and the wall. She tried to twist and turn. Her heart sped as he looked down on her, crowding her breath. He pushed his hips closer, then took both her wrists and held them against the wall by her side.

Raelyn turned her head to the side and gasped. "Stop!"

"I could do anything I wanted to you right now." He skimmed his cold hand up her thigh.

She squirmed, and her voice cracked. "Stop!"

"Raelyn!" Pa's voice shook the room.

Snyder put one finger to his lips to shush her and kneeled in front of her. He grabbed the bottom of her dress, jerked her body in a quick motion, and ripped fabric off with his teeth. Her chest rose and fell fast. Using the silk, he tied her wrists together tight behind her back. He twirled a loose strand of her hair between his fingers. He was more disgusting than a wad of long hair that had been pulled out of a drain.

"Raelyn!" Pa hollered.

She didn't dare speak.

Snyder whispered, "Ah, I need a bit more." He reached down, slid his finger under her dress, and ripped off another piece of gold fabric.

A lump formed in her throat. His eyes were wild as he leaned in and gagged her with the silk. She kicked his shins and grunted.

He pushed her behind a bookshelf. "No talking. Stay here. Do you understand this time?" His sour breath blew in her face.

She nodded. A tear fell from her eye.

"Raelyn?" Pa bellowed from the hole. "What'd you do to her?"

"I sent her away. She's weak and useless."

Silence.

With her wrists tied behind her back, Raelyn felt around for any door or passageway out.

"Where's Liam?" Pa yelled.

Raelyn froze.

Snyder strutted behind a bookshelf. "Oh, that's right. You haven't met your son."

Muffled sounds of a young voice hit her ears. Snyder seized the collar of a boy taller than her and tugged him forward, his mouth covered in fabric too. Snyder snipped the plastic cuffs binding his wrists, and Liam tore the cloth from his mouth, panting.

Raelyn leaned against the bookshelf, sending dust flying. She took in his features. His hair was the color of the sun, and his eyes were sharp with rage, framed with a pair of glasses.

Raelyn met her brother's big blue eyes for only a moment before Liam stomped on Snyder's boot and scrambled, struggling to get out of his grasp.

Pa screamed, "Let me out of this hole!"

Snyder had a firm grip on Liam's collar. "Sure, sure." He sneered. "It's kind of a strange family father-son moment with you down there. Those words do sound wrong, though. A few months ago, you were *my* boy, weren't you?"

Liam pushed a pair of glasses higher on his nose, the same nose Pa had. Snyder shoved Liam back into the shadows.

Pa lowered his voice. "We can figure something out."

Snyder shot another bullet straight at the ceiling. It pinged into a metal pipe above, sending water droplets down. He bellowed. "What the hell are you gonna do? You're ten feet down."

"Let me up. Let's talk about this. We can get what you need together."

"Actually, yeah, let's bring you up. It may be more fun to see your face when I tell you the news." Snyder rummaged through a backpack by a pile of books, pulled out a rope with a loop knotted at the bottom and lowered it to Pa. "So, anyway, why do you care so much about Liam? He could be an awful kid. I mean, he's done some pretty bad stuff. He lies, steals—oh, and his mom hates when he leaves wet towels on the floor."

Raelyn backed into the shelf, sending a book tumbling to the floor.

His mom?

"Don't talk about Mom!" Liam's voice was wheezy as he smacked his body into Snyder's side, making little impact.

"Like father, like son. You both have your priorities in the wrong place."

"You never cared about Mom!" Liam still sounded out of breath.

Snyder turned on his heels fast and slapped Liam across the face. "Don't speak about what you don't know." Snyder threw him to the ground with a thud.

I have to help. How?

"Let me out!" Pa hollered.

Snyder spat. "It's because of me that Jawhara is alive. I saved her life."

Liam's voice cracked, and he gasped as if he couldn't get enough air. "You kept Mom for yourself! You could've sent her home. I could've been with my real family!"

"Oh, right. Your family." Snyder hoisted Pa up one pull at a time.

Pa's wavy hair breached the top of the hole, and Liam rushed forward and grabbed Pa under his good arm. His limp arm hung at an odd angle at his right side. Liam steadied him as groans escaped his lips.

Raelyn didn't dare say a word from the shadows, listening to it all unfold. She tried rubbing her shoulder against the cloth in her mouth to loosen it but it didn't budge. Behind her back, Raelyn kept twisting her wrists in hopes that the binding would snap, but it just pinched her skin harder. At least Snyder hadn't tied her feet together, but if she ran out from behind the bookshelf, would he shoot one of them?

Liam wrapped his long arms around Pa. "I knew I'd find you!"

"My boy." Pa kissed his forehead and shielded Liam with his body. "Are you okay?"

"Yup, I just have severe asthma. All this dust." He sneezed.

Pa nodded. "Let's get out of here."

"You're not going anywhere. Walsh didn't have the file, so you must. Hand it over." Snyder ripped them apart.

Raelyn's heart stopped at the mention of Kody's name but hoped Pa wouldn't say anything.

Pa's eyebrow rose. "Kody Walsh?"

"Walsh was on my team. You know him?"

"He's dating—" Pa cut himself off and backed Liam toward the exit.

Snyder's eyes grew wide. "Oh, this is too good. It's like a triangle of hatred. I was just at his place last week. If I had known that his girlfriend was your daughter, I could've played so many more games. You know, the man fucking your daughter is the one who delivered the threat to your home in Ash Mountain. That soldier started it all."

Pa froze.

"I guess we all do crazy things. Your wife sure did—though, I guess, technically, she *is* mine. I had her in my bed for almost twelve years."

Pa lunged forward. "She's my wife!" Snyder jumped out of the way, laughing, as Pa fell to the floor again, groaning in pain.

Snyder circled around Pa. "You sure about that? She never came back to you. You had her for only seven years. I win."

Pa's mouth dropped. "Did you hurt Joanna?"

"I did what I had to do. She belonged to me. You should've heard her scream—weak. After she couldn't take anymore, she told me about you. Jawhara said you had everything I needed in that little farmhouse." Snyder stepped on Pa's fingers, causing him to cry out.

"Dad, stop."

Snyder's posture went rigid, and his face contorted. "Shut up, Liam! You gave up the right to use that word."

Liam's ragged breathing returned. "Fine. You don't deserve it. You were a horrible father!"

Snyder's gaze snapped to meet Liam's. "You don't know anything!" he barked. "I gave you power and a guaranteed future! You threw it all away. I should've gotten rid of Jawhara earlier. She's a slut. Hell, this guy probably isn't your daddy either."

"At least he cares!"

"I *did* care. She wants this loser!" Snyder kicked Pa with his boot. "I'll never let that happen! Get up so I can look you in the eyes when I kill you."

Grimacing, Pa reached into his pocket with his uninjured arm. "No, you won't kill me. I have the file you want."

"Where?" Snyder jumped forward, pulling Pa by his shirt and started to frisk him.

Pa gestured behind Snyder's back at Liam to leave. "Let my kids leave first."

"You sound so much like Jawhara. Actually, I could give you a sample of her pathetic pleading now. Our clever wife managed to leave me a voicemail three days ago. Listen to her begging."

He pushed a couple buttons on his phone and held it up on speaker mode.

Raelyn's air caught in her throat. She heard Ma's voice through broken sobs.

"Please! Give me back Liam! I'll meet you anywhere. I'll do anything."

Snyder hung up.

The room spun.

Three days ago? She's alive.

30

KODY

Kody pushed his fancy shoe further down on the gas pedal of the stolen limo that jostled over the rugged terrain. At the base of the hill, he halted abruptly and rushed out. He sprinted to Cali standing in the shadows by Yohaan's squad car. The wind started howling, blowing Cali to the side.

He caught his sister, grabbing both her shivering shoulders. "Where's Raelyn?"

Cali's eyes were wide in a frazzled panic as she pointed silently to the warehouse on the top of the hill.

His pulse raced. "What happened?"

Cali's eyes stayed on the stoned structure towering above.

Kody shook her. "Look at me!"

In a daze, her jaw dropped—speechless.

"What happened?" Kody quickly pulled her to the limo and tucked her inside, shutting the door.

"I heard gunshots. Raelyn has a gun."

His heart pounded. "Stay here! I'll be right back."

She managed to squeak out, "I thought the cops were arresting you when I ran out of the hotel room."

Kody took a deep breath. "Cali, stay here." He placed his bullets into the magazine and clipped them into his gun. "Everything will be fine."

Kody ran up the hill, but his dress shoes kept getting stuck in the thick mud, slowing him down. When he looked back, Cali was out of sight, hidden behind the tree trunks at the bottom. All he could see were the old graves speckled around in crosses. The darkness looming around the warehouse looked more menacing than ever.

At the top, he raced to the side, squinting in each direction. Kody pushed his back against the brick wall. He glanced into the window before crossing in front. A loud banging sound came from a metal door on the ground.

Kody pointed his gun at the door and lifted it with his other hand.

"Help!" a young voice cried out. A thick head of blond, wavy hair popped out from the opening. "Hurry! They're wrestling in there. My dad's going to hurt my sister!"

Kody holstered his weapon and reached down to lift the kid up. A tall boy emerged. Bruises spotted his forearms, and his spirited blue eyes shot daggers of fear into Kody's chest.

"Who's your dad?"

The boy froze for a beat. "They both are!"

"Where's Rae—?"

"My dad pounced. So, I ran." The boy paused, scanning Kody. "Wait, who are you?"

"Specialist Walsh." Kody quickly pointed to a line of trees. "Run down, and you'll find a woman named Cali. She'll keep you safe."

The boy stood between the cellar door and Kody. "No. I'm not letting you go down there if you're going to hurt my family." His eyes fearlessly flickered to Kody's gun.

Kody moved the kid aside and stared into the cellar opening.

"I'm here to help. Is Raelyn down there?"

The kid nodded as Kody lowered himself into the hole. A metal spiral staircase descended into darkness. The scent of stagnant, stale air puffed into his face from the dreary interior. He started the swirling descent, twisting around until he met the flat ground. The cold crept up his spine. Shouts escalated to his right, down a long tunnel with a speck of small light in the distance.

As he sprinted down a corridor a voice boomed. "You let Liam get away!" He recognized Snyder's snarl from his nightmares.

Snyder should still be detained.

Kody rounded the bend. The light drew brighter until he stepped into a large library. He stood in the second story, a loft large enough to fit a Blackhawk. Books were stacked and lined on barrels and shelves. Four total exits—below, a sealed off metal door. On his level, there were two high windows. And the tunnel he had entered through. The giant clock with roman numerals on the wall was frozen at 2:22, and cobwebs lined the ceiling.

He peeked below and saw the tops of two heads. Snyder and William.

Where's Raelyn?

William clutched his elbow tight to his chest. His arm looked badly broken.

Kody's eyes whizzed around his surroundings. A ladder in the corner led down to them. When he moved forward, the splintered floorboards creaked under his weight.

Liam's fathers' gaze shot up.

"Who's up there?" Snyder yelled.

Kody leaped forward and kicked dozens of heavy books over the loft, then hurled a barrel over the wooden railing down at Snyder.

Snyder whirled back and shot his gun in Kody's direction. A bullet skimmed the skin over Kody's rib. He stumbled back. He had forgotten he wasn't wearing a vest. He reached one arm to his side and brushed his fingertips over wetness by his ribcage.

Damn it! Ignore it.

"Who's up there?" Snyder hollered again.

Kody backed into the shadows, aiming his gun down at Snyder. He didn't have a clear shot. The wooden banisters blocked his view, and William stood too close. He moved toward the ladder connecting the two floors.

Snyder wrapped his arm around William in a tight hold. "If you come closer, I'll break this guy's other arm."

When Kody dashed over, his shoes slipped, but he managed to keep his eyes on the two men below.

William twisted fast, knocked Snyder to his knees, and grabbed the gun.

Kody shouted, "William, it's Kody! Don't shoot." He scaled down the ladder, a sharp piece of wood slicing into his finger.

Ignore it.

Kody joined them on the lower level, aiming his gun at Snyder.

William's eyes glanced behind the bookshelf, and Kody followed his gaze quick to see the whites of Raelyn's eyes.

Does Snyder know she's here?

"Why shouldn't I kill you right now?" Kody's gun angled toward Snyder's temple. He looked around for anything to tie Snyder up. A rope hung over the side of a giant hole.

"You won't kill me because I'm Zohaib." Snyder's voice cracked slightly. "I have hundreds of men who will hunt your entire family down if you lay a finger on me."

"You're Zohaib?" Kody moved closer.

A muffled moan sound came from where Raelyn stood. Kody turned. She stepped into the light. Gagged and cuffed. Kody jumped to her and freed her mouth.

Raelyn's gasping breath twisted his heart. "Kody, you're bleeding!"

"I'm okay." Kody reached behind her and snapped the fabric knot with his Swiss Army knife.

From behind, a crunch sound came, like a cracking bone. William yelled out.

"Pa!"

"No!" Kody thrust up his hand, blocking Raelyn and shielding her back behind the bookshelf swiftly.

As he turned, a heavy arm pummeled his elbow and grabbed the gun away. William lay in a heap on the ground.

Kody gulped. "Sergeant, let them leave. I'll tell the army during your trial that you didn't attack me that day in my apartment. Everything will go back to normal."

Snyder sneered. "Or I could kill all three of you slowly. You'll be last."

"Why?" Kody's muscles tensed. "What do you want?"

"The damn file! I've said it over and over since September. My entire life is on there! How clear do I have to be?"

Kody glanced down at William, who was unconscious on the floor. His shoulder seemed dislocated, and his other arm was most likely broken. For emphasis, Snyder stepped his boot on William's arm, but there was no response.

Kody licked his lips and spoke clearly, raising both hands in surrender. "Listen, the file's in my Jeep, outside. You and I can go get it together."

Snyder marched toward Raelyn and slowly scanned Raelyn's breasts, full in her tight prom dress. "I'd have fun searching her for it."

Kody blocked his way, and their chests bumped together.

"You forget who has the weapons." Snyder sidestepped him and grabbed Raelyn's wrist.

She struggled and shoved the base of one palm into Snyder's nose, but he had a solid grip on her waist. He pulled Raelyn in close and covered her mouth. "You'd be so easy to tame."

Fury snapped through Kody. "Enough!"

Snyder raised his gun straight at Kody and pulled the trigger. The bullet sliced into Kody's upper arm. He fell back and landed on the ground. Red leaked onto his white dress shirt. It felt like needles were jabbing into his shoulder. The pain radiated through his entire side, making it difficult to focus. Grunting, he pushed pressure onto his bleeding bicep.

Raelyn screeched. She crouched down to where the bulletproof vest laid on the floor, reached into a pocket, and threw the file on the ground at Snyder's feet. "Here!"

"Thank you, darling." Snyder picked up the rope. "Tie up your boyfriend." Snyder snapped, nodding to the bookshelves.

Like hell I'll be tied up.

Raelyn stood strong. "What? You shot him! You got what you wanted! Let us go!"

Snyder waved his gun around. "You're not going anywhere until I confirm this file is real."

Tears welled up as she locked eyes with Kody.

I'll be okay. It's okay.

He opened his mouth to talk, but Snyder kicked Kody in the groin. His air was sucked out of his body.

"Damn it! I'll tie him myself." Snyder kept his finger on the trigger, staring Kody down. "You try anything, and I shoot the girl. I've done it before." He tightened the rope around his shoulders, torso, and neck. "You're wasting my time."

Snyder grabbed a tablet from his backpack and inserted the drive.

Kody groaned as blood dripped from his bicep and onto his tux pants in thick splatters. His ragged breathing didn't help the pain surging through his body.

Snyder leaned over and hissed, "You know, she's actually really pretty. You think anyone would pay ten grand for her?"

Kody writhed, and the rope dug into his flesh. His lips were dry. He could feel a pool of blood collecting under his fingertips.

Water. Please.

A figure flashed above him in the loft, but the room had become blurry. Snyder punched Kody in the gut. Spots blossomed in his vision. He gulped for air, desperate for even a single breath.

"Stop!" Between sobbing sounds, Raelyn screamed, begging him. "Hurt me instead."

"Oh, we have a volunteer!" Snyder snickered.

No!

Kody's nostrils flared as he gripped the rope, trying to tear it apart, but all his energy was draining away. He could barely move.

31

RAELYN

TERROR DRUMMED IN RAELYN's bones as Kody's head hung in weakness. Pa grunted, basically unconscious.

"They need doctors. Let us go!" Raelyn cried.

Snyder ignored her, turned, and swiped on his tablet. "This'll take a few minutes."

"Where's Joanna Bell?" Raelyn demanded.

"You mean, Jawhara Snyder?" Snyder laughed. "Jawhara helps me capture girls to be sold as sex slaves."

Tears rolled down her face as she shook her head.

"I'll make a trade. You for her. I could use a younger version to play with." He stared at her. "Why do you care anyway? Jawhara didn't mention you once. She didn't try to get home to you."

Raelyn rushed at him, ramming her small fists into his stomach. "Take it back!"

"Fuck it! No trade! I'm taking you with me, girl. I can sell you in Tahil."

Snyder rose a hand and stormed forward. His hand cracked against her skin, making her teeth clatter together, and she fell on the cold ground with a moan. The bookshelves looked like they were spinning over her as she tried to meet Kody's gaze, but his eyes were closed, and his head hung.

"Stop!" Pa awoke, groaning. He tried to stand again but only got as far as his knees.

Her pulse quickened as she caught sight of someone scurrying in the loft above.

Snyder pounded his palm on the side of the tablet. He roared, "What the hell? Is this file a fake? Give me what I need, or Walsh will bleed out."

A sob stuck in her throat. She couldn't move.

Snyder pulled out his dagger and walked to Kody. Rubbing the blade against Kody's thigh, he grinned. "Where would you like me to start?" He pushed the tip of the blade through the tux pants and tore a slit into Kody's upper thigh. His head snapped up, and he screamed out.

A gun shot pierced the air from up in the loft. Suddenly, Snyder staggered back. Blood gushed out from the side of his leg. He dropped his gun. Snyder's pained grunts and pants filled the air as he pushed his palm down on his thigh, painting his hand red.

Cali jumped out from behind the bookshelf, sliced through his restraints, pushed Kody over onto his side, and dragged him into the shadows. A trail of blood streaked the floor after them.

Raelyn's heart rammed in her chest as she sprang forward and grabbed Snyder's gun from the ground.

Now there was only a triangle, Raelyn on her feet, Snyder and Pa both on their knees.

To her side, Pa tried to stand on shaky legs. Time stood still.

Raelyn pointed the gun at Snyder.

Aim and shoot.

Raelyn's hands trembled as she aimed and squeezed the trigger.

She jolted back. The bullet grazed the edge of Snyder's upper thigh. A darkness oozed through the other pant leg of his army pants.

Her arms shook.

Aim and shoot.

She pulled the trigger again.

Click.

Nothing.

Empty.

She was locked in a trance with Snyder. He pulled a dagger out, grinned, and arched back his arm. Raelyn stared at the knife, transfixed by the sparkles of light on the blade. Then she snapped out of the spell. With full force, Snyder threw his dagger hard straight at Raelyn's head.

She clenched her eyes shut tight. Pa managed to lunge toward her and collide into her body, pushing her down to the ground just in time. Raelyn's shoulder slammed onto the concrete.

Above, she saw Liam in the loft, who aimed at Snyder and squeezed the trigger again.

Two bullets fired into Snyder's neck. He dropped instantly—lifeless. Her heart slammed against her ribs.

It's finally over.

In shock from Snyder's gruesome body displayed in front of her, Raelyn winced and rolled over.

She took a deep breath, and reached up to hug Pa, but he wasn't standing above her like she expected.

Pa lay on the floor—with Snyder's dagger in his chest. Reality sunk in fast that Pa had somehow jumped between her and the blade.

"No!" Her strangled scream burned her throat. "Pa!"

Raelyn crawled to him fast.

Pa gasped, blinking, looking at her. His hands trembled at his side.

"No! No! No!" Raelyn's hands hovered over the dagger.

Pa's eyes widened as he struggled to open his mouth, but words wouldn't come.

Tears streamed down her face. "It's okay. It's okay—I'm here." Raelyn softly placed her hand over his.

Liam rushed down the ladder. "Oh my god!" He dropped to his knees, and Pa took his son by the back of his head and pulled him closer to his shoulder. A tear fell down his cheek without a word.

Raelyn's breathing quickened as she shook her head. "I'll go get help."

Pa's voice croaked weakly. "Hun, stay … Liam."

Her sobs erupted. "Please, stay." Her heart shattered. "Please!"

Pa gasped on a shallow breath and looked straight at her. "Hun. I love—" His emerald eyes glazed over as the life bled out of him. His body went limp just as his gaze lost their depth.

Raelyn buried her head in his chest and clawed at Pa's shirt. Blood oozed from the edges of the dagger and onto her hands. She wrapped her arms around his lifeless body. Her insides drained away.

"No! Come back! Please!"

32

KODY

Raelyn's bloodcurdling scream vibrated in his bones.

What happened?

Someone strong lifted Kody over his shoulder.

Pain.

He mumbled nonsense, but the man only tightened his grip. Kody grunted as his body bounced from the uneven footfalls through the tunnel. The *thud* sounds pounded against the concrete and into a puddle as water splashed Kody's face. He couldn't open his eyes but heard water dripping from pipes. Pain.

"Stay awake!"

Is that Peterson?

"Damn it!"

Kody slid off someone's back to the ground. Searing hot pain traveled up his leg. Cold and darkness surrounded him. Blackness behind his eyelids. Someone smacked his face. Kody's eyes shot up.

Peterson kneeled in front of him, thick mud smeared onto his face. "Walsh, you have to climb up! You're too heavy."

Kody slumped to the side, closing his eyes.

Thumps echoed down the chamber, followed by heavy breathing and frantic whispers. Four hands grabbed Kody's limbs and carried him in the air for what could have been seconds, minutes, or hours.

"Stay awake!" Peterson's voice faded.

Dreamlike visions began with prom dresses that swirled into images of Snyder pointing a gun at Raelyn. Colors whirled through Kody's mind, memories of Cali singing on stage at a karaoke bar. A spotlight shone down, but instead of lights flooding the stage, blood dripped from the overhead lighting onto their hair. Cali and Raelyn didn't notice the blood. Someone had to warn them. Kody was strapped tightly to the bar chair, screaming, but no one could hear him. In his vision, someone began beating him with pool sticks over and over across his temple. He pulled against the ropes restraining him, but an unexplainable force dragged his chair further and further from the stage as a shape that looked like a red snake pulled the trigger. Blood rained down on both the girls until it was a shower of crimson.

"Kody!" Cali's voice. His sister was somewhere nearby.

He tried to move his hand, reaching toward her. Sticky, thick liquid slipped between his fingers.

Sleep.

A strong cleanser spray met Kody's nostrils, and beeping sounds alerted him awake. He squinted into the assaulting fluorescent lighting, allowing his eyes to adjust. Across from the bed he lay in, a sign by the clock showed "Army Medical Center." Annoying chirps from the cart next to his bed blared like a parrot. Tight bandages had been wrapped around his bicep, and an

IV pumped fluids into his vein. A blanket brushed against his legs, where he could feel another tight bandage around his upper thigh.

No pain.

Cali walked into the room with a tight frown. She looked five years older than when she had gotten ready for prom. Her dress had seen better days, splattered in blood, mud, or both.

"Hey there." Cali smiled weakly, placing her shaking hands on his. "Mom's on her way."

"Are you hurt?" His voice cracked.

Cali shook her head.

Kody shot upright in bed. "Raelyn?" A soreness immediately jabbed his body, but the doctors must have administered pain meds since it felt partially numb.

"Raelyn's okay. She's on her way here with Liam."

Peterson limped out from behind a curtain with a smirk. "No one cares about poor me."

Kody cleared his throat. "Whatever you did to protect them, thank you."

"Anytime." Peterson saluted him sarcastically and walked into the hall. He stood guard outside Kody's door like a soldier reporting for duty.

I owe him my life.

Kody sighed and relaxed back against the pillow and asked his sister, "How long have I been out?"

"Five hours. Peterson carried you, like, a mile and up all those stairs. How do you feel?"

"I'll survive."

"Snyder's dead," she said flatly.

Kody tilted his head back onto the bed, not wanting to ask, "And William—?"

Cali took his hand in hers and tears fell. "He's gone. It's awful. I don't know what to do."

Kody waved his sister closer. "Just be there for Raelyn."

"What if that was you? What if you put yourself between one of us and Snyder?" Her voice trembled.

Kody looked at the white wall.

I would've done the same thing.

"What happened after I left?" Kody's temple throbbed.

"I can't think. Um, Liam kept screaming and wheezing from panic or something. Uh, I don't know. Raelyn got ahold of her cop neighbor, Yohaan. He showed up with his team."

"Come here." Kody hugged her. A layer of the dried blood covered her black dress. Probably his blood. He wouldn't ask.

Cali cried into his good arm, then wiped the tears from her cheeks with her wrist. "So, Liam is her brother. He's eleven or twelve—I don't remember—but he's so tall he looks fifteen. Joanna was pregnant with William's son right before she left on her work trip."

He nodded, trying to take it all in, but his head felt woozy.

Cali continued, "Liam thought his mom's name was Jawhara Snyder until last April."

Kody looked up as voices came from the hallway. He saw Raelyn and Peterson in the middle of a tight embrace.

After he pulled away, Peterson frowned, then nodded to Kody. "All right, then. Time to go. I've had enough of your punk ass to hold me over." He disappeared down the hallway before Kody could respond.

Raelyn and Liam walked in. Cali hugged them, then left toward the hall to talk to Yohaan and other police officers.

Raelyn sprinted across his room, barefoot and muddy, tears falling. "Are you okay?"

I am now.

She rushed next to his bed, and her hands hovered over his skin for a moment, waiting. Her gold prom dress was ripped even shorter on the side, all the way to her hipbone. Black makeup was smeared under her eyes.

"Don't worry about me." He locked eyes with her and took her hand with his good arm. "Come here."

Raelyn's tousled hair stuck to her face. "My pa—" Her breathing quickened, and her chest rose and fell hard. He moved his strong arm around her tiny waist to wrap her tightly against him.

I'll keep my word to him and take care of her and keep her safe. Always.

33

RAELYN

THE RAW PAIN WAS too much to handle. Raelyn moved closer to Kody on the hospital bed, trying to merge into him as one. "Pa is dead."

Overwhelming grief burned into her veins, scorching away her childhood in one night. It felt like Snyder's blade struck her own beating heart and shred it to pieces.

Raelyn wiped her eyes. "Are—are you okay? What did the doctor say? Do you need surgery? Did you lose too much blood? I can donate blood." Her eyes darted to the nurse's station out his door. "Let me go see how I—"

"Raelyn." Kody brushed the strand of sticky hair behind her ear. "Take a deep breath."

Numbness spread through her body as she curled into Kody's chest. She laid her head on his shoulder and let herself dissolve into nothingness.

"I'll be right here." He rubbed her back.

She couldn't talk and struggled to take a breath. Sleeping wasn't an option because she would only see Pa's emerald eyes glaze over. The option of looking at Kody only struck fear deep down that he might leave her too. She moved closer into Kody's warmth and reread Pa's notes in the journal for the tenth time:

Plan

Move to Oak City close near the coordinates

Investigate abandoned warehouse

Pay month to month rent in cash

Cut up credit cards

Don't forward mail

Apply for jobs under different name- Will Bee

Register Raelyn for school under different name- Raelyn Bee

Questions

Who sent the threat?

Where is Joanna's file?

What secrets are on Joanna's file?

What will they do with the information on Joanna's file?

Where are the sand tunnels Joanna researched in her article?

Was the bombing targeting Joanna and her work?

Yohaan

Put a tracker on Raelyn's phone

Make daily rounds to Slate High as a precaution

Follow her when she drives to work at the library.

My little girl

Pros for telling Raelyn the truth:

She could be on the lookout/protect herself

She'd trust me again

Cons for telling Raelyn the truth:

She could get scared

She'll never view me the same way again

She may start investigating Joanna and lead the guys to us by mistake

Pa loved me—unconditionally.

Liam came in and gave her a half hug, then backed away.

Raelyn's voice shook as she tried to make sense of things. "Liam, on the video, Ma said she'd be in a safehouse."

Kody shook his head. "We don't have to go over this right now, babe."

Liam nodded. "Yeah, there's lots of safehouses. I don't know which she's in. I've only been to one in Tahil."

"I have a ticket to Tahil," said Raelyn.

Kody's brows raised. "You do?"

Liam looked as broken as she felt. He sneezed, then took a puff from his inhaler. "I'm going too."

Raelyn couldn't believe how much Liam looked like a younger clone of Pa. She wanted to wrap her arms around her brother, but she was glued to Kody's side. If she were smart and responsible, she wouldn't allow Liam to go with her. But he knew the Tahil area and would be an asset to finding Ma.

Liam lost two fathers tonight.

Goosebumps rose on her arm. How could she go home and sleep knowing Pa would never come back? She stared at the clock, watching the hand tick on like the beating of her heart. Time had lost all meaning. Was it only last night that Pa kissed her cheek before prom? It wasn't real. She had to wake up from this nightmare. Numbness claimed her body.

She stared at Liam. "You killed your dad for me?"

He itched his nose. "No. William was my real father."

"But Snyder raised you."

Liam ran his hand through his thick hair like Pa used to do. "Snyder raised me like a real dad until I was like ten. Then, stuff got weird." His eyes teared up. "Snyder started training me on ways to capture women without being heard or seen. He made me shoot animals, then made me—" Liam broke out in a sob, coughing and crying simultaneously. "He tortured girls and made me watch other things. Stuff I don't want to talk about."

"You won't be like Snyder." Raelyn could tell her voice was flat, emotionless. "He was part of a sex trafficking operation. Is it true, what he said about Ma? Was she a slave?"

Liam looked to the floor. His glasses scooted lower on his nose. "I'm not sure. My dad—I mean, Snyder fell for her, and I thought they were truly married. Last April, Mom told me how Snyder abducted her and about you two. I was desperate to leave Snyder and had to act fast. It was me who tried to give Mom's necklace to that photographer in the market. I knew Mom kept a file in that locket. Emme was the first American I met, the first person I could ask for help. She agreed to help us contact the Embassy."

Liam covered his face with his hands. "I never heard from Emme again, so we tried to run one night. Our backpacks were ready to go. Snyder caught us leaving, so he hurt—he hurt Mom—a lot. I heard her screaming." He stopped and gulped.

Raelyn buried her face in her hands as she listened.

Liam continued. "Because Snyder hurt her so much, Mom told him about the file in the necklace and about our father. Sometimes, I'm not even sure if she knew what she was admitting."

Raelyn patted his back, unsure what to say.

Liam wiped his foggy glasses from his tears on the hospital bed linens. "After I saw how bad Snyder hurt Mom, I had to get her out of there. So, I pretended to sell Mom. She and two other women traveled through tunnels and were supposed to be safe in a cellar, then rescued and taken to the US Embassy. I thought I had it all planned out. I'm so sorry. I don't know what went wrong. I tried."

Liam hiccupped and wiped snot from his nose with his sleeve. "In January, Snyder freaked out when he couldn't find Mom, and everything fell apart. He took me with him, away from our home. At first, he was nice and said he was protecting me from someone and made me stay in some tiny desert camp for a few weeks. Then, he got more suspicious and paranoid, so we flew to America to live in that warehouse. I've been a prisoner in the basement library ever since."

Quickly, Raelyn pulled Liam into her embrace.

Liam needs Ma even more than I do.

He coughed up a bunch of phlegm and hacked it into the hospital sink. "I had to study three languages. At least some of his training paid off. I made that website to find you."

Raelyn sighed. "You sent me those messages asking for help?"

"Kind of." Liam nodded. "After Mom told me our real last name was Bell and that I had a sister and a different father—" He dropped his head and paused. "I uploaded the picture from Emme's Polaroid picture onto the site. Then, I coded the website where I could give certain words that'd alert me of someone on the site. So, words put into the site like Raelyn, Bell, William, Ash Mountain ... things like that ... They triggered an alert we could respond to individually."

She barely understood the technical explanation.

Liam's words rushed out. "But I couldn't monitor it all the time; it was too risky. A girl, Olivia, had access to computers. She helped me and sent those messages to you."

"Yeah, I didn't always understand what the messages meant. I'm sorry. You're really smart." Raelyn had to have hope, or Pa's death was in vain. "We can find her. I have a list of addresses, but it's dated from 2004."

"Joanna's video said that somewhere in the warehouse may be an updated safehouse list," said Kody. "I'll go back to look when they let me leave."

Raelyn squeezed Kody's hand when she said, "Okay, thanks. That's a good idea." She turned to Liam again, "So, was Snyder's name Zohaib?"

Liam stepped back. "What do you mean? Zohaib was Snyder's boss. Why would they have the same name?"

"Snyder isn't Zohaib?"

"No." Liam swallowed. "Snyder is a sweet cupcake compared to Zohaib. There are still bad guys out there." Liam dropped his chin. "I'm sorry about our dad."

"It's not your fault." She held up Pa's journal. "It seems like Pa knew what he was doing and was trying to keep us safe." She sniffed.

Raelyn gripped the thumb drive tight in her palm. "If you can read Arabic, you can help me read the file." She put both her hands on Liam's shoulders. "I'll find Ma for you."

I won't give up.

34

KODY

A WEEK LATER, THEY arrived home from William's funeral. Kody knocked on Cali's bedroom door. Ben Platt's song, "So Will I," blasted from the other side of the door, but it couldn't disguise Raelyn's muffled cries.

"Please, let me in."

Kody cringed as he lowered himself onto the carpet of his parent's hallway, leaned back against the wall, and rested his head, ready to wait for another hour. A rustling came from the other side of the door.

"Raelyn?" Kody rotated, grimacing from the sudden movement. He reflexively covered the bandage on his arm. Snyder had shot him only an inch away from his first bullet wound. Same arm, same muscle.

"What do you want?" The strained rawness of her pain was in each syllable. He could picture her on the other side of the door, only inches away, twisting her plaid shirt nervously and her amber eyes slitting into straight lines. Her hair would be in a bun with a pen stuck inside.

He sighed. "I want to be there for you. Babe, let me in." Kody laid his hand flat against the door. "It's okay to be sad. You can't hide from me forever."

"I'm not hiding." She spoke through the wood, but after a pause, the door knob clicked. Cali's door swung open. Raelyn stood exactly as he had pictured, though large circles smudged the skin below her eyes.

He smiled gently. "I'd hug you, but it took me a while to get down here." Patting the carpet next to him, he said, "Please, come here."

She came out and sat hunched next to him. "You don't have to take care of me."

"I know, but I want to. Talk to me." He gently lifted her chin.

Her eyes glistened, but no tears dropped to her cheeks. "I can't—"

"Crying isn't weakness." He cupped the back of her head into his chest. The heavy weight laying on his mind tripled when her eyes filled with tears. Her body heaved as her shoulders shook. Sobs erupted from deep within, and she melted into him.

"I can't live without Pa." The whispered words almost hid in his shirt.

Running his hand over her hair, he swallowed. "You can. And I'll be here."

I could carry all the weight of her pain if she let me.

Her eyes were red rimmed. "This wasn't supposed to happen."

He hugged her close. "I won't leave your side. I promise. It's okay."

"No—it's not okay!" Raelyn's chest rose and fell heavy and fast. "Have you lost a parent?" She punched the wall. "I've lost *two*!"

Out the window, birds flew away from the sound of her abrupt squeals. She thrashed her arms in his tight hold. He wouldn't let go. When their skin touched, he closed his eyes and imagined sucking out all her pain, letting it seep into his veins. He could carry it. In his embrace, her muscles finally relaxed. She gently rested her forehead against his chest and sighed.

Liam poked his head out of Coop's old room down the hall. "Raelyn, are you out here?" His eyes met Kody's, then the boy smiled softly. He resembled William's features, except for those bright blue eyes.

"She's right here," said Kody.

He saluted Kody, who couldn't hold back his grin. "Ah, the love conquers all moment?" Liam breathed onto his glasses and wiped away the fog on his shirt.

Raelyn rubbed the inside of Kody's good forearm. "Ma spent so much time away from the love of her life. She sacrificed her life with Pa to keep us safe. I don't want to have to sacrifice everything too. I want to be with the people I love—every day. We're going to get her back."

Kody kissed the trail of blue veins under the surface of her wrist.

Liam looked around the corner. "Where's Cali?"

"Getting ready for graduation."

Liam disappeared around the corner.

Raelyn stood and put one hand on her hip. "I need to pack for my flight to Tahil."

It'll be so dangerous over there.

Kody nodded. "I bought a ticket too."

She reached down and helped him up. "What about work?"

"I'm on extended medical leave until the docs clear me," said Kody.

She pointed in his face. "I'm not giving up. I *will* find Ma. You can't stop me. If I have to delay college, I will."

Kody massaged her back. "I know. I'm not going to stop you."

Raelyn scrunched her nose, studying him. "You promise?"

Kody rolled his lips in and nodded.

I can't tell her that Dabbott saw Joanna again yesterday in the market, holding a pile of books. Does that mean Joanna is there voluntarily?

"Okay. I'm gonna go get ready with Cali." Raelyn disappeared from view.

There was a knock at the door downstairs, and Yohaan stood on his porch in full police uniform with bags in hand.

Kody opened the door. "Hey, thanks for bringing her stuff."

Yohaan passed over stuff from William's house, then dripped hand sanitizer between his fingers and rubbed it in. He straightened his police badge. "It's hot for May." Checking inside for anyone listening, Yohaan faced Kody. "I'm sorry we cuffed you at prom. William had called me frantically saying Raelyn was in danger. I couldn't hear everything, so we just assumed—"

"It's okay."

Yohaan cleared his throat. "I'm glad the evidence was clear. Liam admitted to shooting Snyder as self-defense. Snyder's fingerprints were on the dagger. Anything else you need to tell me?"

"Nope."

Yohaan sighed. "At the funeral, their aunt and grandma were arranging where they'll live for the summer. They're planning to enroll Liam in junior high while she starts her freshman year at State."

Kody crossed his arms. "Whatever she chooses to do, I have her back."

Yohaan widened his stance and studied Kody like an investigator. "You're going to let her fly over there, aren't you?"

"It's not about me letting her. She can do what she wants."

"And what about Liam? You think Raelyn will leave him behind while she travels overseas looking for a needle in a haystack? They've been through enough and need to stay near family."

Kody tapped his foot impatiently. "Joanna *is* their family."

Yohaan tapped his fingernail on his gun. "Listen, let us and the CIA figure out what's best for them."

Kody's turned toward the orange sky. "I told her I'd be there for her."

"Don't you want what's best for Raelyn?" Yohaan put a hand on Kody's shoulder, squeezing a bit too tight. "You really think she has a chance in hostile territory? These guys are dangerous. Use your head. Her aunt and grandma have been talking with the detective at my precinct to find Joanna. Let them handle it. You can't protect her forever."

"Thank you for bringing her stuff." Kody stuck out his hand.

Yohaan lowered his chin but didn't shake. "If you need anything, please call me. You're not the only one who cares about them. I lost one of my best friends. You know what that's like?"

Kody rubbed his thumb over his pocket watch. "Yeah, yeah I do."

Yohaan handed out a ripped up red envelope. "Raelyn gave me this envelope to scan for prints. Tell her it had Snyder's prints all over it."

Kody's breath stuck in his throat.

It'd have my prints all over it too.

Yohaan glared. "Is there anything you want to tell me, soldier?"

"No."

A call came in from his squad car. "I need to go." He jogged off, and his car flew up dirt behind as he drove away.

I'll keep them safe, and no one has to know about the box I stole from William's desk.

Raelyn's hips swayed as she joined Kody on the porch. "Okay, so, what's next?"

The sight of the woman he loved approaching him was all he needed in the present moment. While holding bags of her clothes hanging from his wrist, Kody dipped Raelyn and planted his lips on hers.

35

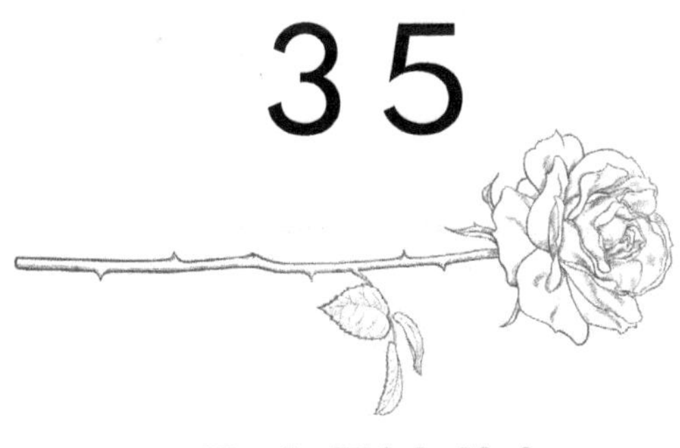

RAELYN

In the tight plane aisle, Raelyn closed the overhead compartment with her one carry-on, but her backpack toppled out, hitting her in the head.

"Ouch!"

Kody helped with his good arm, shoving it above with ease.

He kissed her forehead. "You okay, babe?"

She leaned into him, unsure how to answer. No more Christmases with Pa. Not another birthday or quick phone call or awkward hug. He wouldn't trudge mud inside from his boots again or fall asleep on his favorite chair with his mouth wide open.

For the last week, grief had hollowed a pit in her stomach, but when she awoke this morning, something new was there to keep the grief company. Each step closer to their arrival in the desert lifted just an ounce of weight from her shoulders. Pa was gone, but she had a chance to find Ma. A bit of hope filled her spirit.

Swiping through the pictures she took, Raelyn had to admit that Pa was buried in the most gorgeous location with all the blooming flowers at Ash Mountain's peek. She stopped on one picture of the roses that scaled up the trellis next to Pa's grave. In the background, a small black cabin hid behind the trees. Only when they lowered Pa into the ground had the memory come back to her when she and Pa had buried a time capsule out there. Just like she had thrown soil over Pa's casket, they had tossed dirt over the shoebox together.

Unexpectedly, the sight of Pa's final resting place hadn't terrified her. She knew he would be at peace knowing he saved her life from Snyder's blade. Raelyn would be forever grateful for the man who gifted her with so much more than she ever gave him credit for. Pa would want her living life fully, with joy. Raelyn could see his bushy eyebrows rise and hear his stern voice make her promise to maintain her studies, photography, hobbies, and friends. Pa wouldn't want her to fall into the same trap as he did and turn into a zombie. It would mean too many wasted moments.

I'll be okay—eventually.

She glanced at Liam and whispered to Kody, "I'm not going to give up. If Ma's not at any of these safehouses, I'll keep looking." She tied the plaid shirt around her waist.

"I know."

She sighed. "I can't believe she's actually out there."

"We will find her."

"I can't believe after all this time, Pa will never get to see Ma." The realization squeezed Raelyn's chest tight. He had loved her so much, and to miss this chance because he gave up his life for Raelyn caused the buds of determination to begin blooming in her.

I'll make his sacrifice worth it.

Kody placed his hand on the side of Raelyn's cheek. His warm thumb brushed away a single tear that escaped. He hugged her close.

A flight attendant tried to direct them to sit, but Kody held her tighter.

Raelyn let a stranger squeeze by her in the aisle and gazed into Kody's comforting eyes. "Are you sure you're allowed to come with me?"

"Meadows gave permission for an extended leave."

"That doesn't fully answer my question."

He rubbed his fingers over his temple and sighed. "Babe, let's not worry about that right now. I'm coming with. Plus, they may decide to medically discharge me from the army. My exit counseling date has been set for July."

"Kody, you love the army. I won't let you give that up."

"If they decide to discharge me, I'll try to fight them on it, but you're what matters." He stared out the plan window, deep in thought. "Plus, I've had three injuries to the same arm."

"Three? When was the first?"

"Before I met you. During a jump, I landed rough and needed my shoulder snapped back in. That was a weird day."

Raelyn laid her head on his hard chest as another stranger pushed their way through the aisle.

"Anyway, I need to be back to the Fort by the meeting in July, or I'm listed as AWOL."

Raelyn's brow furrowed. "What's AWOL?"

"Absent without leave. They'd classify me as a deserter and lock me up."

She swiveled on her heels. "Jail? No, you need to stay here."

"Don't worry, I won't let that happen." Kody gestured to Raelyn's seat. "We need to get out of the way."

Cali waved her hand in the air from where she sat in the window seat, which whirled her lemony scent through the stale plane air. "Are you sitting in First Class, Mr. Fancy Pants?"

Kody frowned. "No, I'm right behind you. Someone's gotta watch your back. Plus, I get to kick your seat for thirteen hours."

Cali laughed as she grabbed a magazine. "Lucky me!"

Raelyn squeezed by Liam's legs and plopped herself between her best friend and Liam. She laid her head on Cali's shoulder while Liam wrapped his hand into hers. She was so thankful that her best friend and brother were traveling with them to help find Ma. The safer choice would have been to keep Liam back in the States, but he knew the area, the language, and would be a valuable resource.

Cali folded down the corners of the magazine. She flipped the latch on the plane seat's tray repeatedly without it working, then swiped the plane window shade up and down.

This flight overseas would be drastically different than the one to Tuzlicci. At least Cali sat next to her again.

Raelyn clutched the crinkled paper with a smudgy, handwritten title of "Safehouses" across the top. The jet engines rumbled to life, paralleling a part of her that had awoken, the part now hopeful about Ma returning home with her. A blast of air conditioning blew on her face from above. She turned the little knob away as the plane reversed during the safety speech from the staff. Another jet's trail of white led to a path behind the mushroom clouds.

Everything will be okay. I'll find Ma.

Smiling at Liam, Raelyn asked, "If Ma was here now, what do you think she'd say?"

Liam pushed his glasses up higher. "Probably something about making sure we were wearing good running shoes."

Raelyn smiled. "I know what Pa would say."

"What's that?"

She sighed and let the memories overtake her when Pa taught her how to ride a bike, cast a line, change the oil, and swing a hammer. "He'd say some river metaphor." She deepened her voice to match his. "If the river takes you down an unexpected rough path with white water, just keep paddling until the river is so crystal clear you can see the stones sparkle on the bottom."

"I've been in the desert and don't have much river experience."

"I'll teach you." Raelyn patted his hand. "We have plenty of time for that."

She tucked away her plane ticket that showed, 'Tahil, Iraq,' and pulled down her armrest. The scent reminded her of the old carpet from her childhood. Now that Grandma Viola owned their old farmhouse, Raelyn could go back whenever she wanted to feel closer to Pa.

"Raelyn?" asked Liam. "If we don't find Mom, where will I live?" Liam's facial expressions reminded her of Pa, as if a miniature version of him tagged alongside her, which was simultaneously painful and comforting.

She swallowed hard and patted Liam's forearm. "We'll find her. Don't worry."

There wasn't another option. A life without a parent, especially for Liam wasn't something she would settle with. It didn't matter how long it took, Raelyn would return to Oak City with Ma on one side and Liam on the other.

Pa's compass chain served as a bookmark in his thick journal. She hadn't had time to decipher all his chaotic scribbles yet. She opened the page with his compass. One phrase was written in larger handwriting, underlined, and circled in red ink.

Who stole my marble box?

What box? If only Pa were here to explain …

Raelyn wondered if the box was important and what was inside. It must have been if Pa had circled it. Had he found the answer to that question before he died? She would reread his journal, and if the answers weren't inside, Raelyn would find out who stole the box from Pa.

She stretched out the binding, then ran her hand across a fresh page: an empty canvas. As she plucked a pen from her messy bun, she scribbled in golden ink.

I can't raise him up out of the soil
This hopeful flight will reverse my grief
I'll end the years of longing turmoil
Pa's compass guides to love and belief

Just as the flight attendant asked to buckle seatbelts, Kody leaned over the back of her chair and kissed her forehead. Raelyn reached up and brushed her thumb along Kody's forearm, pulling him down for a kiss. She looked around at Kody, Cali, and Liam, and it dawned on her that maybe everyone she needed to be okay was exactly where they needed to be. Her relationships with them were solidified and strong. A trip to Tahil wouldn't change the connections she had with these three.

Kody's full lips melted into hers until the plane moved down the runway, ready to head east. Raelyn gripped the compass tighter.

I'm coming Ma.

Thank you for reading! If you enjoyed the story, I'd love for you to review online. It helps other readers discover the Golden Chains series. https://www.goodreads.com/book/show/56499805-break-the-stone

Facebook: https://www.facebook.com/CassieSwindon

If you'd like to join the street team: Golden Chain Readers: https://www.facebook.com/groups/408046660350675/

Website: www.CassieSwindon.com (where you can sign up for the newsletter and updates on the next novel)

Please get in touch on social media. I'd love to answer your questions but I won't spill the beans about the sequel. Instagram.com/cassie_swindon_author

The sequel, Hunt the Storm releases August 19, 2021

Acknowledgements:

It takes constant patience and support from an entire team to publish a book. There are so many people I'd like to thank for their role in bringing this book into your hands. Many years ago, my husband randomly asked me if I believed he could run a marathon. Without hesitation, I replied matter-of-factly, "Yes."

Fast forward seven years, the morning of April 4, 2020, right after COVID was settling in as a new reality, I awoke with a dream about two characters. At breakfast, I asked my husband, "Do you think I could write a book?"

Let me tell you, marathons and writing have some challenging similarities. Without Matt's encouragement, unending patience, and willingness to put the kids to bed more than his share, my dream turned into a reality.

First, thank you to my family: Matt, Kyella, Bryson, Aubree, Dustin, Breanna, Mom, and Dad, Anne Marie, Pam, and Tony. There are probably hundreds of people I can list who contributed, yet the following list of people deserve a standing ovation.

Editor: Red Loop Editing
Website: Jen Pavlovitz
Alpha Readers: Dr. A. Anderson & Natalie Proudfoot
Critique Partner: Anna Cackler & Dina Mikule
Military Resource: Retired Sergeant First Class C.T. Ortega
Sensitivity Resource: K Dunigan
Street Team Leader: Kylie R

www.ingramcontent.com/pod-product-compliance
Lightning Source LLC
Chambersburg PA
CBHW070836020826
48982CB00020B/1337/J

* 9 7 8 0 5 7 8 8 4 2 6 3 9 *